Jem and the War

Gordon Thynne

Sketch plans by Helen Smith

AuthorHouse™ UK Ltd.
500 Avebury Boulevard
Central Milton Keynes, MK9 2BE
www.authorhouse.co.uk
Phone: 08001974150

First published by AuthorHouse 11/2/2009

ISBN: 978-1-4389-8407-0 (sc)

This book is printed on acid-free paper.

In memory of my parents,

Olive and Walter,

who would, I think, have recognized in this story

aspects of the West Riding of Yorkshire

they knew.

My thanks to Helen, Ruth and Irene for their help.

Apart from one person who makes the briefest

of appearances, all the characters in the story are

fictional, as is the village of

Althwaite.

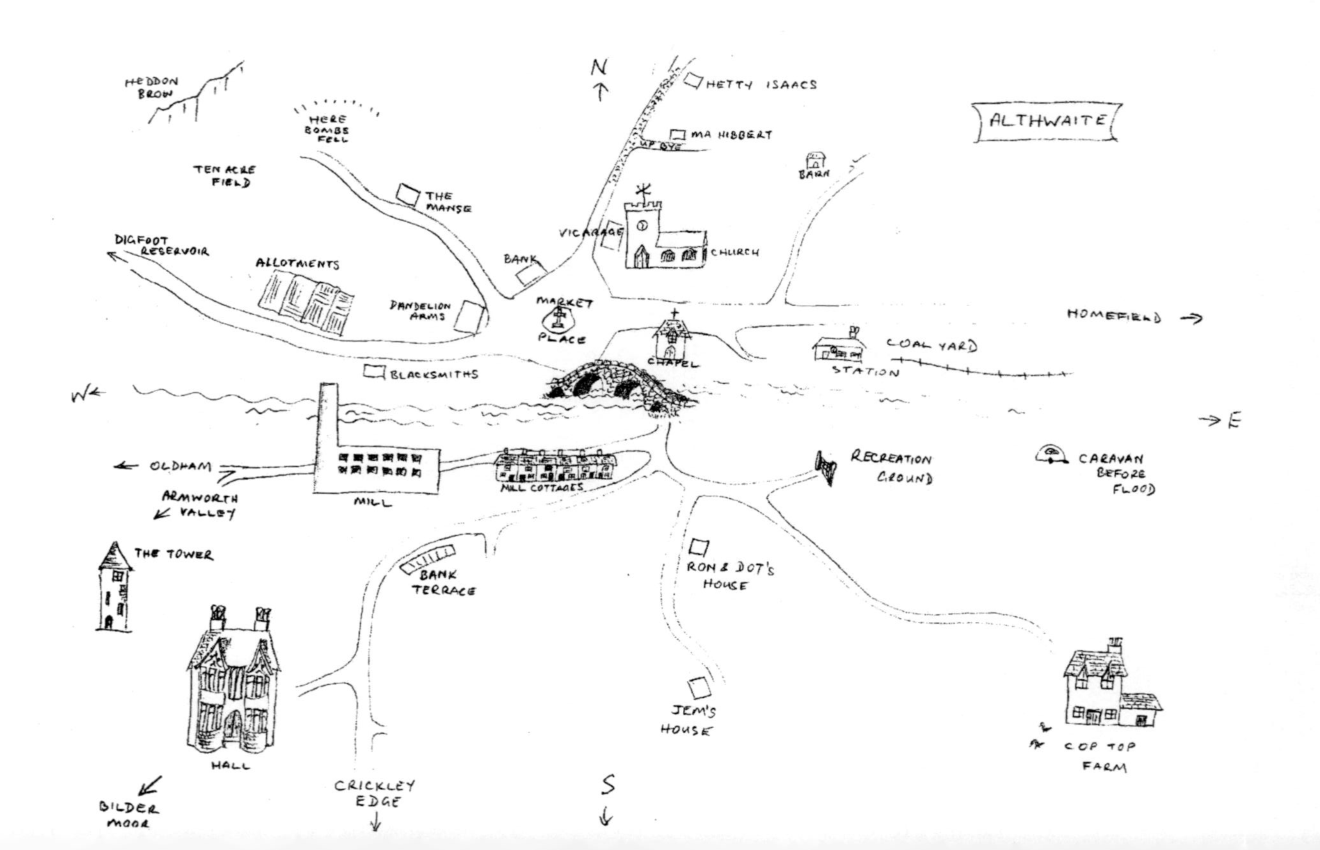
ALTHWAITE
N
S
W
E
HEDDON BROW
HERE BOMBS FELL
TEN ACRE FIELD
THE MANSE
HETTY ISAACS
MA HIBBERT
UP DYE
BARN
VICARAGE
CHURCH
BANK
DIGFOOT RESERVOIR
ALLOTMENTS
DANDELION ARMS
MARKET PLACE
CHAPEL
HOMEFIELD
STATION
COAL YARD
BLACKSMITHS
OLDHAM
ARMWORTH VALLEY
MILL
MILL COTTAGES
RECREATION GROUND
CARAVAN BEFORE FLOOD
THE TOWER
BANK TERRACE
RON & DOT'S HOUSE
HALL
JEM'S HOUSE
COP TOP FARM
BILDER MOOR
CRICKLEY EDGE

Contents

1 THE PUDDING

'Jem! Bring some more logs in, will you love?'

His mother's voice penetrated faintly into the shed where Jem was struggling with the project that he had started in a fit of enthusiasm. In his imagination it had seemed straightforward enough to make a Christmas crib to stand on the sideboard. A thatched stable, with a rear window through which the star would shine, was finished. Now he had turned his attention to the figures, using wood left over from the wreckage of a model glider. But though the wood was not hard, the carving of them was taxing his small talent beyond its limit.

Dropping his pathetic attempt to fashion an angel, Jem opened the door and ran down the garden path. He would never get that crib finished in time, especially being interrupted like this.

After the logs had been got in, it was time for dinner, over which Jem's mother announced yet another inroad into the time available for the project.

'Will you come with me to the Manse, Jem. I've got things to take, and I'll need your help with the shopping on the way back.'

The year was 1937. In those days Mrs Murgatroyd visited the Manse two half-days a week to help with the cleaning and ironing. It was on the opposite side of the village of Althwaite in the West Riding of Yorkshire.

Jem sighed. 'I'll never get that crib finished this Christmas.'

'Yes, you will. You've got all tomorrow before your Grandma and Grandad arrive on Christmas Eve.'

Secretly, Jem was relieved at the prospect of visiting the Manse. Instead of spending the afternoon pitting his limited skill against brutish wood, he could play with Harold, the Minister's son. Both were still nine years old, but liked to think of themselves as nearly ten.

He and his mother set off down the muddy lane, crossed the stone bridge over the swollen river and, with their backs to the wind and rain coming down off the moor, were hurled across the market place. Half way up the hill from there, the Manse confronted the weather with the stolidity of millstone grit.

Mrs Bright, the Minister's wife, answered the bell.

'Come on in, Mrs Murgatroyd. I didn't know whether to expect you on such a wild day. Hello Jem – you'll find Harold somewhere.'

The study door was open, Mr Bright having gone out on pastoral visits. Harold was lying on the floor, setting up his lead soldiers.

'Let's have a civil war,' Jem suggested.

This involved dividing the soldiers into the fancy ones, who might be grouped under the banner of the Cavaliers; and the more soberly dressed, who had no choice but to become Roundheads. So, kilted Scottish soldiers became Cavaliers; and the khaki-clad veterans of the Great War became Roundheads. A few Red Indians formed an auxiliary Cavalier force.

The floor of the study was suited to skirmishes since it was littered with various articles of furniture and piles of boxes, behind which ambushes could be laid. Back and forth the campaign was waged, the victims of one encounter being miraculously revived for the next.

A truce was called whilst Harold foraged for refreshment. Jem stood up, casting his eyes around the room. Bookshelves rose against one wall from floor to ceiling: biblical dictionaries at the bottom, the novels of Sir Walter Scott at the top. On the opposite wall hung a framed photograph of a College group from which a younger Mr Bright looked out. On the mantelpiece was a cast-iron relief of George Stephenson's locomotive, 'Rocket'. Papers and books were neatly arranged on the desk. On the blotter was a single sheet of paper closely covered in illegible script, underlined here and there in red ink. The only words that Jem could read were in capitals at the top: CHRISTMAS IS A TIME FOR GIVING.

A sermon, thought Jem. He knew all about sermons. They were the part of the service where adults were expected to pay attention, but which children could be excused from trying to follow – their turn had already come and gone with the Children's Address. Sermons were a time for mind wandering, for rumination on this and that. Some of Jem's best ideas had come during sermons, - such as the plan, last summer, to dam a nearby stream with grass sods to create a pool almost deep enough to swim in.

The curious thing about sermons was that although, once the text had been announced, the mind switched off to meander on its own, Jem remained faintly aware of their emotional progress. The rising to a climax, the hushed appeal, the reverent drawing to a close: these formed the dim background to more personal concerns.

'Christmas is a time for giving', was the heading for Mr Bright's sermon. In Jem's experience, it was mainly a time for receiving. In fact, that was the chief excitement of Christmas: the anticipation, which sent shivers through his body as he lay awake at night, of the surprises of Christmas morning; the exultation of finding the long-awaited model car or aeroplane placed beside a stocking bulging with minor mysteries. In any case, Jem's pocket money did not extend to the giving in return of anything but token presents.

Harold returned with cocoa and biscuits, and the civil war was resumed until Mrs Murgatroyd had finished her work. On the way home, via the shops crowded with people stocking up as though for a siege, Jem asked about the prospects for Christmas fare.

'Don't worry – there's a big turkey and two Christmas puddings,' his mother replied, thus relieving Jem of a lurking anxiety. The previous Christmas, the budget had run only to a medium-sized chicken and one pudding.

That night, Jem woke with relief from a nightmarish dream in which a train of railway wagons carrying Roundheads and one of dining cars carrying Cavaliers feasting on Christmas pudding approached each other on a single track. A wind was roaring through the dense fir trees at the side of the house. Jem suddenly thought of Benjy. Only the severest of winters drove him to a hostel. When it became too cold to spend the night in the lee of a hedge, he took shelter in barns, disused farm buildings or allotment sheds. You never knew where you might find him, but would come across him in some odd corner – unexpectedly, unless the wind was in the wrong direction and his smell gave advance warning.

The Minister's text took shape in Jem's mind. What could Benjy be expected to give? Who would give him anything except cast-off clothes, a mug of tea and a slice of bread and dripping? Struggling with these conundrums, Jem fell asleep. When he awoke in the morning one conundrum, at least, was solved.

'You'd better get on with that stable, Jem,' his mother said after breakfast. 'You want it finished before Grandma and Grandad arrive tomorrow afternoon.'

Jem went down the garden path to the shed. A miracle was needed if he was to get those figures carved before Christmas Day. But he had no time to spare for that at the moment: he must find out where Benjy was sheltering.

'Seen Benjy?' he asked the first boy he met.

'Smelt him, yer mean!'

Further enquiries produced no intelligence of his whereabouts, so Jem set out on a search. There was no trace of him in the first likely barn, in Ten Acre Field. So he went up to Cop Top Farm where Farmer Ackroyd was loading bales of hay on to a trailer.

'What do you want, sonny?'

'Seen Benjy anywhere about?'

'That rascal! Not seen 'im all week.'

The next port of call was the allotments – plots of ground on which the holders grew vegetables and soft fruit. Not all the plots were in use; and among the huts were some that had been abandoned. Picking his way along the unkempt paths, past a desolation of cabbage stalks, Jem went from hut to hut. In a far corner was an old plot with a hut which had been patched with odd pieces of wood and felt. Approaching it from the rear, Jem caught a whiff of the authentic smell.

There was no need to verify the discovery, so Jem returned home, entering the back garden by the gap in the hedge and strolling up the path from the shed. His father, who combined the care-taking of the Methodist Chapel with gardening jobs, was out. But his mother could be heard upstairs, preparing the spare room for the grandparents. Jem quietly lifted the latch of the door of the outside larder. There was the turkey, resplendent on the largest platter; and the two basins, each covered by greaseproof paper. Taking the smaller of the two, Jem softly let fall the latch, wrapped the basin in brown paper and retreated through the hedge.

Benjy was seated on a box in the doorway of the hut, sunning himself. The soles of his boots were lashed to the uppers with thin wire. Here and there the lining of newspaper poked out. The bottoms of his baggy trousers were tied with string. Thick, hairy, wrists protruded from the frayed cuffs of an old overcoat that was persuaded almost to meet in the middle by a belt of string. A tangled beard protected the throat from draughts. Skeins of uncombed hair, escaping from a trilby hat that had seen better days, did the same for his neck. His hands grasped a penknife and a piece of wood that he had been whittling.

Benjy's eyes, gazing on infinity, became aware that a shape had intervened between them and the sky. They focussed slowly on Jem carrying the brown paper parcel. As became his solitary existence, Benjy was a man of few words. The two stared at each other for a few seconds.

'Hull…hullo, Benjy. A…a Happy Christmas!' Jem faltered.

Benjy glared.

'Who are yer? What d'yer want?'

'I'm Jem Murgatroyd. I've brought you something.'

'What is it?' Benjy asked, eyeing the parcel with suspicion.

'It's a Christmas pudding,' Jem replied, adding, as if to excuse such a munificent gift, 'We had two, so I didn't think it would matter. Anyway, it's the smaller one.'

Benjy stared at Jem and at the parcel.

'Christmas pudding? What do I wan't wi' a pudding?'

'To eat on Christmas day,' Jem suggested.

'Is it cooked?'

'Yes – but it'll need steaming up.'

'I ain't got a saucepan big enough,' Benjy said, a tinge of regret entering his voice. 'Better tak' it back, lad.'

'I could mebbe borrow a steamer.'

'An' where would I steam it? This 'ere ain't a kitchen, tha' knows,' Benjy added in unnecessary comment on the hut.

Surely tramps were up to steaming puddings in the open air, Jem thought. Why was Benjy being so difficult? He saw himself returning crestfallen with the pudding, replacing it in the larder and resuming his hopeless task in the shed.

'I know where you could steam it, Benjy! In the old scout hut. There's a stove there, and I can get the key.'

The old scout hut, a small wooden structure, stood on waste land behind the chapel. It had been replaced by a brick headquarters, but was still used for patrol meetings. Jem's father had a key to it.

'But it'll have to be tomorrow, 'cos we'll need the steamer on Christmas Day,' Jem added.

Benjy graciously intimated that he had no objection to advancing the eating of a Christmas pudding by a day. Jem placed the parcel on the ground beside his seat. He noticed the shavings from Benjy's whittling; and remembered the other purpose of his visit.

'But, Benjy. Christmas is a time for giving. Will you do summat for me in return? Could you do me an angel and Mary and some Wise Men and the rest for a Christmas stable – about so high? I can give you the wood I was using.'

The one harmless activity for which Benjy had any repute was carving pieces of wood into the likeness of human and animal figures, although it was rumoured that he caricatured in wood any farmer who crossed his path and then burnt the figure ceremonially.

'I'll 'ave a go,' Benjy replied, taking the bag of wood.

'Could yer manage any rum or brandy wi' t'pudding?' he asked as an afterthought. Alas, this was beyond the capability of Jem, who lived in a teetotal house.

'Ne'er mind. Beggars can't be choosers.'

So a bargain was struck, and Jem returned home for dinner, light at heart.

'Can I have dinner with Harold tomorrow, Mum?' he asked. His mother looked at him doubtfully.

'It's alright. Mrs Bright said I could.'

'Well, don't be late back, that's all. Grandma and Grandad are arriving at half past three. And there's that stable – are you going to get it finished?'

'Yes, don't worry.'

Christmas Eve dawned with an overcast sky. Shortly after breakfast it began to rain. At ten o'clock, the contents of a rucksack rattled as it was thrust through the gap in the hedge, followed by Jem. At the scout hut, Benjy was already waiting. A large and ancient ground sheet hung from his shoulders. Topping this conical shape was the trilby, with the brim turned down to let the rain run off. At his feet was the pudding, its brown paper covering wet and torn.

With paper and sticks from home and logs stored in the hut, Jem soon had a fire going in the stove. He filled Mrs Murgatroyd's large pan with water from the water-butt, and placed the steamer containing the pudding on top.

Benjy hung his ground sheet from a hook to dry and possessed himself of the only comfortable seat: a sagging arm-chair left over from a jumble sale. He stretched out his soaking boots to the stove, produced pipe and tobacco from an inner recess and proceeded to luxuriate in the ritual of lighting up.

As the rain continued to beat down outside, steam,

tobacco smoke and the fragrance of the pudding mingled with Benjy's earthy smell to produce a fug, the like of which Jem had never previously breathed. At first, he sought relief by opening the door now and then. But this occasioned grunts of annoyance from Benjy. So he forced himself to endure the atmosphere, and concentrated on keeping the stove well fuelled, and the water in the pan topped up. He watched Benjy's rough but deft fingers as they finished the carving of an angel. He tried questions as a means of penetrating Benjy's reserve, but Benjy gave only brief and enigmatic replies.

'How did you learn to carve like that?'

'Ne'er question a gift.'

'How do you manage when it's very cold?'

'Hidden fires.'

'Do you really carve a farmer and then burn him?'

'Farmers and tramps – like oil and watter.'

Jem knew that his mother allowed two hours for steaming. When these were up, he declared the pudding ready. Benjy produced from his knapsack a bent spoon and a tin plate on to which Jem generously heaped two thirds of the pudding. The exquisite aroma overcame the less appealing odours in the hut. Benjy's eyes glistened.

Certainly the proof of that pudding was as much in the eating as in the anticipation. Benjy's hunger had grown during the two hour vigil; and no prior course of turkey and stuffing had taken the edge off Jem's appetite. It was virgin pudding, with no overlay of sauce to distract the taste buds.

At length, regretful, but replete with satisfaction,

Benjy licked the last morsel from his spoon, laid down his plate and re-lit his pipe. He looked at Jem.

'By lad, that were some pudding! Tha' mun congratulate thi mother.'

Jem was not so sure that his mother would appreciate congratulations from Benjy, however heartfelt. And now, the act of charity concluded, he began to feel uneasy about the inevitable interview with her about the pudding.

Apprehension was temporarily suppressed by the excitement and relief of receiving from Benjy a grubby canvas bag containing the carved figures: an angel, a seated Mary, a kneeling Joseph, a manger and three kings offering gifts. Jem handled them with awe. Though roughly shaped, they were convincing and full of character. He mumbled his thanks to Benjy, who proceeded to negotiate occupation of the hut until Boxing Day, promising to leave it in no worse state than they had found it, to be careful not to burn it down, and to place the key under a brick.

It was in a mental state veering between elation and anxiety that Jem crept warily through the hedge. He was just in time for the arrival of his grandparents. After the customary, embarrassing, comments on how he had grown, his mother remarked:

'Jem's supposed to be making a Christmas crib, but he's been out so much, I doubt we'll see it this side of New Year.'

Early on Christmas morning, before it was fully light, Jem stole out to the shed. He brought indoors the stable and figures. Set up on the sideboard, it was a scene to cast a spell.

His mother came down to prepare the turkey for the oven.

'Why, Jem, that's marvellous. How did you do it? Those figures are right clever.'

'It weren't me, Mum. Benjy did them for me.'

'Benjy? The tramp? You're having me on!'

'Honest, Mum. And, Mum, you know that Christmas pudding...the littlest one...well I thought that being Christmas you wouldn't mind Benjy having some of it ...well, most of it.'

His voice trailed away as puzzlement, annoyance and amusement struggled for possession of his mother's features.

'Well, I've heard of some bargains in my time, but this takes the biscuit!'

From the confusion of her feelings, sympathy with Jem's impulse of charity, flawed though it had been, rose to the surface. Even the discovery that the steaming pan was smoke-blackened underneath provoked only a mild expostulation, though it gave Jem another task before the time for chapel.

As on other Christmas Days, Jem was loath to spend an hour or so away from newly-opened presents. But natural reluctance was tempered this Christmas morning by a feeling that all was right with the world. The familiar hymns and carols gave place to the sermon. Mr Bright announced his theme: 'Christmas is a time for giving.' Jem settled down in the pew, a faint smile of self-satisfaction on his face. He closed his eyes, the better to contemplate pudding past and pudding to come.

2 THE HERMIT

Jem's tongue protruded from his mouth as he tried his best to write legibly in the exercise book on the kitchen table.

A hermit was a man who lived by himself so as to worship God without being distracted. There were also lady hermits. They were called 'anchoresses'. In the 13th century St Jude's was famous for a hermit called St Erewold. He lived in a stone hut attached to the church for 30 years. He wasn't officially a saint, but he did miracles and prophesied.

Jem's school class had been studying the history of Althwaite. They had visited the parish church where the vicar had shown them around. He was particularly proud of an Elizabethan monument in the chancel. It showed Sir John Dandelion kneeling opposite his wife. Each had their hands together in prayer. Underneath, much smaller, were their five sons and three daughters. The vicar explained that the surname was pronounced Dandēlion, with the accent on the second syllable. But most village people pronounced it like the name of the flower. In the middle 1800's the name was changed to

Danellion. The Honourable Peter Danellion-Smith, at the Hall, was a descendant.

Jem had been more interested in the story about the hermit. He was both fascinated and repelled.

'How could anyone live cooped up in a small cell for thirty years?' he asked Harold as they walked along the river bank after school the next day.

'I asked my Dad about hermits,' Harold said. 'He said they must have been obsessed – I think that's the word he used – with the love of God. Or else they wanted to run away from a world that was too miserable. Or they may have been – how did he put it, "free spirits"?But I'm not sure what he meant by that.'

Jem had taken in more about hermits than Harold who had made a drawing of the Dandelion monument.

'Between the cell and the church was a little window, so that the hermit could see the services. On the other side was an opening so that he could receive food, and pass out his rubbish and his chamber pot.'

'Chamber pot!' Harold exclaimed, smiling.

'Well he must have had something like that. And he had a boy to run errands and bring his food. An "akalite", he was called. I wouldn't have minded being the boy – people would treat you with respect, being the servant of such a holy man.'

'Benjy's the nearest we've got to a hermit nowadays. I don't fancy being his – what did you say – "akalite"?'

The annual church fête, held in the garden of the vicarage, was an event for the whole village, whether you were Anglicans, Methodists, Baptists or nothing.

Mrs Murgatroyd was involved, anyway, as a member of the Women's Institute. As scouts, Jem and Harold expected to have to look after a stall. But this year they planned something special.

Dear Vicar, they wrote, *Would you like to have a hermit at the fête? We have a friend who would make a good St Erewold. Yours respectfully, Jem Murgatroyd and Harold Bright.*

Two days later a letter arrived for Jem. This was an unusual occurrence.

'Who's your letter from, Jem?' his mother asked.

'The Vicar.'

'Really? What's he writing to you about?'

'It's confidential – at present.'

'Perhaps Jem wants to be a choirboy,' joked his father.

(Jem's singing voice was anything but tuneful.)

Nervously, Jem and Harold presented themselves at the vicarage. They were shown into the study.

'Hullo boys! Now which of you is Jem and which Harold? I remember you were both on the school visit.'

The Reverend Cuthbert Blake was a big man with a booming voice. He seemed to tower over them. But his smile put them at their ease. They explained who their friend was. The vicar laughed.

'But would he be sufficiently presentable? I've heard that he can be a bit- "whiffy" – I think is the word. And could he be depended on to play the part in a respectful way?'

The two boys said they thought they could persuade

their friend, and explained what they had in mind to tidy him up and turn him into St Erewold.

'Well, if you can manage it, it will be a novelty, as well as reminding folk of a piece of St Jude's history. So you carry on, and let me know if there are any problems.'

The next Saturday morning it took them some time to find Benjy. He wasn't in the hut on the allotments. He wasn't in the barn in Ten Acre Field. They asked a walker striding down from Heddon Brow.

'Ay, I caught sight of some sort of shelter, far side of Bluebell Wood.'

Trekking through the wood, they smelt wood smoke, mingled with something else. Sure enough, there was Benjy, seated on some old matting underneath a shelter of branches and bracken. A kettle hung from a tripod over a smoky fire.

'Hullo lads. Though I can't say I'm glad to see yer.'

'Why are you right up here, Benjy?'

''Cos I want to get away from folk for a bit.'

'Like being a hermit?'

'Ay, I suppose so.'

'How'd you like to be a real hermit – for a day?'

'What yer mean – a "real" 'ermit? I'm real, aren't I?'

'We mean – St Erewold, the hermit of St Jude's in the 1200's. For the church fête. You could be dressed up and pretend to say prayers and people might bring you things.'

'What kind o' things? I've 'ad enough of socks wi' holes in them and cast off underclothes!'

'Well, there might be some grub.'

'Ay, but what's the point of an 'ermit these days? People don't believe in all that praying for souls and what not.'

'Well, you could be a free spirit.'

'Free spirits? I could do with some o' them. No good asking you lads if you carry a hip flask? No, I thought not. You'd better clear off, lads. I'm not in t' mood for much talking.'

Disappointed, the boys retreated. But they had not given up. From past experience they knew that Benjy ruminated at leisure on what was said to him. And next time they would go better prepared.

Sundry small amounts of food – taken from this and that so as not to arouse suspicion – accompanied them on their next visit. Benjy was appreciative.

'What about that hermit idea, Benjy?'

'I dunno. I don't want to be gawped at.'

'You'd have a habit – a sort of gown – covering you and a hood hiding your face. You'd just have to sit there, saying prayers.'

'Not really my line, lads.'

'Remember that Christmas pudding?' said Jem. 'There could be another one next Christmas.'

'I can see a bribe a mile off! Do yer think that tramps have no fine feelings?'

Benjy looked cross. There was a pause as he screwed a bit of tobacco from a pouch and put it in his mouth.

'I'll do it, just to show yer.'

'There's just one thing, Benjy,' Jem said nervously. 'You'd have to have a bath beforehand.'

'A BATH? I 'aven't 'ad a bath for more than a year – when I was last in t' doss-house in Bruddersford. I'm not sure I fancy that.'

'You see, people visiting your cell would get quite close to you and ....' Jem's explanation tailed off.

'Yer mean that I smell, don't yer? It's not me that smells, it's you – all that soap and watter! Anyway, I bet your 'ermit smelt! I'd be more authentic as I am.'

Jem ferreted in his brain for the meaning of 'authentic'. Did it mean 'real'? Sometimes he was surprised at Benjy's vocabulary.

'Anyhow,' Benjy continued. 'Where would I get a bath?'

'You could come to our house,' Jem said. 'When my Mum and Dad are out.'

Benjy capitulated. Secretly, he thought a bath after a year would be a good idea. He didn't actually despise personal hygiene. But his role of tramp meant adhering to certain standards. Amongst these was a certain disregard of appearance and cleanliness. In any case, whilst in summer he could take the occasional bathe in a moorland stream, winter forbade such frivolity.

Jem explained the plan to his mother. With some trepidation he asked: 'Could Benjy have a bath here beforehand?'

'Use our bathroom – him! Who says he's got to have a bath anyway?'

'The vicar.'

'Well, let him have a bath at the vicarage then!'

'But it's my responsibility.'

'Not while I'm in the house!'

'Something else, Mum. St Erewold was real – there really was a hermit. But there's also a legend about an anchoress – a lady hermit. What about...'

His mother broke in: 'No Jem. I'm definitely not going to be an anchor...whatever it is!'

The fête was on the middle Saturday in July. During the four weekends leading up to it, Jem and Harold were busy. They painted black lines on some old grey canvas so that it would resemble something built of stone. Jem's Dad helped to fix poles inside so that, when opened out, it could be the hermit' s cell. They painted some posters: *This way to St Erewold, See St Jude's very own hermit, Leave your trubbles at St Erewold's cell.* Some furniture they had in mind would have to wait until the Saturday morning.

For the hermit's habit, Jem got Benjy's measurements. His mother cut and stitched some sacking to make a gown with a hood. Jem and Harold also needed gowns as acolytes. (He'd looked up the proper spelling.) But he wanted them to be made of material better than sacking.

'Why should the servant be dressed better than his master?' his mother asked.

'The acolyte has to go out and about, amongst people. He has to look respectable.'

A compromise was reached with an old grey blanket, which his mother converted into gowns with brass buttons on the front.

What kept Jem awake at night was the problem of the bath. His Mum had said: 'not while she was in the house'. Did that mean it would be alright when she wasn't at home? Friday morning came. His father was going to be out all day.

'Jem, I've got to go to Bruddersford for the Women's Institute for things for tomorrow. If you go out, be sure to put the key under the usual tin in the shed. And don't get up to mischief! I'll be back late. Keep the kitchen fire in, for baths tonight. And make sure you keep the fireguard in front.'

(Friday night was bath night, and the water was heated in a boiler behind the kitchen fire.)

This was the opportunity he'd been waiting for. He and Harold went to the allotments. Benjy had moved there, as it would be handy for the fête. He was sitting on a box in front of the hut, whistling, and whittling away at a piece of wood. This was a good sign! Jem explained the coast was clear for a bath. Benjy feigned reluctance but agreed.

Even though they counted themselves as friends of Benjy, the boys were self-conscious about being seen with him. However, on the way to Jem's the only boy they saw was Charlie Foster, who smirked at them. No doubt he'd have some unkind remarks to make in the school playground on Monday. But it was in a good cause.

Jem sent Harold upstairs to run the water. 'Don't put too much in – remember Archimedes!' In a lesson at school about the ancient Greeks, their teacher had been telling the class about Archimedes noticing that his body displaced an equivalent mass of water; and Benjy's body was bulky. Jem got Benjy to take off his disreputable boots and socks in the kitchen. Then he laid sheets of newspaper on the stairs. With some apprehension, they listened to the splashes and singing. Scraps of 'Charlie is my darling', 'Land of Hope and Glory, 'It's a long, long way to Tipperary' indicated that, despite Benjy's avowed contempt for bathing, he was enjoying himself.

He looked human at last, thought Jem and Harold,

when the operation was complete: his ragged beard trimmed and combed, his bulk squeezed into an old suit that Jem's father had not worn for a few years, his feet finding a new home in a pair of old gardening boots with a lining of horse hair. The job was almost too well done – where was the old Benjy? But no doubt he would gradually revert to his comfortable untidiness. What a pity, though, that he should have to go back to the shed in the allotments – he might get dirty again before the fête. It was usually Jem who had the ideas , but this time it was Harold.

'Benjy could spend the night in our garage. Dad won't be using the car. I could get the mattress from the spare bedroom. No-one would know.'

So Benjy was installed at the Manse, without the Minister knowing that he was earning credit in Heaven by sheltering the homeless. What Harold had not foreseen was the difficulty of secretly providing Benjy with some breakfast.

The morning of the fête dawned bright. Early – for them – Jem and Harold went to the scout hut to borrow the hand cart. It had a pole sticking out from the front and a bar across, so that two scouts could walk behind the bar pulling the cart. It was usually used for going to camps. They took the painted canvas and framework to the church and set it up beside the wall of the chancel. There was a large 'window' opening so that visitors could get a good view of St Erewold. Then they went to the Manse, checked that Harold's parents were not around, and transferred a heavy wooden armchair from the study to the cart. The final call was to the chapel, from which they borrowed a low reading desk and a tall candle holder.

Before escorting Benjy to his cell, Jem and Harold reminded him of his calling.

'No smoking, Benjy, or chewing tobacco. Don't go to sleep. Keep your hood around your face. Look as though you're praying. If children come, reach a hand out, rest it on their head, and say "Pax vobiscum".' (Harold had consulted his Dad who had suggested this Latin blessing: 'Peace be with you'.)

'Thank goodness it's only for an afternoon,' Benjy said. 'But I'll never remember them Latin words!'

At the gate between the vicarage garden and the churchyard, the boys set up the sign: *This way to St Erewold.* The programme of the fête also drew attention to the presence of the hermit. At two o'clock, the vicar and the Honourable Peter Danellion-Smith mounted the platform. The vicar offered thanks to God for the occasion and then invited his companion to open the fete. The Hon Peter was a short, plumpish, man with red cheeks. It was difficult to visualize him wearing armour or fighting in a battle as some of his Dandelion ancestors had done. (The effigy of one of them – a Crusader – lay in the family's chapel in the church.) But what he lacked in physical appearance, he made up for in speaking. His voice was high-pitched and penetrating.

We lived in troublous times, he said. In a year or two, this beloved country of ours might be faced with the most serious threat to its existence since the time of Elizabeth the First. When that time came, we should all depend on the support of each other.

What divided us – church or chapel, God or no God, politics of right or left, status in society – all these were as nothing compared with what we shared. Belief in decency, democracy, freedom, responsibility – this was what mattered. In this fête, the whole village had come together. And we would stick together. We would have need of prayers – including those of St Erewold the hermit, who had come at these troublous times to help sustain us. But we would pull through.

With words such as these, Hon Peter declared the fête open, and wiped his brow with a large white handkerchief.

Jem wandered around, with a notice, *See St Jude's very own hermit* pinned to the front of his grey gown. He took time off from his responsibilities to see how many corks, floating in water, he could stab with a hatpin; and to throw bean bags at a sloping box with holes in it. Then he stood at the gate calling out: 'This way to St Erewold', 'Come and see my master'. Charlie Foster's unwelcome face swam into view.

'We all know who St Erewold is! Not really a credit to the community is he?'

'Happy is he who repents,' replied Jem, playing the part of the faithful acolyte.

Whilst Jem encouraged people to enter the churchyard, Harold stood by the cell, giving warning of pilgrims approaching. Peering through the window, visitors saw a hooded, candle-lit, figure bent over a book on a desk, mumbling his prayers. When Harold whispered, 'Child', the hermit looked up and gave his blessing: 'Pesky vobissums, kid'. Harold, not wanting to let his father's learning down, kept reminding Benjy of the correct words: 'It's "Pax vobiscum", Benjy.' But to no avail.

A little girl complained to her mother that the hermit had called her "pesky". 'I don't think he meant anything nasty, dear,' her mother said.

Harold's Dad came over to the cell.

'Greetings, St Erewold!'

Benjy looked up and saw the clerical collar.

'And pesky vobissums to thee, vicar.'

Mr Bright was bemused.

'Do I recognize that arm-chair, Harold?'

Harold had hoped he wouldn't notice. 'Yes, Dad.'

'A good choice, if I may say so. But don't tell your mother.'

The fête was drawing to a close. Everything had gone well. The games and stalls had been busy. Miss Entwhistle's 'Little Tots' had pirouetted on the stage. The Honourable Peter Danellion-Smith looked pleased with himself after a visit to St Erewold. The Silver Band played its last piece, 'Auld Lang Syne'. When the clapping had died away, a distant baritone voice could be heard singing lustily:

'All things bright and beautiful,
All creatures great and small,
All things wise and wonderful,
The Lord God made them all.

Each soothing flask that opens
Each little drop that sings
And gives me glowing colours
And flies me up on wings.'

Jem felt the responsibility of an acolyte and blushed. He walked to the cell as fast as dignity allowed.

'Not so loud, Benjy!'

'I bet yon 'ermit used to sing when 'e were 'appy.'

It was time to pack up, anyway. Harold and he divested themselves of their habits and helped Benjy out of his. They took stock of the gifts that children had brought for St Erewold: three sticky buns, four jam tarts, a teddy bear, a packet of wine gums, a cauliflower and an old copy of 'Camping for Boys'. Jem guessed that the last had been given by Charlie Foster with a smirk on his face.

Suspecting that somehow Benjy had had something strong to drink, they thought they had better escort him back to the allotments.

'I don't smell right!' Benjy said. 'It'll be ages afore I'm myssen again. Did I enjoy being St Erewold? Well, it made a change. And that Honorary Peter's a real gent. That swig of brandy from 'is flask really set me up! Not one of your pasty teetotallers! Strange there were two vicars though – and that were afore the brandy!'

Another letter arrived from the Vicar.

Dear Jem and Harold,

Thank you so much for arranging for your friend to play the part of St Erewold. It was very well done – I almost thought I was looking at the real hermit. And how nice to hear him singing praises to God at the end! Please convey my thanks to your friend and tell him that there will always be a cup of tea or cocoa at the back door of the Vicarage.

3 THE FLOOD

For two weeks the youngsters of Althwaite had revelled in snow. Every afternoon after school, and at weekends, sledges swooped down the slopes around the village. In the crystal clear air, the valley rang with cries of excitement and occasional injury. The waning light did little to sap the enthusiasm of the bigger boys, amongst whom Jem and Harold counted themselves. In the semi-darkness, Harold's sledge went off course, hit a hump and broke in two, depositing its rider in a drift. Crestfallen, Harold made his way to the Manse, wondering whether his father would be able to fix the two pieces together.

Sorry for his friend, Jem found it difficult to get to sleep. His wandering mind alighted on Benjy. Had the cold weather driven him to the hostel (the doss-house, as Benjy called it) in Bruddersford? Knowing Benjy's detestation of the place, Jem thought it more likely he was in a barn somewhere.

On the Saturday, after carrying logs from the log store into the house, Jem set off for the Manse, pulling his sledge.

'Let's look for Benjy first,' he suggested to Harold, who was agreeable.

They were not surprised to draw a blank at the allotments – there was no hay or straw in the huts there. The barn in Ten Acre Field gave no hint of being occupied. Nor did the one at Cop Top Farm. They went down the field from the farm towards the river. In the centre the water was flowing but, at the edge, thin sheets of ice glinted in the sun. About a hundred yards from the river, on a little eminence, was a shepherd's hut – an old caravan resting on brick supports. A thin spiral of smoke drifted up from a metal chimney. The door opened to reveal a familiar figure.

'Hullo Benjy! You alright?'

'I suppose you'd better come in,' he replied ungraciously.

The hut was cosy. A bale of straw served as a settee. A plank on two logs made a low table. Hay at one end was a mattress. At the other end were a stove and a pile of logs.

'This is nice, Benjy,' Jem asked. 'Does Farmer Ackroyd know you're here?'

'O'course. We've made a pact. In view of the growing threat from Germany…' (Benjy tried to put on the accent of a BBC news reader) '…Britons have got to stick together. Leastways…' (he relapsed into his normal speech) '…that's a good excuse for seeking a bit o' sympathy. I've been splitting logs up at the farm – 'ardest work I've done for years. These 'ere's me wages.' Benjy pointed at the logs.

'You've got a lot of tins there,' commented Harold who had spotted a cache in the corner: Baked Beans, Garden Peas, Mulligatawny Soup and others.

'Ay, well, Mrs Ackroyd came out wi' a cup o' tea. We got talkin' and I told her about my missus. I got quite affected, and so did she. So she 'elped me to stock up my larder.'

'I didn't know you'd been married, Benjy,' Jem said.

'It were a long time ago. Afore I went to France in't war – the war to end all wars they called it. When I came 'ome, wi' a Blighty wound, she'd gone off wi' someone else.'

Jem's sense of delicacy prevented him from prying further into Benjy's history.

'Anyroad,' Benjy continued, 'it's that nightmare o' the trenches that makes me nervous about this chap Hitler.'

Jem and Harold left Benjy, who was obviously comfortable, to carry on with their sledging. Mr Bright had been too busy preparing his sermon to have time to repair Harold's sledge, so they took turns on Jem's.

'Surprising how much Benjy knows about what's going on in the world,' Jem said. 'Last night, my Mum and Dad were arguing about Hitler. Mum said Mr Chamberlain had really brought "peace in our time" – I think it was – when he came back from seeing Hitler at Munich. But Dad said he'd sold out to Hitler over that country, Czechosl…whatever it is. He said we should have pushed him out of the Rhineland when he occupied it two years ago.'

'My Dad says we couldn't have done that because the Rhineland is part of Germany,' Harold commented.

'Well, I don't reckon to understand it,' Jem concluded.

Arriving at the top of a sledging slope, they gladly abandoned their attempt to understand the international situation.

The next day was a Sunday, but it was a Sunday with a difference. The villages in and around the valley took it in turns to perform Handel's Messiah at Christmas. This year the honour had fallen to Althwaite. Lots of folk trudged through the snow to the Methodist Chapel. Jem sat with his parents in the front row of the gallery, near to the conductor. His father had a miniature score, with which to follow the music. Jem's eyes roved over the choir, ranked on steep staging around and above the central pulpit. He was surprised to see the Honourable Peter Danellion-Smith. He had not seen him in the choir before. In fact, this was another of Hon Peter's attempts to get more involved with the community. There were other familiar faces, including the Vicar, Bert, the dustman, and Mrs Bright, Harold's mother. Singers from other villages had come to join in: they all knew the Messiah thoroughly and the way it was sung in the West Riding.

Mr Bright climbed into the pulpit followed by the soloists and the trumpeter. It was fortunate that it was a large pulpit. Having uttered a short prayer, he descended the steps and joined the audience. The familiar strains of the introduction set the performers and the audience on their long journey.

'Comfort Ye, my people', sang the tenor soloist. Jem's thoughts began to roam. He felt comforted by the year that was drawing to a close. There had been plenty of good things. He and Harold had extended their exploration of the country around Althwaite. Within a three mile radius, there was not a footpath they did not know. They also knew many unofficial paths – short cuts across fields or through woods. They knew where there was a badger's sett and a fox's den. Sometimes, Charlie Foster was with them. But Jem was never easy in his company. He was too inclined to make fun of people, not always in a kindly way.

'There were shepherds abiding in the field', sang the Soprano. Benjy would have been at home among the shepherds, Jem thought. He and Harold had got to know him better during the year. But he was still a mystery. He hadn't always been a tramp. He had once referred to a 'cataclysm' in his life. Jem was not sure what that meant. Was it, perhaps, when he returned from the last war and found his wife had left him? Had that turned him into a tramp, or had he always had a bent for the solitary life? Thought of Benjy made Jem uneasy. What could he do for him this Christmas? Last year there had been the pudding. Jem's pocket money did not extend to buying brandy or tobacco, which were Benjy's favourite comforts. Could he invite him to join in their family Christmas dinner? No – his mother was charitable, but even she drew a line somewhere.

Jem was aroused from sleepy musing by everyone standing up. The choir had reached the Hallelujah chorus. He had once asked why the audience stood up for this chorus. He had been told that at a performance soon after the work was finished, King George the Second had been so excited that he had risen to his feet. Of course, the rest of the audience had to follow suit. Jem wondered whether the king had simply wished to stretch his legs, having sat for so long. Jem was glad to do so himself.

After a pause, the Soprano began the aria, 'I know that my Redeemeer liveth'. This was Jem's favourite bit – one to which he actually listened. It made him feel religious. If only his life could continue on such a high plane! But he knew that tomorrow would bring the usual tussles between what he wanted to do and what he ought to do. He had given up making resolutions to be good.

The wooden pew was becoming more and more uncomfortable. His mother had twice told him not to fidget. When the basses launched into the final 'Amen', to be joined one by one by the other parts of the choir, he knew that relief was at hand. After applause and Mr Bright's benediction, the audience gathered up their coats, commented to each other on the quality of the performance, and began to filter out. There was a general feeling that Althwaite had done justice to the Messiah.

In the quieter parts of the oratorio, people had been surprised to hear rain on the roof. They emerged to find that the temperature had risen above freezing under the influence of a mild wind from the south west.

As Jem lay in bed that night, he could hear water dripping from the snow overhanging the gutters. Every so often, snow slid off the roof with a 'whoosh' and hit the ground with a bang. He awoke as it was getting light. Something in his dream had disturbed him. He tried to bring the dream back to life. All he could recapture was a vision of water – lots of it, flowing fast.

He sat up in bed. Benjy! The hut only a hundred yards from the river! He looked out of the window. Already, patches of green showed through the snow in the garden. He got dressed quickly, found his Wellingtons in the kitchen and slipped out of the house, leaving the back door unlocked.

It took him a quarter of an hour to reach Cop Top Farm above the river. The sight both fascinated and horrified him. He had never seen the river so full. The rise in the temperature was melting the snow on the moors rapidly. The water could go only one way: downhill into the valley. After emerging from the village, where it was largely confined by walls, the torrent had freedom to spread itself. Water surrounded the knoll on which the old caravan stood.

'Suppose it rises higher and carries the caravan away!' Jem thought. He ran to the farm-house. Farmer Ackroyd had just come out and was going across to the cow shed.

'What's up, lad?'

'It's Benjy, Mr Ackroyd. Is he still in that caravan?'

'Well, he was yesterday.'

'Come and look at the river!'

'Glory be!' the farmer exclaimed when he saw the scene.

Together they ran down the field. At the edge of the flood, Mr Ackroyd stood still, judging the distance to the caravan and the speed and depth of the swirling water.

'Rope – that's what we need,' he shouted. 'You stay here, but keep above the water line.'

He hastened back up the hill. As Jem waited, he

watched the water gradually covering the bricks on which the caravan was perched. The door opened and Benjy looked out.

'Stay there, Benjy!' Jem shouted. 'Farmer Ackroyd's going to rescue you!'

Benjy surveyed the surrounding water. Jem could almost feel his amazement and anxiety.

'Come on, Mr Ackroyd!' Jem murmured to himself, observing the flood rising almost to the door of the caravan.

At last, the farmer and Pete, his grown-up son, came running down the field. They stopped at a tree which the flood was beginning to lap. Uncoiling a long rope, they tied one end to the tree. Farmer Ackroyd tied the other end around his waist. He stepped into the water and began wading to the caravan. By the time he had reached the bottom of the rise, the water was up to his chest. He disappeared into the caravan. Minutes seemed to pass before he emerged. Now, the rope was tied first around Benjy and then around the farmer. They descended the slope. Benjy was shorter than the farmer, and the water was soon up to his shoulders. He was moving slowly, balancing a bag on his head.

The tree was upstream of the caravan, so that on the return Mr Ackroyd and Benjy had to wade against the current. They needed the help of Pete and Jem hauling on the end attached to the tree. Benjy stumbled and righted himself. Pete and Jem strained to pull them in. More of their bodies rose above the water until they stood panting and dripping on the grass.

Mrs Ackroyd and her twelve year old daughter,

Alice, had now come down the hill with blankets. With these around their shoulders, Benjy and the farmer climbed up the field. Jem carried Benjy's bag, which was so heavy he could only just manage it. At the top, the party turned to look down. The caravan rose gently off its perch. It spun slowly round before being seized by the main body of water. As though in a farewell gesture, a puff of steam rose from the chimney as the water quenched the fire in the stove. Then the caravan sank lower and lower until only the roof was visible.

A blazing fire in the farm-house kitchen was the most welcome sight Jem had seen for a long time. Benjy had to be helped out of his top clothes, which suffered more rents in the process. Mrs Ackroyd produced a small glass of brandy. Benjy gave her an appreciative smile.

'Tha reminds me of my missus as she used to be afore....' Benjy left the rest unsaid.

Before long, Mrs Ackroyd had breakfast on the table. Benjy's immersion seemed to have diluted his smell. Clad in an old dressing gown of Mr Ackroyd's, he looked almost presentable. It wasn't until he had done justice to bacon, fried egg, tomatoes and sausages that he looked around the table.

'That were great, Mrs Ackroyd. I don't know 'ow to thank you all. I suppose it were Jem who gave the alarm.'

Jem blushed as all eyes, including those of Alice, turned on him.

'But where would I be wi'out Mr Ackroyd and his rope and you all? Floating down to Bruddersford, out o' this world, that's what. I were just saying, t'other day, that Britons 'ave got to stick together. Well, you've certainly stuck by me today!'

Jem dreaded going to school the next day. The word of what had happened would by then have got around. As luck would have it, Charlie Foster was the first boy he saw in the school yard.

'Quite the little hero, aren't we!' Charlie said.

'All I did was to raise the alarm,' Jem protested. Then, raising his faith in humanity to a superhuman level, he added: 'You'd have done the same in that situation!'

The following Saturday Jem went up to the farm. Benjy had been installed in an empty cottage. He had a cold, but was otherwise alright.

'What was in that bag, to make it so heavy Benjy?' Jem asked.

'I couldn't leave my siege supplies behind,' he replied, pointing to the tins of baked beans and other things on a shelf.

'Were yer Mum and Dad worried when they found you'd gone out early in 't morning?' Benjy asked.

'You bet! I was going to cop it, if Farmer Ackroyd hadn't telephoned Mr Bright and asked if Harold could go over to our house and let them know I was OK.'

'I reckon they must 'ave been proud of you.'

'Well, they thought I did the right thing.' (It would have been too embarrassing to add that his mother had given him a hug, and his Dad had clapped him on the back.)

'You're mentioned in the paper,' Jem added, producing a copy of the Bruddersford Examiner. A short article described how Farmer Ackroyd, his son and Jem Murgatroyd had saved a tramp from being swept away by the flood.

'*A* tramp! I like that!' Benjy was annoyed. 'I'm *the* tramp of Althwaite Valley.'

It was late on Christmas Eve. Jem lay in bed, unable to get to sleep. The prospect of tomorrow was too exciting. He could hear the Silver Band in the distance as its members made the round of the village, playing Christmas hymns. The night was charged with mystery, like clouds burdened with snow.

"Christians awake, Salute the happy morn!" the Band played. This Christian needed no awaking. But, as his mind wended its way to sleep, Jem was conscious of a problem resolved. Benjy's Christmas was assured. He was still at Cop Top and had been invited to join the family for Christmas dinner. Jem felt a tinge of envy. Was it because of the good cheer he could envisage in the farm kitchen? Was it due to a face which had looked at him with an amused smile? Unable to decide, he drifted into oblivion.

4 THE TOWER

A tall fence surrounded the grounds of Althwaite Hall, The Honourable Peter Danellion-Smith's residence. Boys who climbed trees on the outside of the fence got no more than glimpses, through shrubs, of lawns and flower beds. Such reports as the village had received from gardeners who had worked there suggested a garden of mystery – though the gardeners may have been tempted, by the offer of a pint in the Dandelion Arms, to embroider their recollections. There were rumours of grottoes, a tunnel inlaid with shells, fountains which burst into life on the approach of people.

Some of this was embroidery. But there was a kernel of truth. Hon Peter's grandfather – Sir Quinlan Dandelion – had married a lady with romantic notions. Moreover she was from Ireland, the nearest land of mystery to England. She had tried to devise a garden of surprises as one wandered from one section to another.

The garden had never been open to the public since

Hon Peter's father had died in 1912 from fever caught on archaeological exploration in Central America. His son was a shy, retiring, man whose main interests were his books and roses. He had been in the army in the latter part of the 1914-18 war and had risen to the rank of Captain in the Pay Corps. His main contribution to the local community was as a Justice of the Peace. Now in middle age, he had never married. His elderly mother lived with him. From time to time she tried to persuade him to come out of his shell. She was now making another attempt.

'You really ought to do more for the community, Peter. It needs leaders. "Nobless oblige" and all that!' she said at the breakfast table, interrupting Peter's well-practised feat of reading The Times whilst eating a boiled egg without spilling any of it.

He was inclined to agree. He had been encouraged by the report in the Bruddersford Examiner of the church fête last summer. *The fête got off to the best possible start with a brief but stirring speech by The Honourable Peter Danellion-Smith, one of whose ancestors fought at the Battle of Agincourt*, it had begun. He had been encouraged, too, by the welcome given him when he joined the Althwaite choir as a tenor to sing the Messiah. Almost every week brought disturbing news from Germany about the latest acts or threats of that man Hitler and his gang. The eyes of the portraits of his ancestors followed him around the Hall, as though muttering: 'Rouse thyself, Peter. Nobility *does* oblige, as the old motto sayeth'.

The first indication of Hon Peter's decision to follow a more public life was the announcement that the garden and grounds would be open on a Saturday in May. The entrance fee of one shilling (sixpence for children) would go toward re-equipping the village's recreation ground.

On the day, many people turned out despite a cold wind. The Vicar, the Minister, the Chairman of the Parish Council, the doctor, the village policeman, the owner of the woollen mill, the landlord of the Dandelion Arms and other important people rubbed shoulders with shopkeepers (who had closed for the half day so as not to miss this unusual opportunity), farmers and such lowly people as the dustman and the road sweeper.

Jem and Harold were amongst the young folk who took advantage of the chance to see whether the rumours about the garden were true. Harold had Jonquil, his sister of eight years old, with him. He hadn't wanted to be lumbered with her, but his mother wasn't able to come; and Mr Bright wanted to have some private talk with Hon Peter about the need for money to repair the Methodist Sunday School. Secretly, though, Harold was proud of her. She had auburn hair which fell almost to her waist. A few freckles drew attention to her round cheeks in which dimples appeared on the least excuse. Harold was a bit sheepish about her name. 'Jonquil', a kind of narcissus, was the inspiration of her mother who used to teach botany at Bruddersford High School.

The boys hurried past the flower beds in search of architectural features. At the end of a small lake, there was indeed a grotto, with a statue of some ancient god. They found the tunnel which led under a mound to another part of the garden: it made a splendid echo. But the fountains were so small that even a fresh wind didn't threaten passers by with a wetting. They penetrated beyond the formal paths to the far side, where they found Hon Peter guiding a party of visitors. Unlocking a gate in the fence, he led them through a copse to a field surrounded by trees. In the middle rose a slim, round tower, with a conical top.

Peter had decided to depart from his natural diffidence and wear something festive. His straw hat, linen jacket, red neckerchief and cream trousers marked him out as someone special. The party gathered round him below the tower.

'Lady Dandelion, my great grandmother,' he began, 'came from Ireland. She wanted to be reminded of her native country. So her husband erected this tower. It's like the round towers built in Ireland as refuges in case of raids by Vikings. It became her favourite retreat in the summer. The spiral staircase leads to a room at the top where she used to embroider in the afternoons. The butler would bring her tea. But instead of climbing the staircase, he put the tray in a wooden cradle. If you look up to the window near the top, you'll see a pulley. A rope was passed through it and down to the ground so that the cradle could be hoisted up. There are horizontal bars across the inside of the window to make it safe for her to reach out for the tray. Now, if anyone would like to climb to the top, please do. But a warning: there are sixty two steps!'

The Vicar and some elderly ladies declined the offer. Reluctantly, One-Leg Tim, the veteran of the Boer War, decided that his crutches wouldn't get him up. Bert the dustman was game, as were the younger folk. Harold told Jem to climb up after Jonquil in case she slipped. Charlie Foster followed them.

'Seen any tramps lately?' he asked. Jem ignored him.

As they climbed, the staircase became dark except where an occasional loophole let in a little light. In the room at the top, sunlight streamed through the window, creating bright swathes on the floor. Two rush mats, pale with age, covered part of it. The sun also illuminated dusty corners and cobwebs. There was a low arm-chair, a small table and a faded screen on which knights in armour, dragons and damsels with long hair could be made out. Bert surveyed the room with a smile on his face.

'A right good retreat this! I'll let my missus know. A bit o' spring cleaning an' it'd be just the place for her and her friend to have a natter. Specially if the butler hoisted up tea for them. I could go off to't football match in Bruddersford then wi'out being badgered!'

The party felt their way back down and returned to the garden. One-Leg Tim, who had one of the village allotments, got into discussion with Alistair McAlister, the Hall gardener, on the secrets of growing the best carrots and leeks. After consuming cakes and lemonade at the tent that Peter had had set up on the lawn, Harold and Jonquil took Jem back to the Manse.

'How did you enjoy the garden, Jem?' Mr Bright asked when they had settled down to tea.

'It was very interesting to explore. But the best thing was the tower. I'd never realized it was there. A bit spooky going up. But the room was bright and sort of welcoming – as though it was glad to have people there at last.'

'It was a magicky place!' Jonquil exclaimed. 'I'd like to play up there. Couldn't we have one in our garden, Daddy?'

Mr Bright laughed. 'I don't think the circuit stewards would think it a good idea!'

After tea, the boys set out the railway lines and busied themselves with coupling wagons, shunting and sending the clockwork locomotives on their way. From under the dining-room table, Jem became aware of Mrs Bright reading a bed-time story to Jonquil. He half listened whilst responding to the directions of Harold who had taken it upon himself to be the Bruddersford and Althwaite Railway supervisor.

Jem woke in the night. He had a feeling of great loss, and tried to recapture his dream. He had been climbing a tower but had woken up before getting to the top. The story that Mrs Bright had read to Jonquil floated into his mind. In a few moments, a shiver of excitement ran down his frame. He found it difficult to get off to sleep again. When his mother called up the stairs that he was late for breakfast, the plan was clear in his mind.

He was even less attentive than usual in Sunday School and Chapel. He had not the faintest idea what Mr Bright had been talking about. He grabbed Harold's arm as they emerged into the sunshine.

'I've got something important to tell you. Let's go down to the bridge.'

The bank of the river underneath the bridge was a dry and hidden place where they often went.

'Well, what is it?' Harold asked.

‘You remember that story your Mum was reading to Jonquil last night?’

‘Er…was that the one about Rapunzel, in that book of stories by the Brothers Grimm?’

‘I didn’t know who it was by. But “Rapunzel”, yes. Well, when Rapunzel was twelve, she was shut up in a tall tower by the sorceress. That was after her parents had had to give her up when she was born because they’d stolen a kind of lettuce from the sorceress’s garden. The only entrance to the tower was the window high up. Each day when the sorceress came, the girl let down her long hair and the sorceress climbed up it.’

‘No wonder you were mixing up passenger and goods trains last night, if you were listening to the story so closely!’ Harold interrupted. ‘What happened then?’

‘Well, a prince came by and heard Rapunzel singing. He liked her voice so much, he came every day. But he couldn’t see how to get up the tower until, one day, he saw how the sorceress got up.’

‘How did he know she was a sorceress?’ Harold asked.

‘How do I know? Perhaps he didn’t,’ Jem replied. ‘Anyway, that evening the prince called to Rapunzel to let down her hair and he climbed up and thought her so beautiful he asked her to marry him.’

‘How could anyone climb up her hair without it hurting, or being pulled out?’ Harold questioned.

‘Ah well, you see, she twisted her hair round an iron hook in the window sill.’

‘How stupid of me!’ Harold said, ironically.

‘Are you interested or not?’ Jem asked, becoming impatient.

‘Of course I am. Carry on.’

'There was just one snag.'

'In the hair!' Harold couldn't resist that little joke.

'No. There was no way for Rapunzel to get down. So the prince used to bring lengths of silk which she secretly plaited into a ladder. But the sorceress found out, cut off Rapunzel's hair and took her away...'

'How could she take her away if there was no way for Rapunzel to get down?'

'Because she was a sorceress! Anyway, when the prince came that evening , he was so shocked to find an old hag that he jumped out of the window – but he wasn't killed.'

'Naturally,' Harold said in a withering tone of voice.

'Look, this *is* a fairy story. Although he wasn't killed, he was blinded by thorns. He wandered over the land and at last heard Rapunzel singing, so they were reunited.'

'What happened to the sorceress?' Harold inquired.

'Don't know. Does it matter?'

'Full marks for memory. But what's the point of all this?'

'The point is – the tower in the Hall grounds and Jonquil with her long hair!'

'You're going to imprison Jonquil and let her hair grow down to the ground?'

'Just for a day. She wanted to play in the room at the top. So we take her, we get a rope and put it through the pulley. We make a cradle to haul a snack up. We get her to sing, like Rapunzel. And one of us can be the prince – only he'll have to discover his way up by the staircase.'

'So you're the prince and I'm the sorceress" Harold exclaimed wryly.

'If you like.'

Harold usually fell in with Jem's plans. But he had reservations about this one. To each of his difficulties, though, Jem had an answer. How could they get into the tower? (Jem had noticed Hon Peter looking under a stone for the key.) They'd be trespassing. (They'd be outside the garden, and no one would notice.) Where would they get a long enough rope? (Farmer Ackroyd would lend them one.) What about Jonquil wanting to go to the lav – fairy stories never thought about that. (Take a bucket.)

Harold caved in.

It wasn't until a fortnight later that they were ready for the enactment of the story of Rapunzel. The chief difficulty had been making a cradle for food and drink to be hauled up to Jonquil. In the end, Jem settled for a wooden seed tray washed out as well as he could. He bored two holes in each end and threaded thick string through. He knotted the ends together above the middle of the tray and slipped a metal ring through the knot.

After school on the Friday, Jem went up to Cop Top Farm and asked Farmer Ackroyd for the loan of a long rope.

'What's it for, Jem?' he asked.

'It's just for an experiment.'

The farmer was a bit dubious, but he had a liking for Jem after the rescue of Benjy from the flood.

'Alright, but bring it back before sunset tomorrow.'

At 11 o'clock on Saturday morning, Jem met Harold and Jonquil at the bottom of the steep road leading up to the Hall. It was a fine morning, much to Jem's relief – he wanted the sun to be streaming into the room as it had on the day of their visit. He was burdened with a sack containing the tray, the rope and a bucket. Harold had lemonade, sandwiches and apples in a rucksack. Jonquil carried two dolls and their bedclothes in a bag.

'I told Mum that we were going to your house for a picnic,' Harold said.

They climbed the road. Before reaching the entrance to the Hall drive, they scrambled through a hedge and made their way along the edge of a field of barley. On their left, the high fence of the Hall garden rose above them. At the end of the field, they had to crawl under barbed wire. Jonquil's dress got stuck.

'That's torn it!' quipped Harold who was beginning to enjoy the expedition.

They climbed over a stone wall into the wood which surrounded the tower. Creeping slowly and quietly, they reached the edge of the clearing. There stood the tower, rising serenely into a blue sky. No one was about.

'Bet the key won't be there,' Harold said. He was now becoming nervous, and almost wished for the adventure to be frustrated.

But there it lay under the stone. It took two hands to turn it in the rusty lock. The door swung open, releasing a damp, musty smell from the staircase.

Jem went up first. Again the room at the top, full of sunshine, seemed welcoming. He opened the window, tied a big knot in one end of the rope, fed the other end through the pulley and let both ends drop to the ground. Back downstairs, it was time to assume their roles. From the sack, he drew out a length of black material, left over from his mother's lining of curtains for the black-out.

'That's for you as the sorceress, Harold,' he explained.

Harold didn't think it a very exciting costume, but consented to have it fastened around him with safety pins. For the prince's attire, Jem was content simply to tie a sash round his waist, to hold a wooden sword.

Harold took Jonquil up the staircase with the bucket.

'Now, you're Rapunzel. Look out of the window from time to time to show your hair. It'll soon be time for lunch – I'll haul the tray up. After that, the prince will find you – don't come down by yourself. You can sing, like Rapunzel did in the story.'

Jonquil opened her bag, took out her dolls and began to tell them the tale.

Unlike the characters in the story, this sorceress and prince were on friendly terms. They co-operated in hoisting up Jonquil's lunch and amicably scoffed the remaining sandwiches and lemonade. Then the serious business began. Calling up to Jonquil that they would be away for half an hour, the prince closed his eyes whilst the sorceress crept into the wood. Having counted ten, he began searching. It was very quiet amongst the trees. Only the occasional hammering of a woodpecker punctuated the silence. Like a Red Indian – which he sometimes was – Jem listened for the least noise that might indicate the whereabouts of the sorceress. The crackle of a stick, a dark form, a chase and a scuffle ended with the sorceress prone beneath the feet of the prince.

'Pax!' called Harold, whose black costume was now looking very ragged. 'I say, I found an old quarry over there.'

He led Jem to the edge of the wood furthest from the grounds of the Hall. The quarry, where stone had been extracted for the building of the house, was overgrown and mysterious. Blocks of gritstone littered the bottom. It demanded a detailed exploration. Clambering about, the boys forgot about their role play.

'Hadn't we better be getting back?' Harold asked eventually.

Neither was wearing a watch. Had they been away half an hour, or an hour? They hurried back to the clearing.

There was something strange about the appearance of the tower. The window was shut and there was no rope hanging over the pulley. Had Jonquil given them up and gone home? They ran over to the entrance. What they saw froze them like statues. There was the rope, coiled neatly. To one side was the bucket – empty. There was the seed box 'tray', with an empty lemonade bottle on it. Under the bottle was a piece of paper. Unfolding it Jem read:

The Hon Peter Danellion-Smith requests the prince and the sorceress to have the goodness to call on him after school on Monday. Rapunzel is safe and well."

'Crumbs!' said Harold.

‘Crikey!’ said Jem.

‘Now we’re for it!’ Harold added.

They gathered up their equipment and set off for home. Jem tried to put a brave face on their situation.

‘Hon Peter’s a good sort – I don’t think he’ll be too hard on us.’

‘I’m more worried about Jonquil and what my Mum and Dad will say,’ Harold said, feeling miserable.

Jem had first to return the rope to Cop Top Farm. Alice was in the farmyard.

‘What’s up, Jem?’ she asked. ‘You’re looking glum.’

‘I’ll be alright. Just a little problem.’

‘Want to talk about it?’

‘Not now – thanks. Will you give this rope back to your Dad. Tell him the experiment was partly a success.’

Jem looked back as he shut the farm gate. He returned Alice’s wave. In his mind, he shuddered at the idea of Alice knowing how stupid he had been. On the other hand, he thought she would understand better than his parents.

Four-thirty on Monday afternoon saw Jem and Harold seated in Hon Peter’s study. They were by themselves. Each had a piece of paper and pencil. They were looking around the room for inspiration and scribbling. They had been cowed by the haughty butler and had just managed to avoid trembling in the presence of Hon Peter. He had asked them if they knew what happened in a court of law. This had taken them aback. Was he going to take them to court? They had calmed down a bit when he proposed that Jem should be the Counsel for the Prosecution and Harold the Counsel for the Defence. He had given them ten minutes to prepare themselves.

The door opened and the butler intoned: 'Pray rise for His Honour the Judge.'

Hon Peter made a solemn entrance. He was wearing a red cloak, borrowed from his mother. On his head was a pith helmet. No doubt it had been white when it graced the head of his uncle, who had had a distinguished career in the Colonial Service, ending as Governor of Tonga-Bonga. Now it was greyish-yellow and smelled of moth balls. Nervousness about their forthcoming ordeal overcame the inclination of the boys to smile at his appearance.

The judge took his seat at the desk.

'Counsel for the Prosecution, please state your case. You will refer to Master Murgatroyd as "X" and Master Bright as "Y".'

'If you please, Your Honour,' Jem began. 'X and Y were guilty of trespassing. Also of using someone else's property without permission. And X was guilty of persuading Y to take part when he didn't really want to. Also of forgetting Rapunzel – I mean, Jonquil. To sum up, Your Honour, X was guilty of letting his imagination lead him into something stupid.'

'A list of serious charges. What has the Counsel for the Defence to say?'

Harold rose to his feet. 'Please, Your Honour, the fault really lies with the Brothers Grimm.'

'I don't think I know them. Where do they live?' the judge interrupted.

'They don't. That is, they did – in Germany, a

hundred years ago.'

'Oh, those Grimms! Carry on.'

'Well, X heard the story of Rapunzel being read and was so carried away with it that he got a bee in his bonnet. He had to come up with a plan to let the bee out.'

'You mean,' the judge interrupted, as judges do, 'he was so infatuated with the idea of being a prince and rescuing Rapunzel that he was unable to exercise his common sense?'

'It was partly that. But also, he knew that Jonquil wanted to play in the tower, so…'

'He decided to kill two birds with one stone?'

'Er, yes, Your Honour. But he didn't mean any harm and he didn't do any damage.'

Harold sat down. He thought he had done pretty well for Jem.

The judge was getting warm under his pith helmet, took it off and placed it before him on the desk.

'Having heard the cases for and against, I will now proceed to the sentences. I won't put my black cap on – the case is not quite as serious as that. Harold Bright: you were not as much responsible as Jem. Nevertheless you were a party, and Jonquil is your sister. I sentence you to cleaning the Dandelion brasses in the family chapel in St Jude's. Mrs Carter, the cleaner, will tell you what to do. She lives in the first of the Mill cottages. Now, Jem Murgatroyd: you were the instigator. I sentence you to helping One-Leg Tim to weed his allotment on the next four Saturday afternoons. Do you have anything to say against these sentences?'

'No thank you sir – we're very sorry,' Jem said.

'Well, that's not so bad – though I hate weeding!' Jem said with relief after the butler had shown them out with a grin on his face.

'Not so bad for you! And I don't mind cleaning the brasses. But I'm in dead trouble at home. I didn't tell them where we were going. I didn't take proper care of Jonquil…'

'How did Hon Peter discover her?' Jem interrupted.

'He and his mother were in the garden. They heard singing and went to investigate. Jonquil told them she was waiting for the prince. Some prince! I'm not to have any pocket money for the next two months! I wish I'd never listened to your silly plan. You can get someone else to take part in any more daft schemes!'

Having vented his annoyance, Harold parted from Jem without the usual comradely 'so long'.

Jem wasn't in such deep trouble at his home. In fact, he thought he had caught his Dad hiding a smile when it all tumbled out. But he was angry with himself. And if Harold were to desert him, life would be dark.

As he tried to get to sleep that night, the word 'instigator' kept running through his head. It was not a word he had heard before, but he could guess what Hon Peter meant. He seemed enveloped in gloom. But, like distant stars seen through a gap in the clouds, two possible sources of consolation and encouragement twinkled faintly. They had very dissimilar features: Benjy and Alice.

5 CHARITY

One feature of the episode that especially bothered Jem was his failure to rescue Rapunzel. He had let Jonquil down. Instead, strangers – who were not even in the story – had turned up and released her. What could he do to make amends? He asked his mother what she thought he might do. The result was a bargain between them. He would chop a hundred sticks for fire-laying (being sure to wear thick gloves) on Saturday and she would make a cover for Jonquil's doll's cot.

The week was an unhappy one. Harold paid little attention to Jem at school. Jem saw him much in the company of Charlie Foster. When Saturday arrived, he felt like going to Cop Top farm to see Benjy. But he was busy chopping sticks from split logs in the morning. After midday dinner, he set off for the allotments. It was a grey, uninviting, sort of afternoon. He found One–Leg Tim sitting outside his hut.

'Hullo, lad. I 'ad a message from t'squire that you were turning up. Some sort of punishment is it? Tha looks a bit down in t'mouth. Cheer up! When I were in t'Army, I were on plenty o'punishment squads – didn't do me any 'arm.'

Jem was grateful to Tim for not enquiring into the reason for his 'punishment'. He set about weeding between rows of lettuces, carrots and runner beans. With only one leg, Tim's method of gardening was to squat on a wooden box and reach as far as he could. Then, holding on to the box, he would do something between a hop and a shuffle to another position. His neighbours on other allotments helped him with the heavier work. He was glad to have any help that was offered.

After an hour's weeding, Jem's back was aching. Moreover, he was bored. He straightened up. Tim came out of the hut and smiled.

'Tha's not used to such work! Come and 'av a cup o'tea.'

Jem washed the soil off his hands at a standpipe. Tim poured tea from a flask into two cracked mugs. Jem sat on a wooden box. The sun was starting to come out. This was better, he thought.

'How did you lose your leg, Mr…?'

'Call me Tim. Ay, well it were a long time ago – nigh on forty year. In t'war against Boers in South Africa. Almost a forgotten war these days!'

Tim stared into the distance, as though seeing again the sun-scorched open country – the "veldt" and the little hills, the "kopje".

Bit by bit, over the next few Saturdays, Jem gained an insight into that war, as Tim remembered it. As an artillery man, he recalled the awful labour of getting the guns from one place to another. If the ground was dry, the hooves of the horses and the wheels of the guns threw up clouds of choking dust. If it was sticky, or if they were climbing up hill, or if they were crossing a shallow river, then everyone had to help, pushing and pulling – except the officers who stayed on their horses and urged the men to put their backs into it.

'All wars are tragic, but this seemed specially so. The Boers were fighting for their country. We were trying to get it from them, for the Empire. They were very brave. It were a place called Pardeberg that I came a cropper! We 'ad Boers surrounded in a dry river valley. They'd dug trenches around their wagons. Women and children were there too. We pounded 'em – poor blighters! You could see wagons going up in flames. But their riflemen were well hidden – kept picking our men off. I were sent wi' a message to another company, and got a nasty wound in the thigh. Treatment were delayed 'cos our casualty station came under fire. Eventually, there were nowt t'surgeon could do but take t'leg off. Whilst I were in 'ospital, I treated myself to t'chocolate Queen Victoria 'ad sent for New Year 1900. A tin for each soldier. I'd kept mine for a couple of months. So I ate my little bit while lying in bed and wondering 'ow I'd get on wi' just one leg. I've still got the tin, wi' 'er Majesty's head on t'lid.'

On another occasion, Tim remarked: 'Dreadful things were done in that war. Yer know them concentration camps as that chap Hitler is said to be building? Well, it were our side who invented 'em – for 'olding Boer women and children whilst their menfolk – the commandos – were 'unted down. The number of women and children who died – you'd never believe it!'

These grim tales of a conflict – so far back in time, but fresh in the mind of an old survivor – helped Jem to forget his troubles. He got to like Tim, who talked to him as one grown-up to another.

On Saturday evening, his mother showed Jem the quilt for Jonquil. It was made from patterned pieces of cloth and stuffed with cotton wool. On one side she had embroidered 'Rapunzel'. Jem was nervous on Sunday morning. He wanted to give it to Jonquil secretly. Harold would think he was 'soft', he thought. An opportunity occurred as they were leaving Chapel.

'Look, Jonquil – I'm very sorry I didn't come to rescue you. It was selfish of me. My Mum's made this for your dolls. Keep it a secret.'

'Ooh, thanks Jem. But I wasn't really worried. Then these nice people arrived. Mrs Smith took me to their house and showed me a doll she'd had since she was little. Then Mr Peter took me home in his car.'

Jem hid his disappointment that Rapunzel had not been upset by the prince's failure to show up.

'Friends?' he asked, and received a smile.

Jem's conscience was now much lightened. The following weekend he found time to go up to Cop Top Farm. Benjy was clearing out a pig sty.

'Indecent work for a tramp, this. But, as they say, beggars can't be choosers. Just 'elp me wheel this lot to t'midden, an' we'll 'ave a cup o' tea.'

Benjy's cottage had a stone floor with a few frayed mats. The windows were small, so that it was dark inside. But it was a palace compared with Benjy's habitual residences: hedge bottoms, barns, the allotment hut.

Jem sat in an arm-chair that had seen fifty years of service in the farm-house before being relegated to the labourer's cottage. A blackened kettle stood on the hob. Benjy swung the hob above the fire, and the kettle was soon singing. A much more satisfying way of boiling water than on the top of a gas cooker, Jem thought. Benjy poured out the tea and added a few drops from a small bottle to his mug.

'I 'eard that you were in trouble wi' squire. Serious were it?'

Having thought of Benjy as a possible source of consolation, Jem was nevertheless reluctant to tell the whole tale.

'I let myself be carried away by a story I'd heard. We climbed Hon Peter's tower. Had up for trespassing. But he was lenient – let us off with a bit of hard work. What bothers me is that I was so stupid. I let my friends down.'

Benjy wormed more details out of Jem.

'Tha shouldn't be worried. As for trespassing – I've done more o' that than tha'll do if tha lives to be a 'undred. An' I've done it wi' a feeling o' right on my side. O' course, you don't invade someone's little garden or a farmer's fields. But when someone 'as thousands of acres – moorland or forest, say, or a vast pleasure ground – does 'e really 'ave a right to it? 'Ow did he come by it? Was it fair and square? Or was it 'cos he made big profits from people slaving for 'im? Or by enclosing land that belonged to everyone?Do yer remember the Civil War – them Levellers and Diggers?'

Jem tried hard to 'remember' the Civil War. He could see Cromwell's Ironsides pursuing Royalists fleeing from the bloody field of Naseby. He could see the picture, hanging on the wall of his Grandad's house, of a boy in a satin suit being asked by his Roundhead enemies: 'When did you last see your father?' He could see Charles the First, wearing two shirts so as not to shiver from the cold and appear to be trembling, stepping bravely out from a window of Whitehall Palace on to the scaffold. But Levellers and Diggers had no place in his confused picture of the Civil War.

'They were on the right track,' Benjy continued. 'They thought the land belonged to everyone. And no one 'ad more rights than anyone else. Even the poorest 'ad as much right to a life as the richest. So don't thee worry about a bit o'trespassing for fun.'

Jem took this with a grain of salt. It was all very well for a tramp to have little regard for the rules. But his chapel-going parents would have something to say if he displayed Benjy's disregard for the rights of property-owners.

Benjy poured out more tea and again added fortifying drops.

'Reckon I'll soon be off wandering again.'

'Why? I thought you were comfortable here.'

'Ay. But no tramp can keep his self-respect 'aving to change 'is underclothes and shirt once a week. In any case, when spring and summer come, I get the wanderlust. Secret places in the moor call me. Farmer and missus are very kind – they wouldn't throw me out. But Pete's been called up – by the Army. So they'll need a real farm labourer. An' they'll need the cottage for 'im.'

As Jem left the farm, he looked around for Alice.

She wasn't outside, and he didn't like to knock and ask for her. Still, the visit had done him good. He felt less dissatisfied with himself. But Benjy's intention of tramping off into the wilds was a bit worrying. Jem knew, from news on the wireless and his parents' talk, that war with Germany was likely. When Hitler's troops had marched into Czechoslovakia three months ago, his mother had acknowledged that Mr Chamberlain, the Prime Minister, had been wrong about 'peace in our time', though she still thought he had tried his best. If war did break out and Benjy was wandering about, might he be taken for a German spy disguised as a tramp? Might some trigger-happy soldier shoot first and ask questions later? Well, there was nothing to do but hope for the best. When Benjy took it into his head to do something, he became pretty obstinate.

When Jem woke the next morning, he found that sleep had planted an idea in his head. He had remembered – unusually for him – parts of Mr Bright's sermon. The text had been: 'the foxes have holes and the birds of the air have nests, but the Son of Man hath not where to lay His head'. Mr Bright had described Jesus' wanderings from place to place. He had gone on to talk about the families who would lose their homes if war came, and the refugees who would have to be looked after. Jem had felt an upsurge of pity for these folk. But as for Jesus, wasn't his saying a bit exaggerated? He and his disciples never seemed to have difficulty finding kind people who would offer them somewhere to stay for the night. People were always glad to see him. But Jem could think of someone who, over the next few months, would have no equivalent of a foxhole or a bird's nest. He saw Benjy, in 'secret places in the moors', spending the night under a gorse bush by a stream or sheltering from a storm in a shooting hide. Something ought to be done to send him on his way in good heart. That something was the idea that had come to him. But it was not something he could do on his own. He needed Harold.

He was nervous about approaching Harold, in case he was rebuffed. But he saw him looking in his direction in the school playground and went up to him.

'How do? How's things at home? You still in queer street?'

'No – they're getting over it. I'm getting some pocket money again. Mum took pity on me!'

The ice was broken. After school they sat under the bridge, throwing stones into the river, telling each other what they had been up to. Jem broached his idea for giving Benjy a good send-off when he went wandering. They could raise some money by selling raffle tickets. Then Benjy could be sure to have sufficient supplies, including tobacco and brandy, to keep up his morale. Harold slipped easily into the role of sceptic.

'No one would buy a ticket for Benjy. And what about prizes?'

'The tickets would be for something general – like the poor,' Jem argued. 'We could easily find some prizes. For a start there's that silver teapot that my Mum has said she's going to give to war salvage. It's not real silver, but it looks good.'

Harold took some persuading. He had said he wouldn't take part in any more of Jem's schemes. But all that could go wrong with this one was that it would fail. Like Jem, he had a soft spot for Benjy. So the scheme was launched.

Jem needed Harold not just for his general support, but also because his father had a typewriter. They had to ask Mr Bright for white paper and also for the carbon paper which was interleaved between the white sheets to make copies. Assured that the object was relief of the 'destitute', Mr Bright gave them access to the drawer in his desk. Having to rub out the errors in their typing, the task took a whole Saturday afternoon. In the end they had fifty tickets, which read:

GRAND RAFFLE FOR THE DESTITOOT

FIRST PRIZE: BOY'S BIKE (good condishun – for 8-11 year old)

SECOND PRIZE: BOW AND ARROWS AND KWIVER (in case of invasion)

THIRD PRIZE: 'SILVER' TEAPOT

Price: Children sixpence, Grown ups one shilling

Organisers: J Murgatroyd and H Bright

Draw: Saturday 15 July 1939

Neither boy's spelling was beyond suspicion. Harold's suggestion that they check 'destitoot' came too late – when they were half way through the typing.

Jem was proud of the honesty of the inverted commas around 'Silver'. (His mother had agreed to donate the teapot to his cause rather than to war salvage.)

What had exercised Jem most was the price of the ticket and the number they should aim to sell. The problem had seemed so difficult, he had been tempted to give up the whole idea. It was his first lesson in business economics. He wanted to raise a handsome amount for Benjy, say £5. But his 'market' consisted of children at school and in Sunday School, aunts and uncles and a few grown-up friends. The children could not be expected to pay more than sixpence. Then, was it right to have a higher price for grown-ups? Would that put them off? They might be put off by the prizes, anyway: what would elderly Aunt Florence do with a bow and arrows? In the end, the decision was a compromise. Prices of sixpence and one shilling would raise between one pound five shillings (if all fifty tickets were bought by children) and two pounds ten shillings (if all bought by adults).

Selling the tickets was the hard part. Grown-ups asked who the 'destitoot' were. If Jem knew they were sympathetic, he told them it was Benjy. Otherwise he said it was for 'certain people who are poor like'. Children were more interested in the prizes than who the money was for. Jem took the bicycle to school. Although it was becoming small for him, he could still ride it. Giving it up would be a sacrifice. Harold demonstrated the bow and arrows in the recreation ground. One arrow hit a window of the pavilion and cracked a pane of glass. Harold warned that any of the spectators who 'split' would not be able to buy a ticket. But the accident made the prize more desirable.

Arriving at school the next morning, Jem and Harold found a bunch of the smaller children awaiting them. They began singing:

'Destitoot, destitoot,
Who's going to get the loot?
This old raffle's such a swiz!'

This was repeated a few times, the tune having a resemblance to that of the nursery rhyme, "See-saw, Margery Daw". Harold took it in good part. Picking up a stick at the bottom of a hedge, he bent over and hobbled through the school gate as though he was a very old man. The children followed, in fits of laughter. Jem was less amused. Seeing Charlie Foster grinning in the background, he went over.

'Getting kids to do your dirty work, eh?' Jem said.

'What dirty work? Naturally, everyone's suspicious. If it's not for you two, who's it for? I think I can guess!'

'It's *not* for us. I'll swear it.'

Others gathered round to hear Jem swear, crossing his heart and wishing to die.

Another suspicion that Jem and Harold had to allay was that the draw would be 'fixed'. They needed to find some disinterested person, who had not bought a ticket, to draw the winning tickets. This ruled out their parents, their teacher and Bert the dustman. At four o'clock on the day of the draw a small procession of children, most of whom had bought a ticket, followed Jem and Harold to the allotments. One-Leg Tim had graciously agreed to pull the tickets out of a hat – or, rather, a First World War helmet which he used for measuring out bone meal and other fertilisers.

The tickets, much fewer in number than Jem had

hoped for, were emptied into the dusty helmet. Tim shut his eyes, swished them around and picked out the first. The bicycle was won by Shirley, a shy little nine year old, who seemed taken aback. Boys eyed her enviously. Her seven year old brother was delighted. Laughter greeted the news that Jem's Aunt Florence had indeed won the bow and arrows. Jem calmly produced a letter in which, in her spidery handwriting, she declared that if she won the bicycle or the bow and arrows, she wished a further draw to be made. This self-sacrifice (which Jem had had the foresight to engineer) won admiration. The second draw produced a more appropriate winner: ten year old Donald. More laughter accompanied the award of the 'silver' teapot to Charlie Foster. ('Serve him right!' thought Jem.) Charlie had bought a ticket only because he badly wanted the bow and arrows. He was embarrassed but not too disappointed: Donald was a cousin, so the bow and arrows were at least in the family.

The following day Jem went up to Cop Top Farm. He was uneasy. He knew that, beneath Benjy's hairy and leathery exterior, there was a sensitive soul. Would Benjy take offence at a gift of money, especially one obtained by the devious means of a raffle? He was embarrassed, too, because the amount raised did not seem very much.

Benjy was re-fixing wire to a fence. He took Jem to the cottage. Several weeks of civilized living had transformed him. It still seemed as though a comb would be treated as a trespasser on his head. But his beard was shorter. He had a decent pair of boots. His corduroy trousers and old jacket were like those of any farm labourer. Jem wondered whether he knew that the distinctive smell had disappeared.

A mug of tea in his hand, Jem explained, falteringly, how he and Harold had wanted to help Benjy to be well prepared for his journey into the wilds. But he was sorry that the amount was only eleven shillings and sixpence.

'Well, I'm a bit flummoxed. I'm not one o' them tramps as begs for money. But seeing as it were you and 'arold, I'll say thanks very much. I appreciate the thought behind it. It may not be as much as you'd 'oped for, but it'll be a real 'elp.'

Jem was relieved. He asked when Benjy was going and how long he would be away. Benjy was vague.

'Depends 'ow the spirit moves me. A couple of months perhaps. But this war that's comin' bothers me. I may 'ave to do my bit for the war effort.'

Jem found it difficult to see Benjy fitting into the war effort, but kept quiet.

'That reminds me,' Benjy continued. 'I don't normally leave clues to my whereabouts. But, just in case I'm needed, keep this – they're directions. You're a scout, so you'll be able to work 'em out. If not, ask yer Dad.'

Benjy handed Jem a well-used envelope.

'So long, Benjy. Don't do anything I wouldn't do! See you in the Autumn.'

'Cheeky lad! Don't thee get up to mischief – at least not too much! So long , mate.'

As Jem skirted the mud in the farmyard, Mr Ackroyd and Alice were driving the cows to the milking shed.

'Hello Jem! You're a stranger. Been to see Benjy?' the farmer asked.

Jem didn't want to broadcast his charity.

'Just been to see him before he goes off.'

'Ay, we'll miss having him about. Useful too, when he has a mind to be. And wi' Peter getting called up, we shall be lonelier up here. Come and see us. You can lend a hand and earn a bit o' pocket money. Well, must get these beasts in!'

Alice lingered outside. She smiled at Jem.

'I heard about your raffle. It was a kind thought.'

Jem went slightly red.

'Well, I feel sorry for Benjy sometimes.'

'So do I. But you did something about it. See you soon!'

She followed her father into the cow shed. Jem ran down the lane. There was singing in his head. He felt as though he would burst. To receive a mite of praise from Alice - that was reward enough for all the trouble and problems of the raffle!

6 WAR

After a high comes a low. For a few days Jem's spirits remained at the level to which they had soared. Things seemed to be going well. Jonquil harboured no resentment that he had failed as the prince. He had finished his 'punishment' at the allotments, but continued to do bits of work for One-Leg Tim, whom he liked. He and Harold were pals again. The problems of the raffle were in the past, Benjy appreciated the outcome, and Alice had praised his action. Benjy had entrusted him with information about his whereabouts in the wild, in case the war against Hitler required the assistance of tramps.

Something, though, was not quite right. Jem was aware of a deep-seated worry, which was gradually working its way to the surface of his mind. Walking home from school one day, he realised what it was: the 'Scholarship'.

Earlier in the year most members of his class had sat the Scholarship exam. If they got through, boys would go to the Grammar School and girls to the

High School, both in Bruddersford. Those who did not succeed would go to the Secondary Modern School in Homefield. Although the teachers might be equally good, there was a difference between the Grammar and High Schools on the one hand, and the Secondary Modern school on the other. The former had the élite pupils who could look forward, if they worked hard enough, to carrying on into the sixth form and perhaps proceeding to colleges or universities. The latter had no sixth form, so the leaving age was 15 at most. Jem knew that only a small proportion of his class would be likely to get through. But his teacher had said he had a good chance. So he was hopeful.

The fateful day arrived, just before the summer holidays. The teacher called out to the front of the class those who had been successful. Jem was not amongst them. To say that he was disappointed would be to put it too mildly. Rather, he was dumbfounded. He had not always been a conscientious scholar, but he had realised how much his future depended on getting over this barrier. Now, he had failed. He would be judged a failure by others. The fact that most members of his class had also failed was no consolation. There would be just a chance, in two years time, of transferring to the Grammar School, but he could not rely on that.

Harold had got through. Jem was glad for him, but they would not be in each other's company so much. Alice was already going to the High School, so Jem now had another reason for thinking himself inferior to her. The worst aspect, though, was that Charlie Foster had succeeded. How could he, Jem, have been judged less worthy than Charlie! He could just imagine Charlie crowing to himself, and to others!

Jem's Mum and Dad were disappointed. They had set as much store as Jem on his going to the Grammar School. But they tried to be reassuring. It wasn't the end of the world! He would have another chance. Many people who had not had the benefit of a Grammar School education had gone on to great things. Jem was not to be comforted. A few tears were shed on his pillow that night.

On the first day of the holidays he saw Alice in the village. His immediate reaction was to avoid her, but she caught sight of him and crossed the road.

'Hello, Jem. How's things? Are you going to Bruddersford next term?'

'Afraid not – didn't get through!'

'Oh, I am sorry. I was sure you would. What went wrong, I wonder?'

'Reckon it was the arithmetic paper – not my strong point. Harold's going – which is a good thing. But Charlie Foster as well – that really gets me! Sorry to say that – I've seen you with him sometimes.'

'You don't like Charlie, do you? There's perhaps more to him than you think. He can be sarcastic and unkind. But I think that's because he's unsure of himself.'

'I'm not so sure of myself now!'

Alice looked at Jem. His face was not a picture of happiness.

'You mustn't get too upset, Jem. If Charlie can get through, but you can't, it means there's something wrong with separating people on the basis of one day's exam. You're worth two Charlies! Who has the ideas? Even if they sometimes lead you into trouble!'

Alice's smile was like a ray of sunshine penetrating

the clouds. Perhaps the people who mattered would still have confidence in him!Her encouragement made him resolve not to allow his failure to depress him. In any case, distractions during the next few weeks took his mind off personal problems.

First there was a week's holiday at Scarborough. It was the family's favourite resort, though they had also enjoyed Bridlington and Blackpool. They stayed at their usual guest house, sharing a family room at the back which looked on to the cricket ground. A gap between the guest houses on the other side of the road led to the top of the cliffs overlooking the North Bay. Jem usually went out with his Dad before breakfast: first to the newspaper shop where Dad bought the News Chronicle, and then to the cliff top. There they sat for a few minutes whilst Dad absorbed the news about the gathering storm in Europe, and Jem surveyed the scene. He never ceased wondering at the marvellous prospect. To the right, the cliffs curved round to join the jutting peninsula on which stood the stark remains of the castle. He could imagine the enthusiasm with which Norman soldiers had chosen such a magnificent site.To the left, the cliffs became lower until another height, Scalby Ness, reared up. Beyond that the rising coastline led to Ravenscar.

'We'd better make the most of this holiday, Jem,' his father said on the first morning. 'When war comes, beaches on the east coast will be out of bounds.'

Jem noticed that Dad said 'when' not 'if'. He looked down at the long sweep of the North Bay, with the unceasing assault of the waves. Down all the length of England this was happening: the sea approaching and retiring, nibbling and undermining. Was it possible that these same waves might sweep German soldiers ashore?

The week passed too quickly in a familiar but rewarding routine. A castle was built on the sands and the incoming tide was led into the moat, leading to the collapse of the fortification. The rock pools of the South Bay were explored. The miniature railway was ridden to Scalby. In the rain Jem and his Dad rowed on the lake in Peasholm Park. They braved the open air pool near the Park. They took the train to Whitby and climbed the long flight of steps, Mum complaining about their steepness, to the old parish church and the abbey ruins.

There was one discomfiting experience - an alarming dream. Perhaps it was due to the fish and chips they had had in the evening. Jem woke, crying out and disturbing his parents. Just a few fragments of the dream remained. One was of someone painting a picture, unaware that they were in terrible danger. It seemed to have no relevance to his life, so it soon slipped away from his conscious mind.

On the last evening, they joined hundreds of other folk carrying blankets and refreshments to the Open Air Theatre where they sat on the steep rake of seats facing a grassy stage in the centre of a lake. As the night enveloped them, a musical play unfolded, its participants cocooned in a brightly lit world of romance. Then came the walk back to the guest house, as Jem felt satisfyingly weary and the stars shone faintly above the street lights.

‘Do you think there’ll be war?’ Jem asked Harold.

They were in the Manse garden at the side of the house where Snow in Summer, with its starry white flowers, tumbled untidily down a bank to the path. Snails liked to take refuge there. And Harold’s lead soldiers found it a good place from which to ambush Jem’s mechanised forces – a ‘Dinky’ tank,field gun and lorries.

‘Dunno. My Dad thinks it won’t come to that. Be exciting if it does, though.’

Jem wasn’t sure he shared the prospect of excitement. For one thing, he was afraid that his Dad would be called up into the army.

‘My Dad thinks that when Mr Chamberlain said we’d support Poland - that was after Hitler’s invasion of Czecho…whatever the name is - it made war inevitable. But we had to do it.’ Jem replied.

World problems retreated into the background as they became engrossed in miniature warfare.

On the following Sunday, Mr Bright led earnest prayers for peace.

‘Suppose Hitler is also praying, but for war, how does God decide?’ Jem wondered, and then felt his conscience accusing him of disloyalty to his country.

Most people in Althwaite could not bring themselves to believe that war would come. But preparations in case were under way. Gas masks had already been distributed. Now folk tried to remember where they had stored them and, having succeeded, tried them on and placed them where they would not be overlooked.

Jem, Harold and other boys looked on as bags made from sackcloth were filled with sand and piled up beside the entrance to a room at the back of the Methodist Sunday School. This was to be an Air Raid Wardens' Post. Jem was surprised to find Hon Peter helping. He had come down just to encourage. But, noticing that all the other onlookers were women and children, he had decided the manly thing to do was to take off his tweed jacket, unfasten his cuff links, roll up his sleeves and offer his services. Bert, the dustman, seemed to be the foreman in charge. Lookers-on were treated to the spectacle of the squire being told by a dustman what to do. Hon Peter didn't seem to mind. Bert caught sight of Jem and Harold and winked at them. He was obviously enjoying being the natural leader. A lady emerged from the Sunday School with a tray on which were mugs of tea. Peter was glad of an excuse for a rest. Sipping his tea, he spotted the two boys.

'Aha! So the prince and the sorceress have deigned to visit us!' he said in his loud, high voice, much to the embarrassment of Jem and Harold. 'I trust you are suitably reformed.' Looking at Jem, he added: 'I hear that you and Mr Tim have become good friends. Now, if both of you and that delightful little Rapunzel want to visit the tower again – say as a distraction from the war if it comes – let me know.'

'Don't tell Jonquil that the squire said she was "delightful",' Harold warned Jem, after the work had resumed. 'She's cocky enough already!'

The fathers of both boys had enrolled as Air Raid Wardens. Jem's Dad busied himself one evening making out a rota of Wardens for his part of the village.

Jem helped him to make a glass-fronted case in which the rota could be displayed on top of a post in the front garden.

It was the morning of Sunday 3 September, after service at the Chapel. Jem was in the shed, trying to make a model aeroplane from scrap pieces of wood. He heard his mother calling. From the tone of her voice it seemed to be something important. Jem ran down the garden and entered the kitchen in time to hear a dry, cultured voice coming from the wireless: '…No such undertaking has been received. Consequently, this country is at war with Germany.'

Dad switched the wireless off. No one spoke for a few seconds.

'Those poor Poles!' Jem's mother said. 'There's nothing we can do to help them.'

'There never was,' his Dad commented. 'It was a gesture of sympathy. Now, Hitler will turn his attention to us. The country's ready to face up to him. But I'm not sure our leaders are. We need Mr Churchill as Prime Minister.'

'Will we be invaded?' Jem asked.

'Hitler might have a go. But he wouldn't get very far. When was the last time this country was invaded, Jem?'

Jem thought, and then said: 'The Normans I suppose – in 1066. You can't count William of Orange, 'cos he was invited over to rid us of James the Second.'

'If only the Scholarship exam had been just history, Jem. You'd have sailed through!' said his mother with a smile.

Days passed. The war didn't seem to come any nearer. Jem started going to his new school in Homefield. There had not yet been time to dig air raid shelters, so temporary arrangements were made and tried out. Jem's class went over to a public house opposite the school, where they went down to the vaults below the bar. There they crouched uncomfortably amongst the barrels and copper pipes. Their teacher pointed out a bucket in the corner. Jem was not the only one who found it fun to surprise his teetotal parents by saying he had been into a pub.

The school bus from Homefield deposited its passengers in the market place. Jem's usual walk home took him past a row of houses built fifty years ago for workers at the mill. He hardly ever glanced at them. But one afternoon his eye was caught by a small Union Jack poked out of an upstairs window. A small face looked out – unhappily, it seemed. The next afternoon a little girl was swinging on the garden gate. She had a thin, spotty face and long, straggly hair. She looked solemn, almost cross. Jem didn't remember seeing her around the village.

'Hullo,' he said. 'Who are you?'

'I'm Dot,' she replied. 'I'm a 'vacuee.'

Jem knew that lots of children had been evacuated from the big cities in case of German air raids. This was the first evacuee he had met.

'Where are you from?'

'From Hull – me and my brother and our Mum.'

As though at a signal, a boy came out of the house.

'Who are you talking to, Dot?'

He was probably younger than Jem, but as tall, and stocky. He looked at Jem in a threatening way.

'What do yer want?'

'I was just trying to be friendly,' Jem protested. 'I'm Jem Murgatroyd. I live further up the lane. Have you just arrived?'

'Two days ago. I'm Ron and she's Dot. We don't like it 'ere. Wish we'd never 'ad to come.'

The sound of voices raised in dispute came from the house.

'Our Mum don't get on with 'er that lives 'ere,' Ron said in explanation.

'Day after tomorrow's Saturday. I'll show you around the village, if you like.'

The sour look on Ron's face disappeared.

'Don't want to go round the village,' Dot said. 'All them strange folk staring and pointing at us!'

'No need to bother about them! I'll show you secret places. You'll be surprised.'

Ron eagerly, and Dot apprehensively, agreed to be taken around on Saturday afternoon.

Jem told his mother that he had met some evacuees.

'Poor kids! You'd better bring them to tea some day.'

Jem thought he ought to get to know them before issuing such an invitation. For all he knew, people from Hull might not be familiar with such a meal as tea.

'Waifs and strays' was the phrase that came into Jem's mind as the thought of the strangers. But wasn't that absurd? Dot might be a waif, but not Ron, who was capable of menace. 'Refugees' was another description. But it was only the other side of Yorkshire they had come from, not another country. Still, they had in effect been pushed out by Hitler. For that reason they deserved sympathy and encouragement. These Jem determined to give them – with Harold's help if he could get it. Stimulated, his sleeping mind had produced a small brainwave by the morning.

After running an errand for his mother on Saturday morning, Jem went up to the Hall. Approaching it down the long drive, he began to feel nervous. But he believed that Hon Peter had meant what he said. Still, it would be tactful to go round to the back door.

'Is the Hon..., I mean Mr Danellion-Smith in, please? It's Jem Murgatroyd.'

'Yes, I know who you are, Jem,' Mrs McAlister replied. 'I'll see. Just wipe your feet on the mat and wait here.'

Jem was ushered into the study, where he and Harold had been on trial.

'Ah, Prince Jem. Top o' the morning to you! More maidens want rescuing? More sandbags want filling? Must be something of national importance brings you here!'

The squire's raillery didn't put Jem at ease. But he managed to explain about the unhappy evacuees and asked politely if he could show them the tower. Hon Peter was only too happy, provided the little girl didn't fall down the staircase. As he saw Jem out through the front door he added, as a parting shot: 'I don't imagine she'll be left in the lurch, like Rapunzel!'

Jem went red, and was glad his back was turned to Peter.

In the afternoon Jem and Harold took Ron and Dot on a tour of the village. Highlights were the "Wreck" (the Recreation Ground) where Dot screamed as she was pushed too high on a swing; the bridge over the river, with its secret spot under the arch; and the mill, where bales of wool stood outside and the doors to the boiler room were open. Jem knew, however, that *the* highlight was yet to be revealed. He led the climb up the road toward the Hall. Terraced houses here nestled under a low cliff. Having no back gardens, the front gardens often sported washing lines. As it was a Saturday, there was hardly any washing. But a few of the housewives were gathered outside on the road, talking excitedly and looking up the hill. At a bend in the road, shortly before reaching the drive to the Hall, there was a panoramic view of the village. Here Jem and Harold were surprised to find more of the local women surrounding a younger woman sitting on a stool before an easel. On it was an unfinished picture of the scene below, with the mill prominent in the foreground.

'Nosy Parkers!' Jem muttered. 'Why can't they let her get on with her picture without crowding round?'

He was about to lead his party on, when he realised that the women were not just curious. The artist was being assailed by questions.

'Where do yer come from then?'

''Ow do we know you're telling the truth?'

'Why's the mill such an important part of the picture?'

'You're foreign, aren't yer?'

The artist, who had been trying to ignore this interrogation, was becoming not just annoyed but afraid. She began packing up her paint box and brushes. Two more women arrived, carrying broomsticks.

'Don't let her get away. Grab 'er till constable arrives!'

'Smash her picture!'

Jem had a sudden flash of insight. That nasty dream at Scarborough: the artist in terrible danger! *This* was the situation. He must get her away. Hurriedly he explained his plan to Ron and Harold.

As the most hostile of the women were about to lay hands on the picture, Harold collapsed on the ground, rolling about, holding his tummy and groaning.

'Oh, the pain, the pain!' he cried out.

The ruse worked: the women turned their attention to Harold, who rolled to the other side of the road.

'Come with me!' Jem cried to the artist. She gave Jem a quick look and decided that this unknown knight was her only chance of rescue from distress. Jem hoisted Dot on to his back and grabbed the artist's stool.

'This way, quick!'

The artist followed him to the entrance to the drive, easel under one arm, picture and paint box under the other. Once through the open gate, Jem dropped Dot in order to shut it, then gathered her up again. The women, seeing their prey disappearing, shouted angrily and made after them. On reaching the flower beds, Jem glanced back. The women were through the gate. Ron was using the artist's bicycle and trailer to impede the pursuit. Harold was doing the same with a broomstick held horizontally. But the more energetic women side-stepped these barriers.A large woman knocked Harold down as though he were just a bean stick.

At the end of the garden the gate was open, as Hon Peter had promised. Jem led the way through the copse and into the clearing. As arranged, the key to the tower was under the large stone. The lock creaked, they entered and Jem locked the door behind them. They were safe! In a few moments, there were bangs on the door.

'We know you're in there!'

'We'll soon 'ave you out and 'ave you properly questioned!'

They climbed the spiral staircase, Jem bringing up the rear in case Dot should lose her footing.

'What a marvellous room!' the artist exclaimed, when she had recovered her breath. 'I'd love to paint in here.'

'Typical artist!' Jem thought. 'Escaped near death, and all she thinks about is painting!'

'I'm Lorinda,' she said, holding out her hand. 'Without you, I'd have been in queer street! But what do we do now?'

The women's voices could be heard from below.

'We wait for Hon Peter – the owner,' Jem replied. 'That is, unless Harold's been captured by those women!'

Jem now had an opportunity to look at Lorinda properly. She could hardly have looked more different from a typical woman of Althwaite. Blonde hair escaped from a blue beret down to her shoulders. She wore a baggy artist's blouse, green and smeared with paint; and a pair of maroon trousers which flared out above her canvas shoes, like a sailor's bell-bottoms. Jem wondered how old she was. His own mother was 36. Lorinda's face had fewer wrinkles, the only obvious ones being two vertical lines between her eyes, which were blue.

'I'm Jem. This is Dot. She's an evacuee. I didn't know what the trouble was. I just knew you were in danger. What were those women upset about?'

'Didn't you realize? They think I'm a spy!'

A spy! Jem knew that there was concern around the country about the risk of German spies. But in this far corner of Yorkshire - the idea seemed absurd!

'Perhaps I was dressed a bit too much like an artist, Perhaps it was my hair – you know the Nazis favour blonde hair. Then, my accent could have aroused suspicion. I'm half Czech, you see. And making the mill look important – maybe that was suspicious, though it was just artistic licence. Whatever it was, these West Riding women were really hostile. They put the wind up me! What would have happened if you and your friends hadn't come along, I shudder to think!'

Jem became aware of snuffling beside him.

'I want Ron. Where has he gone? Will he be alright?' Dot was crying.

'Your Ron's bound to be alright. He can look after himself. Do you like this room? Have you heard about Rapunzel, in the fairy story?'

No, she had not. Jem told her the story while Lorinda examined the room and looked out of the window. Dot's tears dried as she listened. Jem had just come to the end when a voice piped up from below.

'Ahoy there, Prince Jem! It's me, Danellion-Smith. Let me in please!'

Jem went down the staircase and unlocked the door.

'Another maiden in distress, eh? Are they a speciality of yours? Some lady artist, I gather.'

Lorinda was not the kind of dumpy, middle-aged, amateur painter that Hon Peter had expected. To his natural gallantry was added a touch of curious wonder. Having heard her story, he led them through the ranks of still suspicious women to the Hall. On the steps were Harold and Ron. Harold's knee was bandaged. Ron had a plaster on a shin. Dot ran to him.

'Have you heard of Rapunzel?' she asked.

'Rap and sell? What's that – door to door salesmen?'

Dot enlightened him. She was happy now.

'Come into the drawing room, my dear,' Hon Peter said to Lorinda. 'Ah, here's Constable Dewhurst, arriving on cue.'

A tall, angular policeman got off his bike and leaned it against the balustrade below the steps.

'Jem Murgatroyd and Harold Bright - I might have guessed! Don't touch that bike!' he said, glaring at them.

The women gathered in front of the house to await the outcome. Jem and Harold felt uneasy under their gaze. Jem had learnt something about the French Revolution at school. They reminded him of the women who gathered near the guillotine and knitted as the blade fell. What were they called? 'Tric…', something.

'You wait, young Jem and Harold! Impeding honest citizens in the performance of their duty!'

'And breaking my new broomstick!'

The boys were tempted to retreat into the hall, the front door remaining open. But that would have been cowardly. They stuck it out, refraining from any response. Jem was confident they would be vindicated. Harold told Jem quietly how, when his sham agony had been seen through, he had wrested a broomstick from one of the women, dashed into the drive and tried to hold the women up. But a rampaging woman, twice as heavy as himself, had simply pushed him over.

'It was like a racehorse, going down at a fence and then being trampled on. Shouldn't be surprised if I've got bruised ribs.'

'Does this sort of thing often 'appen 'ere?' Ron asked.

'Only when Jem's involved!' Harold replied.

After half an hour Hon Peter came out with the constable. From the top of the steps he addressed the women.

'I'm sorry to have kept you so long, ladies. The constable and I have questioned the young woman thoroughly. We have also spoken on the telephone to her parents in Bruddersford and to the police sergeant there. I'm happy to tell you that she is entirely above board – bona fide, as the saying is. Her slight accent derives from her childhood in Czechoslovakia. But she's a British citizen - on her mother's side, as British as you or me. And she deserves our sympathy for Hitler's dastardly violation of her country of origin. However…'

(approaching a piece of oratory, Hon Peter drew himself up and puffed out his chest) '…I do commend you for your vigilance. It was in the best tradition of the energetic citizenship of West Riding womanhood. We all have to be vigilant for "This precious stone set in a silver sea…This blessed plot, this earth, this realm this England", as the Bard of Avon puts it. At the same time, we have to be on our guard against rumour and baseless suspicion. "Watch and weigh" – that should be our motto. Now, if you like to go around to the kitchen garden, I've asked Alistair to give you some cabbages, and a few other things.'

The women moved off, some of them having made a slight curtsey. They were not sure whether the squire's little speech tilted more towards approval or reproof.

'I can't abide cabbage!' Hon Peter said to the youngsters. 'Now, time for tea. You deserve some refreshments.'

He sat them down around the kitchen table, together with Mrs McAlister.

'I think I should apologise on behalf of the village, Miss Vajansky. It really was too bad that you should have been molested like that.'

'Please don't apologise. We're not used to war. We must make allowance for people losing their heads sometimes. Anyway, it's turned out to be an amusing adventure. And I've met such nice young folk.' Lorinda looked around the table, smiling. 'As for your blend of authority and tact, sir – I'm lost in admiration.'

Hon Peter was pleased, but felt that Miss Vajansky was pulling his leg a bit. As everyone tucked into cucumber sandwiches, scones and fruit cake, he and

Lorinda reminisced about Prague, the capital of Czechoslovakia, which she remembered from her childhood and which he had visited in the Twenties.

'Now, if you've all finished,' Peter said eventually, 'I'm going to take Miss Vajansky home in my car. The bicycle is in need of attention after its use as a barricade. I'll get George, the blacksmith, to come up and have a look at it.'

Jem and Harold escorted Ron and Dot back to their house. Their mother was at the gate.

'Where on earth 'ave you two been? I've been right worried!'

'We've just been 'aving tea with the squire,' Ron replied.

'And we've had a lovely adventure,' Dot added. 'A spy and a tower and Rapunzel and scones.'

Her mother had not seen her so animated since they left Hull. Perhaps Althwaite would be alright for them after all.

The word floated up to the surface as Jem settled down for sleep: 'tricoteuses' – the women who knitted whilst watching the guillotine sweep away the aristocracy of France. Or perhaps the women he'd confronted were like Amazons, those female warriors. Suppose their broomsticks had been spears! Sleep overtook him before he could worry about what might have happened.

The parcel arrived a few days later. In it were three small packets addressed to Jem, Harold and Ron, and a larger one addressed to Dot. The letter said: 'With thanks to my heroes and heroine from a grateful artist. I hope to see you again, Lorinda Vajansky.' When opened, the packets revealed clasp-knives for Jem and Harold, a flashlight for Ron and 'The Fairy Tales of the Brothers Grimm', illustrated, for Dot.

7 THE SEARCH (1)

'Drat the black-out!' Jem exclaimed as he stubbed a foot against the kerb. He had forgotten to bring a flashlight to illuminate his return from a scout meeting on a moonless night.

The 'black-out' reminded everyone that there was a war on. After dark, no light was allowed to escape from windows. There were no street lights, and car headlights were partially masked. Unless it was a moonlit night, people carried flashlights (torches) to find their way around. Air Raid Wardens patrolled streets to check that no chinks of light were visible. At first it had seemed exciting and novel. Althwaite did not have many street lights but, even so, switching them off had made a huge difference. The array of stars on a clear night was astonishing. But the inconveniences and risks soon became apparent. Each morning after a cloudy or moonless night, there were usually two or three people in the doctor's surgery with sprains, cuts or bruises.

'Stupid black-out!' Jem muttered again as he stumbled and sprawled on the stony lane leading to his home. What with grazes on his knees and aching shoulders – the result of helping his Dad to dig a hole in the garden for an air raid shelter – he felt like a casualty of the war already.

Most people in Althwaite could not imagine that their remote village would be subject to air raids, but there was great uncertainty about how extensive German bombing might be. Shelters were being constructed in school yards. The bigger houses had cellars which could be used as shelters. The row of cottages where Jem lived had no cellars. His Dad and neighbours were digging holes in their gardens and erecting 'Andersen' shelters: curved pieces of corrugated steel, bolted together and covered with earth.

However, there was something more serious on Jem's mind than his grazes and aches. More evacuees had arrived in the village and were attending school in Althwaite or Homefield. Most, like Ron and Dot, were from Hull. Relations between the evacuees and local children had not been good from the start. When Jakie Andrews had turned up, reluctantly, at Homefield SecondaryModern School, his torn jacket, pullover with holes and his shabby plimsolls had drawn sly looks and nudges. The better clothes that he was then given by well-meaning ladies of Althwaite didn't fit. Taunts that he was now a walking shop model made him sullen. Jem had tried to be friendly with the evacuees. He had succeeded with Ron and Dot. But most of them distrusted friendly overtures. They hadn't wanted to leave the big city of Hull for this untidy village in the back of beyond. They weren't interested in it. The sooner they got back to their familiar streets the better.

What Jem feared was gang warfare. Already he had heard some of the bigger boys at Homefield muttering about 'showing them townies what's what'. He'd heard about Chicago being terrorized by gangs. Of course, it wouldn't be shooting in Althwaite, but fists and missiles could create a lot of damage. Jem sought out Ron. Both he and Dot were attending the school in Althwaite. When out of their classrooms they were nearly always together – so much so that they had begun to be referred to as 'Rondot'. He found them at the Wreck, where Ron was pushing Dot on a swing. Dot jumped off and ran toward Jem. He lifted her up and swung her round. Her face was beginning to lose its spots – perhaps the result of healthier food and the fresher air of the country. She was like the sister that Jem wished he had.

'You're the only Althwaite boy she likes – or girl for that matter,' Ron said.

'How is it between locals and evacuees at your school?'

'Not good,' Ron replied. 'Teacher 'ad to break up some scuffles today.'

'I'm afraid of relations getting worse. What could we do to make your lot happier?'

'Trouble is – they don't feel welcome. O 'course the grown-ups, like your Mum, try to make things better. But some of your lot treat us as though we weren't even English. Like we was Germans! We need cementing together somehow - so that what we 'ave in common is more important than 'ow we differ.'

Dot was staring at her brother. She had never heard him speak so like a grown-up. Even Jem was impressed.

'I think we should go and see Hon Peter,' Jem said. 'Will you come?'

'The squire? Sure!'

''Ooh, can I come?' Dot asked. 'Perhaps we can go up the tower.'

Jem looked doubtfully at her. This was a serious expedition.

'She'll 'ave to come, or I'll never 'ear the end of it,' said Ron.

Jem expected the butler to show them to the study, the place of business. But it was the drawing room to which they were led.

'Master Jem, Master Ron and Miss Dot,' the butler intoned.

Hon Peter was standing before the fireplace, where a fire had been laid but not lit.

'Well, what a treat we have here - three of Miss Vajansky's intrepid rescuers! How refreshing it was to see Art triumphing over Philistines!'

'Here he goes again!' Jem thought.

'But don't you see who's over there – in the window?'

The three of them turned. Seated in a chair was Lorinda. She got up and came toward them, smiling. She shook hands with Jem and Ron, and gave Dot a hug. She was not in her artist's get-up, but was wearing a smart skirt and jacket. Her hair was tidily done up in a bun, with a tortoiseshell comb holding it together.

'How lovely to see you! I hope you haven't been getting into scrapes recently! I expect you got my parcel?'

'Oh yes. It was very kind of you. I would have written, but I didn't have your address,' Jem said.

'Well, I guess this is a deputation of some kind,' said Peter when they were all sitting down. Dot had chosen Lorinda's lap for her seat.

'Is it the Tower, the grotto? It can't be cabbages, can it? Or is the Hall to be commandeered as a recreation centre for evacuees?'

Jem explained his fears that relations between evacuees and local children might worsen to the point of conflict. When he referred to Chicago's gangs, Hon Peter's lips twitched, but he managed to keep a straight face. Ron then described how it felt to be an evacuee, when the boys of the village were unsympathetic, or even hostile.

'Mmm, I see,' was Hon Peter's only comment before pulling the rope that set a bell tingling in the distance.

'Oh dear,' Jem thought. 'Is he going to ask the butler to show us out already?'

The butler appeared.

'James,' said his master, 'please ask Mrs McAlister if she would have the goodness to provide two cups of tea and three orange squash. And I wonder if there's any of her delicious shortbread left?' To his guests he added: 'This is obviously going to require a good deal of thought, so we need to be fortified.'

Jem relaxed. Hon Peter was going to turn up trumps again.

When they had got their drinks and Peter had told them not to worry about crumbs of shortbread falling on to the carpet, he began the discussion.

'It seems to me that the problem is one of alienation...'

Lorinda's soft voice interrupted him. 'Why not use a simpler word, like "distrust"?'

'Quite right, my dear.How do we replace distrust by trust? How make what we have in common more important than differences?'

'By doing things together,' Lorinda suggested.

'And what can we do together? Things that will interest both the evacuees and the local young people. Ideas?'

'What's needed is to show them – us evacuees – that Althwaite's an interesting place. Like Jem and Harold did with Dot and me – showing us around and bringing us up 'ere,' Ron said.

'Stand by to receive the Goths and Vandals!' laughed Hon Peter. 'Sorry, I was only joking! What about a series of visits to see what goes on: the farm, the mill. I could speak to the Water Board about visiting the reservoir.'

'Perhaps I could have a painting class in the tower,' Lorinda suggested.

'I'd come!' Dot exclaimed. 'But…' (here Dot became confused and hid her face).

'Tell me,' Lorinda said.

Dot whispered in her ear.

'You're absolutely right. Dot points out,' Lorinda explained, 'that we mustn't forget to include the local children. And there are more of them than evacuees. So I suggest that a party to visit the mill, for example, should consist of at least half locals.'

'Very tactful!' Hon Peter remarked.

The local stationer volunteered, at Hon Peter's

prompting, to print leaflets. Distributed to evacuees' homes and at schools, these advertised visits and activities during the October half term.

From sheep to cloth. Try your hand at the loom!

(Even many Althwaite children had never set foot in the mill. A few hand-looms were still there, now almost museum pieces.)

From seed to kitchen: the secrets of vegetable growing. At the allotments with a Boer War veteran.

From corn to cows: all you wanted to know about farming: Cop Top is the tops.

From dustbin to tip: how our marvellous dustmen do it. For early risers!

From stream to tap: secrets of Digfoot Reservoir.

From oils and chalks to pictures: painting in the Tower studio.

Those interested had to visit the village hall on Saturday morning to be included in the lists. Jem sat at a table in the hall with his mother and other ladies from the Womens' Institute. It was half past nine and there was already a short queue. Jem raised his eyes from forms on the table and found himself looking into the unwelcome face of Charlie Foster.

'So the tramps' friend is now the evacuees' pal!' he sneered. 'Quite the goody-goody aren't we?'

Jem rose from the table. 'Come outside,' he said.

The thought ran through Charlie's head that Jem wanted a punch-up. Alright, he should have one.

'Look, I know you don't like me,' Jem began. 'I'm not too keen on you, to be frank. But there's a war on. We've got to bury differences until it's over. So no more of this taking it out of each other. Eh?'

Jem waited anxiously for Charlie's response, which was a few seconds in coming.

'Alright – until the war's over. But don't you be so keen on Alice, that's all.'

Having made this concession, allied with a warning, Charlie went into the hall to sign up for the visit to the reservoir.

Jem returned to the hall and busied himself with helping to reconcile demand with supply. Too many children wanted to go to the farm, the mill and the tower, and had to be persuaded to accept the allotments, the reservoir or even the dustmen's round. Disappointment was damped down by the assurance that there would be later opportunities. (Here, Jem was sticking his neck out, but felt justified in doing so.)

On his way home for dinner, Charlie's words recurred to him: 'Don't be so keen on Alice'. The word 'keen' made him uncomfortable. Alice was two years older than Jem, and had more maturity and confidence. His attitude was one of looking up in admiration. The word seemed to demean his relationship with her, and he wished Charlie had not used it.

Differences of class, manners and culture were forgotten when the news of a terrible loss to Britain's Navy was announced. The battleship, HMS Royal Oak, had been sunk by torpedoes fired by a German submarine, with the loss of most of its crew. What magnified the tragedy was that it had occurred not on the high seas, but in the navy's very own harbour – at Scapa Flow in the Orkney Islands. In the school yard at Homefield, Jem joined in agitated debate with other boys, including evacuees, about how this could have happened. How could a submarine have got through the defences – and escaped as well? Mr Churchill, whom many trusted as a war leader, was in charge of the Admiralty. But perhaps he had not been there long enough to get things right.

Harold was now going to the Grammar School at Bruddersford, so Jem saw him mainly at the weekends. Jem was at One-Leg Tim's allotment on Saturday afternoon, clearing away old stalks of that year's peas when he heard excited barking. Looking up, he saw Harold being tugged along by a black and white spaniel on a lead.

'Who's dog is this?' Jem asked.

'She's mine! She's two year old. From the animal rescue place in Homefield. She's a kind of reward for getting to the Grammar School – sorry didn't mean to mention that.'

'That's OK.' Jem smiled as the bitch sniffed him and put up a paw to shake hands. 'She's a beauty. What's her name?'

'Well, the rescue place didn't know. So I've christened her "Raq".'

'Funny name. I've heard of people being tortured on the rack and luggage being left on the rack.'

'No – it's spelt R A Q. She came from gypsies who didn't want to keep her. You must have listened to "Out with Romany" on Children's Hour! Romany has a dog called Raq.'

For years, Harold had been a devotee of Children's

Hour on the wireless at five o'clock. He was now outgrowing some of the features, but the Romany programmes still fascinated him. 'Romany' was a man who came of gypsy stock. He was also a Methodist Minister, like Mr Bright. On the wireless programmes he took friends for walks in the country around his vardo (a gypsy word for a caravan). There was no one like Romany for identifying animal tracks, bird song and birds' eggs. His dog, Raq, was often with them.

Jem finished clearing up the old pea stalks and they wandered off to the river. They sat under the bridge and Harold took Raq off the lead. He dashed up and down the bank, disturbing moorhens.

'How long's Benjy been away?' Harold asked.

'Must be getting on for three months. I was thinking about him yesterday. I suppose he *will* know that war's broken out?'

'What if he's taken ill or had an accident – out on the moors.'

'D'you think we ought to go and look for him?' Jem asked.

'We've no idea where he is.'

'That's where you're wrong. Before he left he gave me a note about his whereabouts, in case he was needed.'

'Needed?'

'For the war effort.'

In his efforts to catch a moorhen, Raq had plunged into the river. Like any spaniel, she swam well. But the bank was steep and the boys hauled her out. She shook the water from her coat, sprinkling them in the process. The question of Benjy was left hanging in the air.

Over the next few days, Benjy kept displacing the evacuees from Jem's mind. The thought of going out to search for him was exciting but also daunting. From Carr Brow, where the Manse stood, there was a wide prospect of the moors. Jem remembered being at the Manse with Harold when visitors by car from Lancashire were leaving. Their route was by the road rising up to the moors west from Althwaite, which could be seen from the Manse garden. The Bright family came out to watch, bringing with them a Union Jack. High up on the road was a bend, from which someone departing would get his last glimpse of the village. Here the car stopped. Its occupants got out and waved. They were mere dots. No doubt it was only the flag being waved by Mr Bright that enabled them to identify the Manse. Then the car resumed its way and was gone.

That road disappearing into the moors led to a land of mystery, it seemed to Jem. Except on a few picnic expeditions to Digfoot reservoir with his Mum and Dad, he had not got beyond the fringes of the moors on foot. He would have liked to think that he and Harold were capable of searching for Benjy. But he knew that the moors could be dangerous, particularly if fog came down. He would have to persuade his Dad to come. This was easier said than done.

'An experienced tramp like Benjy's bound to be able to look after himself. As for the war effort, well, it reflects credit on him to think he might be needed. But it would be a drop in the ocean. Best let him come back in his own good time.'

That was Dad's reaction, and Jem went to bed very

disappointed. But it led him to wonder. Was he really concerned about Benjy, or did he want the excitement of an expedition into the unknown? He decided it was both. He wasn't easily put off. Over the next few days, he pressed the case. Benjy had now been away for three months. That was a long time for him. Did he actually know that war had been declared? He might be hurt if it seemed that nobody cared whether he knew or not. Suppose he had become ill or broken a leg?

Dad was not persuaded by the arguments. On the other hand, he knew that it was only a matter of time before the call up into the armed forces was extended to his age range. It would be good to have a special expedition with Jem before then. It would be something to look back on with pleasure from wherever the war took him.

'Alright, let's have a look at Benjy's note,' he said.

They sat at the kitchen table with Dad's maps and unfolded the piece of paper.

From Grey Nab 10 miles (?) over Blackley Moor to grouse butts above Ashden Clough. Two stunted oaks. Shooter's shelter.

Dad spread out a map and pointed out Grey Nab. It was a high point on the moors about five miles from Althwaite.

'We'd have to go up the Oldham road as far as the bend you've seen from Harold's and then strike off. There's no defined path to the Nab, but I've been up there. Over Blackley Moor will be more tricky. There's ups and downs and boggy patches. We'd have to keep clear of Trembling Moss. Unless we find tracks, it'll be hard going over heather and tough grass. Peat hags will be a hazard.'

'Hags?' Jem exclaimed. 'You mean witches, like the three in Macbeth?'

'Don't be daft, Jem! Depressions in the ground, like miniature cliffs, where the weather has excavated the peat. You'll see.'

'Sounds a bit risky to me,' interrupted Jem's mother. 'Do you think Jem's really up to this expedition?'

'We'll take our time. Have to take a tent and provisions. Take three days over it, perhaps.'

'Can Harold come?' Jem asked, anxiously.

'Well, it'll be a squeeze in the tent. But if his parents don't object – OK.'

Harold was inclined to think, like Jem's father, that Benjy was bound to be alright. But the idea of exploring the moors and camping out excited him as much as Jem. His parents were dubious, but they had confidence in Mr Murgatroyd's good sense. Allowing three days for the expedition meant adding the last of the half-term weekdays to a weekend. Jem would have to miss some of the evacuees' activities, but that couldn't be helped.

About ten o'clock on the Friday morning, Mr Bright's car deposited Mr Murgatroyd, Jem and Harold at the side of the road above Althwaite. Raq jumped out after them. She had nearly not been allowed to come. Harold had had to plead very hard: how could he leave her behind, when this was just the sort of expedition she would enjoy?

They lifted their rucksacks out of the boot and hoisted them on to their shoulders. Jem's Dad had the biggest, together with the tent. Jem had a kettle hanging from his, whilst Harold's had a groundsheet strapped to it. Harold was also carrying additional water for Raq, together with her food and a feeding bowl. Each of them had a walking stick – Dad had said they would be very useful for testing boggy patches. They said goodbye to Mr Bright and set off in single file along a narrow track.

It was a fine morning – breezy with a scattering of cumulus clouds in which the sun played hide and seek. Curlews called and larks sang. Occasionally they startled grouse or partridge – and were themselves startled by the sudden whirr of wings. Raq soon gave up the fruitless effort of chasing after them. Mr Murgatroyd realised that the boys were unused to long tramps carrying rucksacks, so his plan was to stop for a rest every hour. Jem lay on his back on the yielding heather and gazed into a sky studded with sunlit clouds. This was the life! On such a day, he could understand Benjy's urge to roam.

They reached Grey Nab in time for their midday snack. Here, the underlying gritstone exposed craggy surfaces to erosion by the weather. Jem and Harold climbed on top. All around was moor: dark where clouds cast a shadow, brilliant browns and greens in the sunlight. The cry of the curlews emphasised the loneliness.

'Now, you two are scouts. How do we get to where we want to go when there are no paths?' Mr Murgatroyd asked.

'Follow the compass,' Harold replied.

'Right! Let's have a look at the map.'

Dad spread the map out on a flat rock.

'Here's where we are at Grey Nab. Ashden Clough is over here. But we can't get there tonight. I'm aiming for another little valley – Briggen Clough – here. Now, what compass direction do you think it is from Grey Nab? What do you say, Harold?'

'Looks like south west. South would be 180 degrees, west would be – add on 90 that's 270. South west is in between, so that's 225 degrees.'

'Pretty good. I measured it with a protractor last night. It's 220 degrees. So that's our compass bearing. But going across Blackley Moor, we'll have to make detours to avoid marshy bits. Can you see any landmarks to help us keep in the right direction?'

'There's that hump, with what looks like a rock on top,' Jem suggested.

'And down in that dip there's a bush,' Harold added.

They set off, following the compass. Sometimes there were animal tracks or sparse vegetation which made the going easy. At other times they were ploughing through heather or over tussocky grass. The boys soon began to recognize boggy ground by the cotton grass – with its distinctive white fluffs – or the spikes of sedge. They passed near to the thorn bush and reached the hump where the gritstone was again exposed. They skirted around a depression about half a mile in diameter. Water glinted in the centre.

'That's Trembling Moss,' Dad said. 'Anyone who waded into it when it's misty would be in deep trouble. Sorry lads – no pun intended!'

It was mid-afternoon. The boys were beginning to

feel tired. Their shoulders ached with the unaccustomed weight of rucksacks. The 'first fine careless rapture' of the morning had worn off. They were looking forward to reaching Briggen Clough and setting up camp. When they paused for a rest, Raq sat panting, her long, pink tongue hanging out.

'Why do dogs put their tongue out?' Jem wondered.

'It's how they lose body heat – they don't have sweat glands like us,' explained Harold, who had learnt this from Romany.

'Another hour should see us there,' said Dad, thinking it would be an encouragement.

To the boys, however, an hour at that stage in the march seemed a long time. But they found the going easier. There were no more ups and downs. Instead, the moor was gradually declining toward the edge of cultivation. Eventually, they were on the edge of a narrow valley where trees – birches and small oaks – had found sufficient shelter to survive. They could hear the tinkle of water down below.

'Here we are,' Dad said. 'This must be Briggen Clough.'

He felt pleased with himself at having navigated the party across Blackley Moor without mishap.

'Now we need to find a flattish spot for the tent lower down.'

They descended the steep side of the valley, holding on to branches to stop themselves from sliding. Near the stream's edge were gorse bushes. There was no room for a tent.

'I suggest you two look downstream and I'll look

upstream for a suitable spot,' Dad said. 'Don't go for more than five minutes. If you find one, give a shout. If you haven't found one by then, come back.'

It was Jem and Harold who made the discovery. Above a small waterfall stretched a sward of soft grass, wide and long enough for the tent. They hallooed for Dad and heard an answering call.

'Well done!' he exclaimed when he joined them. 'An ideal spot. And away from the trees, too. Let's get the tent up, and then we'll look for dry sticks and branches.'

With their rucksacks off, the boys found they had plenty of energy left. It was not long before the tent was up. They pulled up some heather and bracken to put under the groundsheet. Harold passed up some large stones from the bed of the stream to act as a surround to the fire. Having had some experience of camping with the scouts, he and Jem rigged up a tripod over the fire, from which the kettle could hang. Raq failed to realise that this was a serious expedition, and interrupted proceedings with her insistence on having sticks thrown into the stream to splash after.

It was growing dark. They had had their meal – soup, sausages and baked beans, tinned fruit. They were sipping tea, leaning against their rucksacks and watching the shapes of trees on the other side of the stream merge into each other. Both Jem and Harold thought they had not been so happy for a long time. They looked back with satisfaction on the miles they had walked that day, with the mysterious moors stretching all around them. Another good day lay ahead, one in which they hoped to find Benjy.

'How did your evacuee visit go?' Jem asked.

'It was spiffin!' Harold replied. 'Mr Ackroyd showed us round. Then some went with Alice to fetch the cows in for milking. Mrs Ackroyd took the youngest ones to collect the eggs. Others, me included, went with Mr Ackroyd for turns riding on the tractor whilst he was ploughing. We had a go at steering, sitting in front of him. Instead of straight lines, some wobbly ones! When I came back, one little girl – Jake Andrews' sister – was crying because one of the farm dogs had licked her. Alice took her off to show her how the milking was done.'

'Alice would,' Jem thought.

'Some of the evacuees were real surprised that that was how the milk came! Then we had home-made soup and bread and ended up sliding on hay in the barn.'

'Did it do any good?' Jem asked.

'Well, they all enjoyed it. Some of the evacuees said they'd like to go up again. What did you do?'

'Dustmen's round.'

'Why did you choose that?'

'Well, for one thing, there weren't enough locals to balance the evacuees. And in any case, Bert asked me to go. Thought I might be able to keep order! I had to get up terribly early and rush off without any breakfast. He kitted us out with overalls – much too big for us. We rode in the cart and helped to carry bins out. He kept making jokes – Bert, that is. A couple of lads set a bin rolling down Station Hill – Bert really told them off. They were our lot, not evacuees. We went to the Council tip and then back to the depot. We squeezed into what they call the Mess Room and had a fry-up.

Then Bert taught us a song: "The Dustman's Life's the Life for Me". Not for me, though.'

They were silent as darkness enshrouded them. Dad's profile, pipe in mouth, was lit by the embers of the dying fire. With a pang, Jem suddenly realised that this father of his could be leaving home for the war soon. He had always felt closer to his mother: she was easier to talk to. His father was more reserved and sometimes moody. But there was a strong bond between them. Suppose he didn't come back! Jem tried to suppress the thought.

'Time to turn in,' Dad said. 'We've a long day ahead tomorrow.'

8 THE SEARCH (2)

Neither Jem nor Harold slept well. The heather and bracken did little to cushion their bodies from the hard ground. They were squashed together so that turning over was difficult. Raq disturbed them by resting first on one and then on another. Only Dad seemed oblivious. As dawn showed through the tent, a light rain began to fall. The boys at last fell into a deep sleep. They were roused by Raq barking. He was outside and had spied a moorhen in the stream. Through the open flaps of the tent they could see Dad getting a fire going, using as kindling dry twigs stored in the tent in case of rain.

'Rise and shine!' Dad called. 'One of you fetch some water.'

Jem dipped his face in the cool stream to force himself awake. Brrr! There was an autumn chill in the air, but it had stopped raining.

Breakfast was porridge, boiled eggs, bread and tea.

'Plan of campaign!' said Dad. 'It's about three miles to Ashden Clough. We look for Benjy. Then we set off for home in a different direction – via Castle Rocks.

Perhaps camp near Intake Farm – I know the farmer. So, you two start packing up while I spy out the land.'

Dad crossed the stream, striding from stone to stone, and climbed up through the trees on the far side. Jem cleaned the pans in the stream. Harold removed the stones surrounding the fire and doused the smouldering logs with water to make sure that the fire was really out. They had begun to dismantle the tent when they heard Dad calling from a distance.

'What does he want?' Harold asked.

'Best go and see,' Jem said. 'Come on.'

They clambered up the opposite slope. From the edge of the Clough, gorse bushes gave way to the heather and grasses of the moor. Dad called again. They headed in the direction of the voice. They spied him sitting in what appeared to be a hollow below a grassy bank.

'What's up, Dad?' Jem called out as they approached.

'Thank goodness you heard me, lads! This is a pickle! I seem to have twisted an ankle. Didn't look where I was going and fell off the edge of this peat hag. Ironic – having warned you about hags!'

'Pehaps there *is* some witchery in them, after all!' Jem commented.

'Well, at least I can still smile at your attempt at a joke, Jem! Now then, can one of you go and get my stick, and I'll see if I can walk with it.'

With the help of the stick and with Jem giving support, Dad got down to the tent. He took the boot off his right foot. The ankle was swollen and turning blue. Jem soaked a tea towel in the stream and Dad wrapped it around the ankle. After half an hour it was even more swollen. Dad got out the map.

'I'm very sorry, lads, but I doubt I'm going to be in a fit state to carry on walking today. If you look at the map, you'll see that near Ashden Clough, where Benjy might have his base, there's a farm – High Sykes Farm. I suggest you go there first. Ask if they've got a tractor or something that could get near to where we are. Then have a look for Benjy. Do you remember his directions?'

'Grouse butts, two stunted oaks,' said Harold.

'And shooters' shelter,' Jem added.

'Good. Here's his note, just in case you forget. Now, you take the compass and the map. When you get on to the moor, you'll see a single tree in a south westerly direction. Make towards that. Then you should find a track leading to High Sykes Farm. There's an army range not far off. If you lose your way, make sure you don't cross into it – there's bound to be a wire fence and warning notices. Just take one rucksack with some food and water. Think you can manage?'

The boys nodded and began getting ready.

'Shouldn't we leave Raq with you, Mr Murgatroyd?' Harold asked. 'Then if she hears people, she'll bark and help direct them here. We'd have to tie her up.'

'Good idea, Harold – if you don't mind.'

'Good luck and look out for peat hags!' Dad said with a grin as they set off. Raq pulled at the lead which was attached to a birch tree on the edge of the camp site. She barked and tugged, not understanding why she should be left behind.

Both boys were worried, but tried not to show it. What had started out as an exciting expedition had become a trial – of their judgement and competence. Dad's wellbeing – perhaps his life – depended on them. To their immense relief, they got to High Sykes Farm without difficulty. Now the burden of rescue could be shared with someone else. But relief turned into dismay as they got closer. Windows were boarded up, farm buildings were dilapidated, weeds were thrusting up between the paving of the yard. There was no-one there!

Consulting the map, they saw that there was another farm – Low Sykes Farm – about four miles away. But from where they were it was only a mile to Ashden Clough. If they found Benjy, he might have some useful suggestion. If not, they could go on to the other farm.

They had already seen grouse butts on their way across Blackley Moor so they knew what to look for: circular walls of turf about chest high, from which the 'guns' could shoot at the poor grouse as they were harried toward the butts by the 'beaters'. They saw a line of them on the horizon. On reaching them, they spotted the two stunted oaks. Only about ten feet high, with twisted branches, they were struggling to survive on the edge of the moor. Now, where was the shooters' shelter? They descended the slope toward Ashden Clough and caught sight of something metallic. In a hollow was a shelter of some kind under a semi-circular roof of corrugated iron. Some clothes were spread out on the roof, as though to dry. Peering inside, they could see an old rucksack and other belongings.

'This must be it,' Jem said. 'I think I recognize the rucksack. Best wait a bit to see if he turns up. If not, we can leave a message and go on to the other farm.'

The shelter, erected so that shooters could have their lunch in comparative comfort in poor weather, was long and low. The boys could just stand up in the centre. Down one side were bales of straw. A sleeping bag – no doubt Benjy's – was rolled up in a corner.

Jem and Harold were feeling peckish and decided to have their lunch early. They were just finishing their sandwiches of Spam and tomatoes when they heard footsteps. Fully expecting Benjy's bearded face to appear, they were surprised to see an unfamiliar face looking in. The head wore an army forage-cap. The body was clothed in khaki.

'Hullo! What have we here? Two young fellows having a picnic! What brings you here? It's a long way from the nearest bit of civilization!'

The lanky soldier bent his head and came inside. He had three stripes on his arm, so the boys knew he was a sergeant. He had shoulder flashes with the letters: KOYLI.

'We've come to see Benjy. He's a tramp – sorry, *the* tramp of Althwaite Valley. He's a friend of ours. We wanted to see how he is and whether he knows there's a war on,' Jem explained.

'And he hasn't got a ration book, and he might be needed for the war effort,' Harold added.

'Well, I've never heard of a tramp having friends like you. You're not allowed to pull the leg of a sergeant of the King's Own Yorkshire Light Infantry, you know.'

'Honest. We've come with my Dad. Only, he twisted his ankle this morning, so he's stayed at our camp site.'

'With Raq,' added Haroldwho was anxious that the sergeant should be fully in the picture.

'With who?'

'Raq – that's my dog. She's called that 'cos she's gypsy.'

'A gypsy dog now! This gets more and more bizarre. Do you know where your friend is?'

'No – he wasn't here when we arrived.'

'Well I've got news for him when he returns.'

'Good news?' Jem asked.

'No – bad news. He's likely to be put under arrest.'

'What for?'

'Trespassing on the range. Now, how about this father of yours?'

Jem and Harold explained their quandary: miles from home and Mr Murgatroyd unable to walk – at least not far and perhaps not without crutches. They planned to go for help at Low Sykes Farm.

'Tell you what,' said the sergeant, 'I'll go back up to the range. We've a couple of cross country vehicles. I'll come back down and we'll go in search of your Dad.'

The boys felt as though a great burden had been lifted from their shoulders. They would be alright now: the army had taken charge. The expedition was becoming an adventure. What's more, the sun appeared, putting a happier complexion on the day. They moved outside the shelter to wait. There was one worry, though – the possibility of Benjy being arrested.

'Do you think we should warn him?' Harold asked.

'I was just thinking of that,' Jem replied.

On the back of Benjy's note of his whereabouts, Jem wrote in pencil:

Dear Benjy, Harold and me, with my Dad, came to see how you are. There's a war on. You'll have to collect your rashun book. A Sargent from the range came looking for you. He says you might be arrested for trespassing. We thought we'd better warn you. Best wishes, Jem and Harold.

The next question was where to put the letter so that Benjy would be sure to find it, but the sergeant wouldn't see it. Jem opened the rucksack. On top was Benjy's tobacco pouch. Since he hadn't taken it with him, he was bound to fill his pipe when he got back. Jem put the letter in the pouch. They kept a look-out, but Benjy had not turned up by the time the sergeant returned with an army vehicle.

'No sign of your friend, eh? Have to leave him for tomorrow. Now, show me on the map where your Dad is.'

The vehicle had just two seats. A corporal was at the wheel, with the sergeant occupying the other seat. The boys bounced around in the back. Their route to Briggen Clough was a roundabout one, so as to make as much use as possible of minor roads and tracks. It wasn't until mid-afternoon that they pulled up about half a mile from the valley.

'Raq, hello Raq!' Harold shouted when they got to the edge. A faint, answering, bark showed that they needed to go upstream before descending. When they got within sight of the camp Raq went wild, jumping up and down and shaking the birch tree to which she was attached.

'Well done, lads. What's this – the army? I'm that important am I?' Mr Murgatroyd joked, highly relieved that help had arrived. With his arms around the shoulders of the two soldiers, he managed to climb up the slope without putting the injured ankle to the ground. Jem and Harold packed up the tent as quickly as they could given Raq's excited interference.

At the range, where there was just one small army building, a bandage was put round the ankle.

'No-one stays here overnight, so we can't put you up,' the sergeant explained. 'We could drive you home tonight or you could camp outside the range and we could take you home tomorrow morning. We'd have to make a charge, of course – army time has to be paid for – though not for today: that was a matter of rescue. Or you can ring up a friend.'

'I think you ought to get home as quickly as possible, Dad,' said Jem.

'Let's ring up Mr Bright and see if he can collect us tomorrow. Be a shame for you two not to have another night in camp. Anyway, your mother might be put out if we arrive home a day early!'

'Afraid my Dad wouldn't be able to come tomorrow – it's Sunday and he'll be preaching,' Harold chipped in.

'What about Mr Ackroyd? I'm sure he'd come – he wouldn't be busy on a Sunday.'

Jem's suggestion was adopted. Jem spoke to the farmer on the telephone. He was only too willing to come.

'There's a nice spot for a camp about two hundred yards away,' the sergeant said. 'And there's a stream below. I'll help carry your gear there if you like.'

The range headquarters was well stocked with first-aid material. The soldiers unearthed a pair of crutches, which they said Mr Murgatroyd could borrow till the next day. The sergeant hoisted the big rucksack on his shoulders and led the way to the site.

With Dad's role confined mainly to an advisory one, the boys found that setting up the tent, fetching sticks and water and preparing their evening meal took twice as long as on the previous evening. At length they were able to sit back, hunger and thirst satisfied. The site was on a ledge, just below the moor. The ground fell sharply away, giving an extensive view. As they were eating they had watched the sun set. No longer visible to them now, it painted the clouds in the west with a pink glow.

'Red at night, shepherd's delight,' Dad said. 'I wonder how far back that saying goes?'

He lit his pipe.

'Now, tell me how you got on.'

He was surprised when they said that they had found High Sykes Farm deserted.

'I should have thought of that possibility. These farms up on the edge of the moors are always having a tough time.'

He chortled at their confession that they had left a warning for Benjy.

'Wonder what the blighter was up to, going on the range? After snaring some animal or bird, I daresay.'

Overhead, the sky was almost dark. The brightest stars were beginning to twinkle. In the west, the sky was a pale green.

'You've done well, lads. Good scouts! I'm only sorry that my stupid mishap means we can't trek back.'

They fell silent. Jem's mind went back over the day. What a range of feelings it had produced: expectation, dismay, worry, relief. Sympathy for his Dad was mixed with satisfaction that Harold and he had come through with credit – though he acknowledged that it was largely due to their luck in meeting up with the army.

'If you join the army, Dad, you might find yourself training on the range here!' Jem said.

'If so, I'll have to make sure I don't shoot any trespassing tramp!'

During the second night, roles were reversed. It was now the turn of Jem and Harold to sleep like logs, worn out by the worries and exertions of the day. Mr Murgatroyd slept fitfully, conscious of his throbbing ankle. After breakfast, they moved up to the gate at the range to await Mr Ackroyd.

'You can hang on to the crutches,' the sergeant suggested. 'We sometimes have a vehicle in the Althwaite area, and they can be collected if you let me know where you live.'

Gratefully, Mr Murgatroyd gave him the address.

Rattling over the bumps in the track, Mr Ackroyd arrived in a van. Jem was delighted to see Alice sitting with him.

'Some hikers you are, having to be rescued like this!' he joked. 'Didn't you warn your Dad to look out for peat hags, Jem?'

'It was the other way round – he warned us!'

Alice had to give up her seat and travel in the back with the boys. She wanted to know all about the expedition. Jem asked her whether she thought they'd done the right thing in warning Benjy.

'I don't know, but I'd have done the same!' she replied.

Entering Althwaite, Jem caught sight of boys kicking a ball about. He recognized evacuees, including Ron and Jakie Andrews amongst the local boys. That was a good sign.

'Do you think those visits have done any good?' he asked Alice.

'Well, those to the farm did at least. Lambing time's going to be popular!' she replied.

A few days later, life was returning to normal. Jem's Mum had got over her concern at receiving home an injured husband. Dr McLeish had examined the ankle and said it was just a sprain. With the morning post came a letter marked 'On His Majesty's Service'. Mrs Murgatroyd's heart gave a leap. This must be the call up papers! Her husband opened the envelope.

'Well, I'll be blowed!' was his exclamation.

'What is it Ted?'

He handed the letter to her and she read:

Sir, I understand that your son and a friend of his are acquainted with a vagrant who is of interest to us. I should like to put one or two questions to them in your presence. Would you please let me know by return if next Saturday at 11 am will be convenient. If not, please suggest an alternative time. Yours faithfully, A.C. Clarke (Captain and Adjutant) K.O.Y.L.I.

'What do the initials at the end mean?'

'King's Own Yorkshire Light Infantry – they use the range where Benjy went trespassing.'

Jem swallowed hard when told that he and Harold

were to be questioned by the army. Had they found out about the warning?

'What shall we say?'

'You must tell the truth,' said his mother emphatically. 'We'll stand by you, don't worry.'

'I'd better go and see Mr Bright. Reckon I can get there alright on my crutches,' Dad said.

Harold arrived early on Saturday morning.

'We've got to tell the truth,' Jem said.

'That's what my Dad says. Think we'll get into trouble?'

'Don't see what they can do to us. Can't order us to clean brasses or weed allotments!'

They tried to keep their minds off the impending interview by going into the shed and making catapults with Y-shaped twigs and thick rubber bands. They were both nervous: more so than when called before the headmaster of Althwaite school to receive two strokes of the cane on the palms of their hands. It was even worse than when they went up to the Hall to be questioned by Hon Peter. Then they had been comforted by the thought that he wouldn't be too hard on them. The army was a different matter altogether. They heard the car draw up. Jem's mother called them to come in. With beating hearts and an unusual dryness in their mouths, they went.

Captain Clarke was a young man with sandy coloured hair and moustache. He looked very smart in his well-pressed uniform. They all, including Mum as well as Dad, sat down in the front sitting room. The occasion was too formal for the cosier kitchen. Dad introduced Jem and Harold.

'Hullo boys. Now, I understand that you know a vagrant – a tramp – from these parts called Benjy?'

'Yes sir, he's a friend of ours,' said Jem, thinking that he should be the spokesman since the interview was in his house.

'Do you know where he is now?'

'No. We haven't seen him since he left Althwaite in July. That's why we went to look for him.'

'And you didn't see him when you got to the shooters' shelter near the range?'

'No – he wasn't there. We were waiting for him to come back when your sergeant arrived.'

'And you didn't see him later when you camped near the range?'

'No. We didn't visit the shelter again. We had to set up camp. Then it got dark.'

'I can vouch for that,' Mr Murgatroyd added. 'The lads would have liked to make another attempt to find him. But I put my foot down – not the one with the sprained ankle.'

The captain smiled faintly.

'You see, when Sergeant Briscoe went down to the shelter early the next morning, it appeared that your tramp had made off – with his belongings. Now, the sergeant says that he told you that your friend was likely to be arrested. I may say that he shouldn't have done that – passing sensitive official information to a civilian is an offence.'

'He's not lost a stripe, has he?' Mr Murgatroyd asked.

'No, but he's been reprimanded. Anyway, what I want to ask is whether either of you boys, or both of you, passed that information on to your friend?'

The captain looked intently at them, his eyes seeming to bore into their brains.

'Yes, we did tell him. We left a note. It was my idea,' Harold confessed.

'No – it was my idea as well,' Jem added.

'Well, now we know why he did a bunk.'

The captain paused, glanced at Mr and Mrs Murgatroyd, and turned back to the boys.

'I'm afraid I have to say that that was a foolish and wrong thing to do. You were impeding the army in the performance of its duties. Putting it more simply: stopping us from doing what we had to do. Your friend's trespassing on the range was a serious matter. He might have blown himself up. You may be capable lads, but you're what the law calls minors. So it would be difficult for the army to take any action against you. But I hope that you, and your parents, will realise that you should not have passed on what the sergeant told you. Do you understand that?'

Jem would have liked to argue. Wasn't it the sergeant's fault for telling them? And shouldn't *he* have warned them not to tell Benjy? But he realised that there was no point in disputing with authority in the shape of the captain.

'Yes, sir.'

'Right, well let's hope you've both learnt a lesson.'

He got up to leave.

'Will you have a cup of tea before you go – and your driver?' asked Mrs Murgatroyd, thinking it would be nice to get relations on to a friendlier footing.

'That's very kind, but I have to be getting along'

'I'm going to be joining up soon,' Mr Murgatroyd said. 'Any chance of my getting into KOYLI?'

'We're always wanting good men. Put your preference down.' The captain smiled. 'We won't hold it against you that your son's had a brush with the army!'

'Phew!' Jem exclaimed, slumping down in an armchair. 'Thank goodness that's over!'

'What a nice young man – firm but pleasant. Wish he'd stopped for a cup of tea,' Mum commented.

'That's what a neat moustache does!' her husband exclaimed. 'I'll bet he's a stickler for discipline underneath. If I was under his command, I'd watch my step!'

Harold looked bothered.

'We said we understood why he was telling us off. But did we really do wrong?'

'I'd do the same again,' Jem said. 'Aren't friends more important than anything?'

'I talked this over with your Dad, Harold,' Mr Murgatroyd said. 'He thought that duty to friends can be supremely important. In fact, he gave me a little biblical sermon! About David and Jonathan. Do you remember who Jonathan's father was?'

Jem ransacked his brain.

'Saul,' said Harold who, as the Minister's son, was more conversant with the Bible.

'Right! Well, Saul wanted to kill David. But Jonathan loved David and warned him, so that he could escape. So you see, there was someone who put his friend before the ruler of the kingdom. Mr Bright also mentioned a Greek play about Antig…what was her name?'

'Antigone,' said Mrs Murgatroyd who, unlike

her husband, had had a grammar school education. 'Antigone was the young woman who gave her brother a proper burial, even though the king had ordered that the body be left exposed. She felt that the duty to her brother was more important than the commands of the ruler.'

'That was it,' Mr Murgatroyd resumed. 'Suppose, though, that a friend had done something really horrible – like committing a murder. Would we then be justified in protecting him from justice? That's a puzzle. I don't think I can solve that one. But, as for Benjy trespassing on the range, I can't regard that as serious. I'd have done the same as you lads.'

The following Saturday afternoon there was a knock on the Murgatroyds' door. Jem answered it. There was Alice with a smile on her face. Jem's cheeks reddened from surprise and pleasure.

'Hullo, Jem. I was hoping you'd be in. I haven't called here before, have I? Aren't you going to invite me in?'

'Sorry, I was so surprised to see you.'

'A pleasant surprise, I hope!'

'Of course! Harold's here – we're making a model Spitfire.'

'Good job he's here too – I've brought something for you both.'

Alice took an envelope out of her shopping bag. It was addressed to: 'Jem Murgatroyd and Harold Bright, care of Mr Ackroyd, Cop Top Farm, Althwaite, West Riding of Yorkshire'. The post mark was Oldham.

'That's in Lancashire,' said Jem, puzzled.

'I think it must be from Benjy.'

Jem called Harold and they opened the envelope. The letter was written in pencil in a large, untidy, hand. Jem read it aloud:

Dear Jem and Harold, I'm very grateful for that warning. I packed up and left straightaway. A lot of nonsense – as if I were in any danger on the range – me, a veteran of the Great War. I were merely catching a rabbit – there's a warren in a sandy stretch there. Anyroad, I thought it best to keep out of the way for a time. But I'll be back afore long. Tell Mr Ackroyd I'll be looking for a spot of work. Hope you didn't get into any trouble. Your pal, Benjy.

PS I did know that war had broken out, thanks. I don't understand about rashun books.

'Well, he got clear of that sergeant, anyway,' Jem said.

Mum looked in from the kitchen. 'Alice, how nice to see you! Stay and have some tea?'

They sat round the kitchen table.

'I must have known you were coming, Alice – I made some jam tarts this morning,' said Mrs Murgatroyd.

'Like the Queen of Hearts – but no knave to steal them, thankfully. Unless we're the knaves!' Alice joked.

Jem was happy. Benjy appreciated the warning he and Harold had given him and he seemed in good spirits. Now, jam tarts for tea – with Alice and Harold. One thought, though, cast a slight shadow over his enjoyment.

'I bet Ron and Dot are not having jam tarts for tea! Mum – don't you think there should be a tea-party for the evacuees?'

'Here we go!' thought Harold.

9 THE CHRISTMAS PARTY

It was a month later. Jem was on his way home from school. He had just passed the end of the lane leading up to the church, vaguely aware that some one was coming down it. He was stopped in his progress by a hand grabbing his coat collar.

'Not so fast, young Jem! Fancy not recognizing an old friend!'

'Benjy! I didn't know you were back.'

'Got back a week ago. Just been up to vicarage for a cup o'cocoa. Not that I really needed it, but it's as well to keep in wi' friends against times when yer might need 'em.'

There was something different about him, Jem thought. It was no so much the clothes – though the tweed jacket and corduroy trousers, whilst old, were comparatively decent. His hair still straggled down to the shoulders, he still had the beard – though it was now kept in reasonable trim. Then Jem realised what it was: tufts of hair were no longer growing out of his ears. Scissors had been applied. Why this new concern for personal appearance? Jem thought he had better be discreet.

'You're looking smart, Benjy!'

'Ay, it goes against the grain really. I'm up at Cop Top again – in a loft above t'stables. Wi' Mrs Ackroyd and Alice around, I felt ashamed of the way I'd let myssen go. And then, standing up for Britain against this chap Hitler, we've got to maintain some standards o' decency. When t'war's over, I'll be able to go back to my old ways. You got my letter?'

'Yes, thanks. We'd no idea where you'd got to.' Jem decided not to tell Benjy about the visit from the army captain – it might make him feel guilty.

'I've got summat for you and Harold. Come up to t'farm on Saturday.'

Up at Cop Top, Jem and Harold found Benjy repairing a stone wall. He was glad to interrupt his labour and take them to the stables. Alice's pony occupied a stall. They climbed a ladder to the loft above. In previous times, it would have contained hay – a chute down to the stalls below had been boarded over. Light came from a tiny window looking out on to the farm yard and from a skylight in the roof. There was a low bed and a few other items of furniture. It was the kind of secret place that Jem would have loved to have.

Benjy pulled a bag from under the bed. From it he drew two strange objects. During his sojourn on the moors, he had found twisted roots, each ending in a large, fist-sized, boss. Applying his skill at whittling, he had carved these into the likeness of human faces. On return to the farm, he had borrowed some black paint and a brush. A small moustache and a lick of hair falling over the forehead completed a likeness in caricature of that bugbear of Britain: Herr Hitler. The contours of the two faces were different: one showed a snarling smile, the other was glum. Jem let Harold have first choice and went home with the unsmiling version. He wasn't sure where to keep it. His bedroom seemed an unsuitable place, and he was sure that his mother would not want it downstairs.

'Where did you get that awful thing? It's like something from a witch doctor's kit!' His mother's reaction confirmed his expectation.

Jem explained.

'It's clever, but spooky. I reckon you'd better put it in the shed. It'll frighten the spiders.'

So that was where Benjy's carving ended up.

'Well, I've done it!' said Dad at tea-time. 'Been into Bruddersford to the army office and signed on as a volunteer.'

'Oh dear,' sighed Mum. 'I could see it coming, though.'

'Why?' Jem asked. 'Call-up's only for men up to 27 isn't it, Dad? You're not that young, even though you can jump off peat hags!'

'I'll never live that down, will I? Well, it's only a matter of time before the Government extends the age range. There should be more choice as a volunteer – KOYLI for example. And I think I *ought* to volunteer. I'm not doing anything important here.'

'Looking after Jem and me's not important?'

'Course it is, but you know what I mean.'

A fortnight later another envelope bearing the inscription, 'On His Majesty's Service', arrived. The letter instructed Mr Murgatroyd to report to Catterick Garrison in a week's time. Jem felt despondent. At long last this wretched war had struck home. Why couldn't it have stayed at a distance? Who knew what would happen now? Where might his Dad go, what might he have to do, would he be involved in fighting, would he survive? These thoughts circled in his head. But he tried not to show his feelings. His mother probably felt even worse, and she would need his support.

'Support' was the theme of Dad's parting message to Jem, on a walk to Digfoot reservoir. They sat beside the wind-flecked water, looking towards the rising moor, dark except for the occasional shaft of sunlight.

'Hope it won't be long before I can enjoy this view again!' said Dad, lighting his pipe. 'Sooner that Hitler gets put in his place the better! It'll take time, though. We've got to build up our strength. And maybe we'll need the Americans before it's finished. Glad you're not old enough to be involved, Jem. Except, everyone's involved to some extent. Your job is to work hard at school,be as helpful as you can in the village and look after your mother. Don't get into more escapades than you can help.'

It was a quiet pair who saw Dad off from the station. He tried to brighten the atmosphere.

'If you go on the moors, Jem, look out for peat hags. Some of them have witches' spells on them!'

The guard blew his whistle. Doors slammed. Dad leaned out of the window to give Mum a last kiss. The engine expelled steam in a whoosh as the pistons began to work. Smoke mixed with steam was thrust up from the chimney. With the familiar 'chuff,chuff', the train slowly gathered speed. Arms waved, kisses were blown, and the end of the train disappeared round a bend. The people who were left behind, including Jem and his mother, turned towards the exit to continue their lives as best they could.

During the service in chapel the following Sunday, Jem fell to wondering why ministers and vicars were not called up into the forces. He tackled Harold on the subject after the service.

'Clergymen don't have to do military service,' said Harold.

'Yes, but some of them become chaplains to the forces.'

'Yes, but if they all did, there'd be no one left to run the churches.'

'They could be run by local preachers – laymen.'

'Not for christenings, weddings and funerals – you need a proper minister or vicar for them. Any case, it's not just clergymen who don't have to join up – there's miners and farmers and others.'

'Farming's different – we couldn't do without what they produce.'

Harold thought he had heard his father or some other minister talk about the 'farming of souls', but wasn't sufficiently sure of his ground to bring that into the argument.

They parted with rankled feelings. Harold thought Jem had been unfair. He was sure his Dad would be glad to join the forces if he was free to do so. Jem, too, felt that things were unfair. Clergymen already had God on their side. Now they also had the Government on their side – letting them off having to join up.

Mrs Murgatroyd took over from her husband the duties of care-taker of the chapel. This entailed two mornings a week of hard work keeping the premises clean. Standards had to be kept up even though there was a war on. She also joined the WVS (the Women's Voluntary Service) and went into Bruddersford once or twice a week to help organize the supply of clothing and other necessities to families of evacuees and refugees from Hitler's Germany. Jem's idea of a tea-party for the evacuees was forgotten about. His mother was so busy that he didn't like to remind her.

Going down to the village he passed the house where Ron and Dot were lodging. On an impulse, he knocked at the door. Mrs Weaverthorpe opened it. Wisps of hair had escaped from the bun at the back of her neck. She looked harassed.

'Are Rondot in?' he asked.

'Who? Oh, you mean Ron and Dot! Yes – they're in the back garden – you can go round the side.'

Jem found them feeding Mrs Weaverthorpe's rabbits. There were five hutches, with two in each. A number of people in the village had begun keeping rabbits in order to supplement the food ration.

'We 'ave to collect dandelions and other weeds they like – not that we mind,' Ron explained. 'We feel sorry for them 'cos they're not pets – they're being grown for their meat. But Dot and me are not going to 'ave rabbit pie. We're going to be – what are they called? Conscientious objectors, that's it!'

'Poor things,' Dot added in a melancholy voice, as she put a dandelion leaf through the wire and watched the rabbit nibbling it.

'Our Mum's had to go to Hull, to see to some things. Dot's feeling a bit fed up,' Ron said.

'Let's go up to the Hall and see if we can go in the tower,' Jem suggested.

Dot brightened up. 'I wonder if Lorinda'll be there?'

'Shouldn't be surprised,' Jem said. 'She's often around here these days.'

Mrs McAlister welcomed them at the back door.

'If you've come for my shortbread, I'm afraid it's all gone. But I've got some ginger snaps.'

Jem explained that it was not the inner man which had prompted them to come up the hill. Could they go in the tower? And was Miss Vajansky here?

'Mr Danellion-Smith's gone to Bruddersford to sit on the bench. But Miss Vajansky's painting in the tower. If you see my husband in the vegetable garden, tell him its's time for his morning break.'

'Why's he gone to sit on a bench?' Dot asked as they made their way through the garden. 'Is it a special kind of seat?'

'Silly!' Ron exclaimed. 'It's what magistrates sit on in court.'

Having given Mr McAlister the message, they arrived at the tower. The door was open.

'Hallo!' Jem shouted up the staircase. 'It's Jem and Rondot. Can we come up?'

The window opened and Lorinda looked down.

'Do I spy three quarters of my rescue party? Come on up!'

She was in her artist's gear, though without the beret. She wore an apron marked with all the colours of the rainbow in different shades. Her hair was gathered behind her head in a pony-tail. She had a stain of grey paint on a cheek. On the easel was a portrait of Hon Peter, looking stern and dignified.

'It's very good,' Jem commented. 'It makes you see a more serious side of him.'

'Thank you, Jem. That's just what I was trying to capture. I'm just finishing off the jacket.'

Lorinda pointed to a grey jacket on a hanger suspended from a hook in a beam.

'Can I do a bit?' Dot asked.

Lorinda stood her on a stool and guided her hand as it applied a few more finishing touches. Then Ron wanted a go.

'Will you tell me the story of Rapunzel again, Jem?' Dot asked him.

He took Dot over to the top of the staircase and related it in a low voice. Ron watched Lorinda finishing the picture and answered her questions about his life in Hull.

'We'll have to be going, Dot,' said Ron when the story was ended. 'Mrs Weaverthorpe said we hadn't to be late for dinner.'

Dot's protestations were overcome by Lorinda's promise that if she came the next day she could have a go at painting a picture herself. Jem was about to leave with them.

'Do you have to go, Jem?' Lorinda asked.

'No – not yet.So long, Rondot!'

Lorinda put the brush she had been using in a jar of cleaning fluid and wiped her hands on a cloth. She took off her painting apron and sat down in the low arm-chair. Jem sat on the window sill. He sensed that Lorinda was wondering whether to tell him something.

'You're happy here? That brush with the Amazons of Althwaite didn't put you off?' he said encouragingly.

'I *am* happy when I come here. The Hall, with its occupants, is the best place I know.' She paused and looked at the portrait.

'You're a sensible young man, Jem. I hope you don't mind if I use you like a sounding-board. Sometimes, when you say your thoughts aloud to some one else they – what's the word? "Crystallise", perhaps – they become more orderly. This is in confidence - I know I can trust you.'

Jem felt flattered, but also nervous. Lorinda seemed to be wanting to talk to him as though he was grown up. He was very conscious of being only an eleven year old schoolboy.

'This may seem strange to you. Peter and I have not known each other for very long – as you know. But war somehow speeds things up. He wants me to marry him. He's ten years older. I know he has faults. He's too reserved. He can be a bit pompous – though I think that reflects a lack of self-confidence. But I like him very much. He's a thoroughly decent, conscientious man, with a sense of humour.'

Jem thought of Hon Peter wearing a red cloak and a pith helmet when he 'judged' Harold and himself: yes, he certainly had a sense of humour.

'We seem to suit each other. And I think I could do him a lot of good – enhance his self respect and make him more outgoing,' Lorinda went on. 'I'm sure we'd be happy. But I feel more and more obliged to help win the war - especially because of my Czech background. Nothing's more important at present than defeating Hitler and the Nazis. Not just for Britain, but for the German people themselves. I know many decent Germans. So, you see, I'm thinking of joining the WAAF – the Women's Auxiliary Air Force. But would it be right to marry Peter and then leave for the war? Would that be like desertion?'

Lorinda looked at Jem and smiled.

'Those are the thoughts that are chasing round in my head. I'm sorry to burden you with them.'

Jem felt inadequate. How could he possibly give Lorinda advice? But he had a faint notion that he could say something helpful. He stared out of the window to gather his thoughts.

'My Dad's just gone into the army. You might say he's deserted Mum and me. But that's not how it is. We're with him all the way. And, from what I've heard Mr Danellion-Smith say, he's just as keen on fighting Hitler as you are. Wouldn't he understand you wanting to be directly involved in the war? He'd be proud of you. Especially if you'd got engaged to be married. Isn't there…' Jem added hesitantly, 'Isn't there an old fashioned way of saying that – plighting troth? Like a knight and his lady before he goes off to kill a dragon or something? Except that it'd be *you* going off to fight the dragon!'

Lorinda's face lit up. 'I do believe you've hit the nail

on the head, Jem! I'm so grateful. That's exactly how one should view it.'

She got up from the armchair and gave Jem a glancing kiss on his cheek. 'Whenever the wedding is, we'll invite you to it! Meanwhile, Air Force, here I come!'

Jem was not conscious of descending the staircase and making his way out of the grounds. A grown-up, a lovely person, had just taken him into her confidence about her innermost thoughts. Instead of being embarrassed and tongue-tied, he had managed to say something relevant and helpful. What had inspired him?

Although a tea-party for the evacuees did not materialize, a Christmas party did. German air raids had not taken place on the scale feared, so some evacuees and their mothers had gone home. But thirty children and some mothers were still in Homefield and Althwaite. The two villages formed a joint committee on which Mrs Murgatroyd represented the Women's Voluntary Service. The party was to be held in the parish hall in Homefield.

'I want your advice, Jem,' said his mother as they sat down to supper. 'My sins must be bigger than I thought – I've been given the job of finding a Father Christmas.'

'Well, it's too far to the North Pole or Lapland, so it'll have to be a substitute from Althwaite.'

'Thanks for that helpful contribution, Jem! If your Dad had been here, it would have been easier.'

'You mean – you'd have blackmailed him?'

'I don't think I'd have had to stoop to that, though he would have been reluctant. Now, any serious suggestions?'

'Let's think. There's Bert – he's cheerful and makes jokes. He'd make a good one. But…'

'Not your Benjy, Jem!'

'Why not? He made a good St Erewold a year last summer – even the vicar agreed. And it'd do him good – make him feel he was appreciated by the community. He's much more respectable-looking than he used to be. And he's got quite a normal smell.'

It was the afternoon before the party. Jem had been surprised at the ease with which Benjy had been persuaded. It seemed that he was proud of his performance as St Erewold, and welcomed the opportunity to play another part with a hood over his head. Jem had just returned from Cop Top where he had been giving Benjy a final briefing. All he had to do was to smile through his white beard, and to give out small presents from his bag. All he had to remember was that girls were to receive a present wrapped in pink, and boys one wrapped in blue.

'Do you think he'll be alright, Jem?'

'Don't worry, Mum. He'll be fine, so long as he remembers the colours.'

'Oh, Jem – the presents for the boys – I'm one short. Have you got something decent we can wrap up? Something that doesn't look too knocked about? It's too late to go to the shop.'

Jem went upstairs to his bedroom and began rifling through his old toys and possessions. The lead soldiers looked as though they had been through the wars – even those still with heads and all their limbs were not fit for parade. His 'Dinky' racing cars had raced too often to be presentable. The wooden fort was in a state of collapse, having failed to withstand the siege of time. Jem knew, without having to inspect everything, that there was only one object which would pass the scrutiny of a keen-eyed evacuee and be accepted as virtually new. He pulled the box out from the back of the cupboard. It was another 'Dinky' vehicle: an Army searchlight lorry towing an anti-aircraft gun on a mobile platform. It was a handsome dark green, apart from the lens of the searchlight which was a silvery white. The platform had hinged sides which folded up when the gun was being towed. When not in use, the gun rested horizontally, but in action it could be pointed in every direction. The lorry and platform were each three inches long. In Jem's eyes they were beautiful. The detail was exquisite. That was why, having received them from a favourite aunt a year ago, he had never used them. Harold had urged him to bring them into use when they played wars, but Jem had maintained that they were part of his reserve forces – for use only in dire extremity.

Could he bear to part with them? His instinctive reaction was: No. True, he had never 'played' with them. But he had often had them out of the box to admire, whilst turning the searchlight and gun. The evacuees, though, were worse off than him. They had had to leave most of their treasured possessions behind.

'Found anything, Jem?' his mother called up the stairs.

'Not yet – I'm thinking. Can we leave it till the morning?'

'Alright, but I hope you can find something.'

From his bed, Jem looked at the lorry and platform. They were so handsome! He turned off the light, and they disappeared, just as they would if he sacrificed them. He would never see or handle them again. They would have passed out of his life for ever. In contemplation of this calamity, a tear forced its way out of the corner of an eye on to the pillow. But (oh, why did there have to be a 'but'?) his conscience nagged him. Everyone was having to make sacrifices in this war. His Dad had given up family life. The evacuees had had to give up their homes for the time being – and they might find them flattened when they went back. The calm, smiling face of Alice floated into his inner sight. What would she want him to do? He was pretty sure he knew the answer; and it was not one that pleased him.

'Did you find anything for a present, Jem?' his mother asked at breakfast.

'Yes, Mum. I'll fetch it down after we've finished.'

Jem went upstairs, brushed his teeth and went into the bedroom. He hardly dared to look at the dark green unit. Without pausing, he placed it in the box and went downstairs.

'Here you are, Mum. Wrap it up quick.'

'Oh, Jem – that!'

'It's the only decent thing I could find. Everything else is worn.'

His mother smiled at him. 'Perhaps, when the war's over, we can find another one.'

The party was riotous. The evacuees were determined

to have a good time. All this – the food, the games – had been laid on for *them*. There were no local children, apart from a few helpers, like Jem, present to interfere with their enjoyment. Everyone wore paper hats, even the most staid of the local ladies. Jem was surprised to see Mrs Weaverthorpe looking cheerful under the peak of a black and white check cap. He had always thought her a sombre character. Rondot's mother was back from Hull. To see her smiling and swopping a joke with Mrs Weaverthorpe suggested that a spell of magic had been cast over the event.

Half way through the proceedings, who should enter the hall but Hon Peter and Lorinda! Had it been left to him, they would have wandered around like minor royals, chatting and being pleasant. But Lorinda was determined he should get more involved. Before he was able to protest, he found himself playing musical chairs – walking round a circle of chairs until the piano stopped and then dashing for the nearest chair. Gallantly, when there were only three chairs left for four people, he let a little girl beat him to it. Lorinda had a more competitive streak. In the finals of the Flapping Fish, she flapped her paper fish along the string with patient skill and won, to the cheers of the children.

'Jingle Bells' on the piano signalled the entrance of Father Christmas. Bent under his heavy sack, Benjy came in and stamped his boots, as though shaking snow off. To Jem's surprise and slight alarm, he proceeded to give a little speech.

'Hullo, kids. As I were coming 'ere on my sleigh, one o' my reindeer said: "It's very dark down there –

usually there's lights on". I explained that there's a war on and people don't show any lights for fear of enemy aeroplanes. Reindeer asked: "What if we meet the enemy?" I told 'er that it weren't *our* enemy – Father Christmas is neutral. Anyroad, the sleigh has magic to ward off any planes. Reindeer asked: "Are we going to all t'countries at war?" "Ay," I said, "we're going just as usual. It's not children that's at war. They'll all get their presents if I've owt to do wi' it." So, you see, kids, there'll be children in Germany looking out for me, just like you. Now then, girls first.'

Benjy opened his sack and prepared to hand out the presents. He looked up with an expression of anxiety, casting his eyes around for help. He caught sight of Jem and lifted his eyebrows. Jem realised what was the matter: Benjy had forgotten the colours.

'Is it pink for girls as usual, Father Christmas?' he called out.

A smile of relief was visible through the white beard.

The present giving over, Father Christmas disappeared, having remembered to wish everyone a Happy Christmas. Hon Peter climbed on to the stage.

'Oh dear!' Jem thought. 'He's going to make a speech. They'll all get bored!'

But Peter had more sense, or else Lorinda had given him a hint.

'Didn't Father Christmas treat us to some sensible remarks? We should all remember the poor children of Germany – especially because they're under the heel of that tyrant, Hitler. Now, we need to thank everyone who has helped to make this party a success. I can't thank the vicar of Althwaite because he's gone to take Father Christmas home – I mean to his sleigh. But thanks to the vicar of Homefield and to all the ladies who've been involved. Let's give them three cheers: Hip, Hip, Hooray.'

Paper hats were waved and thrown into the air as the cheers echoed around the hall. Some landed on the few remaining sandwiches and sausage rolls or on the nearly empty bowls of jelly and blancmange.

As the children were leaving, Jem noticed, from the different shade of blue paper that wrapped it up, that the present he had donated had been given to Jakie Andrews. He felt glad. Jakie was one of the evacuees who had still not reconciled themselves to their new surroundings. Perhaps the gift would help. Jem approved, also, of the fact that Jakie was taking it away unopened. Something so special ought not to be gloated upon by all and sundry, but admired in secret or with privileged friends.

'Well, that's a relief,' said Mrs Murgatroyd when they had got home and she was pouring out cups of tea. 'I think it went very well – including Father Christmas. Had you told Benjy what to say?'

'No – honest. It came as a complete surprise.'

'I used to think he was just a lazy layabout. But there's more to him than meets the eye. And you found that out, Jem. Remember the missing pudding?'

His mother laughed, and her laughter was infectious.

His bedroom looked the same, but Jem knew that it was different. Something that had been a treasured part of his existence for a year was no longer there. By an act of will, he had put it out of his life forever. The thing itself would not have altered. If he was invited into the house where Jakie was staying and shown the searchlight lorry and gun on the platform, there would be no sign that ownership had changed. But he would have no right to stretch out his hand and hold it. Being inanimate, it would not realize that it now belonged to another. That was part of the wrench: the prized object being incapable of appreciating how much it had been admired, even loved. But perhaps that was a mercy: how much worse the mutual separation of an owner and his pet, say Harold and Raq. Anyway, Jem concluded, there was nothing to be gained by ruminating on his loss. He had to think positively – of Jakie's delighted surprise on opening the present, and its future in his hands.

10 BURGLARY AT ST JUDE'S

It was a fortnight after Christmas. Jem and his mother were in low spirits, despite the comforting hopes raised by the re-telling of the traditional story. Handel's Messiah had been performed in Homefield. But according to reports (Jem and his mother had not gone) it had not been as full-blooded as usual, since some good singers were away in the forces. Nor had war prevented Althwaite's Silver Band from making its rounds late on Christmas Eve and into the early hours of Christmas Day. As Jem had lain in bed listening, the usual stirring of his spirit, accompanied by goose pimples, had fleetingly occurred. But he had found himself being critical of the lack of harmony: the result of newcomers replacing experts.

The best thing about this Christmas, though, had been Dad's return on leave for four days. He looked different. His hair had been cropped by the army, he looked fuller in the cheeks. He looked healthier, as though the army was good for him. Jem didn't like to comment on this in case it seemed like a reflection on

Dad's previous life at home. But Dad himself had put it down to the training.

'I've had enough square-bashing to last a life time. You wouldn't believe how snappy I've become with rifle drill – I'll show you with a walking stick, Jem. I know I've put on weight. All that handling of rifles and physical training's good for the muscles. But I've also heard more than enough bad languarge. Not least from our sergeant. "I'll have your guts for garters" is mild compared to his other expressions. I'll be glad to get away from him. When I go back I should hear where I'm being posted. I hope it'll be KOYLI- the King's Own. Be fun Jem, wouldn't it, if I ended up under that captain who came to see us?'

Jem hadn't seen much of Dad on Christmas Eve – he and Mum had gone into Bruddersford and left him behind. One result of this was a special present on Christmas Day. Unlike the smaller gifts, which were supposedly from Father Christmas, this was labelled: 'With love from Mum and Dad. Opening the small parcel, Jem found a 'Dinky' box. Inside was a Bren Gun Carrier, with silvery links as the caterpillar tracks. It hauled an ammunition trailer and a field gun. Like the searchlight and gun unit he had given up, it was dark green and realistically detailed. Jem felt his eyes watering as he lifted the unit out of the box.

'It's beautiful – thanks!'

'Mum told me about your sacrifice – I thought, *we* thought you deserved it.'

There and then Jem decided that the Carrier and its attachments were not going to be preserved as part of a reserve force. If Harold wanted to play wars, they would be in the front line.

On Boxing Day they had all three taken a wintry walk to Digfoot Reservoir. No snow had yet fallen, but the ground was hard with frost. On the rutted lane their shoes crunched the thin ice over the potholes. The air was crystal clear. From the rise above the reservoir Dad had pointed out on the horizon the exposed rocks of Grey Nab, where they had had their lunch snack on the search for Benjy. Down by the water, they found shelter from the chill wind at the base of a gnarled oak tree. Mum poured tea from a thermos flask and produced a chocolate biscuit each.

'I don't think there'll be many more chocolate biscuits for a long time – not till your Dad's won the war for us. So make the most of them.'

Dad had fooled about with his walking stick – sloping arms, presenting arms, charging the oak tree with fixed bayonet. Jem had found some flattish stones to skim over the surface of the water. The cry of a curlew reminded him of the great expanse of lonely moors around. On the return home, they had all been quieter. Dad's departure on the following morning loomed ahead, unshielded by other activity. Following behind, Jem noticed that Dad had put his arm around Mum's waist – something that didn't happen often.

Dad's departure had been very early. He had opened Jem's bedroom door and ruffled the hair of the semi-conscious figure.

'So long Jem. Look after Mum. Steer clear of peat hags!'

Now, Mum and he were on their own again. Each felt a need to lift the spirits of the other, but was finding it difficult. Something in the Bruddersford Examiner took them out of themselves. Mum was casting an eye over the pages after breakfast when she spotted it.

'Listen to this, Jem. *The engagement is announced of Aircraftswoman Lorinda Vajansky WAAF, of 84 Moorview Road, Bruddersford and The Hon Peter Danellion-Smith of The Hall, Althwaite.* Isn't that amazing? Everyone thought he was a confirmed bachelor. I knew they were friendly. I remember thinking at the evacuees' party what a nice couple they made. But I didn't imagine the squire would ever put himself under the rule of a woman! And she's joined the Women's Air Force. Good for her!'

Jem read the announcement and smiled.

'Jem! You knew, didn't you?'

'I had an inkling.'

'What a discreet, close fellow you are!'

'Anyroad, it's great news. What are you going to wear at the wedding, Mum?'

'Me! I shan't be invited! And what's this "anyroad"? That's slang you've picked up from Benjy or school. It's summat awful!'

'Not "summat" – "something", old lady!'

'Cheeky lad, I'll wallop you!'

Mum chased Jem around the table in mock annoyance and ended up giving him a hug. Jem felt that he should be embarrassed, but in fact appreciated Mum's display of affection.

The second thing to take Jem out of himself was the news that St Jude's had been burgled. The rumour going round was that all the silver – chalices, plates, candlesticks – had been stolen, together with the

Women's Institute banner. Being Methodists, Jem and his mother were not closely associated with the church. But, like other local people, they were shocked. That sort of thing didn't happen in Althwaite.

Jem pondered on this calamity as he climbed up to Cop Top Farm. It seemed strange that this first theft from the church within living memory should have taken place after war had broken out. It was an invasion of Althwaite's peaceful privacy, just as the appearance of German parachutists would be. Could there be a connection between the theft and the war? Perhaps some person rendered destitute and desperate by the hardships of war time?

Jem had not seen Benjy since the Christmas Party. There was no one about in the farmyard, so he climbed the ladder to the stable loft. His belongings were there, but no Benjy. Descending, he startled Alice who had come into the stable.

'Jem! You gave me a fright! I knew Benjy was out, so it couldn't be him. Did you have a nice Christmas?'

'Yes, but we felt very flat after Dad went back.'

'I heard that the evacuees' party went well. Benjy told us how impressed the children seemed to be by his little speech. He's already looking forward to being Father Christmas again.'

'Do you know where he is?'

'No. He's supposed to be trimming a hedge in Five Acre Field, but Dad said he'd left his tools and cleared off. I think he's upset about one or two people saying that he might have had something to do with the robbery from the church.'

'That's nonsense. What would Benjy do with church silver?'

'I agree. It's absurd and insulting. Just because he still reckons to be a tramp. It's not the silver that's been taken though. I don't know quite what it is, but it's something to do with the squire's family.'

'I just hope that people don't start suspecting evacuees. That wouldn't do relations any good.'

'You're right. Well, I'd better be getting on. But...' Alice hesitated and then continued, with a smile. 'Jem – do you mind me asking something personal?'

'Depends what it is. But I'd always be frank with you, Alice.'

'I like your name, but it's unusual. Where did it come from?'

Jem was relieved. For a split second, until he realised how ridiculous that would be, he had feared a question about his feelings for her. 'It's not my real name. But if I tell you, you must promise to keep it a secret.'

'I will.'

'My real names are George Malcolm.'

'You don't look like a George Malcolm!'

'I've never felt like one either. Ever since I was little, I disliked the names. I made "Jem" up, from the start of "George" and the "M" of "Malcolm". When I was little, I talked to myself in bed. Mum heard me talking to "Jem" and asked who he was. I explained it was me. So she started using it and it stuck.'

'I didn't used to like "Alice".'

'Why not? It's a lovely name!' Jem blushed at the vehemence with which he had spoken.

'It was the association with *the* Alice. At junior school I'd be asked whether I'd seen the White Rabbit that morning or which side of the Looking Glass I was that day. But I've got over all that now.'

A figure passed the entrance to the stable. Alice noticed and went outside.

'Archie! Come and meet Jem.'

A tall man with floppy black hair appeared. He was wearing fairly new overalls and a check shirt. His sleeves were rolled up. His forearms were muscular, but white – unlike a farm labourer's.

'Jem – this is Archie, our new hand. Archie – this is Jem, a friend of ours from the village. He's a special pal of Benjy's.'

Archie held out his hand. 'Any friend of the farm and Benjy's a friend of mine,' he said.

Alice unhitched her pony and led it into the yard. 'I'll leave you two to get acquainted – have to get on with mucking out.'

Jem began walking down the yard with Archie.

'I'm in the cottage where your friend Benjy was before,' he said. 'He didn't take it amiss that I'd displaced him – at least not when he appreciated that my wife, Miriam, and our baby are with me. He's told me what a good friend you've been to him. I wish I'd seen that rescue from the flood!'

For the second time that morning, Jem found himself turning red. Perhaps Archie noticed. He began speaking about himself.

'I understand your Dad's joined up. A brave chap! I'm afraid I'm what's called a 'conscie' – a conscientious objector. Have you heard of them?'

'Yes,' Jem replied hesitantly. He'd been led to believe that they were a low, skiving sort of people, trying to get out of their obvious duty.

'I oppose war on principle. I think fighting and killing is wrong. So I opted for work on a farm.'

'When you were called up, did you just tell them that's what you wanted to do?'

'I wish it had been that simple! No, I had to go before a tribunal – a committee – and answer questions.'

They heard a shout from the other end of the yard.

'That's Mr Ackroyd calling for me. Have to go. Tell you more another time.'

Archie's long legs strode off across the cobbled yard. Mr Ackroyd appeared round the corner of the house and gave Jem a friendly wave. Not for the first time, Jem felt as though he belonged there. Walking back down to the village, he indulged in the day-dream of his mother and himself installed in a cottage near the farm. Then he thought of Archie. It was funny how general ideas often proved inadequate when what they embraced was encountered individually. Evacuees were a case in point. Considered in general, they were an unruly, unhappy, not very likeable lot. But when you met them, they could be interesting and friendly. Now there were the conscientious objectors. Before meeting Archie, Jem had gone along with the common view that they were an unpatriotic lot – some cowardly, others too high-principled, all of them expecting others to do the fighting for them. Now he'd met one, he began to feel that the general picture was perhaps unsatisfactory. Archie seemed a decent, friendly sort of fellow. He was not from Yorkshire – that was clear from his accent, which was more like that of a newsreader on the wireless. But Jem didn't hold that against him. It would be interesting to find out more about his attitude to the war.

A report in the Examiner gave some authoritative information about the theft from St Jude's.

Mystery surrounds the theft from Althwaite parish church of priceless items adorning the history of the Danellion family. Sir Richard Dandelion fought for the Yorkist cause in the Battle of Tewkesbury in 1471. He was wounded, but recovered. After his death in 1483 a monument was erected in the church and his 'achievement' placed above. The 'achievement' – a term from heraldry – comprised parts of his armour: helmet, breastplate, and steel gloves. On Monday last, the church cleaner noticed that they were missing. The police say that there was no sign of forced entry. They appeal for anyone with information to get in touch with them.

The Vicar, the Reverend Cuthbert Blake, told The Examiner that the last time anything was stolen from the church was nearly 300 years ago when some of Cromwell's troops, elated by their victory at Marston Moor, stopped by to deface monuments which were regarded as 'Popish' and took the silver candlesticks from the altar. Fortunately, none of the church silver had been stolen on this occasion, nor had the offerings box been forced open. He was fairly sure that the missing items were still in place when the Sunday morning service took place.

The Hon Peter Danellion-Smith told The Examiner that he was not aware of a vendetta against his family. He regretted the disappearance of the items, though they had become so much part of the furniture that many people had perhaps forgotten that they were there. They had a historical and sentimental value. But if they came up for sale in an antique shop, they might be regarded as not much more than interesting old junk. He appreciated the efforts of the police, but thought they should not spend a great deal of time on the case. They had more important things to do in war time. In the face of the loss, The Hon Peter thus displayed the stoicism which had become a family trait.

Suspicion did indeed alight on the evacuees. They had no feeling for the history of Althwaite and its principal family. What more likely than that a few of the wilder ones would regard the removal of the bits of ancient armour as a clever prank? The police were said to have interviewed some of the older boys. When Jem next saw Ron, he was outraged.

'Constable Dewhurst came to see me. He asked me what I was doing over the week-end, especially Sunday afternoon and evening. I'd the best of alibis for the afternoon, 'cos Mrs McAlister 'ad invited us up for tea in the kitchen at the Hall. Anyroad, none of the evacuees I know would 'ave been able to pinch the things. They were too 'igh up on the wall. They'd 'ave chosen something easier if they wanted to take anything. Not that I think they would 'ave. People from Hull are as 'onest as Althwaite folk.'

Harold came over after school. He admired Jem's new Bren Gun Carrier. They decided to play wars at the Manse the next Saturday. Over cocoa and biscuits, Jem broached the question of the burglary.

'Why should anyone want to steal those old things? They were high up, so they'd have needed a ladder to get them down.'

'Perhaps it was some chap who's daft about collecting things like that,' Harold speculated. 'Just like there's people who'll risk breaking their necks to get rare birds' eggs.'

'There was no sign of a break in. So whoever it was must have been able to pick the lock of the door – unless they'd pinched the key.'

'Yes, but the vicar told my Dad something the paper doesn't mention. The window of the vestry was found open. But it didn't seem to have been forced. The vicar says he never opens that window, and the cleaner swears she didn't open it.'

'It's a complete mystery. I bet the police'll have a job solving it.'

Next day brought a letter from Dad which pushed the burglary to the back of Jem's mind.

'Oh dear!' said his Mum. 'Listen to this, Jem.'

I had some very bad news yesterday. Instead of being posted to KOYLI or some other infantry regiment, I'm being sent to the RASC – the Service Corps. A week ago we were on parade and the sergeant said: 'Step forward any man who can drive'. Obeying orders without hesitation has become so ingrained over the past weeks that I stepped forward without thinking. I was a fool! Now I'll have to drive some…truck.

'Just as well he crossed that word out!' Mum interjected.

I'm down in the dumps about this. I was looking forward to being a real soldier. Still, someone has to keep the army mobile. When I learnt to drive that carpet delivery van, I never imagined I'd be putting the skill to use against Hitler.

'He will be disappointed!' Mum commented. 'He'd rather set his heart on joining the King's Own. But I must say, I'm relieved. He won't be so much at risk, I should think. We want our Dad back, don't we, Jem?'

Jem's feelings were mixed. He could understand Dad being upset. And he'd looked forward to being able to tell people, not least Charlie Foster, that his father was in the King's Own Yorkshire Light Infantry. The Royal Army Service Corps didn't sound anything like as glamorous. On the other hand, he shared his mother's concern that Dad should not be too much exposed to danger.

A fortnight later the Examiner carried a brief item on the burglary. It mentioned the open window in the vestry and assumed that was how the thieves got in. The police had interviewed various people, including some of the older evacuees. But no progress had been made. The police appreciated the Hon Peter Danellion-Smith's advice that they should not spend too much time on the case. If any information came to light, they would re-open their enquiries.

Jem was relieved to see that there was no mention of tramps. He couldn't help feeling, though, that the police were treating the case too lightly. They seemed to be taking advantage of the squire's unselfish advice, and were backing away from something they were finding too difficult. He mentioned these thoughts to Harold when they next met.

'Why don't we do some investigating?' Harold suggested. 'I know you don't listen to Children's Hour much, Jem. But there's these two brothers – Norman and Henry Bones, Boy Detectives. They get to the bottom of cases that puzzle the police.'

Jem stared at Harold. It was usually he himself who made the suggestions. But here was Harold proposing something that he should have thought of.

'Why didn't I think of that? Good for you, Harold!'

Relishing his unexpected role as initiator, Harold continued. 'First thing is to have a look inside the church. Scene of the crime.'

'How do we get in? It's only open for services. We'd look a bit odd turning up for early morning communion!'

'Perhaps we could sneak in then.'

'And get locked inside? No thanks!'

The two would-be investigators seemed to be stumped at the outset. They separated to sleep on the problem.

After school the next day Jem was in his bedroom painting the model Spitfire. The dope he was using smelled strongly. He went to open the window and saw Harold running up the lane. That was strange – Harold was usually slow-moving. Jem went down to let him in.

'I've got it!'

'Come upstairs,' said Jem, aware that his mother was within earshot.

Harold collapsed on to the bed to get his breath back.

'On Saturday mornings the flower arrangers are in the church. I've been to look at the rota in the porch. Next Saturday it's Mrs McAlister and Mrs Dawson, Bert's wife. I reckon they'd let us look around.'

Jem grabbed the tie that he had taken off on return from school. He ceremonially placed it around Harold's neck.

'I hereby award you the ribbon of Order of Detective first class!'

Jem found it difficult to get to sleep on Friday evening. Was this a daft idea? Could he and Harold really expect to find clues that the police had overlooked? Suppose that they got on to the trail of the criminal – whoever it was might be dangerous. Still, there was no harm in having a look.

Mrs McAlister and Mrs Dawson were not too pleased at finding their peaceful arranging of cuttings from evergreen and winter-flowering shrubs disturbed by the entry of two boys.

'What do you want, lads? Oh, it's you Jem. And Harold Bright, isn't it?'

'Yes, Mrs McAlister. Do you mind if Jem and me have a look round?'

'No – but don't get up to any mischief!'

The boys wandered around as though they were genuinely interested in the architecture and the memorial plaques. In the chancel were the monuments to the Dandelion family.

'That's the tomb of Sir John. And look up there,' Harold whispered.

Projecting about five feet from the upper wall of the chancel was an iron bar with a hook at the end. It was from this that the helmet had been suspended. Two shorter projections had held the steel gloves. A lighter patch showed where the breastplate had hung against the wall.

'Look there, just below where that bar comes out of the wall. Are there some marks?' Jem asked.

'Hold on. I've got a flashlight.'

Harold shone the beam on the wall. Now they could see two faint marks, about a foot apart.

'Perhaps that's where the ladder was placed – it might have been dusty.'

'What are you two up to – shining a light?'

They had forgotten about the ladies.

'Oh, we're just having a closer look at something.'

Mrs Dawson came up the chancel steps.

'Yes, that's where the Dandelion things were. Great shame ain't it? My husband were real upset. As a church warden, he felt partly responsible.'

'I know your husband well, Mrs Dawson. He came up trumps when we had those visits for evacuees,' Jem said.

Mrs Dawson smiled.

'I suppose Bert, I mean, Mr Dawson, has a key to the church?'

'Why are you asking? Are you two playing detectives? Well, there's no harm in that. Yes, he has a key. Then the vicar has one, o'course. And the other's held by Miss Hibbert – she used to be a cleaner. She's too old for that now. But as she lives just above the church it's convenient to have a key there.'

'Where would the thieves have got a ladder from? Or would they have had to bring one with them?'

'They may have used the one under the tower. If you look through the curtains at the west end, you'll see it.'

'Thanks. You could perhaps tell Bert, I mean Mr Dawson, that we're interested. But please don't tell anyone else, will you?'

'Mum's the word!' Mrs Dawson replied with a smile and went back to the flower arranging.

'Nice lady,' Harold commented. 'I liked the way you buttered her up with praise of Bert.'

'I meant it! Let's have a look at the ladder.'

They pulled aside the curtain and entered the square space under the tower. Wooden steps led up to a trapdoor. The church had just one bell, the rope for which hung down through a hole in the floor above. An old wooden ladder leaned against a wall. Harold climbed up and rubbed his hand over the top. He showed his hand to Jem. 'Very dusty. This could have been the one they used.'

Mrs McAlister looked through the curtain. 'We're finished boys, so you'll have to come out with us, I'm afraid.'

'Could we just stay on a bit and then lock up?' Jem asked.

'Oh, I don't know about that.'

'They'll be alright,' said Mrs Dawson. 'I'll tell Bert they're here. The key's hanging on the hook beside the door. Be sure you lock up and bring the key down to our house – you know where it is?'

'Yes, thanks very much.'

'Come on,' Jem said after the ladies had gone. 'Let's carry the ladder to the chancel and set it up – see whether it's the one they used.'

The ladder was heavy. It was as much as the two boys could manage to carry it, one at each end, down the church. Raising it against the chancel wall taxed their young muscles. When it was in place, the top coincided with the marks they had noticed.

'This must have been the one,' Harold said. 'I'm taller than you so I'm going up to see whether they could have reached the helmet.'

'Be careful!' Jem was not good at heights. The very thought of Harold leaning out from the top of the ladder gave him a turning sensation in his stomach.

'I could reach the bar holding the gloves – see!' Harold said. 'But where the helmet was – that would be impossible. Look!'

Harold stretched out an arm. His hand was about three feet short of the hook at the end of the long bar. He descended safely, they replaced the ladder, went outside and turned the key in the lock of the heavy door.

'How they got the helmet down's a mystery,' Jem said.

'But we know there must have been at least two of them – to carry that heavy ladder.'

'I'll take the key back,' Jem said. 'If I see Bert, I'll have a word with him. Let's sleep on it and see what we can come up with tomorrow.'

Some non-human force had placed the ladder against the wall. Curiously, it was not the wall of the church, but that of the Methodist Chapel. The preacher had begun his sermon. It was about Jacob dreaming of the ladder reaching to heaven, with the angels ascending and descending. 'Surely the Lord is in this place and I knew it not,' said the preacher, repeating Jacob's exclamation. At that, the top of the ladder came away from the wall. 'It's going to fall on the preacher,' thought Jem. But, having reached the vertical, it stood still, miraculously balanced. It became Jacob's ladder. A bulky angel, with a resemblance to Benjy, climbed up and sat on the top, looking down on the congregation. The angel's wings gradually shrunk into his shoulders until it *was* Benjy. The ladder began to lean, the preacher held out his hands in horror. 'Help!' Jem shouted.

'What's the matter, Jem? You've been calling out.' His mother looked down at him with a worried expression.

'It was frightening. But I think I've solved something.'

'Well, tell me in the morning. And don't disturb my sleep again, there's a good lad!'

Jem was evasive at breakfast. He didn't want to worry his mother by telling her that he and Harold had taken on the role of private investigators. The time between breakfast and setting out for chapel found him in the shed. With bits of wood and small nails, he made a model of the ladder. He tied the middle of a length of string to the topmost rung and stretched each half down to the top of the bench at about a forty five degree angle to the ladder. He placed weights on the ends. The ladder now stood vertical. He moved his fingers up the rungs, as though someone – an angel or Benjy – was climbing up.

Jem listened even less than usual to Mr Bright's sermon. When the service was over he steered Harold away from the people gathered outside.

'I think I've solved it!'

'What – who stole the things?'

'No. How they could have used the ladder to get at the helmet! We need to have another look inside the church. I'm going to see if Bert will let us in.'

Jem thought he had better let Bert know what he and Harold were up to, rather than invent some excuse, like researching the church for school work.

'So which of you is Sherlock Holmes and which is Dr Watson? As if I can't guess!' was Bert's reaction when Jem explained they were taking up the case. 'No, I don't' mind yer having another look inside. But I think I'll come along. Maybe I'll learn summat myssen. I don't mind telling yer that I didn't like squire suggesting t'police shouldn't bother overmuch. I've been a church warden nigh on fifteen year. I feel as though my reputation is sullied as long as thieves are not caught.'

Bert let them into the church after school on the Monday. It was beginning to get dark. To comply with the black-out would have meant drawing all the curtains before switching on the lights. Instead, Bert produced a flashlight with a strong beam. The boys showed him the marks which indicated that a dusty ladder had been leant against the chancel wall. Bert agreed that someone at the top would not have been able to stretch far enough to reach the helmet. Jem proceeded to explain how, if the ladder was stood vertically underneath the hook on the end of the bar, it could be held in position by ropes leading from the top and attached to things on the ground. Looking towards the altar, the most obvious point of attachment was the altar rail. Jem and Harold got on their hands and knees and inspected the rail and the long cushion beneath it in the light of Bert's light.

'Here – look at this.' It was Harold who made the discovery: four wispy and curly pieces of what looked like a very thin string, lying on the cushion.

'I reckon they frayed off the rope where it rubbed against the rail,' Jem said.

'They're valuable evidence. What can we put them in, so we don't lose them?'

'I've got a nearly empty match box. I'll just take these few matches out and you can have it.'

'Thanks, Mr Dawson. Now, let's see where the rope could have been fixed in the other direction,' Jem suggested.

There was no screen between the chancel and the nave. The nearest heavy object was the massive lectern, with a brass eagle on top. Or, if the rope had been long enough, it could have been tied to the front pew. Again, the two sleuths got down for a minute inspection, Bert helping them. Nothing was to be seen under the lectern. Harold squirmed under the pew.

'Shine a light. There's nothing on the floor. But – yes – look here!'

The wood at the bottom of the front of the pew was rough. At one spot there was a splinter. Held in the splinter were three strands of the same thin stuff they had already found.

'More for the matchbox!' Harold said.

'Well, I'm blowed!' Bert exclaimed. 'I bet t'police didn't think of this. But, even with a ladder held like that, I reckon they'd have needed two chaps steadying it whilst another climbed up. And there's no rope in the church, so they must 'ave brought one.'

'And how did they get in?' Jem asked. 'There was that open window in the vestry, but no sign of it having been forced. Apart from the vicar and you, Mr Dawson, the only key holder is Miss Hibbert, is that right?'

'Call me Bert, lads. Ay that's right. And I can assure yer it weren't me that lent a key! Miss Hibbert's a bit odd, but she's devoted to the church. Somebody might have persuaded her to let them look inside. But t'police have already been to see her.'

Miss Hibbert – 'Ma Hibbert' as she was familiarly known – lived up the hill behind the church along a short lane called Up Bye. From the edge of the lane you looked over a stone wall down into the grounds of the church, with a scattering of gravestones below. At the back of the terrace of four houses a rocky cliff rose almost vertically. It seemed a precarious place to live: in danger of falling rocks behind and of tumbling into the graveyard in front.

Jem knew Ma Hibbert by sight, but had never spoken to her. She was small and plump, with rosy cheeks. She wore her hair in a bun or plaited. She looked a harmless, agreeable, old lady. But she was a 'wise woman'. In earlier times she would have been regarded as a witch – but a witch of the benignant, not malevolent, kind. She knew a lot about the use of plants for healing. If they were in deep personal trouble, some elderly people would rather go to her for comfort and advice than to the vicar or Mr Bright.

Jem didn't look forward to visiting her. Her reputation as a 'wise woman' made him feel that he would be at a disadvantage: that instead of him questioning her, she would be questioning him. Still, it had to be done. She was known to have a soft spot for animals, so Harold suggested that they take Raq with them.

The next Saturday morning Jem and Harold, with Raq on a lead, climbed up beside the church and turned into Up Bye. They knocked on the door of number three. Raq barked madly, ignoring Harold's order to 'Shut up'. Straining against the lead, Raq pushed the door. It swung open. The stimulus to his agitation was now evident: three black cats gazed from the foot of the stairs. Raq went wild.

'Oh dear, I shouldn't have brought her,' said Harold, pulling her away from the door.

'She'll be alright. Just a minute,' came a voice from above. Miss Hibbert descended the stairs. She was wearing a black dress which came down to her ankles.

'Come here, lass. Lovely dog. "Raq", isn't it. A gypsy. We like gypsies, don't we pussies?'

Raq fell silent and wagged her tail.

'Come on in, I've been expecting you.'

Ma Hibbert led the way into the kitchen, preceded by the three cats. Three mugs were already set out on the table. She gave Raq a biscuit. She settled underneath the table, watched intently by the cats.

'Dandelion and Burdock alright?'

The boys nodded, rendered speechless by the way Ma Hibbert seemed to have taken charge. How did she know Raq's name? How was it that she had been expecting them – even to the extent of having mugs ready? It seemed uncanny.

'Well now, how are Sherlock Holmes and Dr

Watson getting on?' she asked when they were sitting at the table with their drinks. 'Any clues? When the police gave up, I thought to myssen that there were two bright lads – Harold Bright and Jem Murgatroyd – who might pick up the trail. And then Bert confirmed it. Rum business, ain't it? I bet yon squire, Hon Peter, is right upset, even though he tries to keep a stiff upper lip. Taking an ancestor's accoutrements – have I got the right word, lads? – disgraceful, weren't it? It's natural you should want to know who holds the keys. But then, you're not suspecting the vicar, Bert or me of the crime. That would be a joke, wouldn't it, pussies? Ah but, you say, I might have let someone have the key who had no right to it. And I might, mightn't I?A poor, old woman like me, with only three cats for defence. But I didn't lads. Finished your drinks? If so, I'll show you my garden.'

Ma Hibbert opened the back door and they all trooped out, animals and humans. From the tiny yard, steps led up to a paved area sheltered by a sycamore tree. Here there was a pool.A trickle of water fed the pool at the far end. On a bank of gravel rested a wooden boat about eight inches in length. Seated on it was a clay model of Mr Toad, holding a book. Beyond the pool a few more steps brought them to a grassy area right under the cliff. Here the sun never penetrated. Ferns grew out of the damp rocks; and water seeped out from the foot of the cliff, to be channelled to the pool.

'What a magical spot!' Jem exclaimed. They were the first words he or Harold had uttered since arriving.

'This is where I do my contemplating,' Ma Hibbert said. 'Marvellous what you can see from here.'

Jem and Harold looked around. All they could see was the rock face, the sycamore tree and the roofs of four houses.

'Well, you'll want to be getting on with your investigations. And my spell on Raq is beginning to wear off.'

Raq had begun growling quietly at the cats.

'Let me know how you get on. Bye, lads!'

Jem and Harold found themselves out on the lane. Without speaking they made their way down the lane and across the market place to the bridge. They sat down on the bank underneath.

'Well, I'm blowed!' said Jem. 'She didn't give us a chance to ask any questions.'

'She took the wind right out of my sails,' Harold added.

'How did she know we were coming?'

'And did you notice that she called Raq 'she' from upstairs. How did she know she's a bitch, without even seeing her?'

'But what was it she said? She hadn't let anyone have the key who had no right to it. Was that it?'

'I think so.'

'So who would have a right to it?'

'Someone with genuine business there – the cleaner, the flower ladies, the organist.'

'We didn't manage that very well. We should have asked who she *did* lend the key to. And if she keeps a list.'

'Like as not, she'd have answered us in riddles.'

'I suggest we speak to the people who do go into the church. We've already seen the flower ladies – I'm sure they're innocent. Suppose one of us talks to the cleaner and one to the organist.'

Harold went to see Mrs Carter, the cleaner, whilst Jem went to see the organist. This was Mrs Cawthorn, a retired teacher. What a policeman might have called a 'routine enquiry' gave Jem a shock.

'So you're another one, snooping around, suspecting innocent folk! Which school do you go to – Homefield? I've a good mind to report you to your headmaster. Only yesterday there was another sleuth asking impertinent questions. But he went to Bruddersford School, or so he said.'

'But there couldn't have been anyone else. Harold – my pal – he's not been to see you.'

'Who said anything about a Harold? This one was a Charlie. And a right nosey-parker he was. So I'm not answering any more questions. You can clear off!'

As Jem walked away, he felt almost physically sick, as though someone had hit him in the stomach. Charlie Foster making his own investigation? This was too much. Charlie was poaching on Harold's and his own patch. Jem's mind was a turmoil of indignation and fear. Fear – lest Charlie steal a march on them. Suppose he found a vital clue and solved the mystery? He had a vision of Charlie: triumphant and praised by the local community. The Bruddersford Examiner would have a headline on the front page: *LOCAL BOY SOLVES MYSTERY.* Then there would be a report: *Charlie Foster, a twelve year old resident of Althwaite, has single-handedly solved the mystery of the burgling of Althwaite Church. Superintendent Larkin, head of Bruddersford police, said 'This boy will go far'.*

Jem felt that he would never live down the humiliation. He must see Charlie and warn him off.

11 THE TRAIL RESUMED

Jem knew where Charlie lived. His parents were well off. The house was down the road to Homefield, set back behind tall hedges. Jem felt uneasy as he swung open the iron gate and approached the front door. What kind of reception would he get? He rang the bell and waited at the foot of the doorsteps. A young woman, with a white cap on her head, answered the door. It was the first time Jem had seen a housemaid. Yes, Charlie was in – she would call him.

'Well, what an unexpected pleasure. Come to ask me out to play, Jem Murgatroyd?'

'O'course not! Look, I understand you're investigating this burglary at the church.'

'That's right. Want to give evidence, or own up?'

'No, But it's Harold Bright and me who are doing the investigating. We started days ago. You can't just start up another investigation.'

'Why not? Who gave you the right to say what I can and can't do? The police haven't given you a monopoly. Bet you haven't talked to them.'

'No, but you haven't either.'

'Not personally. But my Dad spoke to Superintendent Larkin. He said he'd no objection to me making a few enquiries. So I'm more official than you. You and Harold had better keep off my patch.'

'It's not your patch. We started first.'

'Anyway, what have you found out? Not much, I'll bet!'

'Why should I tell you? But we have found out something. Bet you don't know how the thieves managed to remove the helmet.'

Charlie stared at Jem. Evidently he had not the faintest idea how the helmet was removed.

'Tell you what,' he said. 'Suppose we join forces. Three heads'll be better than two.'

The proposal gave Jem a start. Join forces with Charlie? He couldn't imagine co-operation between them. He was always butting up against the hard angles of Charlie's awkward personality. There could be no sympathetic understanding. Charlie would question what he and Harold wanted to do; and vice-versa. On the other hand, having to share the limelight with Charlie – supposing they were successful – was far better than seeing Charlie carry off the prize by himself.

'Dunno. I'll have to consult Harold. Tell you tomorrow.'

Harold shared Jem's annoyance that Charlie had barged in. But he didn't dislike him as intensely as Jem. In fact, he had gone around with him when he and Jem were temporarily estranged over the episode of the tower.

'If we go in with him we'll have to share what we've found out. Not that it's very much,' Harold said.

'Yes, but there's one thing I don't want to reveal – yet anyway. Those strands from the rope. They could be vital. Let's keep them a secret for the time being.'

'Detectives working on a case have got to be open with each other. If not, they won't make progress,' Harold objected.

'Just this one thing, please. I've a feeling about it.'

Reluctantly, Harold agreed.

Shivering in the summer house of Charlie's garden – it was still winter – they exchanged their information and views. Charlie had noticed the marks of the ladder on the wall of the chancel. But he had not worked out how the thieves could have reached the helmet. He generously said Jem had done well to figure out how it could have been done. He, too, had been to see Ma Hibbert. Unlike Jem and Harold, he had managed to get a word in. She had let him see her notebook with the names of people to whom she lent the key. As well as the organist and the cleaner, there were a plumber (to mend a burst pipe), an Air Raid Precautions man (to inspect the blackout of the windows) and, surprisingly, One-Leg Tim. The last mystified them. They divided up the tasks. Jems suggested that, as he knew Tim well, he should interview him. Harold plumped for the ARP man, who was a friend of his Dad's. That left the plumber for Charlie.

As it was winter, Jem thought he would be more likely to find Tim at home rather than at the allotments.

He lived in one of the old cottages near the mill. They had been built in the early eighteen hundreds, when Britain had been involved in another war – that against Napoleon. They still had outside lavatories – at the end of the back yards, though they had been converted into flush toilets. Tim was glad to see him.

'I don't get many visitors. It's rather lonely in t'winter. Like a cup o'tea?'

Jem didn't like to confess that he had come to see Tim only because of the investigation. So he let Tim do the talking. He didn't always remember to whom he told particular stories, so Jem was treated again to an account of the battle of Pardeberg, where Tim received the wound that led to the amputation of his leg.

'The fact that we're at war brings back vivid memories. I felt like 'aving my own little remembrance service. So I went to t'church and thought o' them comrades who'd not been as lucky as me.'

Jem was suddenly on the alert. 'Did you have to borrow the key from someone?'

'Ay, from that Ma Hibbert – funny old soul in Up Bye. Odd thing was - she guessed what I wanted it for. "It's a good thing to remember the dead", she said.'

Jem explained about the investigation that he, Harold and Charlie were undertaking. He established that Tim had made the visit a few days before the theft was spotted. He hadn't noticed anything different in the church.

'I wish thee luck,' said Tim as he let Jem out. 'Squire's been good to me. And 'e doesn't deserve the misfortune of losing family treasures.'

The three detectives met in the shed in Jem's garden to exchange their findings. Harold reported first.

'Bill Collinson, the ARP man, laughed and wouldn't take me seriously at first. But he reckoned we could do at least as well as the police. Said if he was younger, he'd join us. He visited the church the Friday before the discovery of the burglary. He inspected the windows and the black-out curtains that had been put up. He noticed the helmet and things. He mentioned that there's an outside door to the tower. I've been to look at it, but it hasn't been opened for years – there's ivy growing across it.'

Jem recounted what Tim had told him. Then it was Charlie's turn.

'You two had an easy time. Finding the blinking plumber – Joe Quarmby – was difficult enough. He lives at the top of Homefield Hill. I had to go up three times before I found him in. He wasn't very obliging at first. Wanted to know what business it was of mine. When he found out that my Dad's the Under Manager at the mill, he calmed down and asked me in. I think he gets work from my Dad from time to time. Anyway, he had to mend a leaking pipe in the heating system. He borrowed a key from Ma Hibbert. But it wasn't the church door key. It was one to the door of the cellar – down some steps at the opposite side to the porch. He said he didn't go into the church, but he could have done, 'cos there's a trapdoor into the vestry. He says he took the key straight back to Ma Hibbert.'

'If he was in league with someone, they could have made an impression of the key on wax and had a copy done,' Harold commented.

'Been reading detective stories?' Charlie asked. 'Well, it's possible.'

'Did the police question him?' Jem wondered.

'He says they did. I got my Dad to have a word with Superintendent Larkin. He said that Joe has something of a past. He didn't say what. But they think he's going straight now.'

'I'll go and get some cocoa,' said Jem.

He came back with three chipped mugs – which his Mum said were suitable for outdoor use – and some raisins. The three sipped and munched, wondering what the next step could be. Jem broke the silence.

'I don't think the vicar or Bert would have lent the key to someone they didn't know. I reckon we can rule out the flower ladies, the organist and the cleaner of being involved. Likewise, Tim and Mr Collinson. That leaves the plumber, Joe Quarmby.'

'And Ma Hibbert,' Charlie added. 'She may have lent the key to someone and not entered the name in her book. She's a strange woman – she'd slip through anybody's fingers if they questioned her.'

'I'll go and see her - by myself,' Jem said, feeling brave. 'I'll take some bits of fish for her cats.'

His heart beating faster than normally, Jem turned into Up Bye. The three cats were on the doorstep. Smelling the fish, they began to miaow and rub against his ankles. The door opened before he had knocked.

'Hullo, dearie. Why I do believe Jem Murgatroyd's brought some fish for my darlings. Now why should he do that? Is he in love with them? Or is he in love with me?Don't mind me, my dear. I thank you kindly. Now, what can I do for you?'

Jem had expected that she would invite him inside.

But, despite the cold wind blowing along the hillside, it was evidently to be a doorstep interview.

'That investigation – Charlie Foster's with us now. You showed him your notebook with the names of people who'd borrowed the key. Could there be someone else you'd not noted down – that you'd forgotten like?'

'Well now. Some people might feel annoyed at being asked such a question. But not me, love. Do you remember what I told you last time?'

'Er, you said that you hadn't lent the key to anyone who had no right to it.'

'That's it, dearie. A detective's got to have a good memory! Now, I'll get this fish ready. As I said, let me know how you get on. That Charlie Foster's got a good head on his shoulders. Not that you and Harold Bright haven't! So long, love.'

The cats had gone inside. Jem found the door closing quietly behind him. He was no wiser than before. He reported back.

'You should have let me go,' Charlie said. 'Bet I'd have got inside at least. I've been thinking, though. There's someone we haven't talked to – your Benjy. He keeps his ear to the ground – in more ways than one, except when he's sponging on Farmer Ackroyd'.

'He's not sponging. He's working,' Jem protested.

Jem felt as though Charlie had won a march on him. *He* should have thought of Benjy. Not that he would have had anything to do with the theft. But despite the solitariness that Benjy valued, he had a knack for knowing what was going on. Jem insisted, though, that he would go and see Benjy. He didn't think Benjy would talk freely if Charlie went. He had a selfish reason too: he didn't want to afford Charlie an opportunity of seeing Alice.

His heart beat faster as he entered the farmyard. But it was from anticipation, not fear. Sure enough, Alice was there, grooming her pony.

'Hello Jem. Nice to see you. How's the investigation going?'

'The investigation?' Jem was taken aback. 'You mean - you've heard what Harold and me and Charlie are up to?'

'Of course!' Alice smiled. 'You don't think all that questioning could be kept secret in Althwaite, do you? I'm glad you've joined up with Charlie. I know you're not keen on him. But it takes all sorts, Jem!'

'Are you ...?'

'What? Do I like him? Not perhaps in the way you're thinking, Jem. Benjy's up there, if you want to see him.'

Relieved of one anxiety, Jem climbed the ladder. Benjy was sitting under the skylight, darning a sock.

'Couldn't help overhearing your chat with Alice. If I were you, I wouldn't worry. Know what I mean? Now, tell me about this enquiry o' yours.'

Jem related all that they had discovered, including the strands from the rope. He took Bert's matchbox from a pocket and showed Benjy the contents.

'Mmm. Interestin'. You've done well. I'm afraid there's nothing I can tell you. Except ...' Benjy laid down his sock and needle and looked intently at Jem. 'If I were you, I'd leave it there.'

'Why? Surely it's a mystery that needs to be solved?'

'Ay, well. Let's say: deep waters. There's no knowin' where summat like that may lead. Leave it over for the time being, anyway.'

Jem left Cop Top feeling elated – it didn't seem that Alice had any special feeling for Charlie. But he was also puzzled. Benjy's advice was baffling. He confided it to Harold, but decided against telling Charlie. He merely told him that Benjy wasn't able to point them in any particular direction. Privately, he saw no reason for taking Benjy's advice and dropping the enquiry. Nevertheless, the three detectives found, like the police, that they didn't know how to pursue the matter further. Jem and Harold on the one hand, and Charlie on the other, agreed that they would keep eyes and ears open. The fact that Harold and Charlie both went to Bruddersford School meant that they could easily communicate.

Weeks passed. Snowdrops came and went. Crocuses peeped above the ground and then opened in the spring sunshine. The Examiner said no more about the church burglary. Jem had reluctantly accepted that he, Harold and Charlie were most unlikely to find any further leads. Visions of local glory had expired into thin air.

Out of the blue came a letter addressed to Jem in a handwriting he had seen once before. Could it be Lorinda? It was. It invited her rescue party (Jem, Harold, Ron and Dot) and Jonquil to tea on Saturday 13 April in the tower.

'What's "RSVP" mean, Mum?' Jem had to ask.

'It's the French: "Répondez s'il vous plaît". Or is it "Reply soon via post"? Either way, it means let her know you can come. Lucky chap – wish I was going.'

Jem wondered whether Rondot would know what RSVP meant. He called after school.

'O'course we know – Hull's nearer to France than Althwaite is!' was Ron's reply.

The day could not come soon enough. When it did, Jem woke to the sound of a downpour. He had so much looked forward to a fine day. But after dinner the sun came out. The afternoon promised to be dry and bright. He called for Ron and Dot. Ron had made valiant efforts to plaster down his unruly hair. Dot was wearing a pretty pinafore dress that Mrs Weaverthorpe had made for her. They met Harold and Jonquil in the village. Jonquil was wearing a new green dress. Its colour was the perfect contrast to her long auburn hair. She was excited to be included in the invitation, not herself having been one of the rescue party. But, as Harold pointed out, it wouldn't be a party in the tower without the princess.

At the top of the hill they pushed open one half of the tall gates and entered the grounds of the Hall. Jem noticed that the gate did not squeak as usual. Someone must have oiled it, he thought. Clusters of daffodils on the lawn made a brave show. Bypassing the house, they went through the copse and gained the clearing. The tower door was open. Red, white and blue balloons hung from a rusty hook beside it.

'Hallo!' Jem shouted up the stairs.

'Come on up!' came Lorinda's answering voice.

Entering the familiar room at the top, they stood entranced. More balloons hung from the rafters. Some of Lorinda's pictures hung from hooks in the stone walls. But what transfixed them was the figure that greeted them. It was dressed in the uniform of the Women's Auxiliary Air Force: grey-blue tunic, skirt and cap; grey stockings; shiny black shoes; white shirt and black tie. Lorinda smiled at their astonishment.

'I thought you'd like to see me in my uniform. Smart, isn't it?'

'Smart isn't the word,' said Jem, when he had recovered his voice. 'It's … it's smashing!'

'I think you look lovely,' Dot piped up. 'I wish I could join the Air Force.'

'I don't think the war will last that long, dear,' Lorinda replied.

'I think I'd rather be you than Rapunzel,' said Jonquil.

'Now that *is* a compliment. Thank you, Jonquil. Anyway, come on in and settle down.'

The children gathered round on the cushions that had been brought from the house. Lorinda sat in the arm-chair.

'What's it like in the Women's Air Force?' Harold asked.

'It's hard work and fun. There's so much to learn. I've joined a maintenance unit. I'm learning how to overhaul the engines of Spitfires and Hurricanes.'

'Cor!' Ron exclaimed.

'If you saw me in my overalls, you wouldn't recognize me. Scruffy and dirty! My hands get all oily, and it's difficult to get the dirt off. Look at them.'

She held out her hands, palms down. Her nails, which used to be shapely, were cut short, with traces of grime under them. Turning her hands over, she showed the darkened fingertips, the scrubbing of which had failed to remove all the dirt.

'They'll recover eventually. But what nails to get married with!'

'Of course, we forgot! Congratulations!' Jem exclaimed. 'It's the best thing to happen in Althwaite in my memory.'

The others joined in a chorus of approval.

'Thank you, my dears. I owe it all to you! Now, I'm going to send Jem, Harold and Ron to the kitchen to carry things here. And I'm going to change. It wouldn't do to get a stain on my best uniform – the Flight Sergeant would be down on me like a ton of bricks.'

Mrs McAlister gave the boys three trays, with bread and butter, sandwiches, scones, cream, jam, cakes and crockery.

'Now, mind how you carry them. I think you'll find that Alistair has set up the hoist,' she said.

Sure enough – the hoist was there. Distracted by the balloons, they had not noticed it on first arriving. In place of the crude tray that Jem had converted from a seed tray, Alistair had made a handsome tray with high sides. It had handles on all four sides. Leather straps were attached to these and met in a metal ring which hung on a hook at the end of the rope, dangling from the pulley above. Lorinda looked out of the window.

'Fill the tray and pull it up. One blow on the whistle means "Stop". Two blows means "Lower away".'

Carefully, the boys loaded the tray.

'Now, heave!' Jem ordered.

The tray travelled up towards the window,

maintaining a level position. The whistle was blown and they stopped hauling. Then two whistles and they lowered it for the second, and final, load.

Lorinda, now dressed in a flowery skirt and jumper, made tea with water boiled on a primus stove. They all began tucking into Mrs McAlister's preparations.

'When I think that I didn't want to be an evacuee!' said Ron in between mouthfuls. 'It's the best thing that's 'appened to us, isn't it Dot?'

Dot beamed her agreement, her mouth full of a sandwich of Spam and tomato.

'Good idea, to use the hoist,' Jem said. 'Do you know where that rope comes from, Lorinda?'

'I think it's usually kept in the room below. It's a store-room. My painting things are there for the duration – the duration of the war, that is.'

The conversation turned to what had happened in Althwaite. It was Ron who commented on the burglary. 'I bet that sort of thing wouldn't even 'ave 'appened in Hull. So I can't understand it 'appening in Althwaite! '

'Harold and Charlie and me's been looking into it,' Jem added. 'But we haven't got anywhere.'

'I didn't know Althwaite had its own CID,' said Lorinda with a smile.

'CID?' Harold queried.

'Oh, sorry Inspector, I thought you'd follow me. Criminal Investigation Department.'

'We're not setting up in business,' Jem explained. 'Leastways, not until we've solved this mystery,'

After the tea, mainly for the benefit of Dot and Jonquil, but enjoyed also by the boys, there were games of ‘Snap’ with cards and ‘I Spy’. The others gave in to Dot, being unable to guess her ‘S’ for squire. She pointed triumphantly to Lorinda’s portrait of Hon Peter, hanging on the wall.

‘It’s been accepted for hanging in the house. Now there’s an honour!’ Lorinda said.

It was time to return things to the house, using the hoist again. Jem studied the rope. On the way back from the house, he nudged Harold. ‘Got your knife on you?’

‘The one Lorinda sent? Yes.’

‘We need to cut a little bit of that rope off.’

Harold looked puzzled. But he was only Dr Watson. When Alistair’s tray lay on the ground after its final descent, and the rope was hanging slack, Harold cut off an inch that was protruding through the knot holding the ring. The knot would still hold, he reckoned.

‘I think she’s too good for the Squire,’ said Ron after the goodbyes and thanks. Lorinda had given them her Air Force address and they had promised to write. When would they have such a tea party again? Perhaps not till the war was won.

Back at home, Jem’s suspicions were confirmed. The rope was a light colour. The strands that they had collected in the church matched it perfectly. After chapel the next day, he revealed his conclusion to Harold.

‘I think we’ll have to go and see Hon Peter.’

It was Peter himself who opened the door when they rang.

‘Ah ha! The two desperadoes – or should I call

you poachers turned policemen? Or avenging angels in disguise? Please come in gentlemen. Umbrellas and galoshes on the coat stand – as my butler would have said. I regret that I've had to dispense with his services – so that Hitler can be defeated. Isn't that the ultimate irony: rise of monster in Germany results in English country gentleman losing his butler! Still, you don't want to hear me ranting. You've obviously come on business of some sort or other. One-Leg Tim needs a new pair of crutches? Your friend the tramp wants a leg up in the world? Let's go in the study.'

Strangely enough, Jem did not feel nervous. He knew that his and Harold's objective – the solution of the mystery – was shared by Hon Peter. They had not been caught in another misdemeanor. They were not asking anything for themselves or someone else. They were allies of Peter in a cause.

'You might have heard, Sir,' Jem began, 'that Harold and me – and Charlie Foster – have been trying to investigate the theft from the church.'

'Lorinda – Miss Vajansky – did mention that. It's very decent of you. I didn't place much faith in the police. That was one reason why I advised them not to waste their precious time on my little trouble.'

'We were forgetting, Sir,' Harold broke in. 'We should congratulate you on the engagement of you and Lorinda!'

'Thank you, boys. I recollect to whom I'm indebted for bringing her into my life. If I were to pop off tomorrow, I'm sure you would find something in my will. Even if it was only a pith helmet smelling of moth balls!' Peter smiled benevolently. 'Now, back to your daring pursuit of the criminals. Carry on, Mr Holmes.'

Jem and Harold described their enquiries into the key holders and the people with a legitimate reason for entering the church. As they explained how the burglars had rigged up the ladder to reach the helmet, Hon Peter's brow began to furrow in concentration. When they came to the identification of the rope, he put his elbows on the desk, rested his chin on his hands and stared at the doodles on his writing pad.

'So you see, sir,' Jem concluded, 'we think the thieves must have known you had this rope in the tower. Somehow they got in and borrowed it. How they got into the church we don't know. Ma, I mean, Miss Hibbert might have lent them the key and forgotten to note it down. Or perhaps it was someone she knew, and didn't want to let on. Or perhaps the plumber was in league with them. How do you think whoever it was could have got your rope, sir?'

Hon Peter took his elbows off the desk and sat back in his chair, looking every inch the magistrate.

'Remarkable - the spirit of England is *not* dead! Just as well you young men are well-intentioned, or you'd be running rings around the police! I think we need Alistair. Harold, would you have the goodness to go to the kitchen and ask Mrs McAlister to send her husband here. If he objects that he's in the middle of planting potatoes, or whatever gardeners get up to in the spring, she can tell him it's a matter of the utmost seriousness. And she might be kind enough to send us some refreshments.'

Whilst Alistair was being sought, Hon Peter maintained an uncharacteristic silence. He smiled to himself and drummed his fingers on the desk. Jem began to feel uncomfortable, but couldn't think of what to say. Alistair came in, not very pleased at having been called away from his potting shed.

'Yes, your Honour?'

'Sit down, Alistair. There, by the window. These young men, and another of their number, are on the trail of the burglars. Submit yourself to some questions.'

Alistair straightened up in his chair. He looked serious. He glanced at the squire and then turned to Jem.

'How could someone have got the rope out of the store-room in the tower, Mr McAlister?' Jem asked.

'Dinna I recollect that twae young rascals got into the tower without difficulty?'

Jem reddened slightly. 'Well, yes, but we'd seen where the key was hidden. In any case, isn't the store-room kept locked? Who has the key to it?'

'It hangs in my wife's kitchen on the key board – as does the key to the tower now.'

At this point, Mrs McAlister entered on cue, carrying a tray with glasses of orange juice and biscuits.

'You may question the bearer of sustenance, Mr Holmes, provided you do so tactfully. It would be tragic if she were to take umbrage and leave us in the lurch,' said Peter.

Jem got up to help Mrs McAlister put down the tray. 'Please, Ma'am, before the burglary in the church, did you notice the key to the tower and the store-room missing?'

'I'm too busy to keep an eye on the key board. It might have been taken for a day or two without my noticing.'

'Thank you, Mrs McAlister, and you too, Alistair,' said Hon Peter, giving them leave to depart.

'That was a splendid hoist you made, Mr McAlister. Much better than ours!' Harold thought it tactful to say.

'Ay, but I got the idea from a couple o' ne'er-do-wells!'

Alistair retreated in good humour.

'I suppose there could be other ropes of the same colour. But those I've seen at Cop Top Farm are all dark brown,' Jem said, having drained the glass of juice. 'It's so unusual. What do you think, sir?'

The squire had got up and was looking through the window. Suddenly he turned as though he had made a decision.

'I'm going to pay you young men the greatest compliment I can. Come with me. Bring the tray.'

He led the way to the kitchen.

'Just taking the keys to the tower and the store-room, Mrs McAlister. I'll borrow the flashlight, too.'

In the store-room, the rope was neatly coiled. On top was the hoist. Hon Peter went to the far side.

'Just help me lift this old carpet.'

They lifted it. The beam of the flashlight revealed a helmet, a breastplate and a pair of steel gloves. They had rusty patches but had been covered with grease. Jem and Harold stared, speechless.

'My ancestor's achievement. Five hundred years old. Wonderful aren't they?'

Jem managed to find some words. 'Yes, but … how did you find them, sir?'

'I'm afraid I'm not at liberty to say.'

'Are they going back to the church?'

'No. Now that I've … found them, they'll stay in my care until the war's over.'

'Why, sir?'

'Supposing the Nazis did invade Britain and took us over. These ancient objects, part of Britain's glorious heritage, are just what some SS officer, or even an ordinary soldier, would love to take back to Germany. Trophies of war. I'm determined not to let that happen.'

'But sir,' Harold chipped in. 'You've been so strong in saying that the Germans would be pushed back if they tried to invade!'

'I have. And I believe it. But the worst *can* happen. So I'm guarding against it. But imagine the effect on local morale if it became known that the squire was secretly entertaining the possibility of a Nazi victory! That must never get out. So you see why I am paying you the greatest compliment I can? I'm trusting you never to disclose what you've seen. The honour of the Danellion-Smiths is in your hands.'

So impressed were Jem and Harold by the solemnity of Hon Peter's reliance on them, that they felt it was neither the time nor the place to ask the questions about the rediscovery of the relics that they would dearly have liked to ask.

'Well, that's that,' Jem mused, as they walked back to the village. 'End of investigation.'

'But still a mystery,' Harold added. 'Why couldn't he tell us how they were found?'

'Perhaps he's shielding someone,' Jem suggested.

'Or perhaps someone's blackmailing him.'

'Anyway, we'll just have to leave it there. Obviously, not a word to Charlie.'

Back home, Jem went out to the shed and continued painting his model Spitfire. So, there was to be no glory. The Bruddersford Examiner would carry no report praising Jem Murgatroyd and Harold Bright - assisted in a subordinate capacity by Charlie Foster - for solving the mystery. Instead, there was the burden of a secret, which would have to be borne until the Germans had been defeated.

12 MORE SECRETS

It was a sparkling morning in early May. Billowy clouds chased each other across the valley, propelled by a strong breeze. Cloud shadows moved down from the moors. They singled out Althwaite for a few minutes and then careered up the other side. It was an invigorating day - the sort that made Jem feel it was good to be alive. Climbing up to Cop Top, as he had done on the last few Saturday mornings, Jem was aware of just one unwelcome feeling. It was one of guilt. He wished it would stop intruding. If it would only go away, he would be entirely at peace with himself and the world. Perhaps he needed to unburden himself to someone. Saying sorry to God was not enough, since God didn't talk back – at least not to him. Ron had told him that their mother, being a Roman Catholic, went to confession on Friday evenings. Jem felt that he, too, would like to enter the dark confessional box and speak to an anonymous, comforting voice.

Jem blamed Miss Arbuthnot for the accusing voice within. She was a formidable lady. Although she did not claim an 'Hon' before her name, she rivalled Hon Peter for what traces of feudal allegiance remained in the consciousness of the village. Her grandfather had been Sir Charles Arbuthnot, the last of a line of land and mill owners. The family had always been Roman Catholics. She was proud of their courage in giving shelter to priests ministering in secret during the times of persecution of Catholics. Being a younger sister, she had not inherited much of the family fortune. She had had to work for her living. She had become a teacher and had retired the previous year from the headship of the Girls' High School.

Unlike Hon Peter, she had never experienced shyness or lack of self-confidence. As a Roman Catholic, she was not in the mainstream of village life, most people being Anglicans, Baptists or Methodists if they were anything. She did not attend the village fêtes in the vicarage garden; she did not attend the annual performance of the Messiah. But she was a power in the village, ready to sally forth if injustices needed righting or standards were falling.

To Miss Arbuthnot, the war was a godsend. She despised Hitler and his crew but she welcomed the war which he had provoked. She would have said it gave her an opportunity to serve her country. But it also provided another basis for the exercise of the power of her personality. Before the village was aware of what was happening, she had become head of the local branch of the Womens Volunteer Service. She was the first of the branch to acquire the uniform: a greyish green tweed suit with a bright red jumper, and a felt hat with a brim. She had dug into her savings to obtain it. Mrs Murgatroyd was still wondering whether she could afford to buy hers.

In Post Offices up and down the country, boxes appeared with a label on the front: "BOOKS FOR THE FORCES". The Bruddersford Examiner began publishing the numbers of books collected in each of the surrounding villages. Great was Miss Arbuthnot's indignation when she read that Althwaite was next to the bottom of the list. Over a space of three weeks, only ten books had been put into the box at the village post office. 'This will not do,' she said to herself, and was immediately galvanized into activity. She was good at delegating. 'Just the job for the scouts,' she decided.

Faced with her penetrating gaze, the local printer agreed to print leaflets free of charge. The scoutmaster, too, succumbed without a struggle. So it was that Jem had helped on successive evenings with the distribution of leaflets and then with the collection: calling at houses, carrying books to the scout hand cart, helping to push the cart up streets and to hold it back from rushing down slopes with a mind of its own. No corner of the village had been left unvisited. The four houses in Up Bye had been included. Jem had himself called at Ma Hibbert's. The three black cats stared from the foot of the stairs.

'I were sure it would be Jem Murgatroyd as would give me a call. Look, pussies, it's Jem the detective. Haven't penetrated the mystery, have you luv? Never mind, it were a good try. Here's a few books that'll restore some poor soldiers to good health. Come and have a drink of my Dandelion and Burdock sometime. Bring your pal.'

Glancing at the books, Jem noticed that they were all about herbs and their uses in healing. He imagined himself in a trench facing the German lines. A fellow soldier collapsed, a bullet through the shoulder. Jem spotted a clump of self-heal growing on the edge of the trench. He picked a leaf and applied it to the wound. Miraculously, his comrade revived. 'Well done, that man,' said the officer who had just come on the scene. Returning to the real world, Jem put the books in the cart.

All the books were taken to the scout hut, there to await the lorry that would deliver them to a depot where they would be sorted. At the end of the collecting, there was time to browse amongst them. Most were books of no interest to Jem. A few were ones he would have liked to keep: 'Children of the New Forest' by Captain Marryat, 'Ivanhoe' by Sir Walter Scott, 'Treasure Island' by Robert Louis Stevenson. He resisted the temptation. But then his eye fell on a small volume with a green cover. The title, in gilt, was: 'Yorkshire County Cricket Club 1937'. Placed in a gilt shield in the centre was the white rose of Yorkshire. Jem picked it up and opened it. Immediately, he was hooked. There was not even the vestige of a struggle against temptation. Looking around, Jem checked that he was unobserved. He slipped the volume into his jacket pocket and left.

In his bedroom he admired the book. He was no good at cricket. When batting, the ball came towards him at an unfair speed. He suspected that his bowling action was laughable. But, like the other boys at school, he was enthralled by the great names of the day. There they were in black and white. Yorkshire v Middlesex,

July 1936: Sutcliffe, bowled Gray 202; Hutton, run out, 15; Leyland, run out, 107.

But now, as he made his way to the farm, he was afflicted by the irksome sense of guilt. He imagined some soldier waiting for the dread call to attack, his morale lifted by delving into the records of mighty deeds on the cricket field. Or an airman in hospital with terrible burns, and a nurse coming into the ward with the book and saying, 'This will take your mind off your injuries'. His selfishness had deprived a soldier of encouragement or an airman of comfort. To guilt was added fear: suppose Miss Arbuthnot found out that he had abstracted the book. He would not be able to stand being shamed and upbraided by her. His legs would be jelly, and he would be deprived of speech.

The sight of Benjy on the back of a horse took his mind off his trouble.

'I didn't know you could ride, Benjy!'

'Nor did I. But Alice is trying to encourage me to learn. Old Dobbin 'ere's not likely to unseat me – so she says. Mr Ackroyd thinks it could be useful – if we run out of petrol for the tractor. I'll just go back to the yard, and we can 'ave a word.'

Jem felt a pang of envy at the thought of Alice teaching Benjy to ride. Not that he needed to feel jealous of Benjy, of all people! And, in any case, Jem didn't fancy riding. He was sure a horse would detect that he was apprehensive.

Benjy appeared, limping slightly.

'Fell off, instead of getting off! Not sure 'orses are my cup of tea. Which reminds me – time for a brew-up.'

Over mugs of tea in his eyrie above the stable, Benjy gave vent to the latest cause of indignation.

'That Constable Dewhurst's getting above 'is station. War time seems to 'ave brought out the worst in 'im. Been snooping around to check whether I'm earning my keep or lazing about. Summat about the Vagrancy Acts and whether I'm an idle or disorderly person. I'd like to idle and disorder 'im! Mr Ackroyd assured 'im I was in 'is employ and pulling my weight. I'm not really – too slow and stiff in my joints. That's what comes o' sleeping out so many nights and waking up drenched wi' dew.'

Jem climbed down the ladder and went in search of jobs. Archie suggested he help clean out the cow shed, and found him a pair of wellington boots two sizes too big. It was a mucky job, and Jem was glad when it came to an end.

'You were telling me about that tribunal you had to appear before,' Jem said when they were washing their hands under the tap in the yard.

'Oh, yes. Well, they asked awkward questions. Didn't I think that *any* useful work would help the war effort? What would I do if the Germans invaded? Could I stand by and see civilians maltreated or killed?

'So what did you say?'

'I said I saw a distinction between helping life to carry on and killing other people. If the Germans did invade, we should resort to passive resistance. In time, if we stuck to non-violent opposition, the invaders might be impressed. In any case, my belief is that what matters in the end is God's love. It extends to everyone, even Hitler and the Nazis. The outcome is in His hands.'

Jem was moved. Archie spoke naturally, not as though he was preaching. If Mr Bright's sermons were like this, they would be easier to concentrate on. His own guilt thrust its way to the surface. Archie was obviously a man who not only listened to his conscience but followed it. Should he ask Archie for advice? It was on the tip of his tongue to do so, but he was distracted by the noisy arrival of a lorry.

Three men got down from the cab, each with a hacksaw. One of them asked where Mr Ackroyd was. Mrs Ackroyd, hearing the commotion, came out of the farm-house.

'Oh dear, you've come to take the railings, have you? Just as well my husband's out. He might have produced his shotgun. Get it done as quick as you can, afore he comes back.'

The farm was surrounded by stone walls, but a previous owner had replaced the walls around the farm-house garden by iron railings. Jem had heard about the campaign to remove railings from gardens and parks so that the metal could be used in the war effort. In the smarter part of Althwaite, where Charlie Foster lived, most houses had railings at the front. His mother had told him that a start had been made on taking them down. Most of the residents were reluctant to see them go. Unless they put up wooden fences, the gardens would be open to dogs and small boys. But they accepted the sacrifice in the interests of providing the forces with the guns and other things they needed. Now it was the turn of Cop Top Farm. As Jem left for home, the men were busy with their cutting.

'You've just missed Mr McAlister,' his mother said. 'I asked him in, but he said he had to get on. He left a letter for you and said he had one for Harold too.'

Jem was mystified. The envelope was addressed to 'Jem Murgatroyd, Esquire'.

'What's "Esquire" mean, Mum?'

'I think it's just a polite way of addressing a man – making out they're important. Who is it thinks you're important?'

Jem opened the envelope.

'It's from Hon Peter.' He read it aloud.

If Master Jem Murgatroyd, erstwhile Prince, alias Sherlock Holmes, would like to take part in a bit of derring-do in the interest of the honour of the Danellion family, let him present himself at the entrance to the grounds of the Hall at 6am on Sunday. Keep this to yourself and those nearest to you.

'The man speaks in riddles,' Jem said. 'What's this "derring-do"?'

'It's what medieval knights got up to in romantic tales – when they were feeling brave and in need of adventure. But six o'clock in the morning! What can he be up to? You'd never get up in time, anyway!'

'I don't think I'd be feeling brave at that time in the morning. But I can't turn it down. If you put the alarm on for half past five, Mum, I'll get up.'

At five to six the next morning, two sleepy boys met at the foot of the road up to the Hall.

'What's all this about, Harold?'

'Search me. We'll find out soon.'

Turning the corner at the top of the hill, they saw a

group of men at the entrance to the drive. Peter came forward to greet them. He was wearing a red and white check shirt, sleeves rolled up showing his white forearms. He had a neckerchief instead of a tie. An old pair of plus-fours and gardening boots completed the outfit.

'Ah ha! Our gallant look-outs. I was sure the youth of England would rise to the challenge, even if rising at this hour meant bidding farewell to a warm bed and comforting dreams. Now, you're going to help to save a bit of the family and village heritage from officious little Hitlers. These gates, which would otherwise be melted down, are going to be saved for posterity.'

Jem and Harold had never looked at the gates carefully before. Now they did so. Hon Peter's grandfather had had them made. They were ten feet high. The upper halves consisted of intricate scrolls, surmounted by the coat of arms of the Dandelion family.

Alistair and Archie were already busy, digging where the iron post of one of the gates was fixed in the ground. They had energy only to grunt good mornings to the boys. Peter proceeded to deploy his look-outs. Harold was placed a hundred yards beyond the drive, where the road went down into a dip. Jem's position was just beyond the bend at the top of the hill: near the spot where Lorinda had been accosted by the suspicious women from Bank Terrace. Each of the boys was armed with an old car horn with a rubber bulb. If they saw a vehicle coming they were to give two blasts on the horn. If they saw a cyclist or a person on foot, one blast sufficed. They were to hide behind bushes when anything went past.

Jem was excited. This was better than going to Sunday School or chapel. His conscience made tender by guilt over the book, he wasn't sure that Hon Peter was right in depriving the war effort of the gates. But it would be a pity if something so fine – now that he had actually looked at them – were to disappear.

Half an hour went by. A strong breeze was blowing, carrying the waking sounds of the village up to where he sat: the slam of a door, a child's voice, the barking of a dog. He began to get bored. Suddenly, he saw a car beginning to climb the hill. His heart began thumping. There was one turning it could take. 'Please turn off,' he prayed. But it kept coming. He grasped the horn and squeezed the bulb twice. The noise frightened him – he hadn't expected such a blast. He dropped down behind a bush and lay there, his heart beating like mad. The car passed him. Jem glimpsed three youngish men. It went round the bend. The engine noise died down swiftly, as though the car had come to a halt. He wanted to go and see what had happened. But, like a good sentry, he stuck to his post. Another car, also with youngish men, came up soon after. Jem's heartbeat quickened only slightly. He knew what he had to do and what noise to expect from the horn.

Another half hour passed. He was beginning to get hungry. He had merely snatched a biscuit before leaving home. He could see a few people crossing the market place, on their way to St Jude's for the early communion service. Smoke blown almost horizontally from chimneys looked like grey flags. He had a sense of the busy, hidden life of the village. So many people, all living their own lives, pursuing their own dreams, interacting with each other – harmoniously for the most part. How different it would be if Hitler's Nazis took over the country. Then, everyone would be ordered what to do.

His musing was interrupted by the distant sound of two blasts. Harold had spotted an approaching vehicle. Its engine became audible – it sounded like a lorry. But the noise died away and no lorry came down the hill. Almost immediately Jem saw a group of cyclists starting the ascent. Hon Peter had said one blast for a cyclist. But what was the signal for a group of them? Jem decided to give one blast and then another after a few seconds. Most of the cyclists dismounted and began pushing their bikes up the hill. Jem was afraid that his hiding place might be spotted by people passing slowly. He hid the horn and sat on a rock above the road.

'Hi there! Nice morning!'

'Watching out for parachutists?'

'Playing truant from Sunday School, sonny?'

Jem grinned fixedly at the greetings and gibes. 'Sonny', indeed! If they only knew what undercover work he was up to!

Another half hour went by. Jem smelt, or imagined he smelt, breakfast being cooked in the Terrace cottages. His tummy began making protests. How much longer would he be at the post? Mr McAlister rounded the bend.

'Jem? Come on laddie. We're nigh finished. Ye mun be famished. We're all awa to Cop Top Farm. We'll ha some breakfast there.'

Jem's spirits revived. The scene at the entrance to the drive surprised him. The gates had been loaded on to a lorry. Farmer Ackroyd and Archie were finishing tying a tarpaulin over them. Hon Peter was looking red in the face from his exertions. He had taken off his neckerchief.

'Sooner we're off, the better,' he said. 'Are you taking the back road, Mr Ackroyd?'

'Ay, we'd best not go through the village.'

'I'll take Alistair and Master Harold. Can Master Jem go with you?'

Jem sat in the cab of the lorry, squeezed between Mr Ackroyd at the wheel and Archie on the other side.

'So it's *Master* Jem!' said Archie chuckling. 'I'll have to treat you with more respect!'

'That's just his way. Don't be surprised if he calls you "Sir Archibald"!'

'I'm surprised to find you and Harold mixed up with this,' said Mr Ackroyd, smiling. 'I thought you were chapel-goers.'

'You'd be surprised at what we really are.'

'No – I don't think I would be.'

The way by the back road was bumpy. Jem heard the gates bouncing. They arrived at the farm to a barking of dogs and Mrs Ackroyd coming out.

'We thought you'd been nabbed. Breakfast's ready when you are.'

A hearty breakfast was in progress. Hon Peter was at one end of the table, Mr Ackroyd at the other. On the sides were Alistair, Archie, Harold and Jem. Mrs Ackroyd and Alice, who had already had theirs, waited on.

'You're perhaps wondering where Benjy is, Jem,'

Mrs Ackroyd said. 'He's got a bad cold, so I've moved him out of his den into a bedroom in the attic. You can go up later.'

'That was splendid, Mrs Ackroyd,' said Hon Peter after swallowing the last slice of four sausages. Reaching for the toast and marmalade, he continued: 'I expect you ladies would like to know how our nefarious bit of business got on. There weren't many alarms, being a Sunday morning. And our sentries didn't fall asleep at their posts – not that I suspected they would, but the flesh can be weak! We were still digging out the posts when the first car came up. My valiant henchmen took cover whilst I lit a pipe and strolled as though taking the morning air. I must say, I enjoyed the little interchange that followed. The car stopped and the young driver leaned out of the window. "Are we right for Crickley Edge?" he asked. I told him it was seven miles further on. "We're going climbing. There's some others following. If you happen to see them, sir, you might tell them they're on the right route." He told me they were from Leeds University Climbing Club. He was about to set off when he noticed the digging around the post, which we'd forgotten to cover up. "Oh dear! Are you going to lose those splendid gates?" he asked. "Yes," I said – without a blush. "They're coming tomorrow to take them. My men have been loosening the posts – they may as well take the whole lot rather than cut them off at the ground." "They're beautiful gates," he said. "If I were you, sir, I'd be hiding them away. But you're like my father – too stoic and patriotic, if I may say so, sir. I expect to be called up soon. But I'll be dashed if I kowtow to authority!" I laughed and said: "Wait till you've met your first sergeant major!" He grinned and said he expected I was right.'

Hon Peter accepted the second cup of coffee that Alice offered.

'Telling me to hide them! Ha, ha! And that I was too stoic and patriotic! I nearly confessed to him. It was so beautifully ironic!' Peter looked round the table with a boyish look of mischief on his face. The others laughed.

'The following car went past at speed. My team had taken cover. I just waved and stuck my thumb up. But the bunch of cyclists were an unpleasant lot. Mr Ackroyd had driven his lorry down the drive so as to be out of sight. The gates were now lying flat on the ground. Again I lit my pipe and strolled nonchalantly.'

Hon Peter broke off and leaned across the table towards Jem. Jem wondered what was coming.

'If you're in a stew, Master Jem, try strolling nonchalantly!'

Jem blushed slightly, not being sure what the word meant.

'Anyway, there was no sympathy from those gentlemen on wheels. Some laughed. "Taking a last look at your ancestral defences?" asked one of them – a wiry little man with a goatee beard. I'll wager he was a communist. "After this lot's all over, stately homes will be public property," he went on. "Hear, hear," said his supporters. Most of them looked as though they were in their late twenties or early thirties. "So when are you lot joining up?" I asked. "We're not – we're Peace Pledge Union." "Well, I hope you get sent down the mines," I said as a parting shot. My apologies, Mr Archie, I don't aim this at you.'

Archie acknowledged this with an uncertain smile. He was about to say something, but Hon Peter had arrived at his peroration.

'So, my deep thanks to you all. When we've won the war, and put the gates back, we'll have a celebration. And, as we agreed, Mr Ackroyd, the home meadow is yours rent free for the duration.'

'I was glad to get my own back, those varmints having stolen my garden railings whilst I was out,' the farmer replied. 'Now, we'd better get the gates hidden in the old barn.'

Breakfast over, Jem and Harold went up to see Benjy. He was lying in bed, looking sorry for himself.

'Hullo, lads. Good of yer to look in. Doan't come near – I've got a temperature. Now, tell me what's been goin' on. I could 'ear that squire laughing from right up 'ere.'

In confidence, they related the morning's proceedings. Benjy laughed.

'We're all the same – tramps and landowners! We'll all defy authority when it's in our interests. But I like squire – he's got some spirit.'

By the time Jem and Harold came out of the house, the gates had disappeared into their hiding place. Hon Peter, Mr Ackroyd, Alistair and Archie were looking up at the roof of the farm-house.

'It's definitely wobbling. See – with that gust?' said Mr Ackroyd. 'If it falls, it might damage the slates. I'll have to get a ladder up and see if I can do summat.'

On the ridge of the house was a central chimney stack with four chimneys. They rose about three feet from a base of bricks. One of the pots had come loose at the base.

'I'll go up,' Alistair said.

With Hon Peter looking on, the others put a long ladder up to the edge of the roof. Alistair climbed it and hauled up a short ladder with a hook on the end. This he pushed up to the ridge, with the hook over the other side. Back down again, he fastened a rope around his waist and draped another over his shoulders.

'See if you can tie the loose pot to the others,' Mr Ackroyd said.

Alistair got up to the ridge and sat astride. Then he shuffled himself along towards the stack. Arrived at it, he made a loop with a slip knot at the end of the rope around his waist. At a second effort, he managed to lasso it around the stack. Now he could safely stand up, his feet on the narrow ridge. The watchers on the ground could see the loose pot wobbling.

'I hope he'll be alright!' said Mr Ackroyd.

'Don't worry about Alistair,' Hon Peter said. 'He was a fine climber in Scotland. He's got a good head for heights and sure feet.'

Alistair took the rope draped over his shoulders. He made a slip knot at one end, placed it over the loose pot, drew it tight and tied another knot to hold it. Then he lassoed the rope around the other pots and made another knot. He neatly coiled the rest of the rope and made it fast. He removed the safety rope and made his way back along the ridge and down to the ground.

'That was expertly done. I'm much obliged,' said Mr Ackroyd.

'Naething to it. I've been in much tighter spots on

the Black Cuillins. That was in my younger days, mind ye. My limbs are not as spry as they used to be.'

'I'll get the builder up tomorrow to cement the pot in place. I wish I had a bottle of whisky to give you, but I'll send one up to the Hall sometime.'

'Dinna fret. But a dram's always welcome.'

Jem gripped Harold's arm.

'Come over here.'

He led Harold around the corner of the house, where they were alone.

'Did you hear that? Alistair used to be a mountain climber!'

'Well, lots of people are.'

'Yes, but this one works for Hon Peter. Think of someone scaling a vertical ladder to get the helmet down in the church. Who better than an expert climber, with a good head for heights?'

'You mean - it was Hon Peter himself who removed the armour, with the help of Alistair? He didn't just find it afterwards!'

'That's what I think. Removing the gates today was much the same – except that he was hiding the armour from the Germans, not the local council.'

'Well, I'll be blowed!'

'Not a word to Charlie.'

'Course not.'

Unlike Jem, Harold had not been excused morning service. If he hurried he might get there in time. Jem went back into the house.

'It's not elevenses time yet Jem!' Mrs Ackroyd said.

'I just wanted to see Benjy again. Can I go up?'

'So long as you don't go too near him, and don't tire him out.'

Jem climbed up to the attic.

'Hullo, lad. I thought you'd 'ave scarpered off 'ome by now.'

'Er, do you mind if I ask you something, Benjy?'

'Now what's coming? If yer going' to ask me if I'm really unwell or just skiving, I've got a temperature to prove it!'

'No, it's not about you. You remember when I told you about our investigation into the burglary at the church? You said we should "leave it". And you said something about "deep waters". What I want to ask is – did you mean that we might find the trail leading to the squire?'

Jem refrained from telling Benjy that Hon Peter had shown him and Harold where the stolen things were now stored – that was a secret. But he explained his theory that a mountain climber would have been just the person to go up a vertical ladder to get the helmet. And now he had learnt that Mr McAlister had been a climber.

Benjy hoisted himself up so that his back rested against the pillow.

'You're right – I did advise you to leave it. Perhaps you tried to leave it, but *it* wouldn't leave *you*. I don't blame you lads for exercising your curiosity. But I ain't goin' to blacken anyone's name. My lips is sealed.'

That was all Jem could get out of Benjy. Evidently he knew the truth. And it was pretty certain that the truth was that Hon Peter had initiated and overseen the 'theft' himself. Perhaps it was Mr McAlister who had borrowed the key from Ma Hibbert. She'd said that she hadn't lent it to anyone who didn't have a right to it. Didn't Hon Peter have a right to remove his family's bits of armour if he felt they would be at risk if the Germans invaded? But he was now burdened with two secrets. There was the secret that Hon Peter had confided to him by showing him that the breastplate, helmet and gloves were in his possession. Now, Jem was sure, there was the secret of who had perpetrated the theft. Hon Peter had said that the honour of his family was in the hands of Jem and Harold. Now, that was doubly the case.

Harold having left, Jem was glad to have a chance of talking to Alice by himself. He found her brushing down the pony in the stable.

'You're looking thoughtful, Jem. Enjoyed the adventure?'

'A bit nerve-racking at times. But it's helped to put something into perspective.'

'That's a big word – "perspective". What do you mean?'

Jem was reluctant to tell Alice about the book he had taken from the collection.

'Come on, you've tickled my curiosity now!'

'Alright, but try not to laugh at me too much!'

Jem described his fall from grace.

'But, now I've seen Hon Peter – the squire of all people- hide his gates from being taken away for the war effort, I reckon my little theft isn't all that serious.'

'I think you're right. My conscience isn't as fine as yours! But perhaps when you've pored over the cricket scores, you could make a big sacrifice and pop the book into the Library box. That way, you could be making up a tiny bit for the squire's unpatriotic action. But, if you keep the book, I won't tell Miss Arbuthnot!'

Jem took his time getting home, knowing that his mother would be at the morning service. She was naturally curious about what he had been up to.

'Sorry, Mum, it's confidential – there's a war on, you know.'

'I expect it'll come out eventually. I'll be patient.'

'Mum – what does "nonchalantly" mean?'

'It means not caring, not being worried. Why?'

'Hon Peter said if I was in a stew, to try walking nonchalantly.'

'So if I see you walking in a peculiar fashion, I'll know you're in a stew!'

'But I don't suppose I could do it as well as him – he's got a pipe to smoke while he's walking.'

'In that case, you'll have to wait quite a few years before you can be nonchalant!'

That night Jem dreamed that he was standing on a stool before a large table. Seated on the other side were three Nazis in black uniforms with the swastika insignia on their lapels. One of them leant forward and fixed Jem with a steely gaze.

'Ven did you last see ze Honourable Peter? Ve know zat he is hiding some vere. He has been wearing a magic armour against which ze bullets of ze Fatherland are of no use. Ve haf reason to believe that you know ver he is.'

'I d…don't know,' Jem stuttered.

'Don't play vith us, little boy. If you do not answer, ve vill tell ze Lady Arbuthnot about zat little book, no?'

Jem awoke, sweat on his brow. His mother looked around the door.

‘I know the war’s disturbing, Jem. But close your eyes and try walking nonchalantly, as the squire said.’

13 ALARMS AND BELLS

To Jem it seemed uncanny. Only two days ago, his Dad had said that it couldn't be much longer before this phoney war ended and the real one began. Now the news on the wireless was that German troops were invading Holland and Belgium.

Jem and his mother had been uplifted by Dad's unexpected visit. He had been given a 48 hour pass. He was on a training course at Sheffield.

'I'm getting over my disappointment about not getting into KOYLI,' he had said. 'It's obvious that transport and supplies are a key part of a good army. So I reckon I'll be doing a real job. We're learning how to drive different vehicles – from ambulances to ten ton lorries. Driving a heavy lorry around those hilly roads in Derbyshire is no joke!'

Through Harold, Mr Bright had learnt that Mr Murgatroyd was home on leave. Harold had been badgering him to take Jem and himself to Crickley Edge. On the spur of the moment, Mr Bright suggested that both families have a run out there, taking a picnic with them. It was a tight squeeze in his small car. Jonquil had to sit on Mrs Bright's lap. Harold and Jem were crammed together in the middle of the back seat.

They sat amongst the rocks at the base of the Edge and watched climbers negotiating routes up the cliff face. Their calls down to companions sounded sharp and clear. Jem was envious of their skill and daring. Would he ever have the courage to entrust his safety to a narrow foothold and a crevice for fingers?

'Maybe some of them are those University climbers,' Harold said to Jem.

'What climbers are those?' asked Mr Bright, who had overheard.

'Oh, just some men who went past the Hall when Jem and me were up there.'

'Been having a busy time lately, you two, haven't you?' Mrs Murgatroyd said. 'What with the church theft and then this mysterious business of getting up early to help the squire.'

'Mum, that's confidential!' Jem exclaimed.

'We're all family here, Jem. Don't worry.'

'So long as they're not getting up to mischief!' Mr Murgatroyd said. 'I'm sure the squire's above board.'

Jem and Harold exchanged meaningful glances.

The conversation moved to the war.

'When will it end? What will people have to go through before then?' Mr Bright asked.

'In my opinion, it won't end until the Americans come in,' was Mr Murgatroyd's reply. 'But there's no sign of that at present. One thing I'm sure of – I bet the Germans are gearing themselves up for an onslaught. Not like Hitler to keep his head down for so long.'

Dad's leave had come to an end all too soon. He had gone back to Sheffield. And now the onslaught had begun. Jem listened to the news on the wireless each morning and evening. Although the announcers emphasized the valiant resistance of allied troops, it was clear that the German army and air force were crushing the opposition. Holland gave up the fight; France was invaded.

Jem and Harold went to the scout meeting. As Patrol Leader, Harold went each week. Jem was a less regular attender. Mr Ash, the scoutmaster, could see that Jem had the potential for leadership if only he would put his mind to scouting. But he often had too many other things on his mind as well. That night it was the flare-up of the war. It was at the forefront of other boys' minds too, together with the change of Prime Minister: from Mr Chamberlain to Winston Churchill. Concentration on first aid and knots was less than total.

'Winnie's not reliable, my Dad reckons,' said Charlie Foster. 'He's changed sides too often and been wrong on things.'

'He'll be better at standing up to Hitler,' countered Ron, who was repeating his mother's view.

Jem knew that his Mum and Dad were also relieved at the appointment of Winston, but he felt diffident about expressing a view himself.

Harold and Jem left the meeting together. Before their paths diverged, they came to the police station. Usually, there was no sign of life. But that evening there was a queue of men waiting to get inside. Mr McAlister, George Wright the blacksmith, Mr Armitage the bank clerk, and Jack Moorhouse the garage man were there along with others the boys knew only by sight.

'What's going on, Mum?' Jem asked on getting home. 'There's a queue of men at the police station. They can't all be helping the police with their enquiries!'

'Oh – I bet it's to do with this announcement.'

'What announcement?'

'Mr Eden – the War Minister – has appealed for men to join a local force to help repel any invasion. The men you saw will be putting their names down.'

'Gosh! So Alistair McAlister and others will be getting rifles and machine guns!'

'Well, if they are, I hope they get properly trained how to use them. We don't want any accidents!'

Mrs Murgatroyd was right. All over the country, men flocked to police stations to volunteer. Within 24 hours, 250,000 had put their names down. There was a buzz of excitement in Althwaite. At last there was something important to be done locally. Caring for evacuees, and collecting books and other comforts for the troops were necessary tasks, but they were humdrum. Forming and arming a local force was stirring stuff. The Government's appeal, though, gave rise to worries. If it was so urgent to create an anti-invasion force, the Government must think that invasion was a real threat.

There was gossip in the village about who had, and who hadn't – yet- joined the Local Defence Volunteers, as they were called. The permitted age span was wide: from 17 to 65. Miss Arbuthnot made discreet, and sometimes indiscreet, enquiries to identify any able-bodied man who had not volunteered. Bert Dawson was indignant when he learnt that she had been asking why he had not done so. He sent her a restrained letter:

Dear Madam, I have been told that you were asking whether I had joined the LDV, and if not why not. I don't know what business it is of yours. But, for your information, I did try to join but was told, to my annoyance, that as I'm Senior Air Raid Warden, I couldn't. If you can use your influence to remove this bar, I shall be most obliged.

Miss Arbuthnot felt guilty at having questioned his patriotism. Also, she was impressed what a well-written letter it was for a dustman. The next day she called on the Dawsons at tea-time. She apologized handsomely to Mr Dawson, presented Mrs Dawson with half a dozen butterfly cakes and was invited to have a cup of tea.

'Fine woman, that,' said Bert after she had left. 'Pity the LDV isn't open to women. She'd make a splendid platoon commander.'

Mrs Dawson laughed. 'You men are all the same. Some lady who's well spoken and with a bit of class pays you special attention. Then you roll on your back like a puppy and let her tickle you. Still, it was nice of her to bring these cakes – made by her own fair hands, as she was careful to mention. Who else can you write a complaining letter to, Bert?'

There was speculation about who would be in charge of Althwaite's volunteers. Some of the men had served in the army in the First World War and knew at least how to handle a rifle. Some had become corporals. Only one of the villagers had risen to the rank of sergeant: George Wright, the blacksmith. His father and grandfather had been blacksmiths. Their work had been mainly that of shoeing horses and repairing farm machinery. With the decline in the use of horses for farming, George had had to diversify into other kinds of work – tools, railings and gates; and the farm machinery now included tractors.

'Sergeant' Wright, as people now remembered to call him, was the favourite for the post of platoon commander. He was a respected figure: a Methodist local preacher, a past member of the Homefield and Althwaite District Council, a leading light in the Althwaite Flower and Vegetable Society and a keen supporter of Bruddersford United Football club. His war experience counted in his favour. He had served with an artillery regiment in France for two years until wounded and sent home. On recovery, he had become an instructor at a field gun training centre. It wasn't just other people who thought that he was a good man to take charge of the Althwaite platoon. George thought so himself.

There was one possible obstacle to this outcome: the occupant of the Hall, The Honourable Peter Danellion-Smith. It wasn't that Peter was ambitious to fill the post. One part of him - the retiring part – would gladly have stood to one side. The other part was anxious not to evade any duty that the needs of the country might put in his way. Naturally, he felt he had to enrol as a volunteer. With his ancestry in mind, he hoped for a responsible position. But if he had to serve in the ranks, he would do so with as good a grace as he could muster.

Exchanges of views in the Dandelion Arms were

not entirely in his favour.

'We're supposed to live in a democracy, so let's have an election for platoon commander,' Jack Moorhouse suggested.

'They'll never stand for that!' riposted Eddie Sykes, the greengrocer. 'The aristocracy may be on t'way out, but it's still got a lot of influence. You can fail the scholarship but still get on in t'world if you've got a handle to your name. Yon Hon Peter, as 'e likes to call 'imself, will end up in command, even though 'e was only a pen pusher in t'last war. I'll bet 'e doesn't know one end of a rifle from t'other.'

'Nah then, Eddie,' Bert Dawson butted in. 'Th'as goin' too far. Hon Peter's the best shot around 'ere. I can vouch for that from being a beater on t'moors in t'grouse season. And 'e's got a good 'ead on 'is shoulders.'

It was not just the men who were outspoken in their views. After a day of Womens' Voluntary Service activities, Mrs Murgatroyd told Jem of her worries.

'There's a lot of ill-feeling about. People are less ready than they used to be to let the aristocracy take the lead. If we're fighting for democracy, then whether you're the son of a baronet or of a shopkeeper shouldn't matter – that's what many say. Others reckon that the squire has talents and the fact that he has a title shouldn't be held against him.'

'I bet you're sitting on the fence, Mum!' Jem said.

'Well, I am, and it's not very comfortable! I think I'll get down on the side of those who think that Hon Peter has some qualities the others don't have. You're such a buddy of his, I'm sure that'll please you!'

Jem was impressed by the fact that so many men

wanted to sign up as defence volunteers. But there were many who couldn't - those who were too old and those who were handicapped. He thought of One-Leg Tim: might he be feeling sore that he was both too old and unfit to join? The next Saturday morning Jem set off for the allotments. It was time he did some work for Tim again, anyway. He found the old campaigner in cheerful mood. Tim was excited by the setting up of the defence volunteers, and wasn't put out that he was excluded.

'I've done my bit for the country. It's others' turn now. But if t'Germans invade us, I'll be one of the resistance, you mark my words! I'll be carrying secret messages in the 'ollow part of my wooden leg!'

Over their mid-morning cups of tea, Tim fell to ruminating.

'Now we've got Churchill at the 'elm, we'll get through. It's a long time ago, but I still think of 'im as 'e was in t'Boer War. 'e were a young man then – went out to report t'war as a journalist. No one like 'im for getting right up tot'scene of fighting. 'e were that brave 'e should have 'ad a medal. 'elped to get an armoured train going that 'ad been partly derailed by the Boers. Got captured and escaped. Newspapers were full of 'im – 'is own reports and escapades. When I think 'ow near 'e must 'ave been to death, I think t'Almighty must 'ave spared 'im to lead us in this war.'

Tim's reminiscences were interrupted by a surprising apparition. It was the figure of Hon Peter wandering among the allotment plots. He was not often down in the centre of the village, and the allotments were an unlikely place to find him.

'Ah, here you are!' Peter exclaimed when he spotted

them sitting on Tim's old garden seat. 'Room for me there? Yes, I don't mind if I do,' he added on seeing Tim reach for the thermos flask.

'Surprised to see me here, I expect. I'm killing two birds with one stone, you might say. Thought I'd see how our friend Mr Tim is getting on. And, as a Local Defence Volunteer, I need to get to know the village better – its nooks and crannies and its outlying haunts, like the allotments.'

Having established that Tim was well and encouraged by the appointment of the ex-Boer War hero, Churchill, Hon Peter turned to the subject that was engrossing the attention of the village.

'I'm with good friends here, so I can be frank. I gather that some people think I might be put in charge of the platoon simply because I'm the son of a baronet. What have you heard, Jem?'

Jem recounted what he had heard from schoolfellows and from his mother about dissension in the village. Tim, though not himself a frequenter of the Dandelion Arms, had also learnt of the feeling against Hon Peter, and passed on what he knew.

'I'm much obliged to you gentlemen,' Peter said. 'It's worse than I imagined. We must have it out in the open. I will bid you good day and leave you to your horticultural pursuits.'

Posters were put on notice boards and displayed in shops.

PUBLIC MEETING

To be held in the Village Hall

At 7 pm on Wednesday 22nd May

under the chairmanship of

Lieutenant-Colonel J. G. Fitzpatrick (Retd.) MC.

To explain the role of the

LOCAL DEFENCE VOLUNTEERS

And to discuss related matters.

Everyone welcome.

Hon Peter had had some difficulty in persuading Colonel Fitzpatrick, the LDV District Commander, of the need for a public meeting.

'I've invited you to head the platoon, Peter, and that should be it,' was his initial response. 'It's simply a matter of military discipline. If any volunteer doesn't like it, he must lump it.' But he had given way to Peter's urgent entreaty.

The hall was full at 6.45 pm. All the men who had signed up were there, together with wives, mothers and older children – the last present out of curiosity. Even some evacuees were there. Rondot had come because Ron had been told that there might be a 'bust-up'. They were squeezed between Mrs Murgatroyd and Mr Bright. Dot hadn't wanted to come, but became more reconciled when she was lifted on to Mrs Murgatroyd's lap so that she could see better. Hon Peter was in the front row between Miss Arbuthnot and the vicar. Jem and Harold stood at the back so that they could slip out easily if the meeting became boring.

At 7 o'clock prompt, the Colonel mounted the platform. He was in uniform and looked impressive. He stood at the lectern and looked sternly at his audience over his pince-nez spectacles.

'Now, you all know why we are gathered here,' he began, speaking with the slightly posh accent of a well-educated military officer. 'To get the Althwaite Local Defence Volunteers off to a good start. Twenty one men have volunteered – an excellent response. What will they be doing? First of all there will be training: drill, use of small arms, explosive devices, map reading. There will be exercises, including co-ordination with other services such as Air Raid Precaution, Ambulance, Police. Knowing the local population, they will be alert to the appearance of strangers. From time to time they will man road blocks. If there are reports of parachutists, they will investigate. In the event of large numbers of parachutists, they will hold the enemy at bay until the arrival of detachments of the regular army.'

Colonel Fitzpatrick went on at some length. As a leader of men, he imagined himself to be inspiring the local people with enthusiasm for the volunteers. However, as Hon Peter realized, the audience was becoming restless. They didn't want all this detail. They wanted to know who was going to lead the platoon and why. Shuffling of feet and coughing ceased as Fitzpatrick got to the part of his address which made even him slightly nervous.

'Now, a platoon has to have a leader. A man in

whom every member has confidence. I know that there has been much, shall we say – speculation - about this. I have invited The Honourable Peter Danellion-Smith to assume this role. I have every confidence that he will carry it out effectively. Before agreeing, however, he wished this meeting to be held. At his request I now invite him to say a few words.'

The Colonel retired from the lectern to a seat at the back of the platform. Hon Peter climbed up. Instead of partly hiding himself behind the lectern, he stood at the front of the platform. Legs slightly astride, shoulders back, one hand in a pocket of his jacket, one thumb behind a lapel, he sought to make up for his short stature. In contrast to the Colonel's stern aspect, Peter looked at the audience in a friendly fashion, a slight smile on his face.

'Good evening, ladies and gentlemen - and young people! As Colonel Fitzpatrick said, I have been invited to take command of the Althwaite LDV platoon. I imagine some of you may say: "Why him? What are his qualifications, apart from having a dubious title before his name?"'

A voice from the back cried, 'You can say that again!'

'Thank you my friend – you confirm what I thought. If I'm an "Hon" and not just plain "Mr", it's because of my ancestors. Should I not be proud of them? To do otherwise would be dishonourable. We all have ancestors we should be proud of. There may be some here tonight who are descended from Harold's soldiers who opposed the Normans at the Battle of Hastings. Some of your ancestors may have been the bowmen of England who defeated the French at Agincourt. The blood of men who fought in Marlborough's glorious campaigns may flow in your veins. Perhaps your muscle, skin and bravery comes down the years from the gallant men who fought under Wellington at Waterloo. Some of you ladies may have forebears who tended the wounded in the Crimean War, inspired by Florence Nightingale. I know there are still men in the village who served their country in South Africa at the turn of the century. There are certainly a number who fought in the last war. "Aye, there's the rub", as Hamlet said. Did I fight in the last war? I confess that I was never in the front line. Not being judged fit enough for the infantry, I undertook the humble duties of a Captain responsible for the pay of a large number of men. Making sure that men are properly paid and that the right amounts are remitted to dependants - that is not a job to be scoffed at, I submit. Where would morale be without it?'

Hon Peter took out a large, white handkerchief and wiped his brow.

'Now, ladies and gentlemen. I don't *claim* the position of LDV platoon commander. I am perfectly prepared to leave it to you to decide by means of a vote. But, if you give me your confidence, I promise to be unremitting in my efforts. Mr Wright, or should I say, Sergeant Wright, will be my right hand man. I will, I am sure, learn from him. And I hope he may learn something from me. Althwaite's volunteers will be the pride of the West Riding. I now leave it to anyone else who may wish to speak.'

Hon Peter went back to his seat amidst hearty

applause, some cries of 'hear, hear' and a single voice from the back shouting, 'Come on George!' Mr Wright got to his feet. A hush fell on the assembled company. Many wondered whether he would challenge the Squire.

'Fellow residents of Althwaite, I'm no public speaker. But no speech is needed. I'm sure that I and the other volunteers will be honoured to serve under Mr Danellion-Smith. Whether he's an Honourable is beside the point. He's the man for the job. He's got that flair for leadership that we all respect. I say three cheers for Hon Peter! Hip, hip, hooray!'

The one or two dissenting voices were drowned under the cheers that rang out. Hon Peter stood up and turned to face the audience.

'Thank you. I am very moved. Now, what I didn't say before, for fear of being charged with bribery, is that Miss Lorinda Vajansky and I will be getting married in a fortnight's time – on Saturday the eighth of June. In the afternoon, everyone is welcome to a little jamboree at the Hall. Please come!'

People filed out of the hall into the evening. Thanks to British Summer Time and the putting forward of clocks, it was still light. Jem hung around until Hon Peter came out with Colonel Fitzpatrick. The latter got into a low-slung sports car and departed with a roar. Peter spotted Jem.

'Can't imagine me driving one of those things! How did it go – the meeting, I mean?'

'That Colonel, sir – he was losing their attention. But they perked up when you started. What you said about ancestors – it seemed to me to put everyone on a level with you. I saw some people smiling.'

'A dangerous gift, that of oratory, Jem. Just think – if I can move people with my poor eloquence, what can that chap Hitler do with his ranting and raging? See you at the jamboree? Oh no, I'd forgotten, you'll be at the wedding itself, won't you? Jolly good!'

Hon Peter had wanted a quiet ceremony, with only immediate relatives, a best man and a bridesmaid. But Lorinda had pointed out that that just wouldn't do. He owed it to the folk of Althwaite to make it more public. In any case, there were certain people whom she was determined to honour with an invitation. Ever mindful of the way in which she had first met Hon Peter, foremost on her invitation list were Jem, Harold, Ron and Dot. Mrs Murgatroyd had been surprised that the stiff, white envelope, addressed in a neat, calligraphic hand, was for her as well as Jem.

'I bet you know what this is, Jem. You open it.'

'I can guess. There we are – wedding invitation. I said you'd be invited as well.'

'They're only inviting me because of you.'

'Nonsense. Lorinda likes you.'

'Oh dear, we'll have to think of a present. But it can't be something expensive.'

'We'll think of summat.'

'*Something*, young man!'

Harold and Ron had also expected to receive invitations and were not disappointed. But they soon began to wish the wedding over and done with. Lorinda called at both households and asked Jonquil and Dot to be her bridesmaids. The excitement of the two girls was intense. There was a trip by train to Bruddersford with Lorinda to buy material for their dresses. Then there were visits to Mrs Berry, the Althwaite seamstress, who lived in Up Bye, near to Ma Hibbert. To Harold and Ron there seemed no end to the transformation of their untidy little sisters into perfect bridesmaids. The talk was about shoes, white stockings, handkerchiefs, decorative headbands; and about their roles, in which they were instructed by Lorinda.

'It's getting beyond a joke,' Harold said to Ron. 'Jonquil was cocky enough already. Now, she thinks she's the cat's whiskers. She thinks and talks of nothing else but this wedding.'

'Same with Dot. But it's doing her a lot o'good. Brought her out of herself. The other day she said: "If it hadn't been for Mr Hitler, nothing of this would have happened." Anyway, let's hope they calm down after it's over.'

Early on Saturday, 8th of June both Jonquil and Dot drew their curtains and inspected the weather. They were dismayed to see low clouds and not a hint of sunshine. Their mothers began to be worried that they would be cold, and that rain might spoil their dresses. But the black clouds massed over the Pennines kept their distance. When Hon Peter and his bride emerged from St Jude's, a shaft of sunlight held Althwaite captive. Those waiting outside were surprised, as those at the service had been, by Lorinda's attire. Instead of a bridal dress of cream or white, she was wearing her grey-blue uniform. The austerity of the costume contrasted with the satin pink of her bridesmaids. Jonquil held her head high, conscious of reflected glory. Dot glanced at people shyly, but smiled.

The church possessed only one bell. Even if war-time regulations had allowed, there could be no joyful peal. But Hon Peter had engaged the Homefield Hand Bell Ringers to create a merry noise. To the surprise of the bridal pair, a guard of honour had also assembled. The ladies from Bank Terrace held aloft broomsticks decorated with flowery garlands. Lorinda was overcome by this unexpected gesture and had to borrow Peter's handkerchief. As she tried to express her appreciation, she was interrupted.

'Don't thee cry dearie. We're all very 'appy for thee and t'squire. You mun forgive us for taking thee for a spy. We should 'ave 'ad more sense.'

Lorinda embraced the formidable figure of Mrs Colethwaite.

'Thank you all so much. But you forget that if I hadn't been threatened, I might not have met my husband.' It was the first time Lorinda had used the word, and a quick flush of pleasure made her cheeks glow.

Jem went to bed early that night. He said he was exhausted, but it was also that he wanted to be on his own to review the extraordinary day. During the wedding service, and afterwards at the reception in the Hall, his mind had kept flicking back to that September day of the previous year when, with the help of Harold and Ron, he had rescued Lorinda and thereby introduced her to Peter.

That he, an ordinary lad, should have been chosen

by Destiny or God or Something to change the lives of those two made him proud, but also fearful. Suppose he had chosen to take Rondot up to the Hall at a different time of the day, after Lorinda had finished her painting or been frightened off by the women? Suppose Lorinda had not decided that day to go out and paint? Suppose the women from the terrace had not noticed her?

He dragged his mind away from the conundrum of freedom of action and destiny to the crowded impressions of the day. They jostled for attention. Jem had never been to a wedding before. When the vicar pronounced the solemn words, 'Therefore if any man can show any just cause why they may not lawfully be joined together, let him now speak, or else hereafter for ever hold his peace', Jem had held his breath. How dreadful if some voice from the back had intervened to spoil everything! Then there had been the agonising few moments when the best man, Major Carruthers, had felt in each of his four waistcoat pockets for the ring, before finding it in a trouser pocket.

The terrace women's guard of honour had been a stroke of genius, he thought. He had been inclined to dismiss them as stupid, after their near assault on Lorinda. But they had redeemed themselves.

What a pity the magical shaft of sunlight had been no more than a prelude to that downpour. A bus had been hired to take the guests from the church to the Hall. But it was too wide to go down the drive, and had deposited people at the entrance, now gate-less. The bridal party had just managed to get inside the Hall before the heavens opened. Mrs Murgatroyd's umbrella had partially shielded Jem and herself, but their legs and feet were soaked. Others, who had neglected to bring an umbrella, were in a worse state. Hon Peter had abandoned his wife to usher folk inside and to organise comforts. Ladies had been sent upstairs to dry themselves with towels. Jem, Harold and Ron had been put in charge of the fireplaces – in the hall, the drawing room, the dining room, the study and the kitchen. As the invited guests had dried off before the log fires and had warmed their insides with mulled wine, their clothes had steamed and the tall windows had become misted over.

To Jem, it had seemed as though the meal would never begin. And even then, the opportunity to heal the aching void that had been his tummy was deferred whilst he and the other older young folk, Alice amongst them, had helped to serve the guests. At last, they had settled down at a trestle table in the study to their share. But they were called to the dining room to hear the speeches before they had had their trifle and jelly.

Jem had feared that Hon Peter, with his liking for public speaking, would spoil the occasion by going on too long. He asked the Althwaite guests to show their appreciation of the presence of Lorinda's parents – at which the distinguished couple nodded and smiled. Her father was inclining to baldness, but it was still evident that Lorinda had inherited her blonde hair from her mother. Peter then sprang a surprise. 'And now, I propose to depart from tradition and hand over to Aircraftswoman Second Class Lorinda Danellion-Smith.'

Amidst much laughing and cheers, Lorinda arose. She blushed at the reception but, looking around and smiling, she recovered her composure.

'Friends – a welcome to you all. It was only on the way from the church that this astonishing husband of mine told me that he proposed that I should give the speech! I've never made one before in my life - except in imagination, telling my Flight Sergeant what I think of him! I'm still almost at my wits' end. So, as I can imagine some Shakespearian character saying: "I pray you mercy".'

'First, thanks to so many people: to Peter's mother for gracing this occasion with her presence; to Mrs McAlister and Mrs Dawson for this lovely meal; to my sweet bridesmaids, Jonquil and Dorothy – sorry, "Dot" [Jem heard Harold mutter under his breath: 'sweet – I like that!']; to Mrs Berry for making their dresses.'

'Now, as you know, I came to Althwaite to spy.'

Mrs Colethwaite's voice interrupted: 'No, yer didn't luv.'

'Yes, with my paint box, to spy on the village, to see if I could penetrate its soul. I can't thank the ladies of Bank Terrace enough for their error. I forgave them long ago, and I think they've forgiven me for leading them into a mistake - their guard of honour this morning assures me they have. And of course, I shall always be indebted to Jem, Harold and Ron, aided by Dot.'

(Here, Jem, lying in bed, twisted his body as he remembered he embarrassment of being smiled at by some of the guests.)

'I've never been a woman who longed for marriage and saw it as her natural destiny. If it came, it would be a blessing. If not, I would continue as an artist trying to see into the souls of things. As it is, the confluence of people and events led me to the magical tower. There, Prince Charming came to my rescue!'

Here, some of the guests nearest to him were pleased to note a slight blush on Hon Peter's cheeks.

'We've all been taken aback by the German advance. We trembled for our men in France, and we're relieved now that so many have been rescued. In a way, it seems shameful for us to be sitting here in comfort whilst the country is in shock, wondering what will happen next. But we know, don't we, that Britain will pull through in the end. The personal happiness of Peter and me, the happiness of you in your families, of people up and down the country in theirs, will be bulwarks to prevent this country from collapse.'

'The weather has put an end to our plans for a wider gathering in the garden this afternoon. But when Britain, with all its allies around the world, has won through, I promise there'll be a grand celebration at the Hall. Till then – keep up the good work and God bless you all!'

Jem had been standing behind Farmer Ackroyd and heard him say to his wife, after the cheering and clapping had died down, 'She's a match for t'squire, and no mistake!'

As for Jem himself, he wished he was a medieval knight, able to lay his sword at her feet and swear a lifetime's devotion.

14 SUMMER INTERLUDE

As the extent of the French and British defeat on the continent became clear, a pall of gloom settled over the village. A feeling of shame at such a disaster contended with relief at the rescue of the bulk of the army. In the queues outside shops, in the Dandelion Arms, at Womens' Voluntary Service meetings and in school playgrounds, there was one overriding question: what would happen next? Most feared that Hitler would follow up his dash to the Channel with the invasion of Britain. People were confident that their countrymen and countrywomen would put up a fierce resistance – they hardly needed Churchill's rousing words to be sure of that. But, with an army battered and exhausted, with the Local Defence Volunteers as yet untrained, how effective could the opposition be?

At the first scout meeting after the news of the rescue of the army at Dunkirk, the scoutmaster tried to raise the spirits of his troop. Mr Ash was not in the forces himself because of his age and lameness in one leg – the result of a wound in the last war. He had retired early from teaching so as to have more time for writing a book about the wild life of Yorkshire, on which he had already been engaged for five years. School children and scouts knew him by the nickname of 'Woody'. The more cheeky called him 'Knobbly', having seen his knees when he wore shorts for the scouts' summer camp. He was often conscious that he didn't cut an impressive figure. He was tall but thin – gaunt, said some. He didn't have the natural authority of Hon Peter. Keeping control over the rumbustious spirits in the scout troop taxed his ingenuity and patience. Nevertheless he relished the challenge of turning his motley crew of teenagers into a trained unit, capable of supporting the Defence Volunteers.

'Now, lads. You all know about the formation of the Local Defence Volunteers. But scouts have a role to play as well. If the enemy invades, the bulk of his forces will come by sea. But he may well drop troops by parachute to seize positions behind the front line, or to cut telephone wires and create confusion. Which of you remembers the name of the town in South Africa defended against the Boers by the founder of scouting?'

The name was on the tip of Jem's tongue, but Ron got in first.

'Mafeking, sir.'

'Well done, Ron. Now, in that defence, Baden-Powell made use of boys as messengers. We've got to train so that if we are needed as messengers, or in support of first-aid teams, we can do so effectively. So, in the next few weeks, we're going to concentrate on communications and brushing up on first aid. And I want everyone here – anyone slacking will be helping the enemy! Next week we'll have a morse code exercise. So now let's test our memories. Harold – what's "A"?'

'Er, dot dash,' he replied and was relieved that he was right.

War is a great generator of rumours. One of these was that Germany had overrun Holland and Belgium so easily because thousands of troops had been dropped by parachute, many of them disguised as nuns, monks and clergy. Hitler might already be up to such tricks. Mr Bright always wore his clerical collar. Going to a hospital in Leeds to visit one of his flock, he had been conscious of a few people eyeing him with suspicion.

The Local Defence Volunteers became known popularly as 'Parashots', since they were to be the front line defence against paratroops. But how were the Althwaite Parashots to deal with paratroops when they had only one gun between three men? That was the question hotly debated in the Dandelion Arms. Pickaxe handles and pitchforks might be alright for close combat, but a German light machine gun would polish a man off before he could get close. Hon Peter had provided his force with three shot guns, keeping the best one for his own use. Colonel Fitzpatrick was getting tired of frequent telephone calls from Peter asking when the promised rifles and uniforms would arrive. Drill could be done using sticks instead of rifles, but Peter was anxious that his men should be equipped to cope with the risk of parachutists.

'How can you expect my scouts to provide adequate support to the LDV unless they practise?'

Mr Ash was at the police station talking to Constable Dewhurst who was proving difficult. The scouts needed to practise signalling by lamps, using morse code. Mr Ash realised that they couldn't do this during the black-out. He had suggested that they use the three quarters of an hour before black-out time started. The sun would have set and it would be beginning to get dark. He reckoned that the lamps would just be visible.

'Oh, I don't know about that. It's getting a bit close to black-out time, that is. I'm not sure I've got the authority,' was the Constable's reaction.

'Well, have a word with your sergeant at Bruddersford.'

'He'll be looking in next week.'

'Next week! Man, don't you realize that this is a matter of urgency? Do you think Hitler's going to put off his plans for landing paratroops until you and your sergeant have had a chat over cocoa next week?'

Mr Ash was working himself up into a state of apoplexy.

'Oh, alright. But make sure you stop ten minutes before black-out time.'

During the week, in the intervals between homework and jobs about the house, Jem tried to mug up the morse code. He could just about go from A to Z. But when his Mum called out a particular letter, he sometimes had to go through the alphabet before being able to answer. He thought of telegraph operators on board ships, including the hero who had stuck at his position on the Titanic. The morse code must be as natural to them as their own language. Perhaps he would be sufficiently expert by the time the German paratroops landed.

Come the evening of the practice, Mr Ash divided his troop in two. Jem found himself in a group with eight others, amongst them Charlie Foster and Will Dicehurst. Harold and Ron were in the other group. He would have preferred not to be in the same group as Charlie, but he welcomed Will's presence. He was one of those lads who treated everything as a joke. This could be irritating at times, but usually it was just amusing.

'We're going to Digfoot reservoir,' Mr Ash explained. 'Charlie will be in charge of Green Group and I'll have Red Group. Green will go to the east side of the reservoir, above the old shooting hut. I'll be opposite on the other side. Red Group will start signalling. Now, let's check we've got paraffin in the lamps and that they'll light up.'

The lamps were ancient. Three quarters of the globe was masked with black paint. The remaining quarter had a shutter which, when slid back, released a glow from the lighted wick, behind which was a steel mirror to enhance the beam.

After 40 minutes of walking, the groups were in position. The sun had set and the pink clouds in the west were reflected in the water. Jem thought of the last time he had been to the reservoir – on that walk at the end of Dad's leave at Christmas.

Suddenly a winking light shone out from the other side: a warning that a message was about to be transmitted. Charlie had Green's lamp and gave the signal: 'Ready to receive'. Everyone had pads and pencils at the ready. Three short flashes – that was 'S'. One long flash – that was 'T'. Short and long – 'A'.

Another long' – 'T'. One short – 'E'. Then the signal for end of word. Both Jem and Will had the word 'state'. So far, so good. The next word was 'your'. Then they ran into difficulties. Red's lamp was signalling too fast. Some had got 'potiton'. Will had 'petition'. 'State your petition' – it made sense, at least.

'What the dickens do they mean?' asked Charlie, crossly.

'It's clear enough,' said Will. 'They're asking what we want – supplies and suchlike. I know what I want – some fish and chips. Let's send that.'

'That's daft,' Jem protested. 'We should be saying something about ammunition or guns.'

Charlie was tickled by Will's suggestion and sent off: 'fish and chips.'

The signal came back: 'repeat your petition.'

'I know,' said Will. 'We forgot the salt and vinegar.'

Off went the signal: 'with salt and vinegar.'

There was a long pause.

'They're wondering how to get the fish and chips over here,' Will suggested.

Then came another signal which Jem took down as: 'stop that nogense.'

'Stop that *nonsense*!' said Charlie, his hands suddenly feeling clammy.

But Red had not yet finished: 'Where are you?'

'Of course,' Charlie said. 'You and your "petition", Will. It's our *position* they want!'

'What a shame,' Will said. 'I were looking forward to fish and chips.'

'Shut up!' cried Charlie, who had realised that

Woody would blame him for the misunderstanding. 'Above old shooting hut,' he sent.

'Any enemy spotted?' was Red's next signal, which both Jem and Will got correctly.

'Tell them Goering looked in but was disappointed there were no fish and chips,' Will suggested. Some of the group collapsed in fits of laughter. Jem tried to keep a straight face, but couldn't hide a smile.

'One landed behind you,' Charlie sent.

Another long pause.

'They've gone to look for him!' said Will.

After some minutes Red signalled: 'return to base'.

The post mortem was not pleasant. Mr Ash was indignant at Green Group's frivolity.

'If you don't get the word, ask for it to be repeated. Don't guess. That could lead to dangerous misunderstandings. "Petition", indeed! And I've a shrewd idea who suggested "fish and chips",' he added, glancing at Will.

Jem and Harold left the scout hut together.

'You should have seen Woody!' Harold said. 'He nearly went off his head when you signalled "fish and chips", especially as some of us couldn't help laughing. He thought you were taking the micky out of him. "German scouts wouldn't dare to be so silly", he said. Then Bert Dawson turned up. Said he'd been tipped off by Constable Dewhurst, and came along to see that we didn't carry on into black-out time. Woody became angry. There was still a quarter of an hour to go by his watch. He said he thought he should have been trusted, and that he was going to have some words with Constable Dewhurst. I was feeling sorry for him. I think we ought to make sure we know the morse code backwards by the next meeting.'

Schools closed for the summer holiday. Normally, this would have been the signal for Jem and Harold, like others, to let off steam. But they didn't feel inclined to indulge in the usual wild abandon. Some element of responsibility had crept into their minds. There was the fear of invasion, or at least of spies being parachuted into the country. France was definitely out of the war, with half the country occupied. Italy had come into the war on the side of Germany. Jem's Dad had made a fleeting visit home and was now being sent abroad. He hadn't been allowed to say where; in fact he wasn't entirely sure. Jem imagined him at sea, his transport ship a prey for German submarines.

Up and down the country, people – many unaccustomed to physical labour – were digging. Members of the Home Guard (as Churchill had now said the Local Defence Volunteers were to be called) were helping to dig trenches across golf courses and other likely sites where enemy planes might land. Allotments were being expanded, lawns turned over to vegetables. Jem's visits to help One-Leg Tim had planted the idea of himself and his mother having an allotment. Harold and Ron said they would help. His mother agreed, though she wouldn't be able to spare much time for it. So there was going to be less freedom during the summer holidays for messing about.

After a council of war under the bridge, Jem, Harold and Rondot had decided that they would, nevertheless, go on an expedition, taking a tent for one night. Rondot's mother had returned to Hull, but she had left Ron and Dot in the charge of Mrs Weaverthorpe who had become a second mother to them. She was anxious about letting Dot join in. Ron said he couldn't go without her. Mrs Weaverthorpe went to see Mrs Murgatroyd and Mrs Bright. They persuaded her that Jem and Harold were sensible enough. But all three ladies agreed that Constable Dewhurst and Hon Peter, as Home Guard commander, should be informed. Jem and Harold were impatient with this molly-coddling. But they saw the sense of letting the Home Guard know where they were going. In any case, they could keep a look-out for anyone suspicious. At Hon Peter's request, Jem, Harold and Ron went to Sergeant Wright's house with their map and showed him where they planned to go.

Jem was all for setting off without delay. But his mother stipulated that the half of the allotment still to be dug over should be dealt with first. They had already planted seed potatoes and seeds for carrots and cabbages. Tim had given them advice about planting the potatoes in trenches on rotted manure – which he gave them – and then covering them with soil to form ridges. Jem, Harold and Ron found it hard work: the allotment was one that had been neglected for three years. One of them had a watch. They kept checking the time to see when they could decently break off from digging up weeds and turning the soil to have elevenses with Tim. Then, taking the thermos flasks they had brought, they joined him.

'Leeks, Brussels sprouts, beetroot and lettuces –

that's what I suggest you put in next. I'll give you some seeds.'

Jem could visualize the whole week being devoted to the allotment. Meanwhile the summer sun shone and the moors beckoned. He was beginning to realize that war meant sacrifices.

'Do you think Hitler will invade, Tim?' Harold asked.

'No, I don't. We'd be naught but trouble for 'im. Anyroad, isn't it living space 'e wants for t'German people? There's no living space 'ere. No, I reckon it's east that Hitler's looking. That pact with Russia won't last. Course, his Luftwaffe can do us a lot of damage – and t'U-boats. But eventually, America'll come in, and then Hitler'll be finished.'

'Don't you think America might just lend a hand, without fighting? Europe's a long way from them.'

Jem envied the maturity of Ron's contribution.

'I mind that they joined in t' last war,' Tim replied. 'And that was under Woodrow Wilson, who was a more peaceable-like chap than President Roosevelt. No, Roosevelt's just waiting until 'e can get t'American people behind 'im. Now, you'd best get back to work, or I'll be accused of 'olding up t'war effort!'

Not for the first time, Jem thought that a lot of knowledge and wisdom lay behind Tim's wizened face. He wasn't a great reader. But he listened to wireless programmes, especially the news and talks.

At last the rest of the allotment had been turned over and sown. Rucksacks were packed, the two tents they were taking were rolled up, and Raq was beginning to get excited, sensing another expedition. Then the spell of sunny weather came to an end. The forecast for the next two days was rain. There was nothing for it but to wait. Something else irked Jem. He and Harold had planned to camp for the night in a little valley, like the Briggen Clough they had camped in with Jem's Dad. But the three mothers had put their collective feet down. Especially since the boys were taking Dot, they had insisted that, instead of camping in the wilds, they should camp near Intake Farm. Jem's parents knew Farmer Whittle. The Brights' telephone was used to ring him up and arrange that he would keep an eye on them. Jem was disappointed, but he had gained something in return. As they would not be camping well away from human contact, couldn't they camp for two nights, instead of one? The mothers had agreed.

The weather forecast improved and the first leg of the journey began: a lift in Mr Bright's car to the start of their walk. Harold sat in the front beside his Dad. He spotted the barrier first - an old telegraph pole resting on X-shaped trestles. Beside it were three men who, together, could claim to be dressed in Home Guard uniform. But, due to the slow arrival of uniforms, they had shared out what was available. Two had regulation forage caps, one had a khaki tunic, two had khaki trousers, one had shiny, new boots. These items of uniform were supplemented by everyday attire. One had a rifle, the other two had pickaxe handles. They were easily recognized as Jack Moorhouse, Joe Quarmby and Eddie Sykes. Mr Bright leant out of the car window and asked what was going on. Jack, with the rifle, approached.

'Can I see your identity card, sir?'

'Sorry, I haven't got it with me,' Mr Bright replied. 'But you know me Jack. By the way, you did a good job last week, the engine's running sweetly.'

'Sorry, sir, but we're manning a road block.'

'I can see that. What's it for?'

'It's an exercise – to see how quickly we can set up barriers around Althwaite. We're just waiting for Sergeant Wright and Captain Smith – he's told us to call him that for the duration. Then we can get back to our real work.'

'I see. Well, let me through, please – I'm taking these youngsters a bit further up so they can start on their little camping trip.'

'Oh, I don't know about that,' said Eddie who had come forward. 'Camping out when there's a war on? Doesn't set a good example for t'war effort, does it? Suppose everyone went camping – where'd we be then?'

'They're only kids. How on earth is the war effort going to suffer?' Mr Bright's Christian patience was wearing thin.

'What about the dangers – German spies and parachutists?' Jack asked.

Jem was getting agitated. He could see the expedition, so fondly looked forward to, being blocked by these stupid Home Guards. He got out of the car. Jack was tall – Jem was only half his height. But he took a leaf out of Hon Peter's book, shoved his chest out and tried to look both bold and pleasant.

'Morning gentlemen! You all know me – Jem Murgatroyd. I'm the organizer. Your platoon commander, Hon Peter, was apprised of this expedition.' (Jem had recently learnt the word 'apprise' and thought it would make an impression.) 'My comrades, Harold and Ron, and me' (too late Jem realised it should have been 'I') 'went over our plans with Sergeant Wright who had no objection and briefed us' (a slight exaggeration, but a good word) 'to keep our eyes skinned for strangers. We've just finished digging and sowing the new allotment. So we're entitled to a little break. Aren't you going to the Lake District next weekend, Mr Moorhouse?'

'That I am, though I'm puzzled how you know that. Moreover,' he added with a smile, 'I'm camping. So, with all respect to you, Eddie, I think we'd better let these suspicious characters through.'

The barrier was lifted and they were waved on.

'Good for you, Jem,' said Mr Bright. 'You really put them on the back foot. I don't think Joe Quarmby agreed with the other two – I could see him trying to stifle a laugh when you were telling them what's what! I think I have the ingredients for a little homily - about using authority considerately, doing as we would be done by and so on. All expressed tactfully, of course.'

'As always, Dad!' Harold commented.

In no time, they were at the bend in the road where Jem, his Dad and Harold had begun their previous expedition. Mr Bright waved them off towards Grey Nab.

'The Lake District – that was a clincher. How did you know that Jack was going there?' Harold asked.

'Oh, my Mum heard that from Mrs Moorhouse at the WVS – she was feeling sore about being left behind.'

Jem and Harold felt themselves to be old hands.

For Ron and Dot, hailing from the flat country of East Yorkshire, a trek over the moors was an adventure. Dot was secretly nervous, but determined not to show it. Jem, Harold and Ron each carried rucksacks. Jem and Ron also had the rolled tents. Harold carried Raq's feeding bowl and food, and a kettle was attached to his rucksack. Raq bounded ahead, sending up grouse and partridges.

They got to Grey Nab without mishap, though Jem had to contain his impatience at the slow progress they made with Dot as a companion. They sat on the rocks and had their snack. Jem remembered how Dad had spread out the map here and outlined the way ahead. Then, their route had been south west, over Blackley Moor and around Trembling Moss. Now, they were going to trek a short distance over the moor until they found a valley heading south towards Intake Farm. The three boys studied the map, having aligned it with the compass. They could see the direction in which the valley should lie, but there were no useful landmarks. They would have to keep checking their direction by the compass.

'How far do you think we've come from Grey Nab, Harold?' Jem asked.

'About a mile, I'd say.'

A dip in the ground meant that they had lost sight of the rocks. Ahead of them were clumps of cotton grass and the spikes of sedge.

'If this isn't Trembling Moss, it's another marshy bit. We'd better skirt round to higher ground.'

They climbed out of the dip. It was hard going over

the heather, and they paused at the top of the slope. Looking back, they could now see the dark rocks of Grey Nab silhouetted against the blue sky. With their backs to it, Jem and Harold scanned the nearer landscape for the valley which would lead them to the farm. In a southerly direction, the tops of some trees were an indication of it. Both boys were relieved. It would have been shameful to have got lost, having Rondot with them.

'I'm tired,' Dot complained. 'When are we going to get there?'

'It won't be long now. But let's have another rest,' Jem said.

Having shared the water bottle, they lay on their backs in the hot sun. The only sound was that of bees and flies. Closing his eyes, Jem imagined he was living in a world of insects. The buzz and hum made him dozy. As he listened, a louder noise intruded into his imagination – that of a ship's engines. Somewhere at sea, perhaps over the equator, the ship carrying his Dad was pressing on. In his mind's eye he saw the intense blue of a southern ocean. Suddenly, a ripple of foam disturbed the flat calm of the sea. The periscope of a U-boat! Jem woke with a start from his doze. He was shivering, though the sun was still hot. What a dreadful thought! He scrambled to his feet.

'Come on, gang. Intake Farm, here we come!' he shouted.

In another half-mile they came to the rim of the valley. Heather and bracken, with ash and birch trees interspersed, clung to the upper slopes. Lower down, the fields and gritstone walls began to parcel up the land in tidy fashion.

'There's someone over there,' Dot said.

'Where?' chorused the others.

Dot pointed. 'On the other side. See where those trees are?'

'I can't see anything,' Harold said.

'I think I saw something moving – just gone behind a clump of birch,' Jem said.

After staring, rubbing their eyes and staring again, they all agreed that there was someone on the other side of the valley. He or she seemed to be moving stealthily, pausing to look behind and taking cover from time to time.

'Tell you what,' Jem suggested, having looked at the map. 'Instead of going straight down into the valley bottom, we could find this path that's marked on the upper edge. Then we can keep him – or her – under observation.'

'Won't he see us?' asked Dot, who was beginning to feel nervous.

'He might, but the sun'll be against him.'

They found the path, which meandered between the heather about a hundred feet below the rim of the valley. Every few minutes they stopped to check on the progress of the other person. He or she was on a parallel course to them, and behaving oddly – stopping to look behind and occasionally ducking down. He didn't seem to have seen them.

For some time, Dot had been hobbling. The heel of one foot was painful. She had repressed the instinct to complain. She didn't want to be regarded as a nuisance. But now the other foot was hurting too. Ron had noticed her discomfort but had hoped it would pass away. It had been his idea that Dot should come as well, and he didn't want her to let them down. But now she was wincing and biting her lip to avoid an exclamation.

'What's up, Dot?' he asked. 'Let's have a look at your feet.'

They sat around whilst Dot took off her shoes and socks to reveal blisters on both heels. Jem thought of his Dad hurting his ankle. Was this expedition, too, going to be spoilt? Harold got out the first aid kit. With plasters applied and Ron helping her along, Dot tried to be brave. But each step was still painful, and the narrowness of the path made it difficult for Ron to support her.

'I could carry her on my back, if it wasn't for the rucksack,' said Ron.

'Council of war,' Jem announced.

They sat down and studied the map. In about a mile, the path they were following would start to descend the side of the valley. It went through a wood, than came out to a lane, where the path from the other side of the valley also emerged. It was then another mile to Intake Farm. So they had about two and a half miles to go. They decided to leave Ron's rucksack, transferring the tent he was carrying to Jem and Harold who would take turns to carry it. They placed the rucksack behind an ash tree.

'How'll we know which one?' asked Ron. 'One ash is much like another.'

Harold took out his knife and cut off a segment of bark. A few, bleached, stones lay here and there in the heather. They gathered a few and put them at the side of the path. Dot gratefully climbed on to her brother's back. Her feelings were mixed. She felt guilty at causing trouble, but was pleased to be the object of care and attention.

Before resuming, they studied the other side of the valley. There was no sign of the mysterious person. He or she would have made progress whilst they had been held up. Perhaps they would meet on the lane.

They made good progress and came to the wood. Sunlight filtered down through the branches. They were glad to have some shade. Ron discovered that Dot was heavier than a rucksack, so Harold and he swopped burdens. Coming out of the wood, they could see the lane ahead. A nearby stone barn was its destination.

'Better be careful, in case whoever it was is down here,' Jem cautioned. 'I'll go ahead and scout. I'll take Raq with me.'

Jem dropped his rucksack, put Raq on his lead, walked quietly down and climbed a stile. He looked each way down the lane. He could see the path climbing up the other side of the valley. There was no sign of anyone. What about the barn? His heart began beating rapidly. But, thinking of the others, and particularly of Dot, he realized he had to investigate. The barn had a large wooden door – big enough to let in a cart. Judging by the grass growing at its base, it had not been opened for a long time. At the side, stone steps led up to an opening – not much more than window size. Conscious again of his heart racing, Jem stole up the steps. The opening gave on to a wooden floor which stretched half way across the barn. At the far end, a ladder was propped.

'Hallo! Anyone there?' he called, his voice seeming unnaturally loud in the confined space. Raq sniffed the air, barked, and was startled when there was a flutter of wings. A pigeon flew out through a gap at the top of the door. Jem looked over the edge of the floor to the barn below. A few bits of old farm machinery were all he could see in the gloom.

Outside, Jem waved to the others to come on. He took a turn in carrying Dot. They were all relieved when the slate roofs of Intake Farm appeared. Harold put Raq on his lead. Two black and white sheepdogs raced across the farmyard to the gate, barking madly. The arrival of humans, and especially another dog, seemed to be a big event. The noise brought an elderly man out of a byre. His shoulders stooped, but he was still tall. Brown eyes were set in the deep tan of his face.

'Hello there! I bin expecting you. I'm Jim Whittle. Now, let's see. This young lad looks most like Mr Murgatroyd – you must be Jem.'

Jem was pleased at this recognition, and introduced the others.

'And what's matter wi' young miss? Just tired feet or a wounded warrior?'

They went through the gate, the sheepdogs whisking around Raq and wagging their tails. Mr Whittle ushered them through the back door and into the kitchen.

'You upstairs, Hilda?' he called. 'Rescue party's arrived, one of 'em needing first aid.' He turned to the young people. 'By "rescue", I mean from monotony. We're very quiet up 'ere.'

In no time they had made themselves comfortable

in the kitchen where, despite the warm day, a low fire made the hearth cheerful. They had been provided with lemonade. Outside, the dogs had settled down. Mrs Whittle, almost as tall as her husband, but thinner, had bathed the blisters. Dot was sitting on a settee with her bare feet dangling.

'They'll perhaps have gone down by tomorrow, but she'd better not walk any more today,' Mrs Whittle said. 'She'd be better staying here tonight instead of camping. She can have the little bed in our Bertha's room.'

'Bertha's our younger daughter,' she added, noticing the curiosity on their faces. 'She's thirteen. She'll be here soon.'

'Nah then, about this camping,' said Mr Whittle, getting up from the arm-chair where he had been contentedly smoking his pipe. 'If I were still a lad, I wouldn't want to be camping too near to t' farm – not just in an ordinary field. I'd want somewhere a bit more romantic like. There's a spot 'alf a mile away which ought to suit. We can take some water there on t' cart – you can ride as well.'

'That sounds fine, but we've got to collect a rucksack first – or one of us has to,' Jem said. He explained about having to leave it behind.

'Is this it?' asked Mrs Whittle, who had been out into the yard. 'I noticed it leant against the gate.'

The four young people stared unbelievingly. It *was* Ron's rucksack, there was no doubt about it. But who had found it, known where it should go, and brought it?

'It's uncanny,' exclaimed Harold, who was the first

to find his voice. 'The only other person we've seen is the one on the other side of the valley. But he didn't seem to have seen us.'

'Can you describe 'im?' Mr Whittle asked.

'Dark clothes, but too far off even to say whether it was a man or a woman,' Harold replied. 'They seemed to be trying to hide from someone. I wondered if it might be a spy.'

'Well, whoever it was, 'e was well-intentioned,' said Mr Whittle. 'A right conundrum it is, and no mistake!'

The boys were still pondering on the seemingly magical appearance of the rucksack as they were jolted across the fields on a flat cart attached to a tractor. The camp site was ideal, apart from the fact that there was no stream nearby. It was a dell with a few bushes and one large ash tree. The ground was soft but not muddy. The farm could not be seen, so they could imagine themselves far from human habitation. They unloaded the two large water containers and some firewood from the cart. As Dot was staying at the farm, they decided that all three of them should squeeze into one tent. Ron hadn't liked to admit, but he was uneasy about being by himself in a tent when there was a strange person around. They had their meal, of Spam, potatoes and beans, followed by tinned peaches. Replete, they sat around the dying embers of the fire. Each was reflecting on the day. They had navigated their way successfully from Grey Nab. They had coped with a setback. They had found a welcome at the farm. Kind hands had taken care of Dot. A miracle had occurred. It was Ron who broke the silence.

'I hope Dot's feet are alright tomorrow. She won't

want to be left out of things. I think she took to Mrs Whittle. She likes being mothered. She misses our Mum, though Mrs Weaverthorpe's kind.'

'What about your Dad?' asked Jem, who had never heard Ron speak of him.

'Mum and 'im separated about two years ago. We used to see 'im before we were evacuated, and 'e writes to us. 'e's in the Air Force, an aircraft mechanic down south – a place called Kenley where they have Spitfires and Hurricanes. Where's your Dad, Jem?'

'On the high seas, on his way to somewhere – Middle East or Far East. Expect we'll hear sometime. If he makes it, that is.' Jem thought again of that vision of a U-boat.

Harold listened uneasily. He was proud of his Dad, of the long hours he put into his job, his care for members of his congregations. But he couldn't match the others' talk of what their fathers were doing in the war.

'You know what I think,' said Ron, turning to the conundrum. 'I reckon that whoever'd been following that chap on t'other side of t'valley switched 'is attention to us. 'e must have been watching when we left the rucksack behind. Perhaps 'e overheard us mentioning Intake Farm.'

'But why should he do us a good turn?' Harold asked. 'That suggests someone who knew us.'

'Let's think of who knew we were coming,' Jem suggested. 'Our Mums, Harold's Dad, Hon Peter, Sergeant Wright, Constable Dewhurst, the three Home Guards on the way up. Can't see it would be any of them. Did any of the scouts know?'

'One or two might have overheard us talking,' said Harold. 'Come to think of it, Charlie Foster seemed to hover near us when we had a chat after the last meeting.'

'Can't imagine Charlie doing us a good turn,' Jem commented in a withering tone. 'More likely, he'd have made off with the rucksack.'

The fire died down. They were tired and turned in. Having tried alternative positions, they found that the best way for the three of them to occupy the tent was for one to lie with his head at the entrance. They tossed a coin. Jem lost. The others insisted he wash his feet. Raq sprawled over the three of them.

Jem woke first. Birds were singing in the dell. Sunlight filtering through the branches illuminated the roof of the tent. He looked at his watch. It was 7.30. The temptation to stay longer in his sleeping bag was strong. But he found that sleep had reinforced the impression of yesterday that there was something familiar about the figure on the other side of the valley. He crept out of the tent without waking the other two. He had not undressed, so he had merely to put on his boots. Raq emerged, wagging his tail. Jem put him on a lead. Then he climbed out of the dell and up through bushes and bracken until he had a view. Smoke was rising from a chimney of the farm. Casting his eyes around, he looked for a sign that he half expected. There it was! A thin spiral of bluish-grey smoke above a clump of trees further down the valley on the far side. He ran back to the tent with an excited Raq. Drawing the flap aside, he shouted 'Wakey, wakey!' to the recumbent forms inside. Then he set about making a fire for their breakfast.

'What's all the hurry?' Harold asked, getting annoyed with Jem for spoiling what could have been a leisurely breakfast.

'Got summat – sorry , Mum, something - to show you. Now, let's get the washing up done.'

Greasy plates were given an apology for a wash in lukewarm water – Jem couldn't wait for the water to boil. Fastening up the tent and taking just one rucksack with water and snacks for the day, they set off across the fields. Harold and Ron had expected to make first for the farm, but Jem led them diagonally away from it to the other side of the valley. Having climbed a few walls, they came to the edge of the clump of trees that Jem had observed.

'Now, follow me and step like Red Indians,' Jem ordered.

Harold slipped the lead on Raq's collar. In single file and avoiding dead twigs, they stole through the trees. Low growing brambles caught at their socks. Jem held up his hand. They stopped and he sniffed the air. The others too, caught a faint smell of wood smoke. Following Jem's example, they now proceeded bent double. The trees thinned ahead and they found themselves in a small clearing. In the centre were the ashes of a fire. Water had been sprinkled over, but one edge had been missed and a miniature column of smoke rose from it. To one side lay a few unburnt logs. Near the fire an area of grass and bracken – large enough for a sleeping bag – had been compressed.

'Dash – we're too late. He's gone.' Jem said.

'Who?'

'Let's look around for clues,' was Jem's response.

It was Ron who found the clue. At the far edge of the site, an opening led to the valley stream a few yards away. The clear water tinkled over small stones. Here, by the opening, a stick had been thrust into the ground. The upper end had been shaped by a knife into a point. On the point was stuck a piece of paper. Ron's shout of 'Eureka!' brought the other two hastening to him. He took the paper off the stick. It had been folded in three. On the outside, scrawled by a blunt pencil, were the words: 'Open up and see if you're rite'. Ron opened the paper and they read*: I bin expecting you, but I can't wait. Your friend, B.*

'Benjy! Just who I thought,' Jem exclaimed triumphantly.

'Come on, Sherlock Holmes, explain yourself to us poor Dr Watsons,' said Harold.

As they walked to the farm, Jem explained that there had been something about the way the figure on the other side of the valley looked around that had reminded him of someone. It hadn't been until last night that the image of Benjy turning his head had suggested who it was. Thinking that Benjy wouldn't have got much further down the valley yesterday, he had looked for signs of Benjy's breakfast fire. If Harold and Ron hadn't insisted on cooking bacon and sausages, they would have got to Benjy's site on time. Still, if they went for an exploration of the area, they could keep a look-out for him.

As they neared the farm, a sight met their eyes which Ron proclaimed as incredible. Dot was astride a pony being led around a field. She waved excitedly to them. They came up to a fence and waited until she came round.

'This is Bertha. She's teaching me to ride. Bertha, this is Ron, my brother, and this is Harold and Jem.'

Bertha smiled. 'Hello. The three musketeers! Or is it two musketeers and D'Artagnan?'

'If you mean, who's the leader of the expedition, it's Jem,' said Harold generously. 'But I don't think he's as dashing as D'Artagnan.'

Bertha studied Jem's face with an intensity which made him uneasy.

'No, but there's something about his face which suggests he doesn't mind a bit of danger.'

In his turn, Jem looked at Bertha. She had black hair which fell to her shoulders in untidy curls. She had rosy cheeks and very dark eyes – it was difficult to say what colour. She was a little taller than him.

'My Dad wants to see you – he wonders what you're going to do today. Dot's blisters are getting better, but Mum thinks she shouldn't do much walking. I'm going to look after her – we'll have a bit more riding, then collect the eggs and do other things around the farm. You're invited for tea – about four o'clock.'

'I've 'eard about 'im,' Mr Whittle said when Jem had announced his identification of the stranger on the other side of the valley. 'Use to 'ave a reputation as a poacher. Weren't much liked by farmers. But I 'eard that e's reformed 'imself a bit since war started. If 'e's a friend of yours, 'e can't be that bad. Nah, I expect you lads wants to do a bit of exploring today. There's an old quarry and some exposed rocks up yonder. I'll show you on my map.'

The quarry and the rocks proved good value, offering scope for some climbing and for hide and seek as German parachutists and Home Guards. Pausing for their snack on the edge of the quarry, they surveyed a wide landscape. Jem and Harold debated which dips in the undulating moor might be Briggen Clough, where they had camped with Jem's Dad, and which Ashden Clough where Benjy had sheltered. They fancied they could make out the low buildings at the army range. They got back to the farm in time for tea.

Mrs Whittle was not very talkative, but Bertha made up for that. She kept addressing Jem as D'Artagnan, and Harold and Ron as Porthos and Athos. Jem felt that she was making fun of him, and regretted that he was not familiar with 'The Three Musketeers' by Dumas, though there was a copy on the shelves at home. He was at a loss how to turn the tables on her. Mr Whittle, perhaps sensing that Jem was embarrassed, turned the conversation to Benjy. Anxious to shine a bit, Jem took courage and told them about Benjy as St Erewold and as Father Christmas. Everyone laughed as he described how Benjy as Erewold kept saying 'pesky vobissums' instead of 'pax vobiscum', and how Jem had to come to his rescue when Father Christmas had forgotten whether pink parcels were for boys or girls. He would have liked Bertha to know how he had helped to rescue Benjy from drowning, but shrank from appearing to boast. Also, he felt rather guilty at painting Benjy as a figure of fun.

'We're laughing at him, but he's deep. And it took courage, after his solitary life, to take on those roles. In any case, he's given up wandering like a tramp – at least until the war's over. He's anxious to do his bit. So he helps Farmer Ackroyd. He's a good friend to us lads.'

'Yes, it takes all sorts. And you can't judge by appearances,' Mrs Whittle commented. 'Remember that other tramp, Jim? What was his name – "Rick"? – I merely gave him a cup of tea outside. But he came back a mile to tell us that some of our sheep had escaped through a broken fence.'

It had been a grand tea, Jem concluded, looking round the table when the plate of scones had been emptied. Everyone seemed content. Bertha had quietened down, and was talking to Dot about horses. Ron was telling Mr Whittle about his Dad joining the Air Force. Harold had discovered that Mrs Whittle was a Methodist and had heard his father preach: such a thoughtful sermon, she had said. Jem was reminded of those times around the kitchen table at Cop Top Farm when a pleasant harmony seemed to reign. There must be something good about farming, he thought.

They were back at the camp site, with Dot. Though made very welcome at the farm, and much as she liked Bertha, Dot was determined not to miss this opportunity to sample camp life. With plasters on what remained of the blisters, she could now walk without much discomfort. All four climbed trees in the dell and imagined themselves on the watch for German invaders. Despite a large tea, they found that they had appetites after all. They made a fire, boiled potatoes and mashed them with corned beef. Dot was given the job of pressing the mixture into balls and then frying them. Darkness was falling as they sat around the fire.

'I think we'll have to take Dot as cook whenever we want to go camping,' Harold said.

Dot wasn't sure this was the sort of compliment she wanted. Wouldn't it be better to be appreciated for what she was than merely as a cook?

Jem came to her aid. 'You did well to keep up with us yesterday, and to keep going for some time after those blisters came.'

Dot beamed at him and blushed a little

Suddenly their quiet content was startled. A noise of footsteps.A shout: 'Ahoy there, my hearties!' And into the circle of firelight stepped a dark figure.

'Benjy!' Jem shouted with relief, having feared some unknown marauder.

'Hello kids! Thought I'd pay you a visit.'

Benjy eased his pack off his back and found a comfortable seat against a tree.

'I set off this morning for a spot on t'moors above Oldham – that's why I left early. Did yer find my message?'

They nodded.

'Good lads. But I decided to come back 'ere and have a yarn with yer. I bet you're still mystified by yesterday, eh?'

'I guessed it was you, Benjy, but not till much later on,' Jem said. 'And we still don't know how Ron's rucksack appeared.'

Benjy chortled. He explained that he had thought it was time he had a little holiday. Mr Ackroyd agreed. Then he had heard from Alice about the boys' planned expedition. That had put him in mind of coming this way en route to the other side of the moors.

Jem had forgotten that they had mentioned their plans to Alice. But her face sprang into his mind.

'I wish I could come. But you wouldn't want a mere girl!' she had said with a slight smile.

'Dot's coming.'

'Well, she'll have her brother to look after her.'

It had been on the tip of Jem's tongue to say that he would look after her like a brother. Fortunately, Alice had continued. 'I couldn't anyway. Mum wouldn't let me. She has some old-fashioned notions. Tell me about it when you come back. And don't get up to mischief!'

Jem remembered how she had uttered these words in mock seriousness. His venture down the alleyways of memory was interrupted by Benjy stirring the fire into a blaze.

'Believe me, I didn't intend following yer. But when I spotted yer, I thought to myssen: "I'll 'ave a bit of fun with 'em". So I pretended I were being followed. Then, when you no doubt thought I were 'iding, I were observing yer with Mr Ackroyd's field glasses that I'd borrowed. I saw yer stop and examine Dot's feet – are they better now, luv? Then I saw yer put a rucksack in t'bracken. I guessed you'd 'ave left a sign of some kind. So I went back round t'ead of valley and got on to your path. I found the sign alright and came on after. I seen yer go into t'farm, so I left rucksack where you'd see it.'

'It was very thoughtful of you,' Ron said. 'It was mine – we'd 'ave 'ad a long slog up to get it.'

'One thing I don't understand,' Harold added. 'Why did you think of leaving a message for us? How did you know we – or Jem – would suspect it was you?'

'I were conceited enough to think yer might associate a good turn wi' me.'

Benjy looked round at them all, with a satisfied smile. His little game had turned out perfectly.

'But, while we're enjoying ourselves, there's a war on. My pal, Rick, who lives in Homefield, tells me there's going to be a big exercise between their platoon and Althwaite's.'

'Did you say "Rick"?' Jem asked. 'Mrs Whittle mentioned a tramp – sorry, Benjy, a wanderer - with that name.'

'That'll be 'im. But e's domesticated now – settled down with a wife who keeps 'im in order. e's in the Homefield platoon.'

An idea stole into Jem's mind. 'Where do they have their meetings, Benjy?'

'In t' sports 'ut on the way to Bruddersford.'

Benjy noticed Jem taking in the information carefully.

'Now, look 'ere, young Jem. If yer get up to summat, I'll deny ever 'aving told yer that!'

They turned in, Harold and Jem welcoming the greater space in their tent now that Ron was sharing with Dot. Benjy had found a place for his sleeping bag in the bracken above the dell.

'Harold – you awake?'

'What is it?' came the sleepy reply.

'What about spying on the Homefield platoon – see if we can get some information about their plans for the exercise?'

'Oh, no! Not another of your schemes, Jem!'

'Well, it was just an idea. Good night!'

15 ESPIONAGE

Jem, Harold and Ron rested under the bridge, backs against an arch. They sat in the shade, watching the reflections from the river dance over the stonework. It was a hot afternoon, a week after their return from the camping expedition. Dot was not with them.

'She's becoming more independent – doesn't want always to be hanging around me,' Ron explained. 'It's a good thing. She wouldn't miss this opportunity of going back to Intake Farm. Mr Ackroyd's taken 'er and Alice. What Dot wants is to see Bertha and ride the pony.'

Jem's imagination was suddenly alight: Alice and Bertha together. What a contrast: one fair and quiet, the other dark and vivacious. He had a longing to be there. Raq's barking brought him back to the present. A moorhen had thoughtlessly come too close, and Raq had jumped into the water. The moorhen skittered over the surface to safety. Raq swam downstream to where the bank was lower, climbed out, shook himself and returned to the arch where he sat, panting.

'Silly dog – never learn will you?' said Harold, scratching him behind the ears.

'It's her nature,' Jem commented. 'Just think – over generations, spaniels have been bred to retrieve water fowl.'

'Like men 'ave been bred to fight,' Ron said.

'That's evolution, isn't it?' Harold asked.

'Talking of fighting,' Jem said. 'What about that idea of mine of you and me, Harold, spying on the Homefield platoon?'

'Oh dear, I was just enjoying this holiday. Does war have to spoil everything?'

'What's this idea?' Ron asked.

'Another of Jem's hair-brained schemes – likely to have us up before a court martial if we're nabbed!'

'What's it all about?'

'Well, it can't involve you, Ron,' Jem said. 'It's OK for Harold and me – we'd just get told off, or given some unwelcome jobs to do. But you might be sent back to Hull.'

'Well, tell us anyway. I might 'ave some ideas.'

Jem reminded Ron of what Benjy had said about a Home Guard exercise involving the Althwaite and Homefield platoons.

'We'd better reconnoitre the sports hut in Homefield to see whether we might be able to overhear their discussions. But first we need to know when the exercise is going to be. Let's go and see Sergeant Wright. We ought to tell him, anyway, that we didn't see any suspicious characters on our trip.'

'Apart from Benjy, you mean,' Ron added.

George Wright eased himself from underneath a tractor and wiped oily hands on a rag.

'Hullo lads! Come to see the blacksmith or the Home Guard sergeant?'

Informed it was the latter, he motioned them to find seats amongst the litter of ironmongery. He listened with interest to their account of the expedition. He smiled when Jem related Benjy's pretence of being followed and his retrieval of the rucksack.

'Ought to be in the platoon, that fellow – though I doubt whether 'e'd be disciplined enough.'

Jem tried to make his inquiry about the exercise a matter of simple curiosity.

'I don't know 'ow you've learnt that there's to be an exercise. But on operations, my lips are sealed. And you'll find the same with other members of the platoon. Now, I must get on. Let me know if you see any suspicious characters about.'

The boys were disappointed. They had drawn a blank, and didn't know where to turn next. Dejectedly they trudged towards the river. Ron broke the silence.

'What about that queer woman who's supposed to know everything?'

'Ma Hibbert - Ron, you're a genius!' Jem exclaimed.

'So, can I be involved?'

'But think of the risk you'd run.'

'Yes, but Althwaite's been good for Dot and me. I'd like to give summat in return.'

Jem and Harold agreed that Ron could take part, but his role would have to be a relatively safe one.

The following morning the three boys made their way to Up Bye. Jem did not feel anything like as nervous as when he had visited Ma Hibbert during the investigation into the church burglary. He recollected that, on the occasion of the book collection, she had invited him to come up again, with Harold. Ron, however, *was* nervous. The odd tale he had heard about her had invoked in his mind the face of an ogress.

The three black cats were sunning themselves on the doorstep. The front door was open. So was the back door leading to the garden. Looking down the connecting passage, they could see Ma Hibbert sitting there. Without seeming to raise her head, she called out: 'Come through lads! The cats won't bite!'

They entered the passage. A gust of wind blew the front door to with a bang. They jumped and hurried along. Ma Hibbert was sitting in the shade of the sycamore tree. She transferred her sewing to a round table.

'I been wondering when Jem Murgatroyd and Harold Bright might come and see me. It's summer holidays and they've plenty of time, leastways when they're not working in the allotments or roaming about the countryside. And this must be Ron, from Hull. What a pity you haven't brought your little sister. Now, one of you go into the kitchen and fetch four glasses from the shelf above the sink, and the other two lift that bench near the table.'

They settled themselves on the bench. Ron looked at the little garden at the base of the cliff in wonder. The only sound was that of water trickling into the pool. A blackbird was drinking at the shallow end, a bottle was almost immersed at the other.

'I see you've noticed the bottle, Ron. Will you do the honours, luv?' When the glasses were filled with Dandelion and Burdock, she continued, 'Now lads, what's the news?'

'I thought you knew all the news Mrs Hibbert,' Jem said.

'*Miss,* not Mrs, though I thanks you for the courtesy. I daresay I know a lot, but I don't conjure it out of thin air. Tell me what the scouts have been up to and how you liked Intake Farm.'

Jem was surprised that she knew about their expedition. He and Harold described the scouts' attempt to learn signalling with Morse, and gave a sketch of their recent adventure.

'Lively girl, that Bertha. She'll be a catch for someone one of these days,' Ma Hibbert commented.

There was a pause. Jem was wondering how to introduce the subject of the Home Guard exercise. Ma Hibbert's penetrating gaze scanned the faces of the three boys, who were sipping their drinks and trying to feel at ease.

'Now, what I'm wondering is whether you've come up here just to see me, or whether you're in need of information?'

'Er...a bit of both,' Jem faltered.

'A tactful answer. But without at least the lure of Dandelion and Burdock, would the cream of Althwaite's young men have come to visit this old lady with her rheumaticky joints and her face ravaged by time?'

Harold looked at the round, rosy face with its blue eyes. 'I think you're still bonny Ma...Ma'am,' he blurted out. He turned red and wished he'd been more discreet. But he meant what he had said.

Ma Hibbert opened her mouth wide in a laugh, thereby revealing her only disfigurement: gaps where the upper incisor teeth should have been.

'If you flatter like that at your age, Harold Bright, you'll go far!'

She looked at the pool. 'As a matter of fact, Harold, you put me in mind of someone I knew a long, long time ago. He made that.'

She pointed to the little wooden boat with the clay model of Mr Toad reading a book. Was it his imagination, or did Harold see tears starting to form? Miss Hibbert lowered her eyes and took her sewing off the table. It was a long strip of cloth, about nine inches wide. The part which was full of embroidery hung down into a basket on the ground.

'This here's my diary. Let's see, now, June… May. Here we are: see these letters? There's "JM" for Jem Murgatroyd and a picture of a book. That was the collection for the war effort. Then, if we go back further…' She pulled more of the strip from the basket. 'Here's January: "JM" and "HB" and pictures of the church and a helmet. That was the burglary. Had to leave that investigation incomplete, didn't you dearies? Now, if we go forward again, just here I'll put a note of your kind visit today.'

Jem noticed something that puzzled him. 'But Ma…Miss Hibbert, you've already sewn some letters and pictures further on. Is that the future?'

'Nothing much escapes you does it, Jem? Ay, them's my presentiments. If they don't turn out right, I pick the threads out.'

'How often do you 'ave to pick them out,' asked Ron, who was becoming fascinated by this old lady.

'Ah, that would be telling, wouldn't it? Trade secret, you might say.'

'Er...is there anything there about the Home Guard?' Harold asked.

'Let's see. No, nothing in that quarter. Why do you ask?'

'Well, we wondered if you might know when the exercise with Homefield platoon is going to take place.'

'Aha, so it's not just the Dandelion and Burdock, or even my bonny face! No, I don't luv. But seeing as how you're fond of me, I'll make enquiries. One of you come back tomorrow afternoon.'

'You won't say that we were asking?'

'Don't worry, "discretion" is my second name.'

'May we ask what your first name is, Miss Hibbert?' Jem asked.

'Julia, my dear.'

Jem had promised to help One-Leg Tim at his allotment the following afternoon, and Harold had to go on errands for his mother. Ron volunteered to return to Up Bye. He was keen to take Dot to see this remarkable lady. The boys agreed to meet at 4 o'clock in the shed in Jem's back garden.

It was 4.30 before there was the sound of running feet. Dot, closely followed by Ron, burst through the side passage into the garden.

'Look Jem and Harold!' Dot shouted in excitement. 'See what that nice lady's given me.'

She unwrapped the paper around a cardboard box to reveal a china doll. Some of her front hair was missing, so that she seemed to be going bald. But otherwise she seemed perfect in her long, silk dress fringed by lace.

'She said she'd had it when she was a girl. And Ron's got the boat to mend.'

'Yes, when I 'ad a close look, I could see the bottom was rotten. So I offered to repair it. See 'ere.'

Out of the pond, it did seem to be in a sorry state.

'Sorry we're late,' Ron continued. 'But Ma…Miss Hibbert was being so pleasant to Dot – telling 'er about going to school in an apron and doing sums on slates.'

'And helping her father deliver the milk – measuring it out into people's jugs,' Dot added.

Jem smiled at Dot's excited state. What a different creature she was from the withdrawn, suspicious evacuee he had first met!

'This social visiting is all very well, but have you got the information?' he asked.

'Week on Sunday, starting at 2 o'clock,' Ron answered.

'So they can have their Sunday dinners first,' commented Harold.

'There's something else,' Ron said. 'Remember she said someone she'd known a long time ago 'ad made the boat? Well, when Dot and me went inside while she searched for the doll, I noticed an old photograph – in that sepia colour – of a young soldier.'

'Perhaps he was in the Boer War, like One–Leg Tim?' Harold suggested.

'Perhaps they were sweethearts, and he didn't come back,' Jem added.

'Oh, that's so sad!' said Dot, her face clouding over.

The great difficulty that Jem foresaw over the attempt to spy on the Homefield platoon was the time of the year. It was summer. With British summertime, it would not begin to get dark until late evening. The operation had to be undertaken in daylight. He made a reconnaissance visit, noted the time of the platoon's meetings from the village notice board, and went to the sports field. Boys were kicking a ball about. He didn't want to be noticed, so he walked around the outside, behind a hedge, till he got to the back of the hut. There was a gap in the hedge, and he slipped through. He dared not go around the front in case he was spotted. Separated from the brick hut by a few feet was a small wooden shed. He would have liked to investigate it, but that would have meant making himself visible to the boys on the field. At the back of the hut the only windows were about five feet up – long and narrow with frosted glass. The only hope for the spies was that, on a hot evening, the windows might be open and voices might be overheard. He went back through the hedge and looked around. Rough, uncultivated ground sloped up to a row of houses about a hundred yards away, with here and there a bush big enough to hide behind. To the right, there was a dent in the slope – a slight depression, perhaps the result of a small quarry years ago. Jem went up to inspect. It was surrounded by trees, but down in the bottom, about ten feet below the edge, the ground was clear. Charred wood and ashes showed that someone had had a fire. Ideas jostled in Jem's mind as he made his way home as inconspicuously as possible.

What Jem called a planning meeting was held the

next morning in a hut in the Manse garden. Ron, who was good at English, was given the job of secretary and provided with a writing pad and pencil. Jem explained about the windows. If they were shut, the only possibility of overhearing what was said inside the hut would be if the front door was open, but that would be unlikely. They needed a second string to their bow. With some pride, but also with some nervousness about how it would be received, Jem launched his big idea. They could light a fire in the old quarry pit and create a diversion. This would attract the men out of the hut, thus giving someone time to get inside and look at their plans. As Jem had feared, the idea met with scorn from Harold and doubts from Ron.

'How would a fire get them out?' Harold asked. 'They might not know there was a fire. Even if they did, they might just send two or three to investigate.'

'And,' Ron added, 'supposing they all left the hut, it wouldn't be long before they were back. Whoever went inside wouldn't 'ave much time to look at their plans.'

'He might be caught red-handed. Then we'd be in the soup!'

Both Harold and Ron promised themselves they would not volunteer for such a daft mission.

Jem had part of the answer. The fire would have to be accompanied by an alarming noise. What they needed was fireworks – bangers going off in or near the fire. Harold was still in scornful mood. 'And where are we going to get fireworks? We're nowhere near November the fifth. Anyway, with a war on, they won't be for sale.'

Jem recalled the words of Jesus that had been the

text for a sermon in chapel recently: 'O ye of little faith!' How true it was!

'Got an idea!' said Ron as a glimmer of light dawned. 'Dot was wanting to take some friends to visit the tower. So I went up to the Hall and saw Mrs McAlister. She said it was out of bounds. The Home Guard are using it to store ammunition.'

'Ammunition? We're going to be killing the Homefield platoon now are we?' Harold expostulated.

'No, don't you see? With this exercise coming up, they're bound to 'ave some fireworks – thunderflashes, to make pretend.'

'Ron, you're a genius!' Jem exclaimed. 'Hull must be a great place if minds like yours come out of it!'

Harold was still not shifted from his role as devil's advocate. 'We'd still have to find a way of getting into the tower without being noticed. It's bound to be locked. And I bet they don't leave the key under a stone nowadays.'

'Remember the keyboard in the Hall kitchen?' Jem said. 'That's where it was when you and me paid a visit to Hon Peter.'

Harold remembered: Peter had taken both the tower and store-room keys from the board before showing them the Dandelion helmet and other things hidden in the tower.

'OK, so how are we going to get the key, or keys?'

That was something that Jem didn't have an immediate answer to. Harold went into the house for lemonade and biscuits to feed the grey matter. When he returned, he had a more cheerful look on his face.

'My Mum's friendly with Mrs McAlister. They

both run the Women's Bright Hour at the chapel. It's not meeting during the summer, and I heard Mum say the other day it was about time she went up to see Mrs McAlister. I could ask to go with her. Say I want to look around the garden.'

It was Ron's turn to be sceptical. 'I can see you asking, "Please Mrs McAlister, can I borrow the keys to the tower? We just want a few fireworks"!'

'Don't be daft, Ron! I wait for an opportunity to take the keys without being noticed, and ask if I can look around the garden whilst they have a chat. At least, it might work.'

At the end of the discussion, Ron read out the actions he had listed.

H takes keys. J and R meet him at tower. Take 6 bangers.

H returns keys

J collects some wood. H collects oily rags from his Dad's garage.

Meet under bridge at 6 o'clock Thursday evening. R brings matches.

J brings sketch-pad and pencils. H brings flag, bangers and wooden box.

If diversion needed, J waves flag. H and R light fire, then go up slope to Stonefield Terrace. Keep watch.

Afterwards, rally at back of Homefield Mill.

'That's it,' said Jem. 'Just one thing, though. Only me and Harold go into the tower. You stay outside and keep watch, Ron.'

He didn't want to run the risk of Ron accidentally finding the Dandelion family things.

Jem's knees were beginning to get stiff. For nearly half an hour he had been crouching behind a grass mower which was covered by sacking. He was in the shed adjacent to the sports hut, having discovered that it had no door: the front was open to the field. It was a warm evening, and he was perspiring, partly from nervousness. What on earth had he undertaken? But there was no backing out now.

He hadn't had much sleep the previous night, partly from feelings of unease and guilt about what they had done at the tower. Harold had managed to take the keys off the board when Mrs McAlister took his mother upstairs to show her the quilt counterpane she was making. He had been given permission to wander in the garden. He had met Jem and Ron at the tower. They had followed the unofficial route that Jem had taken with Harold and Jonquil when they were going to act out the story of Rapunzel. So much had happened since then that it seemed half a lifetime ago, though it was little more than a year.

Inside the tower, the ground level store-room contained a few rifles and some wooden boxes marked: 'Danger – Ammunition'. The first floor store-room was no different from when Harold and Jem and been taken there by Hon Peter. Hoping they were not going to draw blank, they climbed up to the room at the top. They had last been there when Lorinda had her tea-party. Here they found some boxes of thunderflashes. One was unlocked. They took six, so arranging the rest that the theft would not be obvious. Harold said the worst thing was getting back to find Mrs McAlister and his mother sitting in the back garden. How was he to find an opportunity to nip into the kitchen to replace the keys? He had been invited to join them and drink lemonade. The liquid gave him the inspiration: he asked to go to the lavatory, entered the house and replaced the keys.

Everything had gone to plan so far, but now was the real test. Jem looked at his watch. It was a quarter to seven. Members of the Homefield platoon began arriving. Some were in complete uniform, others in partial uniform, some in their ordinary clothes with arm bands. Some carried rifles, some had walking sticks. From his superior uniform and military bearing, he realised that one of them must be Major Rochester, the platoon commander. He was carrying a briefcase. 'The plans must be in there,' Jem thought. Soon after seven, he heard the sounds of drill: stamping feet, rifles and sticks hitting the floor. Then came a roll call, two members hurried up late and the door was shut.

Jem stole around to the back of the hut. To his great relief, the slim windows were open. He stood on the wooden box, the top of his head just below the bottom of the window. He could hear fairly well. The major ordered 'Stand Easy'. Then there was a report – perhaps by the sergeant – about attendance and last week's parade. The major talked about the importance of some future training in map reading. There was to be a visit to an army range for training in rifle firing and the use of grenades. It was clear from questions, and the tone in which they were asked, that many members were fed up with the delay in providing rifles and full uniforms. At last, they seemed to get down to business, with the major telling the men to gather round. Jem imagined a black-board on which a map was pinned. He began scribbling on his sketch-pad. He gathered that the exercise was to centre on a reservoir. Homefield platoon would be defending the valve tower from which the sluices were operated. The sergeant would command a guard at the reservoir, armed with a Bren Gun (borrowed from the army). Parties of men would be deployed at positions around the reservoir, which Major Rochester referred to as 'Alpha', 'Charlie' and other names. The object was to prevent the Althwaite platoon from penetrating this defensive screen. 'Kills' would be scored by visual sighting from a strong position, followed by the throwing of thunderflashes. Umpires would verify kills. Camouflage was important: those who had helmets were to paint a black stripe down the middle or borrow a hairnet from their wives to put over the helmet so that bits of bracken could be fixed in. The major invited questions. It seemed as though the session - or that part involving the exercise – was drawing to a close. Jem realised that his report would be sadly lacking without information on where the positions with code names were. Plan B had to be put into operation. He got down from the box, went through the hedge, picked up the flag and waved it.

The major was about to embark on the peroration to which he had devoted much thought, designed to raise morale and gear his men up for the exercise. Two loud bangs, coming from behind the hut, interrupted him. What on earth was that? Had German paratroopers arrived? Someone squinting through one of the windows discerned black smoke. A crashed aircraft? There was no time for careful orders. Major Rochester led his men out to whatever awaited them. They rushed through the gap in the hedge, rifles and walking sticks at the ready, and charged up the slope. The oily rags were still making a lot of smoke. Bang! Bang! More of the fireworks went off. Men ducked, as though they were being shot at. 'Take cover,' shouted the major, and men dived for stunted bushes and tufts of grass.

Inside the hut, as well as his trembling fingers would allow, Jem copied on to his sketch-pad the plan on the black-board, noting the Alpha, Charlie and other positions. He was so absorbed in this that he failed for a minute or two to realise that the bangs had stopped. It was time to get out. He had reached the door when he heard voices and a shuffle of feet. It was too late! Where to hide? There was a half-open cupboard, but it seemed rather full of stuff. The only other place was the wash-room and lavatories. He dashed inside. There were two cubicles. He went inside one, slid the bolt and sat on the seat. Never had his heart beat so fast, not even at the sight of the first car when he was keeping watch as the Squire and others removed the Hall gates. He put his head in his hands. This was dreadful! If he was discovered with the incriminating sketch-pad, Major Rochester might order a court martial. He felt the need to relieve himself, dropped his trousers and did so as quietly as possible. Then the funny side of his plight caught hold of him. It was as much as he could do to smother a laugh.

There were angry voices from the room. The major was clearly furious at the interruption, saying that he would get the police on to the rascals, whoever they were. Jem was relieved. Evidently, Harold and

Ron had not been captured. There was the sound of packing up. The platoon was called to attention and dismissed. Men shouted 'Good Night, Sir'. There was some further conversation between the major and, presumably, the sergeant. Then the sound of the door being shut and locked.Jem was at once relieved and aghast. Undiscovered but imprisoned!

He waited five to ten minutes in case someone came back, then entered the room. The windows had been closed, but it was easy enough to open one by standing on a chair. He peered out. There was no sign of Harold or Ron or anyone. The trouble was that the hedge behind the hut was not high enough to hide the windows from the view of people living in the houses at the top of the slope. It would be better to wait until dark before trying to get out. It was now half past eight. It would not be dark for another hour and a half. Could he squeeze through the window anyway? A pointing stick rested below the black-board. He put it up against the window and made a pencil mark to indicate the gap he would have to get through. Then he tried to see how the thickness of his body compared. It was going to be a tight squeeze. He might get stuck. It would be easier if the other two came back to help by pulling him. Surely they would return, when they didn't find him at the rallying place!

After an hour, Jem was getting very bored. He tried to stop himself looking at his watch every few minutes. He had read and re-read the notices about cricket fixtures and teams, and the war posters about Digging for Victory, Healthy Eating, and Careless Talk costing Lives. Suddenly, he heard footsteps at the back of the hut. Who was this?

'Jem, you in there?' Harold's voice was between a whisper and a shout.

'Harold! Yes – got locked in. They didn't know I was here. I'm waiting till it's dark before trying to get through the window. I'll need your help. Don't stick around now.'

'OK, be back when it's dark.'

Jem lay on his bed with just one sheet over him. He was very hot. Sleep seemed a long way away. For the umpteenth time his mind went over the nightmare of the exit from the hut. Standing on the table, he had managed to lever his body up so as to get his head sideways through the window. Desperately, his legs kicked in the air as he tried to force his shoulders and chest through. He had had to get back down on to the table to rest and think.'Take some of your clothes off,' Ron had whispered.

With jacket, trousers, shirt, vest and shoes dropped outside to join the all-important sketch-pad, he had tried again. He got his arms through and the other two pulled as he wriggled. He thought of tales of torture, of bodies being squeezed and suffocated. Several times he had to plead with his pals to stop pulling. Finally, Jem's body had flopped into their arms. Although it seemed blasphemous, Harold couldn't help thinking of pictures he had seen of Jesus' descent from the cross.

When Jem got home, his mother said she had been worried stiff. Where the dickens had he been? Why hadn't he at least told her that the scouts were having a late night exercise (the excuse he thought of on the spur of the moment)? He pleaded that he was dog-tired and got upstairs. He undressed and looked at the scratches and bruises on his chest and stomach. There were others on his back he couldn't see. In the bathroom he dabbed Dettol on the scratches he could reach.

Now, as he sweated under the sheet, his body seemed to burn and ache all over. Would he be well enough in the morning to take the sketch-pad to Hon Peter? If not, Harold would have to go. Of one thing he was sure, Peter was bound to commend the three of them for their initiative. On that satisfactory note, sleep overtook him.

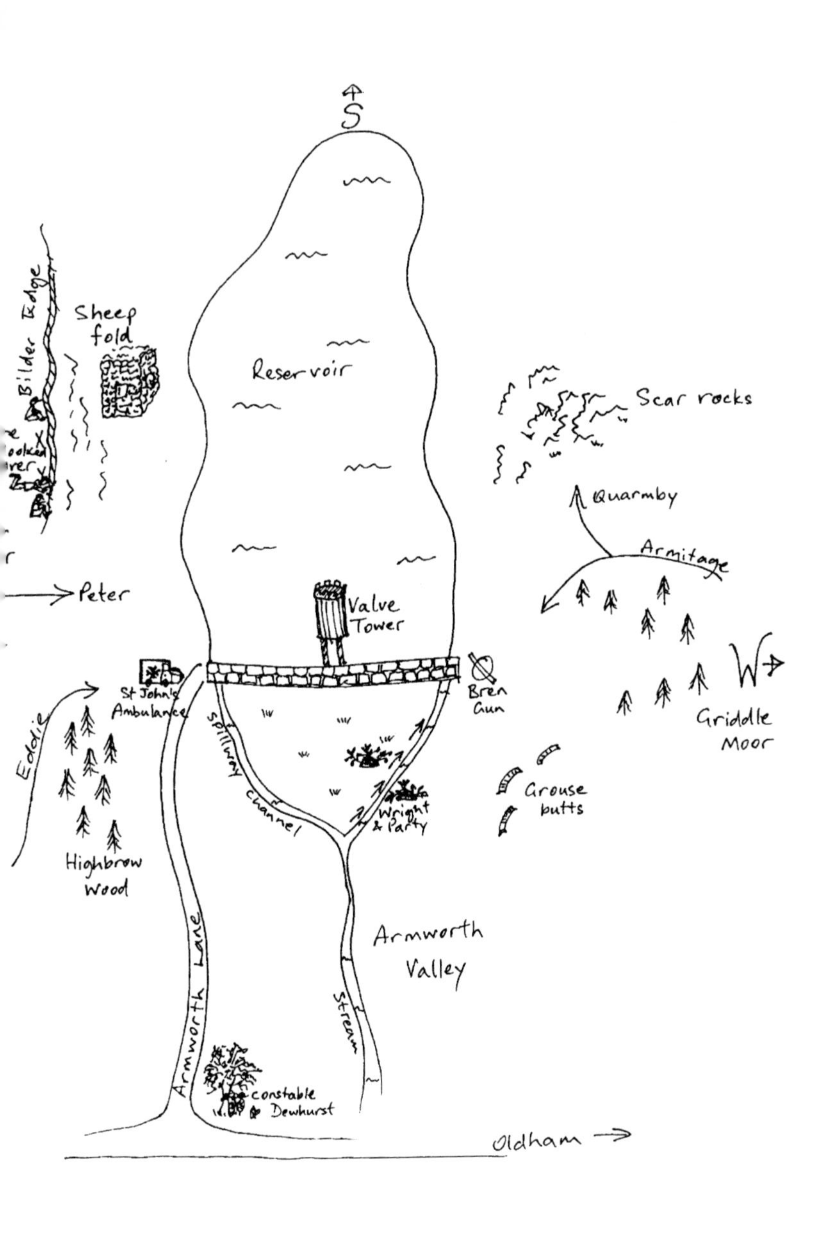
S
Reservoir
Bilder Edge
Sheep fold
Scar rocks
Quarmby
Armitage
Peter
Valve Tower
St John's Ambulance
Bren Gun
W
Griddle Moor
Eddie
Spillway channel
Grouse butts
Wright & Party
Highbrow Wood
Armworth Valley
Armworth Lane
Stream
constable Dewhurst
Oldham
N

16 THE EXERCISE (1)

Jem woke early. Various parts of his body ached, and he felt feverish. It was a great shame. He had been looking forward to observing Hon Peter's delighted surprise and to receiving his congratulations. He just didn't feel like the trek up to the Hall. He would have to delegate to Harold the delivery of the enemy's plans. He heard his mother moving about and began to feel uneasy. If he had to explain everything, she wouldn't share Peter's understanding of how important the operation was.

His mother came into the bedroom, and noticed his flushed face. She felt his brow and got the thermometer from the bathroom.

'Nearly 100. You'll have to stay in bed and have lots to drink. I wonder how you got it?'

She began tidying up the clothes that Jem had taken off.

'What's this? There's blood on your vest, Jem! Let's have a look at you. Take your pyjama jacket off.'

Jem complied reluctantly. He'd been foolish to

think he could have kept his injuries secret from his mother.

'What on earth have you been doing? You've got awful scratches and some bruises on your chest and tummy. Turn over. And your back! Take your trousers off. And bruises on your bottom! Come into the bathroom, young man!'

His mother washed all the scratches and treated them with Dettol.

'I did put some on last night, Mum – those I could reach.'

'Good, we don't want them getting infected.'

Back in the bedroom, his mother sat on the edge of the bed.

'Now, Jem, I want a full explanation. What have you been up to?'

Jem didn't want to worry her unduly, so he left out of his account the theft of the thunderflashes. He explained he had managed to get into the Homefield sports hut when the platoon had gone outside, but they'd come back and he'd hid and then later got out of the narrow window with the help of Harold. He decided not to mention Ron's part in the enterprise.

'Mum, will you take the sketch-pad to Harold, so he can take it up to the Hall? It's a matter of national importance.'

'National importance? How do you make that out?'

'If the Althwaite platoon come out top in the exercise, it'll be good for their morale. They'll be in better shape to deal with German paratroops.'

'What about the morale of the Homefield platoon?'

‘Well, they’ll realize they have to pull their socks up.’

‘There’s something fishy about your logic, Jem. But it’ll do me no harm to go over to the Manse. Now, I don’t want you to think I’m condoning what you’ve been up to. I doubt whether I’ve got to the bottom of it yet. But the first thing is to get you better.’

Nervously, but proudly, Harold presented Hon Peter with the sketch-pad containing the Homefield platoon’s plans for the exercise. Peter at first suspected a prank. But as he listened to Harold’s vivid account of the operation – the signal to light the fire, the platoon’s rush out into the open, how he and Ron had waited anxiously for Jem to appear, their desperate efforts to drag him through the window – he realised that it was true. It had all the hallmarks of a Jem-inspired bit of derring-do. It was a crazy idea, but the lads had pulled it off, though the leader was now in bed with a temperature. It was an enterprise that would not have disgraced his ancestors, he thought. But, to Harold’s surprise, he didn’t immediately take the sketch-pad. It lay on the desk between them. Was it, Peter wondered, a heaven-sent gift or a sinister temptation?

‘This is going to need thinking about, Harold. It might be unfair of me to take advantage of inside knowledge. Better put the temptation out of arm’s reach, whilst I ponder. Would you take the sketch-pad to Mrs McAlister and ask her to lock it away somewhere. I’ll sleep on the matter.’

He looked at Harold, whose eagerness had given way to disappointment.

'I can see you look crestfallen. No doubt you'd expected me to be overjoyed. Please understand – I do appreciate your efforts, though I must say I'm worried about the risks you ran. Now, tell that adventurous captain of yours to look after himself and get better.'

Hon Peter did not sleep well that night. He was faced with what seemed the most difficult decision of his life so far. By comparison, adjudicating as chairman of the bench of magistrates was child's play. Even weighing up whether he had the courage to propose to Lorinda had been far less taxing. His mind went over the pros and cons.

On the one hand, his platoon was badly in need of a boost to morale. The men constantly complained about the lack of uniforms and proper equipment. Also, the platoon was only half the size of Homefield's. Morever, if this was a real contest, he wouldn't think twice about using information obtained from the enemy. And the exercise was intended to simulate what might really happen. Not to use the information would be to ignore an element of reality in the situation. Or was that getting too philosophical?

On the other hand, the information had been got by underhand methods, by trickery. It would be like taking on Homefield platoon with one arm tied behind their backs. Would there be the same satisfaction in beating them as there would be if they were taken on fair and square? Also, a win by underhand means would not be a real test of his men – or of his leadership.

At one stage during the night, he woke and remembered a disturbing dream. He and Jem Murgatroyd were appearing before a tribunal chaired by Lieutenant-Colonel Fitzpatrick. The cricket pavilion seemed a strange venue until he heard the charge was one of not playing cricket. As he stared gloomily into the dark, he wondered what his ancestors would think.

It wasn't until Peter had taken the top off his second boiled egg at breakfast that he managed to come to a decision.

'All's fair in love and war,' he said to himself, realising at the same time that it wasn't.

'What's that you said, dear?' asked his mother who was stirring syrup into her porridge.

'I said the weather's fairing up for the war – I mean the exercise on Sunday.'

'You make sure you take your waterproofs, anyway.'

'Yes mother. Ah, Mrs McAlister' – she had entered the room with a rack of toast – 'would you please let me have the sketch-pad that Harold Bright brought yesterday.'

'Just as well you asked, sir. I was going to put it into the pig waste.'

'You put it into the pig waste!?'

'No sir, I was merely thinking of doing so. I'll get it.'

Hon Peter noticed that in his alarm he had allowed egg yolk to drip on to his copy of The Times. That had never happened before. Just supposing the pad *had* gone into the waste – it would have been one solution to his dilemma!

Jem had been allowed out of bed. He was in the front room reading 'Biggles flies South', when his mother ushered Hon Peter in.

'Don't get up, Master Jem. And you may like to stay, Mrs Murgatroyd, to hear what I have to say to your son.'

He declined a cup of tea, saying he had many things to do.

'So, how is my secret agent getting on?'

He turned to Mrs Murgatroyd.

'I suppose he has come clean about what he was up to?'

'That he has! If ever a lad was born to worry his mother, it's Jem. Anyway, his temperature's nearly normal, and his scratches are not infected. But I didn't sleep for being anxious. And what I'm going to tell his Dad, I don't know.'

Jem felt suddenly cold. Surely, Dad didn't need to be told anything?

'Jem seems to have a power for preventing sleep. I had a wakeful night, too,' said his visitor. 'However, apart from seeing how the sleuth is getting on, I wanted to let Jem know what I've decided to do. Normally, in these sorts of exercises, it wouldn't do to make use of information obtained by subterfuge. But, for this one occasion, I'm going to avail myself of what was discovered. For two reasons: first, to offset the disadvantage that my platoon is only half the size of Homefield. The second reason is more personal. Although there was a lot of support for me at that public meeting when the leadership was discussed, I sense that the men are still sceptical whether I've got what it takes. They believe I have the courage, but they're not sure I've got the sense of strategy and tactics needed. I was only in the Pay Corps in the last war. But

Major Rochester was in the infantry. If I can gain their confidence with a convincing win over Homefield, it will be a happier and more effective platoon. I'm being frank with you, Jem, because I appreciate the valiant efforts you, Harold and Ron have made. You'd do well in the Resistance, if it came to that – which I'm sure it won't.' Peter leant forward. 'But – and this is why I asked your mother to be present – there's to be no more of this risk-taking on behalf of the Althwaite platoon. For one thing, I don't want you getting into trouble. Next time, you might be caught! And, another thing, I don't want to be presented with such a dilemma again! Now, Mrs Murgatroyd, may I suggest you don't bother your husband with this little escapade. If you'll let me have his address, I'll write a short letter saying in general terms that Jem has been helpful.'

'That's very thoughtful of you,' Mrs Murgatroyd said. 'As for the future, this young man is going to have to be more frank with me about his projects!'

Hon Peter got up to leave, and then had a second thought.

'There was one aspect of Harold's story that puzzled me. I don't understand how just setting light to a fire got the Homefield platoon out of the hut. How was their attention attracted to it?'

Jem swallowed. It was a question he dreaded having to answer.

'Sir, can we regard that as one of the tricks of the trade?'

Hon Peter looked doubtful, and then smiled. 'Something out of "Biggles", eh?' he said, glancing at the book on Jem's lap. 'Alright. But obey your mother's advice about getting fit.'

'Best of luck for tomorrow, sir.'
'It's the other side that needs the luck!'

Hon Peter and Sergeant Wright had familiarized themselves with the terrain during the fortnight before the exercise. Approaching the reservoir upArmworth Lane, on the eastern side of the valley, you came out from a plantation of fir trees and saw it half a mile away: a V-shaped, sloping bank of grass, covering the earth and stone of the dam. It was topped by a wall of gritstone blocks. In summer, only a trickle of water emerged from the sluices at the bottom. On either side of the grass slope were spillway channels which allowed the water in the dam to overflow when it reached a high level. The channels were paved with blocks in a series of steps, and the overflow was confined by walls until it reached the stream at the bottom.

Beside Armworth Lane, there was another approach to the dam: a track off Griddle Moor which descended a wooded side valley and emerged at the western end of the dam wall. The objective, the valve tower, stood in the water near the middle of the dam wall, and was connected to it by a narrow walkway bridge.

Since Hon Peter could not use superior force to rush the dam, he had to resort to a surreptitious approach. He and Alistair had ruined a rockery lovingly tended by Peter's mother by creating a model of Armworth Valley. Every morning for the past week he had surveyed it before breakfast, trying to work out a plan. He tried to imagine how Major Rochester would expect the attack to develop. The Althwaite platoon being small, Rochester might think they would stick to one side of the valley. But then he would realise that this was what they would expect him to think. So he would assume that they would plump, instead, for an approach on both sides. But they might expect him to foresee that too, so a united approach up one side would be best. Peter gave up the attempt to put himself in Rochester's shoes: it was too complicated.

The information that Harold had brought had, however, simplified the task enormously. He knew that from the high points occupied by the Homefield platoon any approach to the sides of the dam wall was likely be spotted. The side valley from Griddle Moor would, anyway, be open to ambush. He decided to distract the enemy's forces at either end of the dam wall, whilst Sergeant Wright and three picked men climbed up from the bed of the stream to the dry spillway channel on the western side. Having climbed up the channel, they would be able to get on to the dam wall and dash to the valve tower.

'Do you think it'll work, Alistair?' Hon Peter asked after demonstrating his plan with stones and sticks.

'Ay, it's guid enough. But you ken the saying:

The best laid schemes o' mice and men

Gang aft a-gley.'

'What's that? Oh, your favourite poet, Robbie Burns. Well, I hope *my* scheme doesn't go awry!'

At the final platoon meeting before the exercise, Hon Peter explained the strategy with the help of a map, a black-board and coloured chalks. The platoon was divided into sections, and their appointed leaders were kept back for further briefing. Hon Peter left the meeting thinking that he had at least done his best.

Colonel Fitzpatrick had laid down the rules for the engagement. Not that he had had an entirely free hand. The local fire service had objected that the use of thunderflashes on the dry moor was a recipe for fires. One rule, therefore, was that if one side saw a fire breaking out, it should wave a black and white chequered flag. That would signal a temporary truce in the area, whilst men from both sides suppressed the outbreak. Another rule was that a kill by rifle fire would be within a radius of 100 yards. That of the Bren Gun (a light machine gun) would be 200 yards. Its range was in fact greater than that, but Fitzpatrick restricted its pretended use so as to be fairer to Althwaite which didn't have such a gun.

At Church on the Sunday morning, Miss Arbuthnot added her own petition to the prayers said by the priest. 'Oh God, strengthen the Althwaite platoon. Let them not be defeated.' After all, she thought, if God could favour the Israelites, why not Althwaite? But if God did not lead the platoon to victory, she planned to interrogate not Him, but the Honourable Peter Danellion-Smith.

A kestrel hovering over Armworth reservoir early on Sunday afternoon would have spotted human ants moving into positions on both sides of the water. If it had stereoscopic vision, it would have noticed that most of the ants were settling down on high points. Major Rochester had divided his platoon into seven sections. Two were at either ends of the dam wall. One of these had the Bren Gun borrowed from the Army.

Two were on high points on the western side of the reservoir: Scar Rocks and some grouse butts, the latter slightly downstream of the dam. Two were opposite on the other side: at a disused sheepfold and on the edge of Highbrow Wood. The remaining section guarded the most likely approach to the dam: the wooded valley on the western side which would provide cover for the attackers.

What the kestrel would not have been able to see was the high spirits of the men. This was their first big exercise in the open. It was a beautiful July afternoon. Some of them had been Boy Scouts years ago. It was like being on one of those 'wide games' which had been so exciting at the time. They had confidence in their leader, his plans and their numbers. They possessed the vantage points. So long as they kept a good look-out, the Althwaite platoon didn't stand a chance.

Half an hour after he first observed the human ants, the hovering kestrel would have noted that they were all still, apart from one who strode up and down the dam wall, pausing to scan the scene through his binoculars. This was Major Rochester. Although he exuded confidence, he was nervous. That Danellion-Smith was an odd chap. In the pre-exercise conference they had had with Colonel Fitzpatrick, he had joked about what was a serious exercise. The Althwaite platoon couldn't use force, since they were much smaller. Smith would have some trick up his sleeve. But, for the life of him, Rochester could not guess what it might be.

Constable Dewhurst was not a happy man. After the exertion of working on his allotment that morning, it would have been just the afternoon for a snooze in a deck-chair under the sycamore in his back garden. Instead, he was at the spot on the Oldham road where the lane to Armworth Valley turned off. For a week, notices on the village notice-board, in the church porch and at the post office had warned that the valley was out of bounds on Sunday to anyone not in the Home Guard, the police or the rescue services, and a map had delineated the area. As if that was not enough, Constable Dewhurst had been ordered by Sergeant Milford at Bruddersford to spend this hot afternoon guarding the entrance to the valley. He propped his bike against a hawthorn tree, hung his helmet on the handle-bars, unfastened the top of his tunic and sat in the shade of the tree. Beside him he placed a stone bottle of ginger beer. He was feeling contemptuous of Sergeant Milford. Anyone wanting to get to the area of the exercise could avoid the lane by following footpaths. There were certain lads in Althwaite whom he could imagine doing just that. He wouldn't have put it past some of them to have been involved in that incident in Homefield the other evening. Residents of Stonefield terrace, above the sports field, had been alarmed by bangs and a fire, and had seen boys disappearing as the Home Guard went to investigate. In its Saturday edition, the Bruddersford Examiner had said it was disgraceful for the Home Guard to be distracted by a prank, and had urged readers to be vigilant against troublemakers.

Constable Dewhurst was right in imagining that certain lads would be on their way. But Jem was not amongst them. Naturally, he was keen to see what went on, but his mother was not satisfied that he had got over the feverish attack. The group consisted of Harold, Charlie Foster, Will Dicehurst and Ron. After running risks recently, Harold was concerned to keep on the right side of the law. So he insisted that they keep outside of the prohibited area. That meant a long trek on a lane across Bilder Moor above the eastern side of Armworth Valley, then across country to Bilder Edge, from which they should get a view of what was happening.

If the kestrel had swooped low over the sides of the reservoir an hour after first sighting the human ants, it would have seen that some were adopting postures that were far from warlike. Not having entrenching tools, they had to make do with what natural cover there was available. The men at Scar Rocks were the most exposed, as the rocks themselves were low, and the ground immediately around was grass cropped short by sheep. They lay in a semicircle a few yards below the rocks, where bracken began to grow. Two kept watch, whilst the other four relaxed and drowsed in the hot sun. At the sheep-fold, rifles and walking sticks were poked through chinks in the stone walls. At the grouse butts, two men leaned against the turf tops, whilst the others sat inside, their backs against the walls. The section at the edge of Highbrow Wood was the most to be envied, since it was in the shade of fir trees.

Constable Dewhurst was aroused from a doze by the noise of a vehicle turning into the lane. He jumped up, snatched his helmet from the bicycle and held his hand up. In the front were two men in black and white uniforms and peak caps. On each side of the vehicle was a white Maltese cross. He recognized the St John's ambulance.

'Straight up for Armworth Dam,' he said in reply to a question.

The van lurched off up the bumpy lane. Only when it had disappeared from sight did it occur to him that he should have checked the inside of the ambulance. Troublemakers might have stowed away there.

He had begun to nod off again when there was the sound of more vehicles. He was about to exercise his authority to turn them round, when he recognized Colonel Fitzpatrick at the wheel of his open top sports car.

'It's alright Constable. Fitzpatrick here, and the umpires behind.'

As the second car, a Morris saloon, drove past, he saw that there were four occupants, all with white bands worn diagonally across their jackets. Two also wore clerical collars, the vicars of Homefield and Althwaite having each decided that they would be an additional safeguard of neutrality.

17 THE EXERCISE (2)

The stipulated hour having elapsed since the Homefield platoon drove up the lane, the Althwaite platoon was on the move. As they struggled through waist-high bracken, Eddie Sykes, Jack Moorhouse and three others were wishing the exercise was over. They stopped for a minute to have swigs from their water bottles.

'Drat these flies!' said Jack, 'Are we on course still?'

Eddie consulted the compass dangling from a cord around his neck. 'Yes, still south. That must be the top edge of Highbrow Wood ahead. We have to skirt that, looking out for sharp-shooters.'

Eddie's section was the flank of a force of Hon Peter and five men which was at that moment following in the footsteps of Harold and the others across Bilder Moor. Peter was trying to keep track of the yards they had covered since getting on to the moor. A lot depended on deciding where to leave the lane and strike across to the edge of Armworth Valley. He had to be ready to descend the rough slope between Highbrow Wood and

Bilder Edge when Eddie's section created the planned diversion.

Corporal Armitage, with seven men, entered the area of conflict from Griddle Moor above the wooded side valley. He had a difficult task and was anxious. He was a bank clerk and on the way to becoming a manager. He was intelligent – he had had no difficulty in absorbing his Captain's plan. But he was not used to finding his way across country, not having been a Boy Scout. Like the rest of the platoon, he was liberally camouflaged with bracken and heather stuck in nets over helmets or caps. He was conscious of looking foolish, but no more than the others. The bracken attracted flies. He looked forward to resuming his duties at the bank tomorrow, with all this unreal business behind him.

Armitage's section reached the point in the descent over rough ground where it had to divide.

'Now, let's check watches,' he said to Joe Quarmby, the plumber. 'You remember what you have to do? Your lot traverse…' (he took pleasure in using Hon Peter's word – it sounded professional) '…across the hillside. Scar Rocks'll come into view soon. Keep hidden till 4.05. Then thunderflashes. If you can create a little fire, all the better.'

Quarmby and two others set off, bent double, in the direction of Scar Rocks. Armitage and the remaining three men continued a cautious descent.

The boys left the track across Bilder Moor and made their way towards where they assumed Bilder Edge to be.

'Not a word about what we know of Homefield's positions!' Harold whispered to Ron.

'O' course not!' he replied. Harold had no need to tell him.

A wire fence prevented sheep from falling over the Edge. It was not a sheer drop – and therefore not an Edge favoured by climbers. Instead, it was a steep tumble of rocks for about a hundred feet where it tailed off into a slope covered by bracken. They approached the fence on their stomachs and put their heads cautiously under the lowest strand of wire. The reservoir lay below, its surface sparkling white in the sunshine and light breeze. They could see how the volume of water had shrunk during the summer, revealing banks of mud and stone.

Harold and Ron scanned the scene for Homefield's strong points and soon spotted them. Opposite, about on a level with them, were Scar Rocks. Through his Dad's binoculars, Harold could see men in a half moon shape around the base of the rocks: lying watchful on their stomachs or lazing on their backs. Directly below the Edge was the sheep-fold – a square of walls open to the sky with a gap for the entrance. Men were leaning against the far side and two ends of the look-out. At either end of the dam wall, men were hiding behind boulders, bits of stone walling and bushes. At the far end, facing the side valley was the Bren Gun resting on its twin feet, the operator lying prone beside it. Neither boy could imagine how Hon Peter's men could possibly get to the valve tower against such a defence.

Nothing was happening.

'Your Hon Peter's called it off,' said Charlie Foster. 'He realises he can't win.'

'Don't be daft!' Will Dicehurst replied. 'He'll have to go through with it – like a suicide squad.'

‘Bet anybody sixpence Homefield win,’ Charlie said.

‘You’re on,’ said Harold. His family disapproved of betting, but someone had to show faith in Althwaite. He felt the merest tinge of guilt at benefiting from inside knowledge.

It was hot, and the boys drank from the bottles they had brought with them in rucksacks. From his, Will produced a steel helmet. ‘Be useful when the bullets start flying!’ he said.

It was Harold, with his binoculars, who spotted figures creeping round the end of Highbrow Wood. (This was Eddie Sykes’ section.)

‘They’re going to be seen by the chaps in the sheep-fold,’ he whispered – though the men were too far away to hear a normal voice.

‘We could distract them by dropping some stones,’ Will suggested.

‘No, we shouldn’t interfere,’ Harold protested.

Ron looked at him with a grin, and Harold realised the irony in what he had just said. As if they hadn’t already interfered!

Will put on his helmet. ‘You watch,’ he said. He prised a fist-sized stone from the crumbly earth just below the edge and dropped it. It bounced off rocks and came to rest in a jumble of boulders. The men in the sheep-fold did not stir.

‘Not big enough,’ Will concluded.

He and Charlie found a much larger one a few feet from the top.

‘You lot keep out of sight,’ Will warned. ‘They’ll think I’m one of the Althwaite mob.’

He rolled the stone over the edge. The others heard it crashing down.

Will chortled. 'That's got 'em worried. Came to rest about a hundred yards away.'

Down in the sheep-fold, the men looked up in alarm at the top of the Edge. Was it a natural rock fall?

'There's a chap with a helmet up there – look!'

'It's that Althwaite crew.'

'It may be a trick, but we'd better investigate,' the section leader decided. He ordered two men to climb up one end of the Edge and two the other, whilst he and the remainder watched the top.

Harold borrowed Will's helmet and took a quick look. As well as the Althwaite men at the end of Highbrow Wood, he could now see another defile beginning to descend from Bilder Moor. (This was Hon Peter's section.) The Homefield men detached from the sheep-fold were starting to climb at either end of the Edge where there were fewer rocks.

'It's time to scarper,' he said.

The boys ran towards a knoll about 200 yards away and lay hidden. Harold's heart was beating fast. He was pretty sure that they were not within the prohibited area. Even so, it would be embarrassing to be found, particularly having dropped that stone. They saw the pairs of men put their heads above the top of the Edge and peer around. Not seeing anything, they stood up, walked towards each other, shouted over the Edge to the sheep-fold and, having been instructed to return, disappeared the way they had come. The boys waited for ten minutes and then made their way further along the Edge to see what was going on.

Hitherto, the kestrel above the valley would have had its search for a victim disturbed only by two falling stones and a few shouts. Otherwise all was peaceful. The human ants were either sedentary around their positions or crawling quietly in search of *their* victims. The only sound, apart from the breeze that would have ruffled the kestrel's wings, was the cry of curlews on the moor. At five past four, peace came to an end.

Joe Quarmby, prone in the heather, nervously watched the minute hand on his watch. He struck a match, lit the touch paper of a thunderflash, rose to a kneeling position and flung it as far as he could towards Scar Rocks, which lay about 150 yards away. The bang echoed around the valley. It was followed by other bangs from the direction of Highbrow Wood. Instantly alerted, the men below Scar Rocks sprang to their positions, pointing rifles and walking sticks through clumps of bracken. The leader raised his head and caught sight of a patch of bracken and heather moving suspiciously. He ordered a thunderflash to be thrown in that direction. The three camouflaged Althwaite men wriggled towards the Rocks, throwing the occasional thunderflash. Joe was looking, and hoping, for telltale puffs of smoke. It was the leader at the Rocks who first decided the time had come to up the fires out. He stood up, waved the black and white chequered flag and shouted: 'Truce for fire fighting'. Joe responded with the flag he had taken from his rucksack.

The men from Scar Rocks tackled the flames vigorously, stamping their boots on them, dashing their jackets on them, even sprinkling water from their flasks. Joe and his two comrades acted cannily, pretending to be vigorous, but carefully avoiding the flames. Their job was to keep the Scar Rocks men distracted as long as possible. But at the end of five minutes the flames had all been extinguished. The Althwaite and Homefield men eyed each other warily, uncertain how to resume hostilities, and wondering whether they really wanted to.

'Have a drink,' said Joe, stepping forward and offering his flask, which he had refrained from using in the fire-fighting.

'Might be poisoned,' said the Homefield leader.

Joe drank some of the water and offered it again. It was accepted. The Homefield men were thirsty from their longer exposure in the hot sun, and most of them had sacrificed water in putting out the fire. They sat down, and the flask passed from hand to hand. Eyes turned towards the valley, trying to make out what was happening. This was dangerous, thought Joe. The Scar Rocks men might decide they needed to descend to the dam wall to help their comrades who were being attacked.

'Right, that's enough fraternization!' he announced. 'Give us two minutes to resume positions.'

'Keep outside the hundred yards range,' he whispered to his companions. 'If they advance, keep retreating. If they rush, throw a thunderflash.'

Within a few seconds of Joe Quarmby throwing the first thunderflash towards Scar Rocks, Eddie Sykes hurled one towards the Homefield section on the edge of Highbrow Wood. A Homefield man rushed forward. Eddie pointed his rifle.

'Kill! You're dead,' he shouted, thinking at the same time that this was like a silly game of Cowboys and Indians.

'I shot you first!'

'No! You didn't shout out!'

One of Eddie's pals had meanwhile lit touch paper. He threw the thunderflash at the feet of the advancing foe.

'You're dead now, anyway!'

The courageous, or rash, member of the Homefield platoon sat down, dazzled by the flash. Coming to, he was not displeased to be out of the fray. He could watch developments. He noticed another Althwaite section (Hon Peter's) descending slowly towards the dam wall. Unable, as a dead man, to use his voice, he stood up to attract the attention of his section leader.

'Lie down, you're dead!' Eddie shouted. 'On your back, you piece of garbage!'

The man did as he was bid. Eddie, having recognized him wished he had said 'please'. It was Mr Porteous who lived on the edge of Homefield and had a delivery of fruit and vegetables from Eddie every fortnight. Eddie didn't want to lose his custom.

At each end of the dam wall, Hon Peter on one side and Corporal Armitage on the other were now engaging the enemy. They were trying to keep outside the 100 yard range of the rifles at one end and the 200 yards range of the Bren at the other. Armitage also had to fight a rearguard action against the section which had been guarding the approach down the side valley. He made much use of thunderflashes and managed to create a small fire, which distracted them. But he was in danger of being caught in a pincer action. There were sporadic appeals to the umpires who found the task of judging whether a man was within range of another an almost impossible one. The two vicars had each taken off their clerical collars under the stress of heat and exertion. The easiest thing, they decided, was to allow an appeal from one side, and then from the other.

Up at Scar Rocks, the Homefield section leader had decided that the attack on him was a mere feint, and that he would be more useful down near the dam, where there was a lot of noisy action. He called off the crawling pursuit of Joe Quarmby and led his men in a dash down the hillside. Joe and his two comrades ran after them.

Meanwhile, the crucial part of Hon Peter's plan was creeping up the valley, heading for the spillway on the western side. Sergeant Wright had chosen the members of his élite force: Alistair McAlister for his climbing ability; Toby Middleton, the ironmonger, for his previous prowess at fell-running; and Dr McLeish, who was reputed to have rowed for Oxford. They were elaborately camouflaged. Despite the heat, they wore Balaclava, woollen helmets covering head and neck. Their faces were painted in black and green stripes. As well as rifles or walking sticks, they carried small bushes of willow and alder branches which Wright and Alistair had cut and tied together the previous day. These they held above them, so as to frustrate discovery by the Homefield sections above. Once up to the western spillway, they would be out of sight of the men in the grouse butts; and they hoped that, from five past four, the men at Highbrow Wood would be too distracted to notice them.

The outbreak of bangs and shouts signalled that they could move faster. At the base of the spillway, they discarded their bushes and began to climb. It was hard work. Each step was about three feet high, so they had to lever themselves up. Sweating and out of breath, they climbed up the last step. Here, the channel went under the dam wall, which crossed it like a bridge. Creeping quietly, so as not to be heard by the Bren Gun team near them, they emerged on to the reservoir itself where blocks of stone sloped above the low water level to the base of the dam wall. Hugging the bottom of the wall, they crawled along towards the valve tower. The top of the wall was about ten feet above them. Sergeant Wright knelt down and undid his rucksack. He drew out a grappling iron. He had made it in the forge: a shank with a ring at one end for a rope, and at the other end four branching hooks. The shank and the hooks, apart from the tips, were cased in leather, so as to deaden the noise of using the device. He had practised using it after twilight one evening, so he was pretty confident. He threw it over the wall. It held the first time. Hand over hand on the rope, and feet walking up the wall, he arrived at the top, slipped over and helped the other three up. They were now on the top of the dam midway between the valve tower and the Bren Gun. The latter was in action against Corporal Armitage, who was reduced by casualties to himself and one other. He knew that his day was numbered in minutes.

'Off you go, Toby,' Wright whispered. He and the other two dashed towards the Bren. From twenty yards he shouted, 'Hands up!' The Bren Gun team turned round. To their astonishment, they found two rifles and a walking stick pointing at them. But what really compelled their surrender was the appearance of the attackers: green and black striped faces emerging from Balaclava helmets. For a moment, they thought this was the real thing and that German paratroops had arrived. As Freddie Postlethwaite recounted in The Green Parrot, Homefield's pub, that evening, 'You'd 'ave thought they was demons, straight out of Hell. Made me wish I were a better church-goer.'

A cry of triumph rang out from the valve tower. Sergeant Wright and his team raised their weapons in the air and cheered. Toby had got to the tower without being shot, and had placed at its foot the cocoa tin which represented a charge of high explosive. Colonel Fitzpatrick strode along the dam wall to inspect.

'Well, I'll be damned! Peter's outfoxed them!'

He waved his arms to signal the end of hostilities. An incredulous Major Rochester appeared from the end of the side valley where Corporal Armitage and his men had sacrificed their lives.

The men from both sides converged on the dam wall. They were hot and sticky, dirty and dishevelled. Many would have to ingratiate themselves with wives or sisters so as to get repairs made to tunics, jackets and trousers. The Althwaite men were triumphant, clapping Toby Middleton on the back, and shaking the hand of their victorious Captain. Hon Peter took charge of the cocoa tin, vowing that it would not be the first trophy of the war. The St John's Ambulance men dealt with some sprains, stings and bites. Colonel Fitzpatrick brought about a more equal distribution of morale by producing bottles of ginger beer from his car. He made a short speech, congratulating both sides. Even those who had lost felt heartened. As instructed, the two sergeants each produced a sack and ordered their men to gather up the remains of thunderflashes from each end of the dam. They mutually agreed to forget about those up at Scar Rocks, sensing that an order to toil up there would not go down well.

At the lane end, Constable Dewhurst became aware that the noises up the valley had ceased. He looked at his watch. It was a quarter past five. There was still time for a late siesta in his back garden. He mounted his bike.

The kestrel over the valley would have seen three vehicles drive off down the lane, raising dust. They were followed by the human ants, some limping, all tired. After a quarter of an hour, the dust had settled, the ants had disappeared. The only sign of the recent conflict was a scattering of exploded thunderflashes below Scar Rocks and a few patches of charred grass and heather. The valley was again at peace, the only sounds those of the breeze caressing the trees of Highbrow Wood, and the cry of curlews.

The news that Althwaite had won spread around the village. Miss Arbuthnot heard it when she came out of the little Roman Catholic Church after the evening service. She guessed that the platoon would be gathering in the Dandelion Arms to celebrate. She had been inside the Arms on rare occasions only. This was as important an occasion as any, and she was keen to learn how the victory had been won. As luck would have it, her ex-colleague and friend, Henrietta Isaacs, had arranged to visit her that evening. Mrs Isaacs had been the biology teacher at the school. She was a member of the Methodist congregation, but if pressed would accept a glass of sherry.

The Dandelion Arms had two bars: the Saloon and the Public. Deciding which one to enter was an exercise in self-appreciation. If you were from a certain level in society, you wouldn't dream of going into the Public Bar. If you were from another level, you wouldn't aspire to the Saloon. By natural gravitation, Miss Arbuthnot entered the Saloon, with Henrietta in tow, though she knew that the platoon would gather in the Public Bar. There was just a handful of people in the Saloon – the 'better' sort, Miss Arbuthnot could see at a glance. But the noise from the Public Bar suggested that it was full. After she and Henrietta had settled in a corner with their sherries, Miss Arbuthnot exchanged a few pleasantries with the other occupants: the bank manager and his wife, a retired gentleman farmer and his lady friend. None of them knew anything about the manner of Althwaite's success.

'Hetty, just pop into the Public Bar and ask Captain Danellion-Smith if he would join us for a drink,' Miss Arbuthnot said.

Henrietta Isaacs was used to doing 'leg-work' or, as she sometimes put it, 'dirty-work', for her friend. She acknowledged Audrey's stronger personality. But she maintained a streak of independence, which derived from her wider experience of life: she was a widow with grown-up children, whereas Audrey had never married nor, so far as Hetty knew, been in love.

Hetty went into the Public Bar. She seemed to be there a long time. Audrey looked at her watch: surely Hetty must have been in there at least five minutes. She was wondering whether she would have to demean herself by going into the Public Bar herself, when the door opened and Hetty appeared. Her cheeks were flushed and there was a half-smile on her face.

'I'm sorry, Audrey. That nice Mr Armitage was there and offered me a drink. No, I didn't accept, but it was difficult to get away.'

'He's only a bank clerk,' her friend whispered, not wanting the bank manager to overhear. 'If you want to get tangled up again – though Heaven knows why – you should aim higher than that.'

'He has such kindly eyes.'

'How can eyes be "kindly"? Pull yourself together, Henrietta! The trouble is – you're too susceptible.'

Privately, Henrietta agreed. But it was eight years since Wilfred had died. After the sale of his goldsmith and jewellery business in Bruddersford, she had been left pretty well off. She could afford to marry a mere bank clerk.

'Did you speak to Captain Peter?' Audrey asked sharply, breaking into Hetty's reverie.

'Yes, he'll come in when he's said a few words.'

By propping the communicating door partly open, they heard some of the words.

'... teamwork...great effort...very proud...the

dead played their part as well as the living…here's to the next time…'

There were cheers, followed by Peter's appeal for three cheers for the defeated Homefield platoon. These were more muted.

To Miss Arbuthnot's surprise, Hon Peter brought George Wright with him. Normally, a blacksmith would not be seen in the Saloon. George was reluctant, but his Captain had insisted. Peter recognized that Miss Arbuthnot was a power in the land – or rather in Althwaite and district. He never felt at ease in her company. The way her pale green eyes stared at him suggested that she was penetrating his deficiencies. On this, victorious, occasion, she could hardly find him deficient. But he nevertheless felt the need for support from his right-hand man.

Miss Arbuthnot asked them what they would drink. Having already had a few beers, Peter opted for a ginger ale. George Wright, thinking of the work that awaited him in the forge in the morning, followed suit. After fulsome congratulations, Audrey insisted on a full description of the exercise. Peter gave Sergeant Wright and his team much of the credit. When George described the camouflage bushes they had carried, her habitual seriousness gave way to a smile.

'You must have been remembering your Macbeth, Mr Danellion-Smith.'

Peter had to admit that he hadn't – in fact his recollection of the play was hazy, not having read it since he was at school.

'Don't you remember?' Miss Arbuthnot adopted the teaching role that came to her so naturally.

'Macbeth is told not to fear until Birnam Wood comes to Dunsinane. But Malcolm's soldiers each carry before them a bough from Birnam Wood as camouflage. And so Macbeth meets his downfall.'

Peter was about to say: 'Great minds think alike.' But he managed to appreciate in time the absurdity of comparing himself with Shakespeare, even in jest.

'What role did Corporal Armitage play?' Henrietta asked timidly.

'A glorious one, madam! He and his valiant section sacrificed themselves for the cause.'

Henrietta flushed slightly with pleasure. He might be only a bank clerk but he had character and bravery.

'The Lord must have heard our prayers,' Audrey observed.

'No doubt, but isn't there a saying that God helps those who help themselves?' Peter replied. He didn't like the idea of the Almighty filching the credit due to him and his men. (And Jem, Harold and Ron, he might have added.)

The following morning, Harold saw Charlie on the other side of the market place. Normally they would merely have waved to each other. But Charlie came over, put his hand in a trouser pocket and pulled out a sixpence which he gave to Harold.

'Here you are, Harold. I didn't think that Hon Peter had it in him. But I'm glad Althwaite came up trumps. I've never paid a bet so cheerfully in my life.'

Harold reflected that Charlie's betting life could not be much more than two years old. Still, it was a tribute. Charlie could be unkind, but at bottom he was alright. If only Jem could see him in the same way!

The post mortem was held in Colonel Fitzpatrick's large house on the edge of Bruddersford. The two platoon commanders and the two vicars, representing the umpires, were present.

'Right, plans on the table,' Fitzpatrick ordered. 'You're not adversaries now, but comrades, and we need to see what lessons can be learnt.'

Each commander explained his strategy.

'I can't fault your dispositions, Alan,' Fitzpatrick said to Major Rochester. 'But didn't you think that Peter might send a force straight up the valley?'

'Yes, sir. But the sections at the grouse butts and Highbrow Wood were instructed to look out for that. And they had flags to communicate to me.'

'Instead, the first couldn't see, and the second was distracted. I have to congratulate you, Peter, on your tactics. Especially the camouflage carried by Wright's section. Where did that idea come from?'

'Well, if you remember your Macbeth, sir. Birnam Wood and Dunsinane?'

Fitzpatrick had to confess that he had not looked at Macbeth since school.

'Now what's this about fraternization after the fire-fighting – passing round water bottles and chatting? That's not allowed.'

'It was only at one spot, for a few minutes,' Hon Peter replied. 'It was a comradely act on the part of my men, after the other lot had used their water on the fire. Nothing like as serious as the Christmas truce in the trenches in the last war.'

'Still, it mustn't happen again! Now, umpires, what's the tally of the dead?'

'Althwaite twelve, and Homefield eight. But it was terribly difficult to decide,' Reverend Blake replied.

'Mm…more than half your force wiped out, Peter. Heavy casualties! I think, out of ten points, I'll knock one off for that and one for the fraternization. So eight to Althwaite and five to Homefield.'

Hon Peter felt inclined to maintain that his platoon deserved better than that. But a tinge of guilt about his inside knowledge kept him quiet.

About one month later, an 'On His Majesty's Service' letter arrived for Jem and his mother. It was from Dad who said he had reached a place that he'd always wanted to see, but he couldn't let them know where it was. He now had a certificate from King Neptune – 'a lively old chap' – for crossing the equator. He ended by saying he was pleased to hear from Captain Danellion-Smith that Jem had been helpful to the Home Guard. 'But he didn't say anything about what Jem did. Do I smell a rat, or should I say, a mole?'

What a knack his Dad had, Jem thought, for putting one and two together and making four!

18 UNDERCURRENTS

The fingers of Autumn were touching the valley. Leaves were turning colour, the bracken on the moors was dying. It was the middle of September, but the day was hot. At the railway station, people were waiting for the train from Bruddersford to steam into the terminus. In the quiet before its arrival, they could hear the rails clicking in the sun's heat. The little engine – a 'tanker' without a separate tender – puffed in, hauling two coaches. A railway man got down from the platform and undid the coupling, the engine glided down to the points, reversed into the shunting yard, was turned on the turntable and backed to the head of the train, causing only a tremor to the coaches. Jem and Harold watched this procedure enviously. How grand to wear a blue, greasy cap with a shiny, black peak, and to handle the levers in the cab so confidently. But their eyes were also on the entrance to the platform. They hadn't long to wait. The sound of a car drawing up was followed by the sight of a porter wheeling a trolley on which were four suitcases. Behind him appeared Ron, Dot, Jakie

Andrews and his sister, and Mrs Weaverthorpe. The mothers of the children had decided it was safe enough for them to return to Hull. Ron was in two minds about going back. He had come to like Althwaite, but he missed the busy streets of the city, the movement of ships in the Humber, the tarry smell of the port and the tang of the sea. Dot was heartbroken. From an apprehensive appendage to an elder brother, she had become a person in her own right, valued for her own qualities. She had blossomed in the valley, had made friends and found new interests. The previous day she had been taken to Intake Farm and had bid a sad farewell to Bertha and the pony. Mrs Whittle had invited her to stay in the holidays next year. She was trying to console herself with the thought that she was saying only a temporary goodbye to Althwaite. She would be back, she promised herself.

Jakie Andrew was also in two minds about leaving. He had taken a long time to settle down. He had had to put up with some bullying at school. But he had some pleasant memories, not least of which was the Christmas Party at which he had received from Father Christmas the Dinky searchlight lorry with a mobile anti-aircraft gun attached. Jem's own mind went back to the sacrifice of that treasure. He was tempted to ask Jakie if it was in the suitcase. But he had the sense to realise that it might trouble Jakie to know that it had once belonged to someone else.

The luggage was put aboard the train. It was time for goodbyes – manful on the part of Ron, hesitant on the part of Jakie and his sister, tearful on the part of Dot. Jonquil had come down with Harold. Dot gave her a squeeze and promised to write. Then she put up a wet face to Jem for a kiss.

'Say goodbye for me to Lorinda, when she's here again,' she faltered.

'We'll all meet again in the Tower when the war's over,' Jem said. 'Anyway, Ron's asked me to come to Hull at Christmas, so I'll see you soon.'

The guard blew his whistle. Mrs Weaverthorpe, who was accompanying the children to Bruddersford to see them on the train to Hull, hurried them into a compartment. The guard waved his green flag, and the engine released a cloud of steam as its wheels got a grip on the rails. First one head and arm, and then another, leaned out of the window to say goodbye. Jem, Harold and Jonquil continued waving until the train had disappeared round a bend. It was the end of an episode.

Jem thought of that other time he had watched a train disappearing – as his Dad went off to the war. When he got home, he took out of its small envelope the 'Airgraph' letter that he had received the previous day.

I am writing this on a big sheet of paper in large handwriting. It'll be photographed, the negative will be sent to Britain and you'll get a small copy.

There are lots of interesting things to see out here. Men wear gowns and little red hats. Camels, carrying heavy loads, and donkey carts make driving a vehicle a frustrating business. Trams are packed and people hang on to the sides and back. Every day is hot, and the nights are not much better.

I hope you're looking after Mum and keeping clear of

peat hags. I often think of that expedition with Harold and Raq. When I come back we'll have another! Love, Dad.

The address – Driver E Murgatroyd, 4th Ambulance Car Company, RASC, Middle East Force – didn't indicate just where he was. But Mum had suggested Cairo, Egypt. It was a relief to know that he had got to his destination. His ship had not become the victim of an enemy submarine, as Jem's morbid dreaming had imagined. But now there was news of Italian troops invading Egypt from Libya. Perhaps his Dad's ambulance unit would be in the thick of the fighting.

There were other people in Althwaite with various reasons for worry. At a jumble sale held by the Women's Volunteer Service, Mrs McAlister had mentioned to Mrs Murgatroyd that the squire was not himself. 'There's something preying on his mind,' she had said. Mrs Murgatroyd had passed this on to Jem.

'You're a friend of his. Why don't you go up to the Hall and see how things are?'

Jem was not sure of this. Hadn't he done enough intruding into the business of adults? But One-Leg Tim had some rhubarb he wanted delivered to Mrs McAlister, and Jem offered to take it.

'I won't intrude,' he said to himself. 'But I'll see how the land lies.'

'Hon Peter's at the Tower with Mr Armitage,' Mrs McAlister said after Jem had given her the rhubarb and enquired. 'He'll be glad to see you. But don't go into the Tower – it's got Home Guard stuff in it. Just give them a shout.'

The Tower door was open.

'Sir?' Jem called up the spiral staircase.

'Who's there?'

'It's me, Jem Murgatroyd.'

'Jem? Ah, come on up, my lad.'

Jem climbed up to the room at the top. Hon Peter was standing in the middle, surrounded by boxes. Some had 'Danger – Thunderflashes' on the sides. He was holding a clipboard and pencil. Mr Armitage was investigating the contents of a box by the window.

'I expect you know each other. Corporal Armitage is my quartermaster.'

Mr Armitage straightened up and gave Jem a nod.

'He may not look it, Walter,' Peter continued, 'but this young man's a regular Sherlock Holmes. Has a nose for sorting out mysteries.'

Jem began to turn red. Surely, Peter was not going to spill the beans about the Dandelion family treasures!

'If I had a junior Home Guard squad, I'd have Jem and Harold Bright and that Charlie what's his name in it. Anything under investigation at the moment?'

Jem tried to hide his embarrassment by laughing and saying he wished there was.

'Corporal Armitage and I are just trying to check that we have what we're supposed to have. If Jerry spends as much time as we do on forms and checking, the invasion will never take place! You wouldn't believe how plagued I am by Battalion Headquarters. Got home late the other evening from an exercise. Uneasy sleep. Sound of footsteps on the gravel at 5.30 in the morning. Went down to investigate. Folded piece of paper on the mat: "Please advise Headquarters by return the total number of bootlaces required by your platoon." I ask you! On the other hand, think of the devotion to duty – some poor fellow getting up early and coming out of his way to deliver a message before going off to work.'

Jem noticed that some of Lorinda's pictures were still hanging on the walls, though not the portrait of Peter, which was no doubt in the Hall.

'Have you heard from Lorinda, I mean Mrs Danellion-Smith, sir?' he asked. 'How's she getting on?'

'She's well. Enjoying being part of the war effort.'

Here, Peter looked at Jem, a half-smile on his face.

'Alright if I leave you to it, Walter?' he said.

'Yes, sir. But I'll have to get back to the bank in half an hour.'

'Fine. Come along, young Jem.' Peter handed the clipboard to Corporal Armitage.

Jem had started to follow Peter down the staircase, when Walter called him back.

'Do you know Miss Hibbert, the lady in Up Bye?' he asked. 'Now there's a little mystery for you. But you'd need to be tactful.'

On the way to the house, Jem wondered whether he was going to be questioned about the disappearance of six thunderflashes. Having requested refreshments as they passed through the kitchen, Hon Peter led Jem to the study. Instead of facing Jem across the desk, Peter motioned him to a low chair by the French windows, and seated himself in a capacious arm-chair.

'I've treated you to a few confidences, haven't I Jem? Perhaps unfair of me. But I trust your good sense and discretion. I hope you don't mind if I unburden myself.'

He paused as Mrs McAlister entered with a tray on which were a cup of tea, a glass of orange squash and four chocolate biscuits.

'Them's the last of the chocolate biscuits, sir. I dinna ken when we'll see any more.'

'In that case, Jem and I will take one each, leaving two for yourself and Alistair.'

Peter sipped his tea and continued. 'Lorinda's well, as I said. But we're both looking forward to this war being over, so that we can start living our life together. We've got plans – or should I say, *she* has and I'm backing them up – both for the Hall and the village. But she's also a worry. She likes her job as an aircraft mechanic. I can't help feeling jealous when I hear of the gallant young men on her station. But our relationship's as safe as houses. Come to think of it, though, that's not a happy expression now Jerry's bombing the heart out of East London.But, to get to the point. The powers that be think she may be of more use to the war effort if her Czech background and her knowledge of the language are made use of. What she would be doing is hush-hush. She hasn't been able to tell even me. But I'm worried. It could be some dangerous job. Obviously, there's nothing I can do about it. If she feels that's where her duty lies, it would be selfish of me to try to persuade her against it.'

Jem was nonplussed. What could he say? He imagined Lorinda being parachuted into Czechoslovakia on a secret mission. The chances of her surviving might be slim. But would they be slimmer than those of an ambulance driver in the North African desert? The vision leapt into his mind of a battle, his Dad driving his ambulance at full pelt and coming under fire.

'It seems to me, sir, that you're being asked to share in the worries of lots of other people. Like me and my Mum. Dad's now in Egypt, and there's fighting there. Ambulances have big crosses on their sides and roof. But someone firing a shell from a distance wouldn't see them. Lorinda, though – I can't believe she won't pull through. She's promised to see us all in the Tower after the war. I've got a feeling in my bones that she will.'

'Thanks, Jem. You're a comfort. It was perhaps unfair of me. But I felt that, as you were the divine agent who brought us together, I should share my concern with you.'

'Divine agent'! mused Jem on his way home. That was Hon Peter's way of exaggerating. But wasn't there an element of truth? Surely, he had been the unconscious agent of destiny. Still, he would have preferred Peter to have kept his worries about Lorinda to himself. Now he, Jem, was worried too. The thought that Lorinda might not survive whatever peril faced her was unbearable. She *must* come back!

There was something else buzzing in his mind, too. Hon Peter had said he had a nose for sorting out mysteries. Was that true? That investigation of the church burglary had certainly been exciting. If he had devoted as much thought to school work as he had to that, perhaps he would have got through the scholarship. And what did Walter Armitage mean by the mystery of Ma Hibbert? She was certainly a strange lady – off-putting at first, but kind when you got to know her. Perhaps he ought to get to know her better.

Many people in Althwaite, not just Hon Peter or Jem and his mother, had worries about relatives or friends in the forces. But, as well, there was an undercurrent of general anxiety. September was perhaps turning out to be a crucial month. The German Air Force, the Luftwaffe, had launched heavy attacks on South East England, first on Royal Air Force airfields, then on London, especially the docks in the East End. Was this a prelude to the invasion that many people feared? The prospect of war coming close stimulated people to look into their inmost selves. How would they cope? What had they achieved in life?

Two events brought the war into the heart of Althwaite.

The vicar, the Reverend Cuthbert Blake, had a son and a daughter. Neither was very well known in the village, as they had been sent to boarding schools and were home only in the holidays, when they didn't mix much with the local children. Jack, the elder, went to University but broke off his course to join the RAF soon after the war began. Mr and Mrs Blake were proud of the fact that their twenty year old son was now a fighter pilot. The village felt proud, too. It was a black day when news arrived at the vicarage that Jack had been killed, his Spitfire shot down in an encounter with German planes over Kent. The whole village, it seemed, turned out for the funeral and memorial service, packing the church and crowding the graveyard. The vicar and Mrs Blake were well liked. Everyone wanted to join in their sorrow and share in their pride.

A few weeks later, in the early hours of the morning, a series of bangs woke up everyone except the deaf. Harold felt as though the Manse was going to fall on top of him. His parents hurried Jonquil and him into the cellar which served as an air-raid shelter. There had been no air-raid warning. After a few minutes silence, Mr Bright put a coat over his pyjamas, took his walking stick and went out to investigate. He came back in a quarter of an hour to say that there were craters up the road where the bombs had fallen, a water main was fractured and water was pouring down the hill. The fire brigade and an ambulance were at the scene. But it didn't seem as though anyone had been hurt. He went out again to see if he could be of any help. The other three tried to resume their broken sleep, Jonquil joining her mother in her bed.

In the morning, Harold couldn't wait to go up the road. His mother insisted on breakfast first. For him and most of the other boys of the village there could be no question of going to school when something so momentous had happened. They spent the morning inspecting the craters, the broken windows, the damaged roofs and hunting for pieces of shrapnel. Miraculously, it seemed, the 'stick' of bombs had fallen in fields and on roads, without destroying any houses. Old Mr Quarmby – father of Joe, the plumber - looked smilingly out of a window with no glass on to a crater just twenty or so yards away. The only casualty was said to be a donkey which had been hit by shrapnel, and had in kindness to be put to sleep.

No one could imagine why bombs should have

been dropped on Althwaite. The mill was of little consequence to the war effort. It was assumed that the pilot had lost his way, or wished to get rid of his load before heading back to Germany. For a few days, Althwaite found itself famous in that part of the West Riding. People came from neighbouring villages, even from Bruddersford, to inspect the craters and the minimal damage, and to wonder. As Harold and Jem sat on a gate near the Manse and watched the folk going up the road, they heard someone say to their companion: 'They little know what it all means.' Jem thought that was unfair. His Dad was in Egypt; and he, Harold and Ron had helped the Althwaite Home Guard platoon. They had at least an inkling of what war was about.

Clouds were drifting over the valley from the Pennine Hills. It was drizzling. But the Armistice Day parade had to go ahead. It was 11 November, the date on which, at eleven in the morning, the First World War had ended in 1918. The participants gathered in the forecourt of the mill. First to emerge through the gates was the Silver Band, followed by the Althwaite Home Guard platoon, the Boy Scouts and the Girl Guides. People lining the streets or looking out of their houses were sadly aware that the band was not as tuneful as it used to be. Half the members had joined the forces, and their places had been taken by older men who were out of practice and short of wind. Being below average height, Hon Peter was aware that he didn't cut a very impressive figure as he marched at the head of the platoon with Sergeant Wright. Between them and the body of the men came Corporal Armitage, a tall figure with more of a military bearing than Peter.

The procession passed the bank, where Audrey Arbuthnot and Henrietta Isaacs were standing on the steps for a better view. Corporal Armitage caught sight of them, smiled slightly and then resumed a resolute look to the front.

'Is that your Corporal Armitage, Hetty?' Audrey asked. 'He looks different in his uniform – quite transformed.'

'He looks more officer-like than Captain Danellion-Smith. But he's not *mine*, Audrey.'

Walter Armitage was not the only marcher to spot a face - or faces – and find his mind wandering. Jem, in the Scout troop, caught a glimpse of a face that reminded him of Benjy. But it was a Benjy with a difference. What had he done to himself?

After the service in St Jude's, made more moving than usual by the recent loss of the son of Mr and Mrs Blake, folk gathered outside. The drizzle had stopped, the clouds were dispersing, and it was pleasant to linger in the Autumn sunshine.

'Hullo, young Jem!' said a voice from behind a tombstone.

'Why, Benjy! Saw you in the crowd – at least I thought it was you. I wasn't sure – now I see why!'

'Ay. I never thought as 'ow I'd shave my beard off. I've 'ad it fifteen years. I felt a bit shy about goin' into t' church, so I stayed out 'ere and listened to t' service.'

'People won't know you without your beard!'

'Ay. But if so, there'll be less prejudice against me.'

Benjy's eyes roamed over the folk chatting in groups.

'Who's that woman over there?' he asked.

'You mean the tall one talking to Mr Armitage?'

'No, the smaller one.'

'That's Mrs Isaacs.'

'*Mrs* Isaacs,' Benjy commented in a tone which betrayed some disappointment.

'Yes, but Mr Isaacs died. The tall one, that's Miss Arbuthnot. She was headmistress of the girl's school.'

'She still looks like a headmistress. But her friend seems more sympathetic.'

The Reverend Cuthbert Blake, masking the grief which still gnawed at him, gravitated from one group to another, shaking hands and asking after people's health and about their relatives who had joined up.

'Ah, Mr Benjy isn't it? Good to see you here. I'm glad you took my advice and shaved it off. He looks ten years younger, wouldn't you agree, Master Jem? You'll soon be so respectable, we'll have to find someone else to be the local tramp – if you'll pardon the expression!'

'I'll always be a tramp at heart, vicar!'

'Keep him on the straight and narrow, Jem!' said the vicar as he moved away.

The churchyard was emptying of people. Under one of the yew trees, Jem saw Mrs Bright with her arm around the shoulders of Ma Hibbert, who had a handkerchief to her eyes.Benjy saw them too.

'Yer know, Jem, the folk who've been kindest to me in Althwaite – that is, apart from you and 'arold – are the vicar and Ma 'ibbert. She always makes me welcome at Up Bye - though her cats don't like me. I feel some kind of…what's the word? Affinity? You're a scholar, Jem, what's that mean?'

'Er…near to?'

'Ay, that's it – a sort of fellow feeling.'

In the ensuing days, Audrey Arbuthnot, proud of her independence as a spinster, was annoyed with herself. The face and bearing of Corporal Armitage kept intruding into her private thoughts. She had remonstrated with Henrietta Isaacs when Hetty seemed to have a fondness for him. But, though he *was* only a bank clerk, he had the makings of something more. When the three of them chatted outside the church, she had been impressed by his self-possession. He spoke in a friendly, easy way, not at all intimidated by her self-appointed role as organiser of the women of Althwaite. Asked about his role in the Home Guard exercise, he had been very modest. Perhaps all he needed was the spark of ambition, and she, Audrey, could supply that. Caught in a day-dream, she slapped herself mentally.

'He's Hetty's friend, perhaps her future husband. I've no right to intervene!' she told herself.

Someone else suffered from the intrusion of a face into her thoughts. It was not that of Walter Armitage, but of some other man. She had seen him talking to Jem after the service. He seemed familiar, but also unfamiliar. Henrietta Isaacs was puzzled.

It was Ma Hibbert who intruded into Jem's thoughts. He had asked Harold if he knew why his mother seemed to be comforting her. Harold had no idea. Jem thought of One-Leg Tim. He was of the same generation as Ma Hibbert. Perhaps he would know something of her history.

Having helped Tim to dig up carrots on the following Saturday, Jem approached the subject. He didn't mention Walter Armitage's reference to Ma Hibbert as a mystery.

'Benjy says that Miss Hibbert's one of the people in Althwaite who've been kindest to him.'

'I can believe that. She's 'ad more than a fair share o' trouble. So she's alive to other folks' troubles.'

'You've known her a long time, Tim?'

'Ay. I mind when she were nobbut a lass. Long brown hair, playful manner. She were sought after. But she 'ad only one sweetheart. And when 'e didn't come back from Army service in India, she were never the same again. Some people get over tragedies like that and make a new life. She's never got over it, I reckon.'

'Harold saw a photo of a soldier as a young man in her living room. Could that be him?'

'As like as not. Malcolm Knowsley, that were 'im. A sergeant in the Light Horse 'e were when fever carried 'im off.'

'I wonder if that's why she seemed upset after the Remembrance Service?'

'Could well be. She's always down at this time o' the year. But there could be another reason.'

'What would that be?'

'It's an old story. But it's not for me to tell it. May not be true, anyway.'

That was as much as Jem could extract from Tim. But it was enough to strengthen his interest in pursuing the mystery, if such it was, of Ma Hibbert.

One of the entertaining sights of Althwaite was

Henrietta Isaacs taking her donkey once a year to the blacksmith's to have his hooves trimmed. Most of his life was led in a small field behind her bungalow. She was very attached to Dusty, who would trot towards her to take a carrot or some other delicacy from her hand. Henrietta used to put off the visit because of the difficulty she experienced in getting him there. Some friend, or boy, had to be cajoled into helping. Henrietta pulled, offering carrots as inducement. The friend or boy pushed. She refused to use a stick.

Having deferred the annual expedition for a few weeks, Henrietta decided that she had to face up to it. On this occasion she persuaded her friend Audrey Arbuthnot to lend a hand. Not having witnessed the operation, Audrey had no idea what she was letting herself in for. She imagined herself simply providing Hetty with moral support as the donkey trotted agreeably behind them.

They had not got far down the cobbled lane when Dusty dug in his hooves and refused to budge. Hetty tugged, whilst Audrey looked on.

'You've got to help, Audrey. Give him a shove!'

'I didn't bring my gloves, Hetty,' objected Audrey, who looked after her hands, washing them three times a day in lavender water.

'This is an emergency, Audrey! Give him a slap and a shove!'

The ex-headmistress of the Girls' School applied her hands to the rump of the animal. Dusty shot off, leaving Audrey stumbling forward.

The donkey indulged in more obstinacy outside the bank, much to the embarrassment of the two ladies.

Walter Armitage, glancing out of the window, laughed at the sight. The Manager had just been given his morning cup of tea and was unlikely to emerge from his office for a quarter of an hour. Walter took off his black jacket and, leaving the counter in the charge of the junior clerk, went outside.

'Looks as though you need a hand, ladies. Leave him to me!'

He grasped the leather collar, swung himself on to Dusty's back and dug his heels into the donkey's flanks.

'Come on, Rosinante! Get a move on!'

They progressed in staccato bursts, Walter's long legs almost touching the ground. He got off outside the blacksmith's shop and made a bow.

'DonQuixote at your service, ladies!' he said. 'Not often a bank clerk gets a chance to ride a Derby winner!' He strode off to the bank.

'What a man!' said Audrey Arbuthnot as his lanky form retreated. 'And he's familiar with great literature!'

'He's only a bank clerk, Audrey,' said Hetty with a sly smile.

Back at the bank, Walter dusted down his black pin-stripe trousers, to which some of Dusty's hairs were clinging.

'Mum's the word!' he said to the junior clerk, indicating the manager's office. The junior, who had watched the start of the ride, grinned.

At the blacksmith's, another surprise awaited the ladies. It was the figure of Benjy which straightened itself up from hammering on the anvil.

'Customers, George!' he shouted. 'Morning ladies. I hope he's a docile steed.'

'Oh, we know how to deal with Dusty,' said George Wright, appearing from the back of the shop. 'Mrs Isaacs, let me introduce the deputy blacksmith, Benjamin Oldcastle. You may have known him in another role, when he had more hair on his face.'

'Yes…er…How do you do, Mr Benjamin.'

'I'm going to join a searchlight battery near Halifax,' said George. 'I'll only be here a day or two a week, so Benjy's going to hold the fort.'

'I'm not a complete novice, ladies,' Benjy said, thinking that some explanation was needed. 'I learnt summat o' the blacksmith trade when I were a lad in Oldham. It's all coming back to me. I don't think I've 'ad the pleasure, Mrs Isaacs,' he added, holding out a grimy hand.

Hetty took it automatically, having temporarily lost her composure. *This* was the man who had been talking to Jem in the churchyard. So he was Benjy, the tramp, of whom she had previously heard and had a distant glimpse. She didn't know whether to be displeased with herself or intrigued. She liked his candid, pleasant manner, in which there was a hint of shyness.

Henrietta and Audrey had lunch together and went back for Dusty. Audrey had borrowed a pair of gloves, though Hetty assured her that the return journey would be straightforward. Dusty was anxious to get back to his field. The only trouble was holding him back as they traversed the main street. At the foot of the cobbled lane Hetty let go of the halter. Dusty trotted on. When the friends reached the cottage he was munching thistles in the field.

'What a day!' Audrey exclaimed. 'I need a gin and tonic, Hetty, but I don't suppose you run to that. And, I say, I've just had a thought. If George Wright is moving to a searchlight battery, perhaps he'll have to give up being sergeant of the Althwaite platoon. Do you think Corporal Armitage will get promoted? He'll be a good catch – I mean match – for you, Hetty!'

'No, Audrey. He's very nice. But perhaps he's more your sort!'

'I need your help, Mum,' Jem said as they were having tea.

'What is it now? Been getting into a scrape?'

'No, it's Ma Hibbert – Miss Hibbert – in Up Bye. She's not very happy. I saw Mrs Bright trying to comfort her outside the church, and Tim says she always feels down at this time of the year. And I believe there's some sort of mystery about her.'

'So, it's not that you're feeling sorry for her, it's the prospect of solving a mystery is it?'

'No, Mum, it's both. She's been very good to Harold and me. I'd like to help her.'

'Why don't you go and see what you can do?'

'She'd be more likely to confide in you than in a lad like me.'

'Alright, I'll have a word with Mrs Bright. Then perhaps both of us might go and see her. I could spare a couple of eggs to make a sponge cake to take with me.'

19 THE TRUTH IS MORE COMPLICATED

Jem waited anxiously for his mother to visit Ma Hibbert. He didn't like to press her. She was busy with work for the Women's Voluntary Service, and he knew that she was worried that they had not heard from Dad for over a month. He set himself to exercise superhuman patience. But even that was nearly exhausted by the end of a fortnight. Then, with relief, he found Mum making a sponge cake.

'Er…is that for Miss Hibbert?'

'It is, Jem. Mrs Bright and I are going to see her tomorrow.'

When he got home from school the next day, Jem found the door locked. He went round to the shed to find the key in its usual hiding place, under a tin of nails. There was also a note: 'Gone Up Bye. Start making the tea.'

Jem had the tea almost ready - bread cut, tin of Spam opened, kettle boiling on the hob of the kitchen fire – when his mother appeared.

'Good lad! Now, where's those butterfly cakes I made yesterday?'

'How's Ma, I mean Miss Hibbert?' Jem asked when they were settled at the table.

'She was half expecting Mrs Bright to visit her this week. But me turning up as well rather took her aback – a bit too much like a deputation. And I'm not sure she didn't look on the cake with a bit of suspicion – as though I wanted to get something out of her. She was reserved at first, but by and by she thawed. You're right, Jem, there is a mystery. There's also a tragedy. But I'm afraid I can't pass on to you what I learned. It was told in confidence.'

'But…Mum…!'

'Hold on Jem! Eventually, I said that you and Harold were keen to help her if there was something that needed looking into. She wasn't sure. She said she realised you had wise heads on young shoulders – I must treat you with more respect, mustn't I Jem? But she didn't think you'd got to the bottom of the church burglary.'

'What? We did!'

'Well, I don't know – you've never told me what the outcome was.'

Jem felt frustrated. He could never betray the confidence that Hon Peter had placed in Harold and him. So he couldn't tell his Mum what the outcome was. His mother saw by his furrowed brow that he was perplexed as to what to say or do.

'I can see that you're not happy. But I've a suggestion to make. Why not ask Hon Peter if he's willing to give you a letter of recommendation?'

'Mum, you're a marvel!' Jem exclaimed, getting up to give her a kiss, and knocking over his cup of tea.

'Oh well, it's in a good cause. The tablecloth needed a wash, anyway!'

Jem and Harold sat in arm-chairs in the living room of Ma Hibbert's little house. It was a cold Saturday morning in early December. Jem was nervous. Harold was calm. This was Jem's project and he saw himself as merely providing moral support. She had welcomed them kindly, and the three black cats were rubbing themselves against the boys' legs and purring – a good sign, Jem thought. But it was a crucial visit. Would Ma Hibbert confide in them or not?

As it was a cold day, they had opted for cups of tea instead of glasses of Dandelion and Burdock. But neither of them was used to coping with cup and saucer whilst sitting in an armchair. They were anxious lest a cat jump on to a lap and upset a teacup. As Ma Hibbert read the letter they had brought from Hon Peter, they looked around the room. It was crammed full of furniture, pictures and ornaments. On a highly polished sideboard was a tea caddy, inlaid with mother of pearl. Beside it was the photograph that Ron had seen. It showed the head and shoulders of a smart soldier. He looked young, despite his moustache.

Miss Hibbert finished reading the letter and took off her spectacles.

'My cats are making friends with you, lads. Now what does that mean? Are they trusting you, or are they being sorry for you? This letter's very handsome, I'm sure. So I suppose you did get to the bottom of the burglary? But no doubt your lips are sealed?'

Jem nodded. 'We've no idea what Mr Danellion-Smith says in the letter.'

'Well, you'd better read it, dears.'

She handed the letter to Jem who read it and then passed it to Harold.

Dear Madam,

Jem Murgatroyd has asked if I can recommend the services of Harold Bright and himself as investigators. I have no hesitation in doing so. To my direct knowledge, they have displayed exceptional perseverance and imagination.

Not having any idea of the matter you might wish them to look into, I naturally cannot forecast whether they would be successful. But I believe it would do no harm to try them, and you might be gratified by the result. In any case, I am sure you can rely on their tact and discretion.

If I can be of any further help, please do not hesitate to get in touch with me.

I remain, madam, your faithful servant,

Peter Danellion-Smith

Hon Peter had done them proud. But would she entrust her case to them?

'Now lads,' Miss Hibbert began. 'What squire says is encouraging. But what I'd have to disclose to you is very sensitive – to me. I'd have to work myself up to it. Suppose you come back in a week's time? And thank your mother very much, Jem, for the cake. It's all gone, and the cats had the crumbs!'

At first, the war had been exciting. Jem now felt it was a nuisance.

It prevented him from getting on with his life. There was often terrible news on the wireless. The latest was that the Germans had bombed Coventry, damaging the city severely and killing many people.

'Where's it all going to end, Jem?' his mother asked, letting her mask of optimism fall. 'I think I'd be in despair if it wasn't for that J B Priestley on the wireless Sunday evenings. As he says, we're all in it now -not just the fighting men as in the last war. And when he talks about the future – building up a better world after the war – I don't mind admitting that tears come into my eyes. Some good must come out of all this suffering.'

Jem felt accused: it was selfish to regard his own concerns as more important than this momentous struggle. He decided a visit to Cop Top Farm would help to clear his mind.The first person he saw was Archie driving the tractor. He stopped and switched the engine off.

'Hullo, Jem! Haven't seen you for some time! Heard from your Dad?'

Jem told him that, without having definite information, it seemed that he was in Egypt. But how close to the fighting, they didn't know.

'Well, I may be getting a bit closer myself. I've become uneasy about standing back. I still couldn't bring myself to kill an enemy. But I've volunteered for ambulance work with the Friends' Ambulance – that's the Quakers, you know. Miriam and the baby'll be staying on here. Mr and Mrs Ackroyd have been very good about that. Well, I must be getting on. Alice is in the stable if you want to see her.'

'Hullo, Jem,' Alice said. 'You're just in time to lend a hand saddling up.'

She showed Jem how it was done. First the blanket, then the saddle.

'Bring the girth – that leather strap – underneath and buckle it up on the left hand side. As tight as you can – you don't want to be riding upside down.'

Jem had no intention of riding, whichever way up he was.

'Now, check there's no skin being pinched by the girth strap or the saddle. Up you get, Jem.'

'What me?'

'Yes! Now we pull the stirrups down to the right length.'

Before he realised what he'd let himself in for, Jem was being led out of the stable and being given instruction on using the reins, sitting with a straight back, trying to relax and feel confident. After a few circuits of the stable yard, he was relieved to dismount, but felt proud that he had not fallen off.

'Not bad for a beginner,' Alice commented. 'Now, I'd better give him some real exercise. By the way, are you going to come to the High School's "As You Like It"? I'm playing Rosalind and Bertha Whittle is Celia.'

Jem was both intrigued and perturbed by this news. He couldn't imagine anyone having the courage to act in public. He was much too self-conscious, and felt envious of Alice. The thought of both girls being on the stage both pleased and worried him. He admired them both. Would the sight of them together leave him more mixed-up?He needed to be brought back to earth from this intoxicating, but unsettling vision. He found what he needed in Benjy who was still lodging above the stables. Benjy explained that he was dividing his time between the farm and the blacksmith's shop.

'You'll 'ave to come along and see me at work, Jem.

Takes me back to my younger days in Oldham. O' course, when I left school, I went into the mill – most lads did. But I couldn't stand the noise. So when I saw an advertisement for a blacksmith's apprentice, I applied. Smithing's noisy, too. But there's a deal of difference between noise you make yourself and noise you've no control over. In any case, iron on iron's a musical sound.'

Before the week that Ma Hibbert had stipulated was up, Mrs Murgatroyd received a letter from her. She said that she didn't feel easy about confiding her trouble directly to Jem and Harold, but she asked the two mothers to explain it to them. If they can help, I'll be grateful, but I don't hold out much hope, she concluded.

After his mother had been in touch with Mrs Bright, she and Jem went up to the Manse. They were shown into the front room, where Harold joined them. Through the window, Jem looked across the village to the road rising up to the moors. It became lost in mist before the point where Mr Bright had dropped him, his Dad and Harold at the start of the expedition to find Benjy. That was only just over a year ago, but so much seemed to have happened since then. It was chilly in the front room. Mrs Bright apologized: Mr Bright was in the dining room, which also did duty as a study, composing a sermon; and Jonquil was in the kitchen. There wasn't enough coal or logs to light a fire in the front room as well.

'That photograph you've seen of the soldier,' Mrs Bright began, 'was Malcolm Knowsley. He and Julia Hibbert had known each other since they were children. She was 18 when they realised that they loved each other. But for some reason there was a quarrel. Julia blames herself. Instead of their becoming engaged, Malcolm went off to join the army. He could ride, having been brought up on a farm. So he was drafted into a cavalry regiment and found himself sent to India. He came back on leave two years later. He and Julia had made it up in letters, and they became engaged. The plan was that he would leave the army in a year's time to work on the family farm, and they would marry. After Malcolm had returned to India, Julia found that she was expecting a baby.'

Jem and Harold began to feel uncomfortable. They realised why Ma Hibbert might have felt too embarrassed to tell them herself.

'You see, lads,' said Mrs Murgatroyd, taking up the tale, 'in those days it was a shameful thing for an unmarried woman to become pregnant. Julia was happy at the prospect of having Malcolm's baby, but she was also worried about the reaction of her parents. They were very strict, and they were horrified when she told them. They felt that they would be shamed, too. They decided she must be kept out of the way until after the baby was born. Her mother had an old school friend who'd married Elias Whittle of Intake Farm – the Mr Whittle you met in the summer is their son. So she was packed off there.'

'So, did the baby stay there?' Harold asked.

'No,' said Mrs Bright, feeling that it was her turn to carry on. 'This is where the story becomes tragedy. Julia's parents wouldn't hear of her bringing up the child herself. They wanted Julia to come back to Althwaite as though nothing unusual had happened. They insisted she get the baby adopted. Julia held out against this. She loved the child – a boy. But then came news that Malcolm had died of fever. In those days she wasn't as strong-willed as she is today. She was in such despair that she allowed her mother and father to overcome her own feelings. So, at six months old, the baby was adopted by a couple without children. They lived in Oldham.'

'Didn't she see the baby again?' Jem asked.

'We're coming to that,' Mrs Murgatroyd said. 'For the first three years, Julia managed an annual visit. Then her parents died, she herself was very hard up, and she couldn't afford the journey. She had replies to letters for a further three Christmases, then a fourth letter was returned, marked "Gone Away". Julia – Miss Hibbert – has lent you some papers. You'll have to be careful with them.'

It was a week later. Jem and Harold were at the Manse. They had laid out the rail track on the floor of the dining room and had sent the battered clockwork locomotive back and forth a few times. But their interest soon palled.

'Let's decide what we're going to do to help Ma Hibbert,' Jem suggested.

They went up to Harold's bedroom. Harold produced an old exercise book with some empty pages.

'First thing is to see what we know,' he said.

After studying the papers lent to them and some sucking of his pencil end, Harold wrote:

Date of birth – 18 May 1895

Name – Raymond Hibbert

Date of adoption – 15 November 1895

Name of foster parents – Joseph and Hilary Oldcastle

Occupation of Mr Oldcastle – ironmonger

Last known address (1901) – 25 High Mill Place, Oldham

Age of son now – 45

'Seems a shame he couldn't have been called "Knowsley", after his father,' Harold said.

'It wouldn't have been allowed on the birth certificate, as they weren't married,' Jem replied. 'We haven't got much to go on. Did they just move house and keep on the business? Or did they leave Oldham? There must be some way of finding out what happened to them.'

'Perhaps we ought to find out from the Library whether there are records of businesses,' Harold suggested.

Neither Jem nor Harold was on good terms with Mrs Postlethwaite, the Librarian. Too often she had had to admonish them for chatting despite the notices enjoining SILENCE. But when she found out that they were apparently really interested in the history of local businesses, she stopped her checking of overdue books and explained that they would have to go to the library in Bruddersford, as the Althwaite library was too small to house books of reference like that. In spindly handwriting, she wrote a letter which she said they could give to one of the librarians in the Oldroyd Library.

Harold got permission from his parents, and Jem from his mother, to go into Bruddersford on the train. Neither had been there very often, and Mr Bright drew a map to show them the way from the station to the library. They both thought that permission to visit the town would be wasted if they did not also use the opportunity to go to the 'pictures'. The film, 'Robin Hood' was being show again at the Odeon. Each boy had already seen it, having nagged their fathers to take them a year ago. The previous Christmas, Harold had been given the book of the film. With many photographs from the film, it was a prized possession. Having enough pocket money to pay to get in, they were given leave to include the cinema in the expedition.

The Oldroyd Library, the result of a benefaction by Sir Hector Oldroyd MP, a wealthy owner of an engineering firm and several mills, was an imposing building with a pillared portico. Entering the vast, panelled Reference Library, Jem and Harold felt very small. Had they not been able to present Mrs Postlethwaite's letter of introduction, they would have felt extremely nervous. They presented the letter at the counter.A pleasant young lady read it, and smiled at them.

'Research for a school project?' she asked.

'Something like that,' Jem replied.

She showed them a shelf with a row of Directories of Businesses going back fifty years. They selected a couple and sat down at a long table where adults of various ages where reading books or newspapers.

'Shsh…,' a neighbour admonished them when they began whispering about some of the entries.

They made a show of writing some notes as though for a school project, and then left. They were satisfied that if there were similar directories in Oldham, they stood a good chance of finding out whether the Oldcastle ironmongery shop had continued.

The visit to the Odeon put out of their minds the question of the next step. Robin Hood's sword duel with Sir Guy Guisborne on the staircase of the Great Hall of Nottingham Castle was as exciting as they remembered. They again fell in love with Maid Marian. They laughed at the quarterstaff duel between Friar Tuck and Little John.

On the return journey, they discussed the film. Jem thought Errol Flynn was his favourite actor. He persuaded Harold to lend him the book of the film. It was only as the train was approaching Althwaite that the main purpose of the visit recurred to them. How were they to consult Directories of Business in Oldham without visiting the library? Though just over the Pennines, they saw as much likelihood of being able to get there as London. Harold, who rather prided himself on his composition, suggested they write. He offered to prepare a draft. He produced it the next day.

Dear Sir (or Madam), it read,

We wish to find out if the ironmongerry shop of Mr Joseph Oldcastle went on after 1901 AD. It might have been at 25 High Mill Place. We'd like to know if it staid there or went somewhere else. We will be much obligated if you will tell us.

Harold was disappointed that Jem was not impressed. He was particularly fond of the word 'obligated', which sounded grown-up.

'It's too short. Doesn't explain that the question's important, not just curiosity. But I don't think I could do any better. Tell you what – let's ask Hon Peter to write.

He told Ma Hibbert he'd be glad to do anything.'

They visited the Hall and found Peter in the unusual activity of gardening. His face was flushed. He unbent and straightened his back.

'Am I glad to have a diversion, lads! Alistair has decided to join up, though he's not obliged to. Most of the garden will go to rack and ruin. But so long as I can keep the vegetable plot going, that will keep Mrs McAlister happy. I hadn't realised what hard work it is though - as you'll have found out Jem, helping our friend Tim. Now, what brings you here? I see some important project in your serious expressions. Let's adjourn to the study.'

Peter took off his gardening boots outside the kitchen. When Mrs McAlister brought a coffee and two orange squashes into the study, Peter apologized for the lack of biscuits. The boys explained the mission that Miss Hibbert had entrusted to them. They showed Peter the birth certificate and the copy of the adoption certificate. Harold produced the draft letter, and explained that they thought Hon Peter could do better.

'That's very handsome of you,' he said, and suppressed a smile as he read it.

There and then he wrote a letter to the Town Clerk of Oldham. Jem and Harold watched in admiration as the fountain pen flowed fluently over the paper. It filled a whole page before signing off with a flourish. He didn't show it to them, not wanting to hurt Harold's feelings.

'That should get a bit of attention though Town Clerks are busy, like other local government officials, with war matters. We shouldn't expect an early reply.'

'How's Lorinda?' Jem asked.

'Thank you for asking. So far as I know, she's well. But she decided to go into the secret work I mentioned to you. So naturally I worry about that. Won't it be marvellous when it's all over, and the Hall and the village can get together on something constructive?'

The following Saturday morning, Jem decided he would look Benjy up at the blacksmith's, as he'd been invited to. A pony had just been brought in. Jem watched as Benjy heated a shoe in the glowing fire, hit it into shape on the anvil, plunged it into water, creating steam, and repeated the process until the shoe could be fitted to the pony's hoof with nails. As he was leaving, he saw something which gave him a start. Over the entrance the words, AND BENJAMIN OLDCASTLE, DEPUTY, had been added to the name of GEORGE WRIGHT.

'Is that your surname, Benjy?'

'Ay. I reckoned I 'ad as much right as George to put my name up, what with him being away at the searchlight battery so much.'

Jem was about to ask further questions, but thought he had better consult Harold first. He hurried up to the Manse and arrived breathless.

'Is Harold in?' he asked Mrs Bright.

'Sorry, Jem, he's gone to Bruddersford with his father. They'll be back before dinner.'

'Will you ask him to come over this afternoon?'

'Something urgent is it, Jem? Yes, I'll tell him.'

It was nearly tea-time before Harold turned up.

'What's up Jem? Mum said you looked agitated.'

'I've found out who Ma Hibbert's son is.'

'What do you mean? Peter's only just written to Oldham.'

'Do you know what Benjy's surname is?'

'No – he's never let on.'

'It's "Oldcastle".'

'Well?'

'Don't you see? That's the name of the foster parents.'

'Could be a coincidence. It's a common enough name.'

'Yes, but think on. Benjy was brought up in Oldham. And what sort of age do you think he is?'

'Difficult to say, perhaps mid-forties.'

'There you are then! What's more, he told me that he felt there was some sort of sympathy between Ma Hibbert and him. "Affinity" is the word he used. You're at the Grammar School, Harold – what's that word at the end of geometry theorems?'

'You mean "QED" – "Quod erat demonstrandum"?'

'That's it. Demonstrated!'

'Not so fast, Jem. There could be plenty of Oldcastles. And it might be a coincidence that Benjy also came from Oldham. And his Christian name isn't "Raymond".'

'The foster parents may have changed it.'

'Then – Ma Hibbert's sympathy. That could be because she's that sort of person. There's only one way to test your theory – ask Benjy who his parents were.'

'We can't do that without letting on that we're

looking for Ma Hibbert's son. And, if he is her son, we couldn't let him know without her knowing first. So perhaps we ought to tell her what we think.'

'What *you* think, you mean, Jem. But supposing you're wrong – you'd be raising her hopes, only for them to be dashed. We ought at least to wait for a reply from Oldham.'

'Perhaps we ought. But I'm dead sure I'm right. It seems so fitting.'

'Aren't you jumping to conclusions?'

'I'll bet you I'm right – anything you like from what I've got for anything I like from what you've got.'

'Alright. I'd like that model of "Cock o' the North".'

'And I'd like that telescope.'

The model that Harold coveted was of the famous LNER – London and North Eastern Railway – locomotive. It was about six inches long, of solid metal and on a metal plinth. Jem had been given it by an Uncle whose hobby was collecting anything to do with the railways.

Jem didn't find it easy to concentrate on school work as they waited for a reply from Oldham. His mind would keep wandering to a grand reunion scheme in which a happy, tearful Julia Hibbert accepted Benjamin Oldcastle as her long lost son. Looking on were Hon Peter, Jem's Mum, Mrs Bright and Alice (though how she came to be there he wasn't sure). Everyone congratulated him and Harold, but particularly himself, as the one who had put two and two together.

There was something, though, that succeeded in distracting his mind: the approach of the performance of 'As You Like It'. Although not involved, Jem found himself becoming nervous on behalf of Alice and Bertha. Suppose one or the other forgot her lines? If they had not been playing the parts, he would not have been very keen on going to see the play. He was finding 'Macbeth' hard going at school, though he enjoyed the scenes with Banquo, the ghost.

The night after the play, Jem couldn't get to sleep for hours. Images of Alice as Rosalind and Bertha as her dear friend, Celia, thronged his mind. Having only the sketchiest idea of the plot beforehand, it had taken him some time to realize what was going on. But he felt affronted by the banishment of Rosalind, and moved by Celia's determination to accompany her. Disguised as Ganymede, Alice made a handsome young man. He was envious of Orlando, her lover. He was not surprised that Oliver, Orlando's reformed brother, could fall in love so rapidly with Celia.

For days afterwards, the scenes in the Forest of Arden kept intruding into his brain. He was astonished that he could claim two confident actresses as friends. Shy of projecting himself publicly as they had, he felt a sense of inferiority. How they could have any regard for him? But, he reflected, he had done some things of note: he'd helped to rescue Benjy, and Harold and he had come so near to solving the mystery of the church burglary that the perpetrator had as good as disclosed himself. And he believed he was near to finding Ma Hibbert's long lost son. He remembered from Bible readings in chapel that St Paul had said something about people having different gifts. The recollection made him feel better.

But Jem was left with a conundrum: which of the two girls did he like the best? He didn't know Bertha so well, but her lively, sometimes mischievous manner appealed to him, as did her dark eyes and her shoulder-length black hair. Alice he had known for a long time. Tall and fair, quieter and more reserved than Bertha, she was more distant but capable, he felt, of more sympathy. He left the problem unresolved.

For the first time in the memory of Althwaite and district, the Messiah was not performed in the customary way at Christmas. Too many men and women were in the forces or away on war work. But Handel was not entirely forgotten. The choirs of St Jude's and the Methodist chapel presented a selection of choruses from the oratorio, the audience being invited to join in. Jem thought of Benjy. He had now moved from Cop Top Farm into one of the mill cottages, in the row where One-Leg Tim lived. His mother had once before rejected the idea of inviting Benjy to their Christmas dinner. But he had made himself more respectable since then.

'Alright, Jem. He's certainly made an effort to spruce himself up,' his mother said. 'What his table manners are like, we'll see.'

Jem conveyed the invitation to Benjy, confident of it being thankfully accepted. He was surprised, therefore, when Benjy seemed embarrassed, flushing slightly and scratching his head.

'That's very kind o' your Mum. But I'm going somewhere else on Christmas Day. How about Boxing Day? Mebbe you could save a bit o' pudding for then, eh?'

It was a different Benjy from the one Jem had got to know three years ago who knocked on their door at twelve o'clock on Boxing Day. He was wearing an old, but still decent, tweed suit that Farmer Ackroyd had passed on to him. He was wearing a tie, and his stout shoes had a shine to them. He had had his hair cut recently.Although he was balding at the front, he still had a good covering, and there were only a few flecks of grey.

Mrs Murgatroyd was pleased at his obvious attempt to pass muster as a respectable citizen. Once she had invited him to sit beside the living room fire and to smoke his pipe if he wanted to, Benjy began to feel at ease.

After the first course of cold turkey, the Christmas Pudding was placed on the table.

'I know this is goin' to be good, as I've tasted one of your puddings before, Mrs Murgatroyd,' Benjy said.

'Yes, we know all about that,' she replied. 'Jem confessed. It's become a family joke.'

'You may wonder at me becoming less of a tramp,' Benjy began when the dinner was over, the washing up was done and they were sitting in front of the fire. 'I used to pride myself on being a tramp – the tramp of the Althwaite Valley. It was uncomfortable and cold at times, but it gave me a status. And I liked my freedom. But eventually it dawned on me that I couldn't go on like that. It were partly the war. It made me feel that being a tramp was selfish. Then, there was the kindness of the Ackroyds. Living at the farm, I felt I 'ad to be more presentable. And there's my old pal, Rick, at

Homefield. I began to envy 'im – a nice, little 'ome and a cheerful wife. My own marriage, long ago, didn't work – though I tried 'ard. That's partly why I took up tramping. So you see, Mrs Murgatroyd, I'm trying to change my image – not just my image, but myssen. Am I succeeding?'

'You are that, Mr Oldcastle – or may I call you Mr Benjy?'

'Benjy will do very well, ma'am. Another thing – you may wonder why I couldn't come yesterday. Fact was, I were invited to 'ave dinner with Mrs Isaacs – Henrietta.'

It was with difficulty that Mrs Murgatroyd repressed a smile at this surprising news.

'A lovely 'ouse she has – no disrespect to you o' course – very comfortable. She's a cut above me, but we get on. When I was there, and now I'm 'ere, that vagabond life o' mine seems a world away!'

'Well!' Mrs Murgatroyd exclaimed when Benjy had gone. 'He was really very pleasant, and his table manners were better than I expected. But fancy his becoming friendly with Mrs Isaacs! What will her posh friend, Audrey, think about that?'

The second New Year of the war was welcomed by Althwaite people with a mixture of hope and misgiving. The war had already gone on longer than many had expected, and there was no prospect of it ending. There was encouraging news, though, from North Africa. General Wavell's soldiers were pushing the Italians out of Egypt and towards Libya. For Jem and his mother, though, this news was a cause for anxiety. Was Dad mixed up in the fighting?

Jem had begun to despair of a reply from Oldham to Hon Peter's letter. Then, on a Saturday morning in late January, Mrs Murgatroyd answered a knock at the door. It was Hon Peter. She had her apron on and felt embarrassed.

'Sorry to take you by surprise, Mrs Murgatroyd. Is young Jem in?'

His mother called him from the shed where, wearing an overcoat to keep warm, he was painting a model aeroplane – a Hurricane fighter. Though he had wiped his hands, he brought with him a smell of the dope he had been applying.

'Splendid news about the fall of Tobruk, isn't it?' Peter said.

'Yes, but it's somewhere in North Africa that Jem's Dad is – in the Ambulance Corps.'

'Well, he's safer there than in the infantry. I do hope you hear from him soon. Now, I've a reply from the Town Clerk of Oldham. I'll read it out.'

Dear Sir,

Thank you for your letter of 2 December 1940. I have caused enquiries to be made and have pleasure in reporting as follows.

Mr and Mrs Joseph Oldcastle moved from 25 High Mill Place, Oldham, to 36 Moor View Road, Oldham on 14 July 1904, keeping the shop at High Mill Place and letting the floor above the premises. Joseph Oldcastle joined the Army in 1915. It appears that the ironmongery business was kept going by Mrs Oldcastle, perhaps aided by her adopted son, Raymond. Joseph Oldcastle was killed in France in July 1918. His wife sold the business towards the end of 1918, and she and Raymond emigrated to the United States of

America in January 1919. Nothing further is known about them.

I hope this information is of assistance,

Yours faithfully,

J O Thompson, Town Clerk

'So,' said Hon Peter, 'the mystery thickens! We're now on American territory. I'm not at all sure how best to proceed. I could try writing to the American Embassy to see if their immigration service has any record of the address that Mrs Oldcastle went to. Would you like me to do that, Jem? Or would you and Harold like to write?'

Jem thought of Harold's draft of a letter to the Town Clerk and said he'd be glad if Hon Peter would write. When Peter had left and he had resumed his painting of the Hurricane, the thought hit him. Raymond Oldcastle had gone to America. Benjy had never said anything about living in America. So, were Benjy and Raymond different persons? Was he wrong in believing that they were one and the same? There was only one way to find out.

The next day was a Sunday. Jem pressed his mother to agree that he needn't go to Sunday School or Chapel, pleading the enquiry on behalf of Miss Hibbert. His mother gave way reluctantly.

'I'm soft – your Dad would have been more strict. But don't be late for dinner,' she said.

It was a cold morning after overnight frost. The sun was making only a feeble effort to penetrate a blanket of cloud. The lane leading to Mill Cottages was not made up, and the potholes were coveredwith ice. In previous years, Jem would have delighted in stepping on them and crunching the ice into splinters. Now, he noticed how the colour of the ice changed from white at the edge, to grey and black at the centre of the holes. He skirted around them. He was not sure which of the six cottages was Benjy's, and had thought he might have to knock at One-Leg Tim's door and ask. But he saw Benjy leaning on a wall opposite the cottages, looking at the river, here corralled between high banks.

'Hello, Jem! Come to see my new abode? It's a grand spot this, though I 'aven't got used to the sound o' the river at night. I expect you've 'ad your breakfast. I 'aven't. So, 'ow about a second one?'

It was nearly ten o'clock, only two hours since Jem's breakfast. But he didn't say no to the bacon and eggs that Benjy produced. Jem sat at the side of the kitchen table nearest to the fire. It was just big enough to prevent him from shivering. Perhaps Benjy's previous outdoor life had given him an indifference to cold, he thought. The breakfast, concluding with toast and hot tea, put him in the mood to broach the important matter that had to be resolved. He realised, though, that he would have to approach it tactfully.

Benjy almost took the wind out of his sails by himself posing an unexpected question.

'Ever thought you'd like to go to America, Jem?' he asked.

'Er, not really.'

'My pal in Homefield lent me a book by a chap called Davies. Described himself as a super-tramp. Perhaps 'e was a bit big-headed. But if 'is story is true, 'e deserved to be. Went to America and became a hobo – what they call a tramp. Rode on couplings of freight trains, or 'anging on underneath. 'ad to 'ave a foot amputated. Came back 'ere and became a famous poet. Makes my tramping look very ordinary.'

'So, you've not been to America, Benjy?'

'Never 'ad the chance. What makes you think I might 'ave?'

'Well…'

'You alright, Jem? You look a bit hot. Too near the fire?'

Jem gazed into the fire, which was giving off little heat.

'I've been a fool,' he said, looking up at Benjy and forcing his mouth into a slight smile.

'Out with it!'

'Harold and me – we've been trying to help Ma Hibbert to find the son she had to give up to be adopted.'

'And you thought I might be 'im?'

'Well, there were some clues. Your surname's the same as the foster parents', and you seemed the right age, and you said that she and you got on specially well.'

'Well, I'll be jiggered! This takes some beating!'

Benjy paused, noticing that Jem looked very unhappy. He stifled an impulse to roar with laughter.

'I can see it would make a lovely headline. "Wise woman of Althwaite acknowledges tramp of the Valley as 'er son". But I 'ave to disappoint you, Jem. I know very well who my mother and father were. Tell me what you know about Miss Hibbert's son.'

Jem told him what he knew.

'Ay, there were two or three families called Oldcastle when I were a lad in Oldham. I mind Joseph Oldcastle the ironmonger. I remember the news coming that 'e'd been killed. People felt very sorry for 'is widow. I think she 'ad a relative in America. That'll be why she decided to make a new life there.'

Benjy put some more coal on the fire, which was almost dying away.

'I tell you what, young Jem. I've still got friends in Oldham. I could go and make some enquiries. See if anyone knows where she and Raymond went to in America.'

Jem left Benjy's with mixed feelings of shame and hope. Thank goodness only Harold – apart from Benjy – knew what an ass he had been in jumping to conclusions. But out of his mistake had come new hope, now that Benjy was enrolled in the search.

On the way home, a thought pierced Jem to his stomach. The bet with Harold! There was no going back on it. Now he would have to sacrifice Cock o' the North. But it would be a just punishment for his folly. He went to see Harold in the afternoon, taking the beloved model with him.

'I'm sorry, Jem,' Harold said when Jem had explained how wrong he had been. 'I don't like taking something you value so much. But it was a bet. Suppose I have it for just a year?'

Jem was so relieved by this generous offer that his sense of humiliation receded into the background.

Before he woke the next morning, Jem had one of those late dreams, so vivid and pleasing, that make the return to the real world unwelcome. Ma Hibbert's son, Raymond, was a Duke in the Forest of Arden which was located, strangely, in the Rocky Mountains of America. Alice was there in disguise as a cowboy. Benjy arrived, having ridden as a hobo on a freight train. Benjy discovered the Duke's real identity, and sent a telegram to Jem. Was the dream a favourable omen, Jem wondered?

20 THE DOWNWARD SLOPE

It dawned on Jem that he and Harold ought to report to Ma Hibbert on how they were getting on. They took Raq with them, as she had previously been made welcome. As they turned into Up Bye they saw Mrs Isaacs shutting Ma Hibbert's garden gate. She approached them with her eyes on the ground, but they could see that she was smiling to herself. Raq ran towards her. She was momentarily startled, and then bent down to rub her behind an ear.

'Hullo boys! I was miles away. But I shouldn't be surprised at meeting you. Julia – Miss Hibbert – said she was expecting a visit from Jem Murgatroyd and Harold Bright. And here you are – on cue! What a marvellous old lady, isn't she? She told me you were helping to trace her son. I do hope you manage it.'

She was about to leave them when a thought seemed to strike her.

'You know my donkey – Dusty? He doesn't mind being ridden around the field. If you feel like a bumpy ride, pretending to be cowboys, come up some time. You know where I live – up the hill? Goodbye boys!'

The front door was open, despite the cold wind off the hills. The three black cats eyed Raq with suspicion, but were not hostile.

'Come in lads, and shut the door,' Ma Hibbert shouted from the kitchen. 'I thought it might be you.'

Jem gave her the reply from the Town Clerk of Oldham. As she read and re-read it, his gaze wandered around the cluttered room. It alighted on a Toby jug on a shelf. One eye was half-closed and the mouth was twisted up into a cheeky grin. Was the Toby trying to say something to him? If he was, it would not be something reassuring. More likely it would be some sarcastic comment on his motive: to make a mark on the world, rather than simply to help an old lady.

'Oh dear,' said Miss Hibbert, putting the letter down. 'Have we come up against a blank wall?'

Jem explained that there were now two trains of enquiry: Hon Peter would write to the American Embassy about immigration records, whilst Benjy would visit friends in Oldham to see whether they knew of anyone who might have maintained contact with Mrs Oldcastle in America.

'Now why didn't I think of that? I knew Benjamin came from Oldham! I'm not such a wise woman, after all. Or maybe,' she added, looking at the photograph of her fiancée, Malcolm, 'I'm only wise when thinking about other people's problems. Well, thank you lads. We'll just have to be patient.'

'I wonder why Mrs Isaacs was looking so pleased with herself before she noticed us,' Harold mused, as they descended the hill.

'Perhaps she'd been for a consultation, and got some good advice.'

'Yes, but about what?'

'Dunno. I say, I wouldn't mind having a ride on Dusty,' Jem said, recalling his brief experiment at Cop Top Farm. 'But – "pretending to be cowboys" – she must think we're kids!'

When Jem arrived home, he found his mother sitting in an armchair looking into the kitchen fire. She was holding a letter, and seemed hardly aware of his return.

'What's up, Mum?'

'Nothing's up, Jem. Here's a letter from your Dad. He's well and cheerful. You read it.'

How are you, love? Not over doing it with the chapel caretaking and the WVS? Thanks for the parcel. Taking into account the length of the journey, the fruit cake was in good condition and much appreciated – not just by me. The Lifebuoy soap added a bit of extra flavour! As you'll know by the news, the war out here has become interesting. Driving my old ambulance long distances is no joke, but at least there are no traffic lights! I spent a whole day recently cleaning the sand away from underneath, but now it'll be just as bad. There's some splendid chaps in my crew. The other night, we went round describing what kind of holiday we'd like when we come home. Most of them didn't want to go far afield. I said we'd go to Scarborough. On return, we'd have a picnic at Digfoot Reservoir. Then perhaps you'd give Jem and me leave to go for a tramp – avoiding peat hags! I hope Jem's going to try for the transfer to the Grammar School. Lots of love to you both.

'Well, that's fine, Mum, isn't it?'

'Yes, but I can't help worrying, with all that fighting going on. I bet he's involved in things he doesn't tell us about. And he's obviously so keen to be back home.'

'Are you going to the WVS this afternoon, Mum?' Jem asked in an attempt to turn her mind from worrying about Dad.

'Yes.'

'Are you going to put your new uniform on?'

Mrs Murgatroyd had managed to save enough to buy the outfit.

'I should, shouldn't I? If only to impress Miss Arbuthnot!'

After dinner, she went upstairs to change. When she came down in her green tweed jacket and skirt, red jumper and green felt hat, Jem was astonished.

'If Dad saw you, he'd desert the army like a shot!'

'And *be* shot, as like as not!'

In ensuing weeks, as winter still held the valley in its cold and moody grip, the village needed some distraction from the season and the uncertainties of the war. One came in the form of Wings for Victory Week. Homefield and Althwaite, as part of the same Rural District, adopted a joint target of £50,000, enough for ten Spitfire fighters. Audrey Arbuthnot, was the President of the local National Savings Committee. When it was suggested that she should launch the campaign, she leapt at the opportunity to enthuse the community.

The Week began with a parade, starting in Althwaite and then carrying on to Homefield. It was led by the Silver Band, behind which marched the Home Guard platoons, the Air Raid Wardens, the Women's

Voluntary Service, the scouts and guides. It ended at the Alhambra cinema in Homefield where Audrey addressed the responsible and curious. She began by reading a greetings telegram from Sir Kingsley Wood, the Chancellor of the Exchequer.

National Savings have played a vital part in sustaining the war offensive. I look confidently to Homefield and Althwaite to increase still further our national resources. Best wishes to you all.

There was also a message from the Secretary of State for Air. Many in the audience assumed that it was Miss Arbuthnot's influence that had prompted communications from these important men. Others, more cynical but more realistic, attributed them to lowly clerks in the Treasury and the Air Ministry.

Hon Peter generously admitted that Audrey Arbuthnot's powers of oratory were equal to his own.

'The object of this campaign,' she said standing confidently on the stage in her best WVS uniform, 'is not just the raising of vitally important funds. It's also to show Herr Hitler that he faces an implacable foe. There are some who say it is for the Government to find the money for aircraft and armaments.'

She was interrupted by a voice from the back: 'And so it is!'

'Of course my friend,' Audrey continued, 'but where does the money come from if not from the people? Who is fighting this war – the Government or the nation? We are all involved. The least we can do is to mobilize the small savings of people like ourselves.'

The man at the back, like some others, reflected that Miss Arbuthnot's savings were no doubt much greater that those of most folk in the locality, but he held his peace.

'So let us show Hitler, and the rest of the West Riding, what Homefield and Althwaite can do!' she wound up to applause.

Audrey had been right in her speculation that if George Wright went to a searchlight battery, his place as Sergeant of the Althwaite Home Guard platoon might be taken by Walter Armitage. Walter sat in the audience, proudly conscious of the three stripes on his uniform. 'What a woman!' he thought, as he listened to her rousing speech. His mind harked back to the admiring glances she had seemed to give him after he had alighted from Dusty outside the blacksmith's. Could he aspire to such a height? The thought made him sit up straighter. With Audrey Arbuthnot behind him, he could see himself as Bank Manager and Councillor Armitage.

After the launch of the campaign, people adjourned to the recreation ground at Homefield where a damaged German Junkers bomber had been put on display. It had crash-landed in the south of England, and was one of a number of trophies that went the rounds of the Wings for Victory Weeks.

It fell to the scouts to deliver leaflets about the Week. Jem offered to take those for the part of Althwaite which included Cop Top Farm. He hoped to see Alice, and was not disappointed.

'Come for another ride, Jem?' she asked with a smile.

'You know I'm not keen on horses, Alice. Nor them on me, I bet. I've just come to leave this leaflet about the Wings for Victory Week.'

'Not to see me?' she asked, raising her eyebrows in mock disappointment.

'Yes, of course,' said Jem, regretting his lack of tact.

'Seriously, though,' she continued, 'I've been meaning to ask if you're going to try for the transfer to Bruddersford.'

Jem was approaching thirteen, at which age the most promising pupils at Homefield School were given a second opportunity to get into the Grammar School.

'I suppose so. I'm quite happy at Homefield, but I know Mum wants me to try, and Dad mentioned it in a letter we've just had.'

'What was your weakness in the scholarship exam?'

'My arithmetic.'

'Well, maths is one of my good subjects. Could I give you some coaching?'

'Yes please!' Jem exclaimed. The transfer exam was suddenly transformed, from a hurdle he thought he should make a vain attempt to get over, into a challenge he was determined to overcome.

Jem was to remember those late afternoon and early evenings in the large kitchen at Cop Top with fondness. The fire in the range and the curtain over the yard door kept the room cosy. One or more of the cats would be snoozing on vacant chairs. Mr Ackroyd would often be reading the newspaper beside the fire, or attending to accounts at an old desk. Mrs Ackroyd would be in the adjoining scullery or darning socks by the fire. Jem sat at one end of the scrubbed table, whilst Alice sat at one side. She would begin by posing some sums for Jem to do in his head – to get the blood flowing into the grey matter, she said. Then she would introduce work she had done in her first year at the Girls' High School. His attitude to the exercises she gave him to do at home was very different from that towards school homework. He wanted to show Alice that he wasn't stupid, and to justify her faith in him.

Audrey Arbuthnot had good reasons to be satisfied with her efforts at galvanizing the two villages into contributing to the war effort. The Bruddersford Examiner carried the news that the target of £50,000 had been surpassed. A staggering sum of £65,000 had been raised – enough for thirteen Spitfires. One lady had thrown a gold ring into a collecting box. One envelope contained only one shilling and three farthings, but it included a letter from a five year old boy. 'To help fight Hitler, I have saved this,' it said.

February arrived. Going outside in the early morning, the people of Althwaite felt uplifted by the sense that spring was in the offing. The patches of snow on the high moors were getting smaller, nights were milder and there was the smell of something fresh in the air. Such a morning, one Saturday, inspired Jem with the thought that he should visit the allotments. He was guiltily aware that the family's allotment was in need of attention. But he thought he should first see if One-Leg Tim wanted some help. He found him seated on a wooden box, and digging with a trowel.

'Eh lad, tha's a sight for sore eyes!' Tim exclaimed. 'I

can't dig deep enough. There's a spade in t' shed.'

For and hour, Jem dug and weeded until his back was protesting.

'Time for a break, lad,' said Tim, seeing Jem putting his hands on hips and pushing his shoulders back. 'Tha's not used to 'ard labour, but tha keeps at it.'

Jem found that Tim no longer brought a thermos flask. He now had a spirit stove and a kettle in the shed. With the tea made, Jem expected to be treated again to Tim's recollections of the Boer War, kept fresh by repetition. But there came a shout from the gate into the allotments. They saw Benjy approaching.

'Looks like I've arrived just in time – or is tea only for workers?'

'I'll get another mug,' Tim replied.

There was barely room for the three of them on the bench outside the hut. After enquiring about Tim's health, and before Tim could embark on his recollections, Benjy began to explain what had brought him there.

'Your mother said I'd find you 'ere, Jem. I got round at last to visiting my friends in Oldham – got back yesterday.'

Jem was suddenly alert. Would Benjy's report be encouraging or dampening?

'Ay, it were good to see 'em again. They 'ardly recognized me wi'out my beard, and looking smart in Mr Ackroyd's cast-offs. To cut a long story short, Joan – that's the wife – knew an elderly lady, Priscilla, who she thought 'ad kept in touch for a time with Hilary Oldcastle in America. So we went to see Priscilla in an old folks' 'ome. God preserve me from an old folks' 'ome, Jem! I've no doubt they're looked after well, but

I'd rather shift for myssen, even if I'm blind and batty. Anyroad, this old lady told us she used to write once or twice a year to Hilary after she went to America in 1919. But after 1935 she didn't get any replies, so she didn't know whether Hilary 'ad died or what. She gave us the address she used to write to. Priscilla's going to write there again, and also to the mayor of the town. We thought they must 'ave mayors in America. So we've done what we can. But don't be too 'opeful, Jem.'

Jem was relieved that Benjy had at last managed to get to Oldham. Knowing how busy he was at the forge and at Cop Top, he hadn't liked to remind him. It raised his spirits to know that enquiries were afoot. Surely there must be some trace of Hilary Oldcastle and her 'son' Raymond!

Some weeks later, a proud and excited Jem rushed up to Cop Top Farm when the results of the transfer exam were announced. Alice was not in the stable, but her pony was there. He knocked on the farm-house door. There was no reply, and no sound of anyone moving inside. This was most unusual. He was about to look into the neighbouring fields when a voice called.

'Hullo there! What do you want, laddie?'

Jem turned. Two women were coming out of the cow byre. They wore green jerseys, fawn corduroy breeches, brown stockings, and boots. One had straight, brown hair, the other curly, fair hair. It was the fair-haired one who had shouted and who came towards him with a grin.

'Who are you?' she asked.

'I'm Jem Murgatroyd. But who are you?'

‘I’m Jeannie and this is Marge. We’re the Land Army. Arrived last week.’

‘To help fight the war in this god-forsaken place,’ added Marge, looking Jem up and down.

‘Where’s the family?’ Jem asked.

‘They’ve all gone to Intake Farm, somewhere in the wilds. Did you want to leave a message?’

‘Er…will you tell Alice that I got through.’

‘Through what – a hedge backwards? Your hair wants a brush, laddie.’

Jeannie’s scornful words were spoken with a Scottish accent.

‘She’ll know what I mean.’

‘Don’t you listen to Jeannie. She’s got a chip on her shoulder,’ said Marge. ‘I expect you’re one of Alice’s admirers, like that nice young man – what was his name, Jeannie? Was it “Charlie”?’

‘She’s a special friend, yes,’ said Jem lamely, not knowing how best to deal with these cheeky women.

‘Don’t worry, luv, we’re only pulling your leg,’ Marge added as Jem turned to leave. ‘So long!’

Jem kicked some stones aside as he went down the lane. He felt discomfited by the encounter. What right had these strangers to intrude into comfortable and friendly Cop Top Farm? But he soon realised how foolish this was. With Archie gone, and with Benjy spending half his time at the blacksmith’s, Mr Ackroyd needed help. Jem had heard about the Women’s Land Army , but these were the first members he had seen. He decided that when he met them again, he would try to chaff them as they had chaffed him. But the information that Charlie – “that nice young man” – had been up to CopTop was disturbing.

As well as Wings for Victory Week and the approach of spring, other developments stirred the interest of Althwaite folk. First there was the decision of the powers that be to amalgamate the Althwaite and Homefield Home Guard platoons. The Althwaite platoon had never grown much beyond twenty. Together they would make a platoon of fifty. For a time, local patriotism prompted a feeling of resentment. It seemed as though Homefield was taking over, particularly since Hon Peter was no longer in charge. He did his best as deputy to Major Rochester to instill a wider outlook into the minds of the Althwaite men. A local emergency helped to weld the two ex-platoons into one.

It was Benjy who gave the alarm. The signs of spring had got into his bloodstream. He felt the familiar urge to be up and off, into the wilds. But to go for a week would be to let Mr Ackroyd and George Wright down. So, instead of the extensive roaming for which his nature called, he confined himself to a long day's excursion. He particularly wanted to see if he could find the cave at the foot of Crickley Edge where he had once spent some nights sheltering from the cold of winter.

He found the cave. The dead bracken he had strewn for bedding was still in place. But there was the stink of fox. Apart from that, it was an ideal camping place: a stream below and the vast, curving moor beyond. He returned over moorland where there were no footpaths. He recognized landmarks he had used in the past: a stunted ash tree, some shooting butts, a broken-down hut where an attempt to convert the acid soil into pasture for cows had failed. Suddenly, he was aware of something unusual glimpsed from the corner of an eye. Turning to face it, he saw what looked like a white sheet spread over the young shoots of bracken. In the soft breeze, it rose and fell as though inflated from below. It was segmented like something he had seen in pictures. A parachute! The realisation made his whole body tingle with fear and excitement. A further thought prompted him to sink down to the ground: suppose the parachutist was still there? If so, was he one of ours or one of theirs? If he was a German, wouldn't he have folded the parachute up and made it inconspicuous before making off? But perhaps he was lying there injured? If so, he might still be dangerous – perhaps with a pistol in hand.

Benjy picked up a fist-sized stone and crept forward. The parachute billowed up. Alarmed, he stopped. But the movement had shown that there was nothing lying beside the parachute. Gingerly he lifted the folds. Underneath was not the dead or injured body he had expected, but a long, canvas bag with a harness around it. He was assailed by another unsettling thought. Suppose it was a booby trap, liable to blow to smithereens whoever was foolish enough to tamper with it? He returned to his pocket the knife with which he was about to cut the bag free from the cords of the parachute. Better to let an explosives expert have a look, he thought.

He looked around. That part of the moor was rather featureless. He had to be sure that he could guide troops to the spot. Gathering some bleached stones where a stretch of heather had been burnt, he built a small cairn. A quarter of a mile away was a mountain ash. In the distance beyond, and almost in line with the ash, was an electricity pylon. An imaginary line through them would guide him back to the cairn. He set off for Althwaite as fast as he could.

Early the next morning, an army truck outside the village hall signified that something unusual was afoot. Inside the hall, Colonel Fitzpatrick, Hon Peter, Benjy, Sergeant Walter Armitage, Corporal Joe Quarmby, Constable Dewhurst and an Army sergeant – an explosives expert from the KOYLI range – were studying a map pinned to a black-board. Benjy was much better at reading the actual countryside than a map. He knew he could lead the party to the spot. But to pinpoint it on the map so that the army vehicle could get as close as possible was another matter. Fitzpatrick decided that Benjy and Joe Quarmby should set out on foot by the route that Benjy knew. Once at the spot, they would set off a maroon and both wave flags. The rest of the party would drive on moorland tracks to get as near as possible to the area that Benjy had indicated.

After an hour's tough walking, Benjy and Joe arrived at the cairn. By then Joe had decided that the exercise he got as a plumber – squeezing his body into small spaces in kitchens and bathrooms – was not the kind needed to keep up with Benjy over rough ground. The parachute and the bag were as Benjy had left them. Joe loaded the signal gun, pointed it in the air and pulled the trigger. A deafening bang was followed by a streak of purple smoke rising into the sky. He and Benjy stood on the highest ground nearby and waved white flags. A pistol shot from some distance away indicated that they had been seen. They continued waving flags at intervals, until they spotted the rest of the party topping a rise a mile away.

Fitzpatrick and Hon Peter, being older than the others, had found the cross-country trek very hard going. Fitzpatrick was cross. It would have been better to have left the vehicle at the edge of the moor and come up with Benjy. Everyone shared his puzzlement at the sight of the canvas bag. They withdrew fifty yards and lay prone whilst the Army sergeant examined it.

'It's OK. No danger!' he called out.

The bag had a metal frame inside to which the canvas bag was stitched. The contents were straw stuffing and oilskin packages containing papers and maps. The writing was German.

'Better get these back to HQ and get in touch with the Army as quickly as possible,' Fitzpatrick said.

'May I make a suggestion, sir,' said Peter. 'Instead of going into Althwaite and perhaps creating a stir, why don't we go to the Hall. It's this side of the village, and we can telephone from there. I can rustle up some refreshments, which I'm sure we're all in need of.'

The prospect of a comfortable arm-chair and perhaps a glass of Peter's sherry clinched the matter as far as Fitzpatrick was concerned. He and Peter decided they would walk back with Benjy, leaving the others to carry the parachute and bag to the lorry.

'Officers go first class, as usual!' grumbled Joe Quarmby, as he toiled up a slope carrying one end of the canvas bag.

'No mutinying in the ranks!' Walter Armitage

commented with a smile. 'Think of some nice grub in Mrs McAlister's kitchen.'

'I reckon you must know the country around here better than most people, Mr Benjamin,' said Hon Peter as they left the mountain ash behind and headed for the edge of the moor. 'Why don't you join the Home Guard? It's men like you we need.'

'Well, squire, you know my vagabond life. Some people disapproved of me. Thought I was just a lazy layabout.'

'Maybe. But aren't you a reformed character now? Farmer Ackroyd speaks highly of you, and George Wright trusts you to look after his business. Only the other day, Mrs Isaacs was suggesting to me that you would be an asset to the platoon.'

'Well, I'll be blowed!' Benjy exclaimed.

He mulled the matter over during the next half mile. He felt flattered and encouraged by what Hetty Isaacs had said. Perhaps the platoon would not take it amiss if an ex-tramp joined them.

'I don't know as I'd be much good at drill, sir. But if you think I'd be useful, I'll be glad to join,' he said at length.

'Good man!' said Fitzpatrick who had overheard the conversation.

Mrs McAlister was disturbed from her knitting by the sound of boots and voices. Looking out of the window, she was suddenly alarmed for the cleanliness of her kitchen. Hon Peter was about to open the door, having supervised the placing of the parachute and bag in an outhouse. Mrs McAlister beat him to it.

'Boots outside, please,' she commanded.

'That means you and me too, Colonel,' said Peter. 'Mrs McAlister's in charge here.'

Stockinged feet thronged the kitchen. Fitzpatrick was denied the arm-chair to which he had been looking forward, since Peter decided that they should all, officers and men, stay in the kitchen. But he was offered sherry, whilst the men had beer or tea. Mrs McAlister felt obliged to sacrifice the fruit cake she had made for Comforts for the Forces.

'Some real soldiers will have to go without, whilst this lot feed,' she said to herself.

It transpired over the next few days that other 'phantom' parachutes had been found in various places in England and Scotland, some in tops of trees, or on roofs of houses. The content of the bags was the same. The documents purported to be orders addressed to commanders of parachute regiments to carry out operations like blowing up bridges and railway lines, and poisoning reservoirs. The maps were mostly of the areas where the bags were dropped – copied from British maps and over-printed with German wording. Some were of other areas, indicating that the planes carrying them had lost their way. The purpose of these 'spoofs' was not clear.

'Most likely to spread alarm and tie up troops,' was Colonel Fitzpatrick's opinion.

He proposed to the Army regional headquarters that his men should scour the countryside for more parachutes and bags. The platoon therefore spent the next two weekends combing the surrounding country for other drops. Benjy was in demand as a guide across the remoter parts and to eminences from which the area around could be scanned with powerful binoculars. Only two more bags were found. But most of the men enjoyed the arduous trekking around in the fine weather of early spring. Benjy's acquaintance with the country was appreciated, and most of his new colleagues welcomed him into the platoon.

'Another step on the road to rehabilitation,' thought Hetty Isaacs when she heard that Benjy had joined. She went outside with carrots for Dusty.

'You'd like a man about the place, wouldn't you, Dusty?'

She was glad that no human was present to perceive the blush she felt in the cheeks.

'You're a fool, Henrietta Isaacs,' she said as she went back indoors.

Jem, Harold and other members of the scout troop were disappointed that they had not been called upon to search the countryside for phantom parachutes.

'Sorry, lads,' said Mr Ash, when asked why they couldn't join in. 'I've been advised it's dangerous. It's just possible that there may be some real parachutists as well.'

'I bet Woody didn't want to go trekking over the moors – his knees wouldn't stand it,' Will Dicehurst observed unkindly.

It was now two weeks since Jem had been up to Cop Top and left the message for Alice. He had not had an opportunity to go up again. In the village one Saturday morning, he saw Alice approaching. He was pretty sure she had seen him, but she turned into a shop. He loitered outside. When she came out he smiled at her, expecting to receive her congratulations. He was taken aback when she looked at him with a serious expression.

'I suppose I have to congratulate you, Jem,' she said. 'But why couldn't you have come and told me? Instead, I had to read the results in the paper and hear nothing from you – after all the work we did together.'

Jem was flabbergasted. Something seemed to sink in the pit of his stomach.

'But I did come up! The very day I heard the news. Only, you weren't there – none of you. So I left a message with the Land Army girls.'

'They didn't tell me.'

'Well, they should have done!'

'Yes. Anyway, I'm relieved. Sorry, Jem. I *am* glad for you.'

After Alice had left him, Jem was still in a turmoil. It was awful to think that Alice should have thought he had neglected to tell her, due to those stupid women. He felt like marching up to Cop Top and telling them off. But he soon realised that he would make himself ridiculous.

Jem had another worry, too. He brought it out from the back of his mind. It concerned the lack of progress in finding Ma Hibbert's son. The reply that Hon Peter had had from the American Embassy had not been promising. It explained that the war meant there was little effort available for pursuing enquiries of that sort.

Benjy had heard nothing from Joan in Oldham. Jem thought of Julia Hibbert waiting hopefully at Up Bye. It would be awful to let her down.

It was the day after the celebration of Jem's thirteenth birthday. There hadn't been much to celebrate. His mother and he were still waiting for further news from Dad. He hadn't had the nerve to invite Alice to the tea party, being unsure whether she was still friendly. Ron and Dot were too far away to come. Harold, Jonquil and Raq had been the only guests. Jem reminded Jonquil that it was two years since she had been Rapunzel in the tower. She had laughed: 'Fancy you boys acting out a fairy story!' Being now ten, she thought she had grown out of the stage of make-believe.

For the first time as a thirteen year old, Jem surveyed his face in the mirror. It was not an encouraging sight, he thought. His dark hair stuck up, refusing to obey comb or brush. He had some spots, though his mother said it was just a phase, and they would disappear. He didn't like seeing himself in profile. His nose turned up (a feature inherited from Dad), and his chin receded too much. It was not an impressive face or head, he felt. Moreover, he had a tendency to look glum, except when animated. 'Cheer up,' someone would say, when he didn't feel he needed cheering up. Conscious attempts to look pleasant didn't last. How could Alice see anything in him? For her, looking in the mirror must be a pleasure – not that he would accuse her of being vain. It was ridiculous to think that she would ever again regard him as a special friend. But it was difficult to accept that the smiles and encouraging words she had once had for him were just part of the past.

The summer holidays arrived. The fact that Germany had invaded Russia in June had made an invasion of Britain seem less likely. But there was still a lingering fear of real German parachutists, and parents warned children not to stray too far from the village. Jem and Harold would have liked an overnight expedition to the moors. But Mr and Mrs Bright, and Jem's Mum, put their feet down. A trip to Scarborough was out of the question. Mrs Murgatroyd didn't have the money. In any case, the beaches were out of bounds due to anti-invasion devices. It seemed to Jem that the summer would be dull.

'What are we going to do?' Jem asked Harold as they sat in the shade under the bridge, whilst Raq scuffled about in the shallows of the river, which was low.

'What about going up to Mrs Isaacs'?' Harold suggested. 'She said we could ride Dusty. It might be fun.'

They toiled up the lane in the hot sun, past Up Bye, until they reached Mrs Isaacs' bungalow, almost the last house. From there they looked down on the village. Sounds, including the hammer on the anvil at the forge, rose up in the still air. The hills around were indistinct in a heat haze.

'It's a hot day to climb up,' said Mrs Isaacs. 'You'd better have some lemonade first.'

They took turns in riding Dusty around the field. He went in spurts. He seemed obstinate, then suddenly he was off. Then just as abruptly, he stood stock still for a few minutes. Mrs Isaacs came out whilst Harold was trying to manage him.

'Yes, he is very contrary,' she shouted to Harold. 'Try talking to him nicely.'

She and Jem laughed as Dusty sprang into action, almost unseating Harold.

'Jem, do you mind if I ask you something?'

Jem felt uneasy. Was this going to be something personal?

'You know Benjamin Oldcastle well, don't you? He's told me what a good friend you've been. We can all see that he's trying to shake off his past – not that there's anything dishonourable in being a tramp. But he's trying to be useful, especially because of this awful war. He's a good man at heart, as you know. What I'm wondering is…well, will he revert to being a tramp when the war's over? Will he settle down – *could* he settle down?'

Jem smiled to himself. He had an inkling why Hetty Isaacs was putting this question. But he had to reply honestly. He thought about some of the conversations Benjy had had with him.

'I don't think it's just the war. I think – I know – that he wants to lead a more normal life. I've heard him talk about his pal, Rick, who used to be a tramp. He's settled down now. When Benjy's been to visit him, he comes back a bit envious. "Nice home, cheerful wife," he says. But I don't think Benjy'll ever lose his urge to get out into the wilds from time to time. Any…friend would have to understand that.'

He looked at Hetty, whose eyes seemed to be directed towards something beyond Harold and Dusty.

There was a faint blush on her cheeks. She turned to him.

'Thank you, Jem. You don't know what a relief it is to hear that. Between ourselves?'

Jem nodded.

When Jem had seen Dot at her home in Hull after Christmas, she had reminded him that Mrs Whittle had promised to invite her to Intake Farm in the Summer holidays. Jem hoped that Mrs Whittle would not forget. Dot would be terribly disappointed if she did. He hoped that Ron would come to Althwaite, too. There had been air raids on Hull in the Spring and early Summer. A postcard to Mrs Weaverthorpe had said that the family was alright. But it would be a relief to see them both.

It was unusual for Jem to get involved in any cooking, except when camping with the scouts. He woke one morning with a desire to make some chocolate buns. His mother checked that the larder contained the necessary ingredients, and said he would have to do without eggs. He had just weighed the flour and the cocoa when there was a ring at the door. His mother went to answer it. He heard feet running down the passage. The kitchen door burst open to reveal a smiling Dot. She reached up to give him a kiss. Jem, not used to kisses, was pleased at this show of affection. He lifted her up and swung her round.

'You've got an apron on!' Dot exclaimed. 'What are you making?'

Jem explained and invited her to help. He was not embarrassed at being seen in an apron by Dot, but the arrival of Mrs Weaverthorpe in the kitchen was a different matter. But she put him at ease.

'Don't mind me, Jem. I'm not stopping. Will you bring Dot back? You can see Ron then – he's doing some errands for me.'

Over the next few days, Jem learnt about the raids on Hull. Ron admitted that he had been frightened, as well as Dot. They had spent many nights in an air raid shelter. Their school had had a near miss. Their mother had been in two minds whether to send them to Althwaite, but kept hoping the raids would end.

Jem, Harold and Ron set out one fine day for Intake Farm, where Dot had gone to stay. Jem had to assure his mother, and Harold his parents, that they wouldn't go on the moor. They would keep to lanes, even though that would take longer.

'Here's D'Artagnan and two of the musketeers!' Bertha cried, as they reached the field where Dot was gently cantering a pony.

After his first encounter with Bertha the previous summer, Jem had taken 'The Three Musketeers' off the shelf of the glass-fronted bookcase at home, thinking that he should be better prepared for her teasing. But he had found the intrigues and frictions between the French King's Musketeers and those of the Cardinal tiresome. He had given the novel up, thinking that he would have another go when he was older. So he was no better prepared than he had been.

Bertha's black hair, down to her shoulders, was untidy but still curly. Jem was again struck by her charm, but felt that as a friend she would be unpredictable –

not someone you could rely on to sympathise with your moods and concerns.

Ron and Harold wandered over to the fence to watch Dot.

'Is Celia still in love with Oliver?' Jem asked Bertha with a smile, thinking of her part in 'As You Like It'.

'As much as when we were married! Why, you're not jealous are you, Jem? Oh, I forgot – Alice is your favourite! Seriously though, what's the matter between you and Alice?'

'What do you mean? It's true there was a misunderstanding. But we sorted that out.'

'Well, I dunno. I saw Alice last week and she seemed not to want to talk about you – even that you'd passed for the Grammar School. Charlie Foster was at Cop Top, by the way – having a ride on Alice's pony.'

Jem was unusually silent as he, Harold and Ron returned to Althwaite after tea in the farm kitchen. The turmoil that had engrossed his mind after his meeting with Alice in the village had returned to trouble him. Didn't Alice believe his explanation that he had asked the Land Army girls to pass on his message? Then there was the thought of Charlie riding the pony. Perhaps Charlie was a natural rider, like the knights of old, whilst he was doomed to be a mere foot soldier.

He returned home depressed. Nothing seemed to be going right. The search for Ma Hibbert's son was sinking without trace. His friendly relationship with Alice was being undermined. There were, he had to admit, some gleams of light: Dot's pleasure in seeing him again, and the unlikely romance between Mrs

Isaacs and Benjy. But the things that affected him most deeply seemed to be turning, not to gold, but to rust.

21 TROUBLE

At a meeting of the scout troop Mr Ash announced an unexpected diversion.

Between Althwaite and Homefield was a lake used by a sailing club. With the advent of the war most members had joined the forces, and the club's regular weekend sailing had come to an end. Mr Ash announced that an ex-naval Petty Officer, Mr Ferguson, was willing to teach some lads the rudiments of sailing. Petty Officer Ferguson had been invalided out of the Navy, having suffered severe burns to his left arm when his destroyer came under attack. He had told Mr Ash that he would take ten boys to start with. He was to be assisted by Donald, an elderly member of the club.

As most of the troop were keen, lots had to be drawn for the first training sessions. Jem was relieved when both he and Harold drew pieces of paper with crosses from Mr Ash's hat. Not so pleasing was that Charlie Foster was also successful. Most of the boys, Jem included, expected to start sailing straightaway. But Mr Ferguson was a man who believed in starting from the basics. 'Understand the theory, and you'll be better able to practise' was his guiding principle. He brought a black-board and a model of a sailing dinghy down to the sailing club hut.

Demanding concentration – he had not been a Royal Navy Petty Officer for nothing – he explained the points of sailing: the correct positions of the sails around a whole circle, given the wind from a particular direction. He was not satisfied until the slowest boys were able to position the sails of the model correctly, and to say whether the centre-board should be right down or half down. For the next session he brought a mock-up of the stern of a dinghy: a seat, a tiller and a rope representing the 'main sheet' which controlled the boom. Everyone had to take turns in practising the movements when Mr Ash called out: 'tack', 'go about', gybe', 'luff up', 'bear away', 'let go'.

Jem's mother found him practising at home with a stick for the tiller and a length of washing line for the main sheet, muttering commands to himself.

'Goodness, this is serious!' she exclaimed. 'I hope I'm not going to be subject to naval discipline!'

'It's alright, Mum. You can just be the landlubber, preparing the grub that sailors need.'

'If that's a hint to get the cake tin out, there isn't any till the weekend.'

Next came a visit to the swimming bath in Bruddersford where, dressed in old clothes and wearing buoyancy jackets, the boys had to show that they could swim at least 50 yards on their backs. At last came the exciting day when two dinghies were wheeled out of the boat park on launching trolleys. Much of the morning was spent learning how to rig the boats and what to do in the event of a capsize. The boys could see the whole morning disappearing without any sailing. But their nervous impatience was at last satisfied.

Mr Ferguson and Donald took out two boys at a time, and gave them each a few minutes at the tiller. When it was Jem's turn, he felt desperately keen to show that he was a promising sailor. There was a soft breeze – enough to keep the boat moving without heeling over. But Jem found it was far from straightforward to keep the boat on a steady course. The telltale sign of the luff of the jib sail beginning to flap showed that the boat was veering too much into the wind. But which way to move the tiller? In two minds what to do, Jem found that the boat was in irons, sails flapping and the boat unable to progress. Donald backed the jib, and the boat sprang to life. Then came the order, 'go about'. Which way did that mean moving the tiller? Jem began pulling it towards him, but realised in time that he had to push it away. The boat went round on to the other tack. 'Sheet up', Donald called, and Jem hauled on the main sheet until the boom was over the corner of the stern. 'Not bad', said Donald, and Jem began to relax. But he was surprised to find that on climbing out of the boat on to the jetty his knees felt wobbly.

The capsize practice, which Jem and Harold had thought would be a bit of fun, had its troubling moments. The wind was stronger than on the morningwhen they had first gone out. Mr Ferguson and Donald got a rescue boat, with oars, out of the boat park. Jem, Harold and Charlie were detailed to capsize one of the dinghies, and show the younger boys how to bring it upright.

Clad in swimming trunks and buoyancy jackets they stood up in the boat, clung to the mast and leaned out until the boat went over. Jem, as the helmsman, had the job of working his way around the stern to the bottom of the boat, kicking his legs and hanging on to parts of the boat. The main sheet, trailing in the water, tangled round his feet. As he tried frantically to free himself, Charlie and Harold shouted to him to hurry up. Having got around to the centre-board, he began hauling on the jib sheet that the other two had flung over to him. He got the board down to a level where he could climb on to it. But all his pulling failed to bring the boat upright. Mr Ferguson shouted to Charlie to go round and help. He seemed to Jem to be round in no time, having avoided getting tangled up in the main sheet. Together they hauled the boat upright and fell into it, on top of Harold.

'Free the main sheet and start bailing,' Mr Ferguson shouted.

By the time the dinghy was back at the jetty and emptied of most of the water, Jem felt exhausted. He felt crestfallen, too. Charlie, of all people, had had to come to his assistance, as the other boys had witnessed.

'Let me know when you're in trouble again, Jem,' Charlie said, giving him a look in which Jem thought he detected some contempt.

Two weeks later all the boys, save one or two, were feeling pretty confident. It was becoming second nature to keep an eye on the luff of the jib when sailing close-hauled, and to move the tiller in the correct direction when changing course. When the wind was not very strong, Mr Ferguson had let them sail without himself or Donald, though the rescue boat was at the ready. Jem thought he was making progress, but he was taken aback when he overheard Mr Ferguson saying to Donald, 'That Charlie'll make a good sailor.'

With only a fortnight to go to the end of the summer holidays, Mr Ferguson said that, if the weather was alright, they would spend the whole of the next Friday at the lake, perhaps picnicking on the island. He told the boys to bring sandwiches and drinks. The day dawned bright, though Jem's mother quoted the saying, 'Red in the morning, sailors' warning', after she had been outside. She asked Jem to help carry things down to a WVS sale in the village, and to help set up tables in the village hall. This meant he would be late for the lake, but as there was a whole day of sailing ahead, Jem was not too bothered.

When Jem came out of the hall, he found that the day had taken a turn for the worse. The sun had gone in, black clouds were massing over the Pennines and a strong breeze had got up. For a different reason, Charlie Foster was also late. He and Jem arrived at the lake at about 11 o'clock. They found both dinghies tied up at the jetty, and the other boys in the process of taking down the sails.

'What's going on?' Charlie asked.

'Fergie says it's going to get nasty,' Will Dicehurst replied. 'He's told us to get the boats in. We're going to picnic in the hut and have a quiz. He's gone off home for something.'

'Well, there's time for me and Jem to go out.'

'You'll get into trouble,' one of the younger boys piped up.

'Just once round the island, eh Jem?' Charlie suggested.

Jem could see that Charlie was daring him. If he didn't agree, Charlie would think – and no doubt say – that he was scared. On the other hand, Mr Ferguson had said the boats had to be brought in. To disobey an ex-Petty Officer would be a serious thing. If he returned before they were back at the jetty, he would be very annoyed. Also, he and Charlie would be setting the younger boys a bad example. Jem felt suddenly furious. He'd looked forward to the day, and now here he was faced with a cruel dilemma.

Meanwhile, Charlie had got the sails back up and re-fixed the rudder and tiller. He looked up at the jetty, where Jem had got as far as putting on a buoyancy jacket.

'Ok, Jem? Do you want to helm first?'

Jem thought of Alice: what would she expect him to do? Would she think him cowardly, or sensible, if he refused the challenge? Another thought occurred to him. Charlie seemed determined to go out. With the wind getting up, it would be safer to have two people in the boat – for handling the sails and for the extra weight. Charlie was anything but a friend of his, but to let him go out on his own would be selfish.

'You helm, I'll crew,' Jem said, committing himself to an outing which he hoped would be brief. He undid the painter and stepped into the boat, with Charlie at the tiller. Immediately, the wind caught the mainsail and slung the boom across. With the wind behind them, the dinghy began careering towards the island.

'Keep the centre-board down,' Charlie ordered,

alarmed by the speed of the boat and concerned that it might go over if the boom swung across to the other side.

Harold watched their departure with misgiving. He was glad that Charlie had not challenged *him*. He helped to get the other dinghy out of the water and into the boat park where its cover was put on and fastened down. By now, the sky had become dark. Storm clouds were racing from the hills. The trees near the jetty began to thresh and moan. He and others went to the edge of the lake to see how Charlie and Jem were coping.

'Better leave the rescue boat here,' said Will. 'We might need it.'

'They went behind the island a few minutes ago,' said one of the younger ones.

All eyes were trained on the end of the island where the dinghy would reappear. Minutes went by.

'They must have capsized,' Will said. 'We'd better go out in the rescue boat.'

'There they are!' someone shouted.

'Where?'

'There, in front of the trees.'

It was not the boat they saw, but Jem on the island, waving to them, as though beckoning. He had his hands cupped to his mouth, and seemed to be shouting, but his words were drowned by the noise of the wind.

'One of you go and telephone Fergie,' said Harold, feeling that someone should take charge. 'There's a phone box at the end of the lane, and he'll be in the book. Here's some coppers for the call. Come on, Will, we're the biggest. Let's take an oar each.'

The picnic in the hut was a mournful affair. Everyone felt more or less guilty.

Mr Ferguson blamed himself for not staying and seeing the dinghies safely ashore, Donald having had to leave for an Air Raid Precaution practice. Harold and the others who had disapproved of Charlie going out felt they should have spoken up more firmly, or have prevented the painter from being untied. Others, who had thought it an amusing escapade, now saw their mistake.

Will and Harold had rescued Charlie and Jem alright, though it had been desperately hard to row back against the wind. What deepened the gloom in the hut was that the dinghy was tied to a tree at the far side of the island, its mast broken.

'We thought it'd be sheltered on the far side of the island,' Jem began to explain. 'But the wind must have shifted. Even with both of us leaning out, the edge of the boat…'

'The gunwale, you mean,' Mr Ferguson corrected.

'…the gunwale was almost under water. Then came an almighty gust, and the mast came down, wrapping us in the mainsail.'

'If it hadn't broken, we'd have been over,' Charlie added. 'The jib was down too, but after we'd got out from under the mainsail, we untied the paddle and managed to get to the island. It was all my fault, sir. I dared Jem to come out. Otherwise, he wouldn't have come.'

'Nevertheless, you both disobeyed orders, and you see what the result can be,' Mr Ferguson said.

By the time everyone had finished their sandwiches

and lemonade, Mr Ferguson had calmed down a lot.

'Really, I ought to tell Charlie and Jem that's the end of sailing for them this summer. If this was the Navy, they'd be for the high jump. However, I think we can all learn some lessons – me too. There's no excuse for Charlie and Jem taking the boat out when I'd ordered the dinghies ashore. The state of the weather should have told them not to, anyway. But at least, when the mast broke, they managed to get the boat to the island and made secure. You were right, Harold, to tell someone to phone me. It would have been better if you and Will had waited for me before taking the rescue boat out, given the strong wind. But you did well in getting to the island and back. So, for the wrong sort of initiative – a black mark. For the right sort of initiative – well done. When Donald gets back from the ARP practice, we'll go out and tow the dinghy back. Then we'll see what the damage amounts to. Hopefully, Charlie and Jem'll be able to pay for the repairs out of their pocket money!'

Mr Ferguson reached into a brief case he had brought with him.

'Now, when we began this course, I said that if you got through, there would be a certificate. I'm glad to say you've all got one. You've all done well. Some better than others, but some are older than others. You can all feel encouraged to continue sailing. When the club re-opens after the war, you can become junior members. Now, in alphabetical order: Harold Bright…Will Dicehurst…'

Jem felt his heart pumping. What would his certificate say? When his name was called out, he took it with a trembling hand.

Jem Murgatroyd has attained the basic standard with a performance meriting

FAIRLY GOOD

Only FAIRLY GOOD! What had the others got? Harold seemed pleased and showed Jem that he had been given a GOOD. Charlie had a satisfied expression on his face. As they were leaving, Jem could not contain his curiosity.

'What have you got, Charlie?'

'Well as a special friend, Jem, I'll show you.'

Charlie unrolled his certificate to reveal *VERY GOOD.* Jem felt a sudden pang of something he interpreted as a mixture of disappointment and envy.

As he and Harold walked along the lane, he felt disinclined to talk. He was glad that Charlie had owned up to being the one who was most responsible for the disastrous outing, though he could hardly have concealed it when all the other lads knew. But that Charlie Foster should have done so much better than himself was hard to bear. He was sure that Charlie wasn't cleverer. But he had a natural ability for sailing that Jem lacked. Perhaps it was the same with horse-riding? He knew from Chapel and Sunday School teaching that envy was a sin. But how could he help feeling as he did?

Harold broke into his thoughts. 'Perhaps Fergie wasn't really serious about pocket money,' he said, trying to be helpful.

'Gosh – I'd forgotten about that. How much do you think a new mast costs?'

'No idea. But… if it was £20, divided between you and Charlie, that's £10. How much do you get a week,

Jem?'

'Sixpence.'

'Same as me. Twenty shillings in a pound. Times ten pounds is two hundred shillings. That's four hundred sixpences. That's about eight years.'

'Holy smoke! That's almost a life sentence!'

'Perhaps Fergie'll take pity on you,' was Harold's crumb of comfort.

'What a day it's been!' his mother exclaimed when Jem reached home. 'It got really squally. You surely didn't go sailing in that weather?'

'By the time I got there, sailing had been cancelled.'

'Oh dear. Well, cheer up, Jem. I've got a treat for our tea. Pikelets – will you toast them?'

Jem got the long fork, put a pikelet on the end and held it before the glow of the kitchen fire. The pikelets were round, with holes into which butter or margarine would run. When he had toasted four, he and Mum settled down to their tea. Jem loved the crunchiness of the outside of a pikelet. But he couldn't concentrate on that pleasure. His mother sensed that something was bothering him.

'You've finished the course then, Jem. Did everyone get through?'

'Yes, but I didn't do as well as I'd hoped. Only Fairly Good.

'Well, that's better than Poor.'

'True, and I'll get better with practice. But it's what actually happened that's the trouble.'

Jem described the fateful outing.

'I don't think Mr Ferguson was serious about you

and Charlie having to give up your pocket money,' his mother said when he had finished.

'It's not that that bothers me. I'd be ready to give it up. Not, it was going against his orders. But I couldn't have let Charlie go out on his own, could I Mum?'

'Mmm. I'd be inclined to say it was his own fault if he did. But I reckon your Dad would have agreed with you.'

The thought that his Dad might take the view that he had done the right thing lightened the burden of guilt. But Jem still had a wakeful night, punctuated by a nightmare in which the boat capsized, the buoyancy jackets he and Charlie were wearing floated away, and a monster fish began nibbling at their feet.

By the time Jem got up in the morning, later than usual, the postman had been. He found his Mum sitting at the kitchen table, staring into the fire, a letter in her hand.

'What's up Mum? Been sacked from the WVS?'

She turned to him with an attempt at a smile on her face.

'Is it…is it Dad?'

'It's alright, Jem. He's only been hurt.'

Hurt – that could mean anything. It could mean a scratch, or that he was near death.

'You'd better read it, Jem.'

Jem took the letter reluctantly. He felt as though he wanted to be shielded from the worst.

To: Mrs E Murgatroyd
5 Moor Lane

Althwaite, Near Bruddersford
West Riding of Yorkshire
Dear Madam,

I am sorry to have to inform you that your husband, Corporal Edward Murgatroyd, 4th Ambulance Car Company, Royal Army Service Corps, has suffered an injury to an eye. He is being treated in a military hospital in Cairo. He will return to the UK as soon as can be arranged. Please be assured that he will receive the best medical attention.

I remain, Madam,

Yours faithfully

C.J. Carstairs

Captain, Family Liaison Officer

The War Office, London

A handwritten postscript added: *I am informed he is in good spirits.*

'Does that mean he might lose the sight of one eye, Mum?'

'It might be as bad as that. It could be much less serious.'

'But the fact that he's going to be returned to England must mean it's not just a slight wound.'

Saying his Dad was in good spirits was also not a good sign. It could mean that the wound was serious – as though he was facing up to something bravely. But Jem thought he should not trouble his mother with this thought.

'You may be right, Jem. But even if he does lose the sight of an eye, think how much worse it could have been. He's alive, he's out of the fighting. He can walk. Lots of people cope with just one eye.'

'At least, he'd have an excuse for stumbling into a peat hag!' Jem added, his concern alleviated by Mum's comment.

Word had got around that Mr Ash wanted a good turn-out at the next scout meeting. Someone important was going to be there. Imaginations were set alight. A Spitfire pilot with a 'kill' of ten German bombers? A small boat sailor who had helped to rescue the army from Dunkirk?

There was disappointment, even mirth, when the gangly figure of Constable Dewhurst made its appearance. He entered the hall rather sheepishly and took off his helmet.

'Now, scouts,' Mr Ash said, 'Constable Dewhurst has something important to say to us. So listen carefully. Then we'll see what we can do to help.'

Althwaite's policeman was not used to public speaking. He looked and felt awkward, even before an audience of boys – perhaps particularly before such an audience, knowing how mischievous boys can be. He wiped his brow with a clean handkerchief and tried to conceal his unease by glaring at them.

'You may have noticed, lads, from reports in the Bruddersford Examiner, that there's a spate of war crime in the district. Coal from railway sidings, pigs from pig clubs, rabbits, hens and eggs, all stolen. Grocers burgled. Whoever's doing this is helping Hitler. Now, with men called up into the forces, police resources are limited. Of course, there's the Home Guard and the ARP men. But they have their own duties and exercises. So, lads, I want your eyes and ears.'

As he got into his stride, the Constable became more at ease. He was aware that the boys were listening intently.

'I'm not asking you to be detectives, though some of you fancy yourselves.' (Did Jem and Harold only imagine that he cast a glance at them?) 'But be aware that these things are going on, and let me know of anything suspicious. But – a warning! Don't get involved. If you see someone acting suspiciously, perhaps mooching around for something they can pinch, don't go up to them. Contact me. You all know where the police station is. Thanks Mr Ash. Now I'll leave you to get on with your knots and what-not.'

Constable Dewhurst picked up his helmet, and left the hall feeling that his little speech had gone down alright.

Mr Ash told the troop that he didn't intend to organize any watching or guarding. But everyone should be alert for strangers or unusual happenings. He repeated the constable's warning not to get personally involved in questioning or interfering.

As the troop dispersed, Charlie made his way to Jem and Harold.

'What about joining forces again?' he asked. 'Perhaps we'd have better luck than with the church burglary.'

Jem felt reluctant to commit himself. 'Whoever's doing these things, it's likely to be when we're in bed.'

'Can I go out late tomorrow, Mum?' Jem asked. Harold had persuaded him that they ought to cooperate with Charlie. Friday night was the one that they selected. They would be able to sleep in the following morning. It was also a moonless night, more likely to be favoured by thieves, they thought.

'What's on, Jem?'

'It's a scout duty – going the rounds of the village. There'll be Harold, Will and Charlie Foster as well.'

'This is what Constable Dewhurst has put you up to, is it?'

'We won't get into trouble. We're going to wear our uniforms, so we look official.'

'Well – I'm not happy about it. I expect your Dad would say no. But…alright. I shan't get to sleep until you're back, though.'

It was midnight when the boys met outside Middletons' ironmongers in the market place. Jem was beginning to regret the decision, though he would never have admitted it to the others. Because of the black-out, none of Althwaite's few street lamps were on. Due to clouds, there was not even any starlight. Jem had never been out so late, except when carol singing. Then the number of folk around him dispelled any fear of the night. Now, it was a different matter. At any moment they might come across a gang of men who would think nothing of using force to keep them quiet. Harold and Charlie felt just as uneasy, but were determined to put a brave face on the expedition. Will still thought it was a bit of fun.

The coal yard was at the railway sidings. It was

surrounded by a tall, wooden fence. The boys crept around, looking into the yard through chinks in the fence. All they could see was blackness. From the coal yard they made their way to the allotments. They each had a torch, but had decided to use them only in an emergency, so as not give their presence away. Now and then, though, they were forced to switch one on to check where they were.

The Air Raid Precaution unit had a pig club on a plot of waste ground near the allotments. The men had invested in ten pigs. They had a rota for collecting pig swill from the special bins placed around the village for vegetable peelings and food scraps. One of the pigs had been stolen, and the men had since put up a higher fence. The boys smelt the pigs long before they reached them. They looked through the metal gate. A short burst of torchlight showed snouts protruding from wooden sties. The pigs seemed to be sleeping peacefully.

'Smell puts you off eating bacon,' Will said.

'They're supposed to be really clean animals,' Harold commented.

'Never heard a rasher statement!' said Will. '*Rasher*…got it?'

The others groaned.

The last port of call was the hen runs at the end of back gardens near the recreation ground. All was quiet save for the occasional cluck as hens dreamed or shifted their roosting places.

It was getting on for one o'clock when they got back to the market square. Suddenly they were blinded by the strong beam of a large torch. Four hearts leapt, and four figures froze. Had they disturbed a gang?

'What are you lot doing 'ere at this time of night?'

Never had they been so relieved to hear the voice of Constable Dewhurst.

'We're keeping a lookout, as you asked,' Harold replied.

'Well, I'll be blowed! I said keep your eyes and ears open when you're about. I didn't say go the rounds of the village in the middle of the night. Now, did I?'

'Well, not exactly,' Jem admitted.

'But we thought it'd be helpful,' Charlie added.

'I appreciate that. But I'm more concerned about the danger. There's some thugs about, and I don't want you getting clobbered – although I'll admit I've thought of clobbering some boy scouts myself in the past. Anyway, where've you been? Seen anything?'

The boys told him where they had been.

'Right, thanks. But don't come out again at night. Now, get off home and catch up on your beauty sleep!'

Constable Dewhurst was pleased with his final sally, and continued his beat in good humour. After a little while, his thoughts became more serious. He shuddered to think what might have happened if the boys had surprised some thieves on such a dark night. He would have been held responsible for prompting their expedition. He had not suggested nightly excursions. But maybe the effect of his speech had been more powerful than he expected. Perhaps he possessed some power of oratory. Fascinated by this thought, he pursued his lonely, and fruitless, vigil.

When Jem got home from school on Monday afternoon, his mother was sitting in the kitchen reading the Bruddersford Examiner.

'Listen to this, Jem,' she exclaimed.

In the early hours of Saturday morning two burglaries took place. Both were into ironmongers, one in Homefield, and the other in Althwaite. Drums of paraffin and boxes of candles were amongst the items stolen.

'Poor Mr Middleton. That was the night you were out, Jem.'

'We started off at his shop. But we didn't go down the back lane. I bet that's where they forced an entry.'

'They can't be local people. They must be gangs coming from somewhere else. Can't the Home Guard do something?'

The same thought was going through the mind of Hon Peter as he sipped the cup of tea that Mrs McAlister had brought him. It was all very well defending the country against non-existent parachutists. The real danger was close at hand and from his own countrymen. 'Scoundrels!' he said to himself. 'If I'm on the magistrates' bench when their cases come up, I'll jolly well make sure they get maximum sentences. But the first thing is to apprehend them. Constable Dewhurst needs more active help.'

Peter drained his cup and decided to telephone Major Rochester. The thought of Jem Murgatroyd and Harold Bright entered his mind. He smiled. 'We'll get them yet!'

Jem and Harold wandered disconsolately out of the village the following Saturday afternoon. Constable Dewhurst's appeal to the scouts had been like a call to arms, an opportunity to do something for the country, or at least for this corner of Yorkshire. But his astonishment at seeing them out at dead of night and his telling them to go home – like little boys – had been a discouragement. Did he want help, or didn't he?

In search of a diversion, Harold had borrowed his father's binoculars, saying that he and Jem were going bird-watching. Raq had been left at home, though he had whined to come with them.

'I'll make it up to her tomorrow,' Harold had said.

They took the lane that led towards Armworth Valley. But instead of turning up the Valley to the reservoir, they kept on. A noisy van approached from behind. They had to press against the hedge as it burst around a corner, raising dust.

'They could have slowed down!' Jem complained, licking the back of a hand where thorns had scratched it.

They turned up the next valley, which led to Griddle Moor. Dr McLeish, who knew more about birds than anyone else in the village, had told Mr Bright that eagles could sometimes be seen there. Tyre tracks in the dust of the lane suggested that the van had taken that route.

'Why should anyone want to come up here?' Jem asked.

'There's a farm at the far end – Scantlands, I think it's called.'

On the western side of the valley, crags known as Griddle Edge pricked the skyline. It was here that eagles were most likely to nest and be seen. Jem and Harold left the lane and began climbing up through bracken. They emerged on to tussocky grass. They had a view of the profile of the Edge: rocks rising steeply, with here and there a precipice. They sat and took turns with the binoculars to scan the face for eagles. None were visible. They climbed higher and went along to the top of the Edge. The whole valley was spread below them. Scantlands Farm was towards the far end. Through binoculars it seemed dilapidated. Some of the outbuildings were ruinous. Did anyone now live in that lonely spot? As if to answer the question, the van emerged from the back of the farm and started down the lane on the floor of the valley. It became lost to view in a plantation of fir trees.

Tired from their climb, the boys lay back on heather and stared at the cirrus clouds sketched against the blue. They knew they were a sign of good weather. The sound of a scuffle of feet on rock broke their reverie. Sitting up, they saw two men toiling up the slope. One pointed at them. Jem and Harold were mystified, and also a little worried. Were they guilty of trespassing? The men came up to them. They both seemed of middle age and looked well dressed for farmers.

'Hullo, lads! What are you up to then?' the burlier of the two asked.

'Up to? We're not up to nothing,' Harold replied, forgetting his grammar under the stress of the encounter.

'Nice field glasses, those' said the leaner man.

'They're my Dad's,' Harold replied, clutching them tightly.

'And who may he be?' the burly one asked.

'Mr Bright, the Methodist Minister in Althwaite.'

'Parson's son, eh? So, why are you using them up

here?'

'Looking for eagles.'

'Eagles – that's a nice story!'

'It's not!' Jem exclaimed. 'Dr McLeish has seen them.'

'A doctor now. Aren't we well connected!' Said the lean man in a sneering tone.

'OK. Now listen lads,' the burly one continued, with a hint of menace in his voice. 'The valley's not safe. The army's been using it for exercises, and there's some unexploded ammunition left lying around. So I'd go looking for eagles somewhere else if I were you. Alright? Come on, Ed.'

The men began their descent. Almost immediately, the lean man stumbled.

'Ouch! Twisted my ankle. Give us a hand, Bert.'

They continued at a slower pace, Ed with his arm on Bert's shoulders.

'Come on,' said Jem. 'Quick!'

He led the way back along the ridge until they could descend without being spotted by the men.

'What's the idea, Jem?'

'We've got to get to the van – take its number.'

They reached the edge of the fir plantation, and crept quietly through the trees. The van was parked on the lane. They could see a woman at the wheel.

'I haven't got anything to write with, or on. Have you, Harold?'

'No.'

'509 WY. You remember the figures. I'll remember the letters. Got them? We'd better wait till they've gone.'

They hid in the plantation until the van departed. In the lane, Harold used a stick to draw "509 WY" in the dust.'

'Now, if we forget, we can come back.'

'We should have had something to write with, like proper scouts,' Jem said. 'Suppose we'd come across a German spy and had no pencil and paper to make a note of what he said.'

'Think he'd have spoken English?'

'Well, if he was a spy, he'd have been able to.'

'Did you spot any eagles?' Mr Bright asked after they had got back to the Manse and were having tea.

'No, but…ouch.' Harold grimaced from the kick that Jem had given him under the table. 'Next time we might.'

Jonquil had noticed the kick. 'I think they've been up to something,' she said.

'We might have been trespassing a bit when we climbed up to Griddle Edge,' Jem said. 'But I bet Dr McLeish has been up there.'

Harold glared at Jonquil. Jem gave her a wink, and she smiled. Neither parent pursued the matter.

After tea, they retreated to the garage.

'Jonquil's getting too big for her boots,' Harold complained.

'She just wants to join in a bit.'

'She can't join in this! I got into enough trouble over the Rapunzel business.'

Jem didn't like the way Harold referred to that episode, but he kept his peace.

'Do you think the army *has* been leaving unexploded ammunition in Griddle Valley?' Harold asked.

'I reckon that was meant to scare us away. They wouldn't have climbed all the way up to see who we were unless they were up to no good.'

'Scantlands Farm!' Harold exclaimed. 'I bet they're using it as a hide-out. We'd better tell Constable Dewhurst straightaway.'

Jem thought of the way the Constable had treated them as youngsters who ought not to have been out late at night.

'I've got a better idea,' he said. 'We'll go and see Hon Peter.'

'Go along to the tower and shout up at him,' Mrs McAlister directed them.

They hailed him and waited for the door to be unlocked from inside. The tall, uniformed figure of Sergeant Armitage appeared.

'I could ask you the password, but you wouldn't know it. You don't carry matches, do you? No. Right, you're to come up.'

Hon Peter had a clipboard again, and looked harassed. His hair was untidy, as though he had been scratching his head.

'You're a welcome diversion, boys. Walter and I were just wondering if we'd have to start all over again. There's not enough room to do a check methodically. I can see this isn't a social call. Something important to tell us? Let's sit down.'

Hon Peter chose a long, bulky box on which was printed in yellow letters *Northover Projector, Mark 1.* Walter seated himself on *Smoke Generators, Mark 2.*

Harold chose a box marked *Thermos Bomb*. Jem thought he'd be safer on *Thunderflashes Quantity 20.*

'That story about the army is nonsense,' said Hon Peter, when Jem and Harold had told their tale. 'They didn't realize they had a couple of bright lads to deal with. There's obviously something fishy going on. Now, I appreciate you coming to tell me first. But I'd better go and see Constable Dewhurst right away. You'd better come with me – we'll go in my car. Can I leave you to carry on Walter? Lock up after us.'

Walter Armitage followed Jem down the staircase.

'So you took up that hint of mine about Miss Hibbert's mystery? Audrey – Miss Arbuthnot – was telling me what a good job you and your pal were doing.'

'It's Benjy, really,' Jem managed to say feeling his cheeks turning red.

'That's the last inventory we'll be doing in the tower,' Hon Peter said as they walked to the garage. 'We're moving all the stuff elsewhere.'

'Isn't it safe enough there?' Jem asked.

'Oh, it's safe enough. Safe for other things, too, eh?' He glanced at Jem with a confidential smile. 'No, the powers that be think it's not convenient. Once we've cleared the room, I might ask you and Harold to help in putting it to rights. I'd like Lorinda to find it as it used to be, when she comes back.'

In the back of the car with Harold, Walter Armitage's words reverberated in Jem's mind. 'A good job', Audrey Arbuthnot had said. Fancy being recognized by such a formidable person! Who had told her? Mrs Isaacs, no doubt. Jem felt pleased, but also guilty. There would be no pats on the back if the search came to a full stop. But he felt a sudden surge of hope and resolution: it mustn't fail. He, Harold and Benjy *had* to justify this confidence, and not let Ma Hibbert down.

22 REVIVAL

'I'm beginning to wish Alice hadn't helped me to get through the transfer exam,' Jem said to his mother, having unloaded text books and exercise books from his satchel.

'Why?'

'It's such hard work. Look at all the homework I've got! I don't really feel I belong, either.'

'You will in time. Be patient.'

At Homefield School, Jem had been well up in his year and had felt that he was somebody. At Bruddersford Grammar School he had been placed in form 3C – next to the bottom academically. Harold was in 3A, as was Charlie. He felt that he was a very small cog in a vast machine. And he was feeling the pressure of the greater expectations of the teachers. It was good, though, to travel on the bus with Harold. Not so good was seeing Charlie every day. But, since their joint mishap on the lake, he had become less unfriendly and had stopped being sarcastic. Jem would have liked to know whether he was visiting Cop Top Farm.

Charlie came over to him and Harold in the school playground.

'Heard the latest?'

'What's that?' Harold asked.

'Police and Home Guard raided a farm below Griddle Moor.'

'Did they find them?'

'Them? Who?'

'Ed and Bert – the two men with the woman.'

'Oh! Been doing some investigating have you? If we'd done it together, we might have caught them. The farm was empty. Seemed that the birds had flown.'

'Look,' said Jem who had come to a difficult decision. 'I think you're right. We should be in on this together. After all, there is a war on.'

He proceeded to tell Charlie about their encounter on Griddle Edge.

'They may have moved out of the district altogether. But there could be something they still have their eye on here. What they don't know is that we've got the van's number. It's 509 WY. We'd better get all the scouts looking out for it.'

'We ought to patrol all the streets and roads,' Charlie suggested. 'Let's go and see Woody after school.'

The upshot was a rota for all scouts over ten. Areas of the village were to be patrolled in pairs before school and after coming home until it got dark. Each scout had the van's number pencilled on the inner side of a wrist in indelible ink. At first the scouts were enthusiastic. They felt enrolled into the war effort. The mysterious men with the van took on the aspect of spies and saboteurs.

They were almost as much enemies as Germans. After a week with no sign of the van, the patrolling palled. The younger ones, particularly, found more interesting things to do. Three weeks later, only half a dozen were still keenly on the look-out, amongst them Charlie, Jem, Harold and Will.

What with trying to keep his head above a flood of homework and patrolling the streets, Jem had little time for other important things. One Saturday morning, though, having done an errand for his mother, he went in search of Benjy. The forge was closed, so he went along to Mill Cottages. There was an autumnal feel in the valley. Leaves of the trees by the river were beginning to turn yellow. A few dropped into the water and were swept away. Despite the chill in the air, the door of Benjy's cottage was open. Three upright chairs and a folding table stood on the garden path.

'Hullo, Benjy! You there?' Jem shouted.

'Ay, lad. Wait a minute!'

Benjy appeared wearing overalls – not the dirty ones he wore at the forge, but an off-white pair which made him look like a baker.

'What's going on, Benjy? Not moving are you?'

'Nay, lad – not yet at least. I'm doing an autumn clean. There's corners in this cottage that 'aven't seen a brush or a duster since the flood – and I mean Noah's, not the one you rescued me from. But come on in – it's time I 'ad a break.'

It was the front room that was the object of Benjy's assault on dirt. In the living room behind there was a fire. Benjy made some tea.

'I were going to come and see you,' he said with a smile. 'I've 'ad a reply from my friend in Oldham.'

Jem's heart leapt. 'Is it good news?'

'You'll see – here it is.'

Jem took the letter with fingers that trembled.

Dear Benjamin, old man. How's tricks? It was good to see you last February. I hardly recognised you without your beard. But as it were the vicar who advised you to take it off, I suppose you'll stand a better chance at the pearly gates without it.

Enough of this nonsense! We've got some news for you and your friends. Joan went to see Priscilla at the home yesterday. She'd had a reply a few days ago from Hilary Oldcastle. I'm enclosing a copy of it. So our shot in the dark reached its target – though in a roundabout way. Joan and I are glad to have been of some help. Don't leave it too long before trekking over the Pennines again.

Your pal, Percy.

'Found her – how marvellous!'

'Ay. Now read the letter from America.'

Copy of letter from Mrs Hilary Williams

2520 Union Street
West Sector
Cleveland
Ohio, USA
25 August 1941

Dear Priscilla,

I can't tell you what a lovely surprise it was to hear from you. Your letter was dated in February, but it was only last month I received it. You naturally addressed it to the farm where I was when we were last in touch. That must be about six years ago. The people there now had lost my forwarding address. So it's lucky the mail service was able to find me.

You must think me awfully remiss not to have kept in touch. The fact is, I had a lot of trouble. You know I married again – in 1922. Jake was a good husband for a few years. Then he took to gambling. At first he was lucky and we lived the life of Riley. But then he began losing. The last two or three years that I wrote to you, we were living in misery, though I didn't let you know. We had to leave our lovely farm and move into a run-down tenement in this enormous city. Jake got a job at the steel works, but it undermined his health and he died in 1935. So there was I, having to look to my son, Raymond, to support me, and he was miles away in Toronto. Yes, he's become a Canadian. He liked the country and the people and decided to throw his lot in with them. He has a job with the City Council. He's been a good son.

That brings me to the question in your letter – would Raymond like his real mother to get in touch with him? Up to ten years ago I'd have felt jealous about that. But after what I've been through and with this terrible war raging in Europe and elsewhere, I realize we have to be more respectful of people's feelings, even if their interests are not the same as ours. I can therefore say, Priscilla, that I've no objection to Miss Hibbert writing to Raymond, provided that he wants her to. I'm writing to ask him. It will perhaps come as a shock to him to know that his mother is still alive. Of course, he knows that he was adopted – we were careful to tell him as a boy. But by then we'd lost contact with Miss Hibbert. You told me you are now in a home for the elderly. Raymond has asked me to go and live with him. If I go I'll send you the address. Thank you for writing. Do so again. I still think a lot about my life in Oldham. I will let you know what Raymond says.

Your friend, Hilary Williams (Oldcastle)

Jem finished reading the letter and sat back, looking into the fire. He had the uncomfortable feeling that he had been peeping into someone's life when he had no right to; even worse, that he was guilty of helping to stir up things which might best have lain dormant. Suppose Raymond *did* wish to meet his mother. What would be the result? Suppose he *didn't*, and Ma Hibbert had to be told! It was all very well putting the enquiry in train. But now various outcomes were in prospect, he began to feel a weight of responsibility.

'You look worried, Jem,' Benjy said. 'Good news isn't it?'

'Of course. But…supposing Raymond says he's not interested.'

'Well, at least we'll 'ave tried. And Julia Hibbert will know that Raymond turned out alright.'

'I expect you're right, Benjy. I'd better take the letters to show her this afternoon.'

'Ah, well…I've got a suggestion to make, Jem. You know how anxious she's been about hearing from

America. I've a feeling she'll be upset, even though it's good news. I think it's more a task for a woman to give it to her, rather than us men. Suppose we ask Hetty Isaacs to go and see her?'

Jem was disappointed. He wanted to convey the news himself and to receive Ma Hibbert's personal thanks. But Benjy was right.

'I agree. I could go up to Mrs Isaacs' after dinner.'

'Well, as a matter of fact, she's coming 'ere this afternoon.'

Jem grinned. 'So that's the reason for the autumn clean!'

'Well, I don't want the place to be a disgrace!'

The following day Jem wondered whether Mrs Isaacs had yet been to see Ma Hibbert. But he was too much occupied with Sunday School, seeing Harold and catching up with homework to climb the hill to her bungalow. In the middle of the week he received a message.

'Mrs Isaacs was at the WVS meeting this afternoon,' his mother said. 'She's got *her* uniform too, and very nice she looks in it. She asked me to tell you that Miss Hibbert would like to see you and Harold. I expect it's about the reply from America.'

Not till the Friday evening did he and Harold have the opportunity to go to Up Bye. Harold took Raq. The three black cats were at the bottom of the stairs. Raq wagged his tail tentatively, as though to say: 'I'll make friends if you will.' The cats gave no response. Miss Hibbert took them through to the garden. The sun had gone down but there was still a glow in the sky.

Three deck chairs were set out.

Jem remembered the first time that he and Harold had been there – when they were on the tracks of the church burglar. He had been rather afraid of Ma Hibbert then. Now he knew that, though eccentric, she was one of the kindest people in the village. The garden was the same: the almost perpendicular cliff, the tiny stream issuing from its base and flowing into the pool, the overhanging sycamore. There, too, on the gravel bank, was the little wooden boat that Ron had mended. Mr Toad was still sitting in it, reading his book.

'Now lads,' Miss Hibbert began, 'I've asked you to come up because I wanted to thank you for finding the whereabouts of my son, Raymond. I know you'll say that it was Benjamin Oldcastle who did it. But it was you two who had the idea and got people looking. Without that, I'd have just continued moping.'

'We're glad if we've been of some help, Miss Hibbert…'Jem began.

'Call me Julia, dear.'

'…Julia. But what if Raymond's not interested in his past?'

'If that should happen, you're not to blame yourselves. I'll have the satisfaction of knowing that he's made a life for himself. But I've an intuition – call it a fancy it you like – that he *will* get in touch. I've sent my thoughts winging from this little garden over the Atlantic all the way to Toronto. Yesterday evening, after it got dark, there was a bird singing loudly. It had such a varied song. Small, with a pale breast – I think it must have been a nightingale. Never heard one here before. Was that a reply? I can see from your smiles you think me odd – or even batty? But strange things happen in this world. Now, Harold, I've got something to say to Jem. Would you and Raq go into the house?'

Jem wondered what on earth this could mean. Special thanks? Or a warning not to meddle too much in other people's affairs?

'It's naught to worry about, Jem. So there's no need for that anxious look on your face! One good turn deserves another, doesn't it? I don't pry into other folks' lives, as some people think. But I keep my eyes and ears open. Something tells me you and Alice Ackroyd are not the friends you used to be. I don't know the reason, and I'm not asking, Jem. But I'm sure it's based on a mistake. So what I suggest is, if you want to be a good friend of hers again, you've got to do something about it. There's no point in harbouring resentments, or moping – as I might have continued to do over Raymond if it hadn't been for you and Harold. Now let's join him. I've got some old mementoes to show you. Perhaps when you come up again, you'll bring Alice with you.'

Going down the hill, Harold turned to Jem. 'Suppose you don't want to tell me what she wanted you for?'

'Afraid not, Harold. At least, not yet.'

Jem replied calmly, but inside he was elated. Perhaps what had come between Alice and him *was* just a mistake. If so, it could be corrected.

He was nervous about what he had to do, and lost some sleep over it. But it had to be faced up to. Early on Saturday morning he excused himself from errands and chores, promising his mother that he would do them later. He set off for Cop Top. It was not Alice he wished to see. In fact, he hoped not to see her. It was those Land Army girls he was after.

On the outskirts of the farm he saw them in a turnip field. Marge spotted him.

'Here comes trouble,' she said to Jeannie.

They both straightened up and watched Jem approaching between the rows of turnips. He was a foot shorter than them, but the expression on his face showed he was determined not to be browbeaten.

'It's Master Jem, isn't it?' Jeannie asked in her Scottish brogue. 'How are ye, laddie?'

Jem hated the word 'laddie', but tried not to show it.

'Do you remember I gave you a message for Alice – in July, two months ago?' he asked, looking from one to the other.

'What might that have been?' Jeannie countered.

'About me getting through the exam.'

'Do you remember that, Marge?'

'Er...'

'You must remember. You made a joke – at least you thought it was a joke – about me getting through a hedge backwards.'

'Oh dear! Has that been troubling you all this time?'

'Of course not! But you didn't pass my message on to Alice.'

'Does it matter all that much? Couldn't you have told her yourself next time you saw her?'

'You don't understand. She thinks I overlooked the need to tell her – that I forgot how much I owed to her. Poor sort of friend she thinks I am! She's not been friendly since – all because of you!'

Jeannie and Marge looked at Jem's flushed face.

'Come on, Jeannie,' said Marge, speaking for the first time. 'This has gone on long enough. I told you it wasn't right. You see,' she added, turning to Jem, 'that Charlie was up here. We guessed that you were competing to be in Alice's good books. We both took a fancy to him…'

'Charlie didn't ask you not to give Alice my message, did he?' asked Jem, who was on the point of exploding.

'No, he knew nothing about it,' Marge continued. 'We thought we'd do him a favour by not passing on your message. It was Jeannie's idea, but I went along with it. We've seen Charlie since a few times, and we're not sure he's all that nice a lad – a bit too cocky.'

'I'm sorry if we've upset things,' said Jeannie, who had begun to look embarrassed during Marge's explanation. 'It was a silly thing to do. How can we put matters right?'

'By telling Alice!'

'It may cost us our jobs, but we'll have to do it, eh Marge?'

Jem was so relieved, his face broke into a grin. 'If you'll do that, I'll put in a good word for you. And I'll give you a hand with the turnips!'

At the end of an hour pulling turnips and chopping off the roots, Jem felt that his back would break. He said he had to be getting home.

'You're not as tough as you think, Jem. But we never got any help from Charlie, did we Jeannie?'

'So long, and don't worry,' Jeannie called, as he made his way to the lane.

Trust Charlie to have the good luck, Jem thought. The History master was trying to explain why Charles the First had been obliged to call a Parliament. But Jem's thoughts were elsewhere. In the mid-morning break Charlie had told Harold, Will and him that he had seen the van. He had gone out before breakfast. He had started walking up the hill beside the church. A brown van had come down and turned into Up Bye. As it did so, Charlie had realised that it bore the registration they were looking for. By missing breakfast he had had time to go to the police station before catching the bus.

'But Up Bye's a cul-de-sac! Did they take a wrong turning?' Jem had asked.

'I went along,' Charlie had explained. 'The van had stopped and a man was opening the gate. I didn't want him to see me, so I turned into Ma Hibbert's front garden. The door was open, so I called to her. I told her what was up. She said there's a barn in the field beyond the end of Up Bye. She's going to keep a look-out.'

'Constable Dewhurst's been here, Jem,' was his mother's news when he got home at the end of the afternoon. Normally such news would have been alarming, but it was just what Jem had hoped for.

'He wants you and your "pals", as he called them, to go down to the police station. He said he's already called at Charlie Foster's house. He assured me that it's nothing you've done. A matter of urgency, he said. So what are you up to now, Master Jem?'

'It's to do with the thieves. They've been spotted. I'd better go now.'

'What, without any tea?'

'I'll take a sandwich with me.'

Jem was excited. He had feared that by the time they got home from school it would be all over: the police would have collared the men. Now, there was a chance that he and the others would be in on the kill.

At the police station he found Harold, Will and Charlie waiting for him. Constable Dewhurst surveyed them across the counter.

'What a pity I'm not running you in!' he said. 'A pleasure to come, perhaps. You'd better come into the office – the operations room, rather.'

In the small room were gathered Police Sergeant Milford from Bruddersford, Hon Peter, Dr McLeish, Walter Armitage and Joe Quarmby. Constable Dewhurst and the boys squeezed in.

'First, congratulations, Charlie,' said Hon Peter, who was obviously in charge. 'We're really on their tail now. Let me put you in the picture, boys. Constable Dewhurst…may I call you Reginald, Constable?'

'Reggie, sir.'

'Reggie went up to Miss Hibbert's, after having had the good sense to change into mufti. Apparently, she'd seen the van a few times during the past week – she assumed Farmer Hebblethwaite, who owns the field, was making use of the barn there. Reggie did a reconnaissance. Tell us again what you saw.'

'The barn's in a dip, so it can't be seen from the gate. There's a bumpy track leading to it. I got into the next field and went along behind a hedge till I could see the barn. The van was there. I saw three people. One of them was a hefty chap, another tall and thin. I assume they're the ones who climbed up to Jem Murgatroyd and Harold Bright. The third was a woman. They were carrying things from the van into the barn, but I couldn't see what. I went back to Miss Hibbert's, and we both kept watch. While we waited she repaired a tear in my trousers where I'd caught them on barbed wire. Through an open window we heard the van. She suggested she should go outside and pretend she'd lost one of her cats. They were opening the gate. She deserves a medal that lady. By leaning out of an upstairs window – I'd put a cloth over my head so that I looked like an old woman – I could see what was going on.'

Jem and Harold were looking down at the floor, trying to contain their mirth at the image of Reggie (they had not known Constable Dewhurst's Christian name before) with his darned trousers pretending to be an old woman. Will had his handkerchief between his teeth.

'She weren't at all afraid. Made out she were right distressed about her cat. Of course, they said they hadn't seen it. She said she wondered if it had got into the barn in the field, and couldn't get out. Could she go and have a look? Oh no, they said. They'd been in the barn and they hadn't seen a cat. She went on imploring them. "It could have been hiding from you, but it would come to me," she said. They were getting desperate to be off, but she was barring the way. I went downstairs to the front door ready to intervene if they got physical. You may ask why I didn't go out and arrest them. First, I'd no evidence. Second, the three of them could have overpowered me, even with Julia …I mean Miss Hibbert…there as well. Then they'd have got away and as like as not we wouldn't have seen them around here again.'

Constable Dewhurst was anxious to defend his honour. It wasn't that he lacked courage. He would have been prepared to have a go, but had judged it unwise.

'You did quite right, Reggie,' Sergeant Milford said, realising he needed some reassurance. Hon Peter nodded his head.

'So then the thin one said, "Look, lady, we'll be back this evening and we'll have a proper look." The big chap said, "Ed" in a sharp tone as though he didn't like what Ed had said. Then the van went off. I went down to the barn. It was padlocked. I thought it better not to break in until we'd decided what to do.'

'Now we're all up to date,' Hon Peter said. 'This is the plan that Sergeant Milford and I have devised.'

The sun had set an hour ago and the moon had not yet risen. Jem and Charlie were twenty yards apart in the field at the other end from the entrance at Up Bye. Each of them had found a bush to crouch behind. Harold and Will were at a similar distance on either side of them. After the briefing, they had all dashed home to change into scouts' uniform and to ask mystified mothers for some grub to take with them. Charlie and Jem were nearest to the gate at this end of the field. At Charlie's suggestion they had taken stones from a wall and placed them in two rows on the ground.

'I'm getting stiff,' said Jem, standing up. 'How about you, Charlie?'

'I wish something would happen. Do you think part of war is getting bored?'

They heard the engine of a vehicle. It died to a low putter.

‘Here they are,’ Jem whispered. ‘I bet they’re opening the gate now.’

The engine revved up, became louder as it approached and then cut out.

‘They’re at the barn!’ Charlie said.

From their position, the barn was hidden in the dip. It was getting too dark to have seen it, anyway. Nothing happened. Time went by. Jem and the others crouched down again. Surely the plan wouldn’t have gone wrong, Jem thought. The two policemen and the four Home Guard were the frontal attack. Their job was to follow the van down the field to the barn and, at a suitable moment, catch them red-handed. The scouts were, as Hon Peter put it, an ‘outer cordon’: in case any of the party escaped seizure and made for the other end of the field and the gate into a lane. The scouts were to use whistles and torches to signal, and to confuse anyone trying to get away. But they were forbidden from impeding a person physically. Jem felt for the whistle and torch, both hanging round his neck. The torch was from home, but the whistle was one issued by Constable Dewhurst. He had insisted on the boys signing receipts: he wasn’t going to have police property purloined, he had said.

Suddenly the silence was broken. The engine of the van started up and then died down. Cries rang through the air: ‘Get him!’ ‘There she is!’ ‘Ouch, you blighter!’ ‘Cut him off!’ ‘Gotcher!’

Then: ‘Scouts, look out!’

There was heavy breathing and the thud of feet as someone ran up the slope from the barn towards the position of Charlie and Jem. Each waited tensely, whistle in mouth and torch in hand. A figure loomed out of the darkness. Jem switched on his torch and pointed it. He blew his whistle.

'What the devil…?' exclaimed a woman's voice. An arm lashed out. Two bodies fell.

Jem came to after a few seconds. He was lying on a shoulder which seemed to be a power house of pain, sending shoots of agony down his arm and into his chest. He tried to turn on his back, but the devil inside him leapt. He was aware of someone else on the ground, a few feet away, groaning.

'Did she get you as well, Charlie?' Jem managed to ask.

'No! We've got her. Dr McLeish'll be here in a minute. Just hang on.'

Jem drifted into semi-consciousness, a blissful state where the pain receded into the background. He was hauled back into hurting awareness by fingers feeling his shoulder. He heard the voice of Dr McLeish.

'Alright Jem, laddie. Move slowly on to your back. That's it. Now what have we here? Collar bone broken, I think. That'll mend alright. So there's no need to worry. We'll get you over to Miss Hibbert's. Then I'll get my car.'

The accent was the same as that of Jeannie, the Land Army girl. But her voice had seemed harsh, whilst the doctor's was soothing.

Walter Armitage and Joe Quarmby clasped hands to form a seat, and Jem was lifted on to it. As gingerly as possible they carried him across the field. In the light of a torch, Jem saw two men sitting against the wall of the barn, hands and feet tied. Constable Dewhurst was standing in front of them with his truncheon at the ready. They went through the gate into Up Bye. Ma Hibbert was there.

'Bring the poor lad in. It's Jem isn't it? I had a premonition it'd be you. Mind cats - out of the way!'

'Dr McLeish said to give him a hot drink, Miss Hibbert,' said Joe. 'He's had a shock.'

Jem had never before felt so relieved to sink on to a sofa. If he kept his shoulder still and took only shallow breaths, the pain was bearable. He felt the warm rasp of a cat's tongue on the hand that extended toward the floor.

'Cats can show sympathy, like humans,' Ma Hibbert said, helping him to sip tea.

Dr McLeish entered.

'I'm going to take you to Bruddersford General, Jem. They'll be able to set your collar bone. We'll collect your mother first. Now, I'll just give you an injection to reduce the pain.'

Jem afterwards looked back on that first, brief stay in hospital as satisfying. He was the object of attention. His comfort was important. Doctors and nurses showed a brisk sympathy. He was sorry that he was allowed to stay only one night. An ambulance took him home the following day. He was conscious that he was going to look very odd in the village and at school. A large piece of wood in the shape of the letter 'T' had been fixed to his back with adhesive bandages. In addition, he had an arm in a sling. His mother found an old shirt of his father's, large enough to cover his expanded frame.

‘I’d rather stay at home until I get this thing off, Mum,’ Jem pleaded. ‘It’s not that I mind appearing funny. But it’ll be embarrassing, folk pointing me out as a wounded warrior.’

‘The hospital said it’d be about three weeks. You can’t miss school for all that time. You’ll just have to put up with it. But they did say you should rest for a couple of days. I only hope it’s off before your Dad comes home. I don’t want to justify letting you be put in the line of fire, so to speak.’

It was Hon Peter who felt the need to justify, or rather, to excuse, himself. The euphoria of the capture had worn off by the next morning. He had dreamed of Jem being severely hurt, even disabled. He was horrified that he had put boys into potential danger. It was unforgiveable. If something dreadful had happened, he would have been the man primarily responsible, with his grand plan of operations. But it wasn’t the image of being hauled over the coals that troubled him. It was the thought of irreparable harm to others.

Mrs Murgatroyd had just made Jem comfortable in bed, with pillows propping him up and ‘Just William’ within reach when Hon Peter called. Her heart beat a bit faster. Peter might be the ‘squire’, but she was determined to say some hard things to him. She was disarmed, though, by the expression on his face. It was similar to that on Jem’s face when he’d done something wrong. Seated by the kitchen fire, he confessed his guilt at having exposed the boys to possible injury or worse.

‘I’m not expecting you to forgive me, Mrs Murgatroyd. All I can do is express my penitence and promise not to make such a mistake again. And if Mr Murgatroyd wants to remonstrate with me when he's back, I'm prepared to face the music.'

'I don't think I'll be telling him – I don't want to add to his worries. I think you *were* wrong to involve the scouts. I wanted to tell you that. On the other hand I wouldn't put it past them to have got involved anyway. So I'll just put it down to your boyish enthusiasm running away with itself, if you don't mind me saying so, sir.'

'You take a weight off my mind, Mrs Murgatroyd. Now might I see Jem?'

After he had gone, Mrs Murgatroyd felt dissatisfied with herself. She should have been more severe. Instead, she had allowed herself to be mollified by his penitence. For his part, Hon Peter was both relieved and impressed. Jem was fortunate to have such a sensible mother.

Another visitor was Constable Dewhurst. He came grudgingly, though he tried not to show it.

'I've got summat for you, young Jem,' he said. 'I don't like writing off police property. But Sergeant Milford thinks you four deserve a memento each. So here you are.'

Jem unwrapped the piece of paper to find a police whistle.

The first day that Jem went back to school, he felt self-conscious. He was unable to get his jacket over the 'T', so he wore a large pullover of his Dad's. To the many enquiries, he merely said he'd had an accident. With the younger boys, he joked that he was turning into Frankenstein, and made a face to match. During the morning break, Charlie joined him, Harold and Will. Jem learnt the reason for the delay in arresting the party. They had begun loading the van, and Sergeant Milford had let them finish, so as to save the police and Home Guard the task of loading it themselves. They were just starting to leave when the policemen, backed up by the Home Guard – Armitage and Quarmby had fixed bayonets to their rifles – pounced.

'What about the woman?' Jem asked.

'Dr McLeish attended to her when he'd seen to you,' Charlie replied. 'She'd stumbled against one of those stones we put on the ground. She'd wrenched an ankle and might have some broken ribs. She had to be helped across the field.'

'She was quite young,' Harold added. 'She looked scared. I almost felt sorry for her. But she lashed out at you, Jem.'

'Not knowing I was just a …'

'A little boy scout who wouldn't have harmed a flea,' Will suggested.

Jem grinned. He wasn't warlike, but he was a bit fiercer than that.

'What I don't understand is why they should have chosen a hiding place in the centre of the village. Surely they'd have realised it was risky?'

'Sergeant Milford said they were trying to be clever,' Charlie explained. 'They thought no one would dream of looking for them so close.'

'And Hon Peter thought they were just too cocksure,' Harold added.

It was the following Saturday morning. There was

a knock on the door.

'Perhaps another well-wisher,' his mother said.

Jem went to the door. It was the well-wisher he had dared to hope might call.

'Hullo, Jem. Can I come in?' There was a tentative smile on Alice's face.

'How lovely to see you, Alice,' said Mrs Murgatroyd. 'You two have a chat, then I'll come and join you.'

Jem was grateful for his mother's tact.

'You'll have to tell me all about your adventure, Jem. But first, I must have my say. Marge and Jeannie have confessed to me. I felt so annoyed, but also relieved. It was like a cloud being lifted. I still feel angry with myself, though. I blame myself for not trusting you when you said you'd left a message. I've no excuse. But I'd like to be forgiven.'

Jem was riveted to his chair. This was music in his ears. Tears came into his eyes. It was a few moments before he could trust himself to speak. When he did so, he felt the words to be inadequate. 'Let's forget it, Alice. Be friends like we were?'

'Of course, unless you think I deserve to be thrown over!'

'What about Jeannie and Marge? Are they in trouble?'

'No. I've promised to keep it to myself.'

Mrs Murgatroyd reappeared. 'You both seem happy! Something to celebrate? I've not had the chance, Alice, to thank you for helping Jem to get that transfer. I'll just put the kettle on. Then we can hear how things are getting on at the farm. I hope those Land Army girls are behaving themselves and not skiving.'

'They were a bit of a handful at first. But they're settling down. They'll be alright. They think highly of Jem – he helped them pull turnips.'

Alice looked at Jem. He knew what she meant. There was no need to tell anyone else about the girls' behaviour. That, and what flowed from it, was over and done with.

23 REUNION

Since the War Office report of Dad's injury there had been only one letter from him. He said that he would soon be on the way home – the long way round. That meant via South Africa, Mum had said. It was now November: surely he would be back soon, Jem thought. Returning from school on the fifth of November, he regretted the ban on fireworks. But he found his mother's face glowing.

'There's a letter from your Dad!'

Jem plonked his heavy satchel on the kitchen table and sat down in front of the kitchen fire. Mum gave him the letter.

Ward C5,

Royal Victoria Hospital,

Netley,

Hampshire,

3rd November 1941

My dear Margaret,

At last I'm back in dear old England. Arrived

yesterday on board a splendid steamer, though it wasn't exactly first class accommodation. I'm having a bit more treatment at this hospital near Southampton. If you can get down it will be lovely to see you.

Your Ted

'I'll have to go, Jem. Perhaps you could stay with Harold. I'll have a word with Mrs Bright.'

'Couldn't I come too?'

'Sorry, love. They might not welcome young folk. And I'd rather see what your Dad's like by myself.'

The prospect of Dad's return was both exciting and unsettling. Jem had dreamt of his return for so long that he had a feeling of intense pleasure in envisaging him being home at last. But he began also to be worried. How extensive were Dad's injuries? Was it more than the loss of an eye? Had he suffered in his mind – was he still suffering in that way? He thought of someone else who had gone through the experience of being wounded in battle. He suggested to Harold that it was time they paid One-Leg Tim a visit.

It was unlikely they would find him at the allotments on such a raw, murky morning, but they went there first. Tim's patch looked weedy and neglected. They picked some of the Brussels sprouts and proceeded to Mill Cottages. Tim came to the door wearing a dressing gown, cap and muffler.

'Come in, lads. I'm right glad to see yer. I don't get many visitors. I've got a cough that won't go away, so I'm biding indoors, as doctor says I should.'

They followed Tim into the kitchen where a coal fire was burning in the grate. Sitting near it, the boys felt their fronts warm, but were aware of draughts at their backs.

'You ought to get your windows sealed, Tim,' Jem said, thinking of his mother's attack on draughts at home.

'Ay, well, Benjamin Oldcastle said 'e'd come in and do it. If you see 'im, just remind 'im. What's the news of your Dad, Jem?'

Jem explained about the injury Dad had received. 'We don't know how he's been affected by it – in his self, if you see what I mean.'

'I knows just what yer mean,' Tim replied. 'But being wounded affects people differently. There's some as it's like water off a duck's back. They put the experience behind them and carry on as best their injury allows. There's others who take a long time to get over the mental shock. They feel they've been…what's the word…violated. They feel resentment at being singled out.'

'Was it water off a duck's back for you, Tim?' Harold asked.

'Ay, I were one o't' lucky ones. I 'ad a positive outlook. The loss of a leg weren't goin' to stop me living! Knowing your Dad a bit, Jem, I reckon 'e'll get over it pretty quick. But you and your mother'll need to be patient – and understanding. There's one thing, though. If 'e's got the use of 'is limbs, 'e's fortunate. I'd rather 'ave lost an eye than a leg.'

Tim began coughing and said they had better leave him. He thanked them for the sprouts, and said they could go to the allotment any time, do a bit of weeding and help themselves to what there was.

'It's been quite an experience,' Mrs Murgatroyd said, sipping a cup of tea in the Manse kitchen on her return from her journey to Hampshire.

'How was Mr Murgatroyd?' Mrs Bright asked.

'They've tried to restore the sight of his left eye but without success – so far. He has scars down his left cheek, and he's walking with a limp. But in himself, he's cheerful.'

'When will he be home, Mum?' Jem asked.

'Quite soon. We'd best start dusting the flags. But that hospital – it's enormous! Ted said it's more than four hundred and fifty yards long. It looks out over Southampton Water – built in the last century. Wards and wards of injured men – and women. It makes you realize what a cruel thing war is. So many lives afflicted, damaged, destroyed. We're so lucky that Ted's been only slightly hurt compared with many.'

As the end of 1941 hove in sight, many people in Althwaite were worried about the progress of the war. No one would admit – even to themselves – the prospect of defeat. But things were not going right. The German army was now attacking Moscow. In North Africa we had defeated the Italians. But the German army there was now commanded by Rommel, a star general, and he had pushed the British army back towards Egypt. Germany had invaded Yugoslavia and Greece. Air raids on Britain were continuing. How were we going to win this war?

There was excitement at Bruddersford School on the eighth of December. The previous day Japanese planes had attacked American warships in Pearl Harbour in the Hawaian islands. It seemed a dastardly thing to do. The Japanese Government had not even declared war beforehand. Charlie was one of those who seemed to have a grasp of the situation.

'Don't you see? Now America's in the war, we're bound to win. It seems like a setback – the Japs joining Hitler. But the Americans are up in arms. They'll be backing us all over the world now.'

Jem was not so sure. He had a feeling that the Japanese would be very tough enemies – soldiers and airmen prepared to sacrifice themselves for their Emperor. Most people, though, felt relieved. They were appalled by the Japanese attack, and felt sorry for the Americans. But the fact that America, with its enormous resources, was now actively with us meant that Hitler's defeat was certain, sooner or later.

On one thing, everyone was agreed: the thieves had got what they deserved. The two men had been sent to prison for a year. The woman claimed that, as one of the men was her husband, she was forced to cooperate. The court decided not to send her to prison, but fined her £50. Hon Peter had not been on the magistrates' bench when the case came up. At first, he thought the woman's defence was outrageous. If *he* was engaged on a criminal act, he would expect Lorinda to protest and to refuse to join him. But, the thought then came to him, would he not have been disappointed if she had declined to help with the removal of his ancestors' pieces of armour from St Jude's? Perhaps the woman did have some defence, after all.

Jem had often imagined Dad's home-coming. Usually it was to a public welcome. If the silver band – its ranks depleted by the war – was not at the station, there would at least be a crowd of well-wishers to greet the train from Bruddersford. His actual arrival was different. On a Saturday morning a fortnight before Christmas Jem was looking out of his bedroom window. He saw a car draw up. A man in khaki uniform got out, and the driver helped him with his bags. Dad was here! Jem flew downstairs, shouting out to Mum. There followed a confusion of greetings and hugs.

'There was no time to let you know, love.'

'You could have sent a telegram.'

'Telegrams bring bad news. In any case, I fancied giving you and Jem a surprise.'

'Well, you've done that alright, you rascal!'

For a couple of weeks a feeling of euphoria prevailed in the Murgatroyd household. It was a pleasure to see that Dad was so pleased to be back. Jem was relieved that the injuries were not as marked as he had feared. Dad wore an eye patch. The scars on his left cheek, where the shrapnel that had blinded him had cut grooves in the skin, were unsightly, but they might become less so. He still walked with a limp, the result of shrapnel in his left thigh. But at least he was active. He took a stick and enjoyed walking around the village, greeting and being greeted. It was like being a local hero. A reporter from the Bruddersford Examiner arrived to interview him. He was disappointed in not getting from Mr Murgatroyd the graphic account of the war in the desert that he had hoped to write up.

Christmas was celebrated in low key fashion. Some of the choruses and arias from Handel's Messiah were sung in St Jude's, where the chapel congregations joined with the church folk. The stalwarts of the silver band kept alive the tradition of playing Christmas hymns around the village in the early hours of the morning. But presents were few and cheap. Jem and his mother, however, were treated to gifts from Cairo: a trinket box covered with tiny pieces of mosaic for Mum, and a wallet embossed with scenes of ancient Egypt for Jem.

As January progressed, Dad went out less often. He no longer regaled Jem and his mother with an account of how far he had walked and who he had seen. Snow fell, and Dad had good reason to stay at home, so as not to risk his bad leg. But the snow soon melted, and still he did not venture out much. He became less communicative; his usual liveliness was absent. At meal times, his attention was sometimes elsewhere. Jem came into the kitchen from the shed where he had been painting another model aeroplane, and found Dad staring into the fire.

'Hullo, son,' Dad said, turning to Jem with an attempt at a smile.

'What do you see in the fire, Dad?'

Dad was silent a few moments. 'I see things I wouldn't want you or your mother ever to see, or even to know about.'

'Things you saw in the desert? Men being killed?'

Dad nodded. 'And worse – death's not always quick.'

Both his mother and Jem hoped that Dad was just

going through a reaction from which he would soon emerge. But his mental state seemed to get worse. He began waking from nightmares. He moved into the back bedroom where his cries in the night would be less disturbing.

'What can we do, Jem? Who can help us?' his mother asked.

'Perhaps Miss…Julia Hibbert might have some ideas.'

'And I've had a thought. I'll mention it to Audrey Arbuthnot at the WVS this afternoon.'

'Do you think Dad would take to her?' Jem asked in astonishment.

'Not her, but her friend, Walter Armitage. He's an intelligent, sympathetic fellow.'

Ma Hibbert listened to Jem's account of his Dad's state of mind. It was a question, she said, of finding new interests which would displace his vivid memories.

'But if he's not interested in finding new interests, how do we start?' Jem asked.

'Leave it to me. I'll try to think of something.'

The clouds casting a gloom over Mr Murgatroyd lifted temporarily as he shared Althwaite's interest in a local manifestation of the war. Eight Air Force men got lost on the moors. They had been guided by Benjy to a spot where a Fleet Air Arm aeroplane had crashed. The body of the pilot had already been removed, and the men were now going to bury the wreckage.

'A daft idea,' said Benjy in recounting the expedition. 'How they expected to bury big pieces of metal with just spades on ground covered by heather, I can't imagine.'

Benjy had said he would return at four o'clock to guide them back. They were not there, and he hastened back to Althwaite to raise the alarm with Constable Dewhurst and Hon Peter. Search parties were organized from the Home Guard, ARP men and farmers. Car headlamps were unmasked to shine across the moor. But it was not till morning that the party was discovered.

'We thought it'd be easy finding our own way back,' said the RAF Sergeant in charge, after the party had been given breakfast in the Dandelion Arms. 'But I reckon we must have walked in circles once it got dark.'

'It's as though there's no connection between the world I've left and this one in Althwaite,' Mr Murgatroyd said.

The vicar, warming his hands around the cup of cocoa that Mrs Murgatroyd had made before disappearing upstairs, nodded. Being a Methodist, Mr Murgatroyd had been surprised when the Reverend Cuthbert Blake was ushered in.

'I felt something of the same thing when our son was killed,' Mr Blake commented.

'I was very sorry to hear about that. It must have been devastating.'

'Yes. It certainly tried our faith. But tell me more about your experiences. It's not good to keep them bottled up.'

In the confines of the kitchen, the vicar moderated his booming voice. His large face had a benignant expression, which Mr Murgatroyd found encouraging.

'Well, of course, at first it was exciting. Foreign places - the sights, the smells, the sun of Egypt - the training, the feeling that we were going to help push the Germans out of North Africa. Then there was the desert – extraordinary world. I've known silence on the moors, but it's never complete. There's always something to be heard – hum of a bee, cry of a curlew. But the desert – no sound at all. You can almost touch the quietness. And the desert stars – so vivid. No wonder the Wise Men were led by a star. But the desert's like the sea. One moment it can be utterly peaceful, the next a storm's brewing, and then all hell breaks loose. I wouldn't wish my worst enemy to be lost in a sand storm. You have to find a bit of shelter – it might be a fold in the ground – cover yourself up best you can, put your back to the storm and hope to ride it out. Of course, we had our ambulances to shelter in, but sand percolates everywhere. Then when the storm dies down, you have to dig the vehicle out and try to get moving over tracks that have almost disappeared.'

'That must have been trying. But then, the real war – how much did you see of that?'

'That's what's difficult to talk about. Why I stare into the fire and see images. Why I'm disturbed in the night.'

'Try and tell me.'

'Being in a motor ambulance company, we had to be up near the fighting. Picking up wounded and taking them to the nearest MDS – Main Dressing Station, and from there to the CCS – Casualty Clearing Station. Some of the injured were in a horrible state. In great pain – despite morphine – and hanging on to life by a thread. I expect, Mr Blake, you had occasion to imagine what it must be like for the crew of an aircraft if it's hit and catches fire. It's the same for a tank crew. A desperate struggle to get out. Twice we were near enough to the front to see a tank hit. The screams of those inside will be with me to my dying day; and the silence when they'd died. There's an awful expression – a brew-up. It makes me shudder even to utter it.'

'War is dreadful. I often wonder how people keep their faith when they are up against its realities. But now you're out of it. Isn't it possible to start putting it behind you?'

'Not yet, it seems. I know folk here are concerned about the war and the men fighting in it. But the desert war is a world away from Home Guard exercises, the WVS collecting comforts for the forces, airmen being searched for. I don't want to decry these things. But people don't realise how horrific war really is.'

'I wonder. We're not far from places that have been badly bombed and where men, women and children have been killed and wounded. People have got to try to carry on with their normal lives. In any case, suppose they did take to heart how horrific war is, how differently would you expect them to behave?'

'That's it – I don't know.'

'Perhaps, if you don't mind me saying so, you regard your experiences as so vivid and important that you overlook that others may be suffering too, even though they don't show any outward sign of it. They may be fearing the worst for relatives and friends who are on the front line, not necessarily abroad, but in cities liable to be raided.'

'There may be something in what you say, Mr Blake. I'll think about it.'

'Come and have a chat anytime. I find composing sermons difficult, so I quite welcome an interruption.'

'Thanks very much for coming, vicar.'

'That was a long heart to heart,' Mrs Murgatroyd said when Mr Blake had gone. 'Are you going to be an Anglican now Ted?'

Ted smiled. 'No risk of being such a heretic! No - we talked about the war. I was able to tell him about things that bother me. He's a wise chap – may have helped me to get things into proportion.'

The vicar was not the only important visitor. The following day Hon Peter Danellion-Smith put in an appearance.

'Haven't seen you about so much recently, Mr Murgatroyd. What are you doing with yourself? Are you going to be recalled?'

'No sir, I've got my discharge papers. The army says thank you, but we don't want you any more. I've really got to make shift to find some occupation that'll keep the wolf from the door.'

'I hear the mill is looking for a storekeeper. That might suit you, for a time at least. And, if the army has released you, what about joining the Home Guard?'

'What about my disabilities?'

'Well, I won't say the Home Guard is a refuge for the infirm, but we do make allowance for some falling short of a peak of fitness. I'm sure you're sufficiently capable. You can see. And if your leg doesn't allow you to trek on the moors, we need men who can drive and man headquarters. But there's another thing. Whether you join or not, I want you to come down to HQ and tell us about the desert war. Will you do that?'

'I will, and I'll be glad to.'

'Good man!'

'Why are all these august people suddenly taking an interest in me?' Dad asked over their next meal. 'Have you and Jem been up to something, love?'

'Hand on heart, I haven't been to the vicarage or the Hall, have you Jem?'

'No, Mum.'

'What about that trip I want us to take to Bruddersford? Could we go tomorrow?' Mrs Murgatroyd asked.

'Sorry, love, not tomorrow. I saw Walter Armitage this morning – he popped out of the bank. He's asked me to go fishing – at your sailing lake, Jem.'

Mum gave Jem a knowing look. Their initiatives were beginning to bear fruit.

His friendship with Alice being now on an even keel, Jem had resumed his visits to Cop Top Farm. He exchanged banter with the Land Army girls, trying to give as good as he got. Miriam told him that Archie had been sent to Greece with the Friends' Ambulance Company. Their baby was now a toddler, wandering unsteadily around the farmyard, disturbing the hens and cats. Jem had wanted to take Alice to Ma Hibbert's ever since their reconciliation. Alice was so busy at the weekends – cleaning out the stable, exercising her pony, collecting eggs, helping her mother in the kitchen

-that the visit kept being put off. At last, on a Saturday afternoon in the middle of February, when yellow crocuses brightened Ma Hibbert's tiny front garden, they knocked at the door.

'Beware cats!' Jem said.

Julia opened the door and looked at them for a second or two before breaking into a smile.

'Forgive me, my dears. I was a world away. Come in. It's alright, cats. It's your friend, Jem, with Alice.'

Jem asked if he could show Alice the back garden. She marvelled, as Jem, Harold and Ron had done, at the secluded space beneath the cliff, with its little stream running into the pond, where Mr Toad waited in his boat for a wave to launch it from the bank. By the time they had looked around and made friends with the cats, the kettle was boiling.

'Good job I made these scones! Though I wasn't expecting anyone – not yet at least.' Julia smiled mysteriously. 'I've got something to tell you, Jem. I was hoping to see you soon.'

'About Raymond?'

'Yes! Just a few days ago, I had a letter from him. A lovely letter. He's so pleased to make contact. Says it fills a gap in his life. I'm afraid I can't show it to you, it's too private. I must have read it fifty times, and I still start weeping. I'm a silly, old woman you see, Alice.'

'Nonsense. You're like any doting mother.'

'I am that. And judging by the way he's turned out, I've good reason for doting. Though I realize I have to give credit to his foster parents. But I haven't told you the exciting bit. He says that when the war's over, he's going to come to England to meet me. I just hope I'm spared that long.'

'That's marvellous,' Jem exclaimed.

'When he comes, I'm going to introduce you to him as the young man who set about bringing us together.'

'I hope you'll introduce him to Benjy as well.'

'Of course.'

Jem started. It was only one of the cats making a dash at one of the others. But for a moment he thought it was something else. Julia noticed and stared at him with a serious expression.

'What's up, Jem?'

'I thought…it was so quick…gone in a flash. Is Raymond tall and burly?'

'So you've sensed it, too. It's a confirmation, isn't it? We're already in touch.'

'I don't believe it - it was my imagination.'

'Where imagination stops and reality takes over is often difficult to recognise.'

'I'm not sure what all this is about,' Alice interrupted.

'There's no need for you to know, my dear. But Jem perhaps has an inkling. Now Alice, I know all about Jem. What about you? What's happening at the farm? How are the Land Army girls behaving? And how's that poor wife of Archie and their bairn?'

As Alice, encouraged by Julia's sympathetic interest, responded, Jem looked around the room. The Toby jug on a shelf was still winking and grinning in his knowing fashion. There was the photograph of Malcolm Knowsley in his India Army uniform. Leaning against the frame was now another photograph. It showed a man of middle age wearing a cowboy hat, standing beside a long, ornate car. Raymond! Judging by his size relative to that of the car, he was a big man. Jem had the sensation of having seen him before.

'She *is* a kind woman, as you said, Jem,' Alice mused as they headed down to the centre of the village. 'Up till now, I'd thought of her as just an odd person. But I didn't understand what was going on between you and her – that stuff about imagination and reality.'

'I don't understand it either. Had her mind flashed across to mine a picture of Raymond? There was a photograph, which must have been him. But I wasn't aware of noticing it before that impression I had.'

'Are you going to make a career of telling people what's going on in their minds, or what's going go happen to them?'

'I don't mind you poking fun, Alice. But what is it Hamlet says to Horatio? I should know – we were reading it in class last week.'

'Er...could it be, "There are more things in heaven and earth than are dreamt of in your philosophy"?'

'That's it. Now why couldn't I remember it?'

As weeks went by, Jem and his mother observed with relief a change coming over Dad. He was emerging from his trauma. He himself was conscious of reviving powers, of a renewed enthusiasm for life. The memories were still there, and occasionally his mind visited them. But they didn't hold him in thrall. He was able to put them in the perspective of the life that continues. He had applied for, and got, the storekeeping job at the mill. It required discipline and attention to detail: qualities that he had developed in the Army. He had talked again with Mr Blake, and had acquired a strong respect for him. He almost wished he was a member of St Jude's, but his loyalty to the chapel was too long-standing. He had joined the Home Guard, and enjoyed the matiness and what Hon Peter liked to call the 'corps d'esprit'. His leg was less painful, and he looked forward to a moorland expedition with Jem and Harold in the summer. The doctors had concluded that nothing could be done to restore the sight of his eye, but he revelled in what he could see with the other – apart, that is, from the sight in the shaving mirror of the scars on his cheek. But Margaret said that, together with his eye patch, they made him look like Long John Silver, or the pirate captain in Peter Pan.

It was when all three walked to Digfoot Reservoir that Jem realised that Dad had at last come back to them. It was one of those uncertain days in late spring when nature is seen to be bursting into life despite a chill wind, reminding us that winter has not entirely given up the ghost. The wind puckered the surface of the water into a myriad of wavelets. Here it shone silver in a shaft of sunlight, there it glowered grey under a threatening cloud. As on that visit before Dad had gone overseas, Mum had brought a thermos flask. But there were no chocolate biscuits, only plain oatcakes.

'After drill last night, some of the lads were talking about an exercise up Armworth Valley, before the amalgamation,' Dad said. 'Summer before last. They still boast of the way the squire led them to victory over the Homefield platoon. Sounded like David overcoming Goliath. Did you hear about it Jem?'

‘Er…yes, Dad. As a matter of fact, some of the lads went up to Bilder Edge to see what was going on. But I was unwell in bed.’

‘That was a shame. What was the matter?’

‘I was a bit…under the weather.’

‘He’d been…’ (Jem held his breath – what was Mum going to say?) ‘…overdoing it.’

Jem breathed again.

‘I bet there’s lots you got up to that I haven’t heard about yet.’

‘And that *I* haven’t heard about, either,’ Mum added.

Jem would have loved to tell Dad about his role in that affair, but he owed it to Hon Peter to keep quiet. Perhaps after the war he might make a clean breast of things and enjoy his astonishment.

He and Dad skimmed flat stones across the water to see who could get the largest number of bounces. Dad won with sixteen to Jem’s twelve.

‘That’s what comes of being one-eyed,’ Dad said. ‘It concentrates the mind.’

They set off home. Following behind, Jem saw his parents join hands and swing their arms. Like kids, he thought. Dad had had a mercifully short war. He had emerged damaged, but not beaten. Life at home was going to be alright.

‘Like to come to the tower on Saturday with Harold and me?’ Jem asked Alice. ‘Hon Peter’s asked us to help him clean the top floor.’

‘I’ll come up after I’ve exercised my pony. But why this mania to have it clean?’

'Dunno. But I expect he's got something up his sleeve.'

Having been used to store the Home Guard's ammunition, the room was in need of tidying up. Empty, damaged boxes had to be carried down the spiral stairs and along to a corner of the vegetable garden where Peter planned to burn them. ('If there's a few grains of gunpowder left, it should make an interesting spectacle,' he said.) Jem and Harold carried buckets of water up and scrubbed the floor. Alice arrived in time to help re-furnish the room from the store-room on the floor below.

'One other thing,' Hon Peter said, having arrived to inspect. 'We must test the hoist. The tray that Alistair made is down below. Here's the rope.'

Harold opened the window and threaded the rope through the pulley, whilst Jem went down to attach one end to the tray. He found three bottles of lemonade on the tray. He shouted up to Harold, who hauled them up.

Hon Peter sat in the arm-chair. Its upholstery had been repaired and stuffing no longer peeped out.

'What's all this preparation for, sir?' Jem asked. 'It's not the end of the war yet.'

'There's no knowing when the room might be needed.'

'Is Lorinda coming back?'

'Ah, who can tell?'

'It's a wonderful place,' observed Alice, who had never been in the tower before. 'Why not have village children in for a summer party?'

'I like the idea, but I'm not sure it's big enough.

We'll have to see.'

They let the tray down, hauled in the rope, shut the window and descended the stairs. Harold and Alice went on to the Hall. Jem lingered whilst Peter locked up.

'The Germans are not going to invade now, sir, are they?'

'Most unlikely. Hitler's got his hands full in Russia. And America'll be helping to fortify the island.'

'So, you could return your ancestor's things to the church without any risk of their being pinched by the Germans.'

Hon Peter smiled. 'It's not as simple as that, Master Jem. Do you remember me saying that it must never get out that the squire had thought that the invasion might happen? Well, it's just as important to local morale now, that I'm not seen as someone who was preparing for it. So Sir Richard's achievement remains hidden till the war's won. And our secret has to be maintained, eh Jem?'

'Of course, sir.'

'I'm very glad, by the way, that your father's joined the platoon. He's going to be a great help. The men are already becoming more expert at first aid.'

'He's up to something, I'm sure,' Jem said as he, Alice and Harold went down the hill to the village. They went past the terrace of cottages backing on to the cliff. Two women were in the front gardens, taking washing off their clothes lines. They exchanged friendly greetings.

'You wouldn't think they were some of the women who attacked Lorinda, would you?' Jem said when they were out of hearing.

'But who made a guard of honour at her wedding,' Harold added.

'Look at this Jem,' his mother said when he had returned from school.

Jem took the envelope and drew out a card with gold, crinkly edges. It was obviously something important. He read:

Benjamin Oldcastle and Henrietta Isaacs

invite

Mr and Mrs Murgatroyd and Jem

to their wedding

on Saturday, 16th May 1942

at 2.30 p.m.at the Methodist Chapel, Althwaite.

And afterwards in the School Room.

RSVP

'Who would have thought it?' Mum exclaimed. 'We've seen it coming, of course. But think back just a couple of years – who'd have imagined Benjy the tramp being respectable enough to marry Hetty Isaacs! This invitation's to you really, Jem. You're his pal. Dad and I are only invited as hangers-on.'

'Oh, I don't know, Mum. Think of the Christmas Pudding!'

The village had watched the growing friendship between Hetty and Benjy with disbelief, amusement and, latterly, with sympathy. People wanted a happy ending. Now they had got it. The Bruddersford Examiner carried the news under the headline: *Althwaite Valley Tramp is no more.*

As the day approached, one aspect of the wedding became the subject of amused speculation. Audrey Arbuthnot, ex-headmistress, President of the WVS, and local notable, was Hetty's best friend. Would Audrey deign to be Matron of Honour at Hetty's marriage to an ex-tramp?

Hetty had chosen her wedding outfit with extreme care. She was a widow, so white was out of the question. Above all, she didn't want to add to Benjy's inevitable embarrassment on the day by wearing anything 'showy'. It had to be discreet, whilst making the statement that she was proud to be marrying him. Everyone who saw her acknowledged that she had done herself justice. A long skirt of dark green, a jacket of dark maroon, a straw hat with a dark green ribbon, grey gloves, black stockings and low-heeled shoes: Benjamin was entranced when he turned and saw her coming up the aisle. For a moment he wondered if he was in a dream. He was wearing a dark grey suit, a white shirt and dark blue tie. The best man, Benjy's ex-tramping pal, Rick, had had to help the bridegroom to fasten his cuff-links – 'dratted things', Benjy had exclaimed.

And, Yes! Audrey Arbuthnot was the Matron of Honour. Taller than Hetty, she had wanted to avoid appearing to rival the bride. Her grey dress was thought by some to be drab, but that was the effect she wanted. Contrary to what many people might have thought, she had had no hesitation in accepting Hetty's nervous invitation to be her principal support at the wedding. Three years ago she would have crossed to the other side of the road to avoid the tramp of Althwaite Valley. But the Benjamin Oldcastle who had reformed himself, who had helped Julia Hibbert to find her long-lost son, and who had found favour with Hetty, was a man she now respected. His manners and speech might still be rough, but he was intelligent and outgoing.

The marriage ceremony, conducted by Mr Bright, was dignified. The reception, in the adjoining Sunday School room, had moments of uproarious laughter. When Benjy rose to say his few words, he fingered his tie nervously, brought out of his pocket a piece of paper, looked around the assembled company, then crumpled the paper up.

'I mind those preachers who thought it wrong to prepare their sermons beforehand. They preferred to wait for the inspiration of the Spirit when they stood up in the pulpit. I'm no preacher, but I'm looking for inspiration, And I think I see it. It's in the faces of you all, as I look around. You're smiling, you've kindly expressions. You wish Hetty and me well, I know you do. I want to thank you for 'elping me back into the fold. I was something of an outcast – by my own choosing. I rather prided myself on being a loner, a misfit. But there's them 'ere as 'ave extended the 'and of friendship to a man who didn't deserve it. I'm not goin' to name names. But I know just when it began. It started with a Christmas Pudding. Now, I said I was back in the fold. But an animal that's been tamed can still 'anker after the wild. I've got a dispensation from my wife...' (at this first mention of the word there was laughter and cheers) '… from my wife to take myself off into the moors for a fortnight every summer. Who knows, I might invite 'er tosample a night in the open, with the stars above! Now, our especial thanks to Mr Bright for joining us together, and to Hetty's best friend, Audrey for gracing us with 'er presence.'

Benjy sat down to cheers, and wiped his brow. Hetty squeezed his hand under the table. She had been nervous because he was nervous, but she had been sure he would manage. And he had done more than that: he had touched people. She wasn't the only one in the room, she was sure, whose eyes were wet. Even Audrey, who prided herself on her public speaking, was impressed. Jem had been startled by Benjy's mention of 'Christmas Pudding'. He looked fixedly at the table. Only his mother, glancing at him with a smile, was aware of his confusion.

Two weeks later another invitation arrived. It was from Hon Peter for a 'celebratory occasion' at the Hall: half past two for three o'clock on Saturday the 13th of June.

'What does "half past two for three o'clock" mean, Dad?' Jem asked.

'I suppose it means you can turn up from half past two, but nothing will happen till three o'clock. Very unmilitary – I'm surprised at the squire.'

'I wonder what it's for?'

'He likes his little mysteries, doesn't he?' Mum commented.

Jem reflected that he liked his big mysteries, too.

'Mrs Weaverthorpe mentioned to me that Ron and

Dot are coming over,' his mother added. 'I wonder if they've been invited?'

A knock at the door a few days later heralded the arrival of the pair from Hull. Dot looked shyly at Jem. She looked more grown-up, but she was still his 'little sister'. Jem picked her up and swung her round. But Dot didn't seem to take the same pleasure as before in such an exuberant welcome. Ron explained that they had been asking their mother if they could come to Althwaite. Then, the arrival of an invitation from Hon Peter to a celebration had settled the matter.

'Why has he invited us? Is he getting all the evacuees back together?' Ron asked.

'I bet it's something to do with Lorinda,' Dot said.

Jem confessed that he was in the dark.

Two days before the event, Jem announced that he, Harold and Ron had been asked to help with the arrangements in the morning.

'Well, don't eat all the best sandwiches before we get there,' his Dad joked.

Jem caught up with Harold and Ron on the climb up to the Hall. Dot and Jonquil were with them, having refused to be left behind. Presenting themselves at Mrs McAlister's kitchen, they were delighted to find Lorinda there. She greeted her 'rescuers' with smiles, shaking hands with the boys and kissing the girls.

'You didn't know I'd be here, did you?'

'I did,' said Dot.

A marquee had been set up in the garden by volunteers from the Home Guard, attracted by the reward of beer and sandwiches. It was in camouflage colours of brown and green, having been borrowed from the army. The young folk were kept busy, setting up tables in the marquee and carrying plates of food from the kitchen.

In the early afternoon, those who had been favoured with an invitation began wending their way up the hill. Gorse was in flower at the side of the road. In the warm sun, it attracted the bees. People stopped from time to time to look down at the village. The scene was peaceful. It was difficult to believe that, elsewhere on the globe, war was being waged, and that men and women were being killed and injured. Women living in the terrace cottages came out into their front gardens to see who was passing. They were surprised at the identity of some of the guests. They speculated enviously: why her, why him?But they took comfort in the fact that Bank Terrace would be represented in the person of Mrs Colethwaite.

When the camouflaged marquee came into view, the joke went around that Hon Peter didn't want the party to be spotted by an enemy reconnaissance plane. As the guests gathered and observed who was there, it became clear that it was not just a gathering of local notables and friends of Peter and Lorinda. He had made an effort to bring together a cross-section of the village. Sergeant Walter Armitage and Benjamin, as the husband of Hetty, were there by personal invitation. But the Home Guard was also represented by two chosen by ballot. Joe Quarmby, the plumber, was one of them. There were two shopkeepers, one of them being Eddie Sykes the greengrocer. There were a spinner, a weaver and a boilerman from the mill. Mr Ash, the scoutmaster was there, as was Jack Moorhouse, the garage man. There were a dozen children of the age of Jonquil and Dot. It was a motley assemblage. At first, like oil and water, the higher and lower elements didn't mix. People gravitated to their like, or to those with whom they were on familiar terms.

'Come on, Audrey,' said Walter Armitage. 'We must shake them up.'

Audrey found herself being propelled towards Bert Dawson and his wife, and was soon having an interesting discussion about the surprising contents of dustbins.

'That'll be the next wedding,' Mrs Murgatroyd said to her husband, indicating Audrey and Walter. 'She's at last found a man she doesn't want to dominate. He's a good influence. She's been more willing to listen to others at WVS meetings.'

It was true: after many years of waiting, Audrey Arbuthnot had at last found her chevalier. As for Walter, a new life beckoned. His ambition was fired. He would settle for nothing less than manager of the bank's branch in Bruddersford.

The tables in the marquee were covered with Mrs McAlister's best white cloths. She had jibbed at this, but Hon Peter had said that only the best was good enough. Accustomed to the limited range of food that rationing permitted, the guests were surprised by what was on offer. Not just tinned Spam, but real ham; sausages – contents unknown, but their appearance inviting; Scotch eggs; lettuce and fish paste sandwiches; jellied trifle; blancmange; fruit cake; ginger cake; currant buns; and other delights. But no one dared to begin the assault on the tables until the host appeared. Where was he?

Jem's Mum came up to him.

'It's ten past three, Jem. I wonder why he's not here? Any idea?'

'Come on,' Jem whispered to Harold.

They hastened to the kitchen. Mrs McAlister was just about to go along to the marquee.

'Have you seen Hon Peter and Lorinda?' Jem asked her.

'Aren't they there?'

'Are they in the house?'

'I'll see.'

The boys waited.

'No, they're not,' Mrs McAlister reported. 'I last saw them going out of the kitchen – but that was nearly an hour ago. I wonder...'

Before she could finish her sentence, Jem had pulled Harold's arm, and they had set off at a run.

'Where are we going?' Harold asked.

'The tower. It's just a chance.'

They ran to the end of the garden, dashed through the copse and came tothe clearing. The window at the top of the tower was open. Hon Peter's arms extended through the bars. He was trying to flick the looped end of a rope over the key in the door.

'Thank goodness! Rescue is at hand,' he shouted. 'We're on our way down.'

When they emerged, Jem thought Peter looked shamefaced, like a boy caught stealing rhubarb from an allotment. Lorinda looked worried, and her cheeks bore the traces of tears.

'We managed to lock ourselves in,' Peter explained. 'Tried shouting, but the Hall's too far away. I was making my fiftieth attempt to lassoo the key. Had it not been for the bars over the window, I could have climbed out and down the rope. It's the fault of the war. We had a new lock fitted to protect the Home Guard stuff. It snapped to.'

'It was my fault,' Lorinda said. 'Come on, Peter, we must hurry. It's too dreadful.'

'Tell them to start, Jem,' Hon Peter instructed, as he and Lorinda went into the Hall to tidy themselves up. That was all very well, Jem thought, but how was he going to attract attention? His voice was not loud enough, and he shrank from getting up on one of the tables. He looked around the marquee. Walter Armitage was the tallest. Having bent down to hear Jem's message, he tapped a spoon on a plate until there was silence.

'I have it on good authority that our host wishes us to attack the tables. He'll be here shortly.'

There was a surge towards the food. 'It was like a dam bursting,' Jem's Dad said afterwards. Everyone had something on their plates by the time Peter and Lorinda arrived. 'It's Lorinda!' the word went around.

'It had crossed my mind it was the second anniversary of their wedding,' Mrs Murgatroyd said to Mrs Colethwaite. 'But there had been no news of her coming home.'

'To think I was one of the guard of honour, and I'd forgotten the date!' Mrs Colethwaite exclaimed.

Lorinda was not in uniform but in a light summer

suit. No one, seeing her smiles, would have guessed that half an hour ago she had been shedding tears at her and Peter's plight. During the busy morning, Jem had stolen glances at her. He had wondered whether her face might show signs of dangerous missions. The two lines between her eyes were perhaps more pronounced. But, with her blonde hair and light blue eyes, she seemed to him to be still beautiful. Was her leave, though, a prelude to another secret visit to occupied Czechoslovakia?

However, it was as though she had no worries at all that Lorinda made the rounds of the guests, trying to speak to everyone. She joked with Mrs Colethwaite about the uplifted broomsticks. She noticed the engagement ring on Audrey Arbuthnot's finger, and congratulated her and Walter.

By the time guests had progressed to the dessert items, Hon Peter thought it was time for his few words. He had had a shallow box placed underneath a table. He drew it out. Standing on it, he was on a level with Miss Arbuthnot, which was satisfying.

'Friends! First let me apologise for our late arrival. Lorinda and I had gone to the tower to check that it was in order for a later stage in the proceedings. I managed to lock us in.'

'Peter!' Lorinda interrupted. 'I can't have that.'

She got up on the box beside him.

'Gallant as always, my husband is protecting me. He told me to take the key out of the door before we climbed up, but I forgot. It was all my fault. And, as an air force mechanic, I'd been taught to be so careful about tools! So it's me who has to apologise.'

'There's no need, Lorinda!' Mrs Colethwaite's strong voice spoke for everyone.

'All's well that ends well,' Peter continued. 'And it ends well thanks to two young men, whose names I won't mention to spare their blushes.'

Jem hoped that no one was looking at him, as the colour rose in his cheeks.

'Lorinda and I are glad to see you all on this occasion of our second wedding anniversary. But there was another reason for asking you to come together. Althwaite is not special – though many of you who have lived here all your lives may think it is. But it *is* typical. We have the qualities of courage, endurance, charity and humour which make this country such a tough nut for the likes of Herr Hitler to take on. There's a long way to go before the war is won. Hitler is mired in Russia, but he still occupies the continent of Europe. We shall have to push him out. And our American cousins will help us to do that. The Japanese have to be pushed back in the Far East. Life may be drab, food may be plain…'

'Not today!' came a shout, followed by laughter.

'…I'm sure Mrs McAlister, Mrs Ackroyd and Mrs Bright will be pleased by that tribute to their conjuring skills. But what I wanted to say was that we have to continue to show the resolution we've shown so far. We've got to stick it out. Just like the citizens of Canterbury, Bath and other cities in the front line are doing now. That way, Hitler and his Nazi thugs will be chucked into the dustbin of history…Do I feel a gentle tug at the back of my jacket? Lorinda thinks I've said enough. I've great faith in her judgement. So I'll stop and wish you all well. Now, the young folk are invited to follow Jem and Harold in ten minutes or so to the tower, where there's a little surprise in store for them.'

Prompted by Audrey's elbow in his ribs, Walter Armitage said a word of thanks and asked everyone to show their appreciation. If there had been rafters to the marquee, they would have rung. As it was, the clapping and cheers startled the pigeons which were waiting outside to feast on the crumbs. With a clatter of wings, they flew to a distance.

After ten minutes, Jem and Harold led a crocodile of children through the garden to the tower. Alice and Ron brought up the rear to ensure that no one got lost. In the room at the top, Lorinda sat in the low armchair. She had changed from her suit into a long, light-yellow gown on which white swans were embroidered. Dot and Jonquil sat at her feet, together with the young children. Harold and Jem stationed themselves beside the window, ready to hoist the tray when Lorinda should give the signal. A few adults, who reckoned they were young at heart, had followed out of curiosity.

'Have you got the book, dear?' Lorinda asked Dot.

Dot proudly handed her the book which she had been asked to bring.

'*Rapunzel*, by the Brothers Grimm,' Lorinda began. '*Once upon a time there lived a man and a woman who, for many years, had been wishing for a child, but to no avail. One day the woman began to feel that God was going to grant their wish…*'

As he half listened to the familiar words, Jem's mind travelled back to that escapade of three years ago when he and Harold had enacted the story, with Jonquil.

What a lot had happened since then: adventures, secrets, setbacks, triumphs. His life had become so involved with others: Benjy, One-Leg Tim, Ma Hibbert. He imagined them listening to the tale with him. In her long gown, Lorinda seemed like Rapunzel herself. He noted that her nails were again shapely, and there was no trace of oil on her fingers. Evidently, she had not been doing the job of an air force mechanic for some time. But suppose that, on a secret mission, she was caught by the German SS and tortured by having those nails pulled out! He shivered. The thought was too terrible. He tore his mind away from it.

'…A *few years later it so happened that the son of a king was riding through the forest. He passed right by the tower and heard a voice so lovely that he stopped to listen…*'

Jem looked around the room. Dot and Jonquil at the front hung on Lorinda's words. Harold and Ron were absorbed. He caught a glance from Alice, and they exchanged smiles. His Mum and Dad were sitting at the side. Dad's eye patch and scars were towards him. But he was alive, and a summer expedition lay ahead. Jem felt content. The only cloud in the sky was the possible danger to Lorinda. But she had promised a party in the tower when the war was over. Surely she would be spared to keep her word!

'…*The prince wandered around in misery for many years and finally reached the wilderness where Rapunzel was just barely managing to survive with the twins – a boy and a girl – to whom she had given birth. The prince heard the voice that was familiar to him, and so he followed it. When he came within the sight of the person singing, Rapunzel recognized him and wept. Two of the tears dropped into the princes' eyes, and suddenly he could see as before, with clear eyes. The prince went back to his kingdom with Rapunzel, and there was great rejoicing. They lived in happiness and good cheer for many, many years.'*

Lorinda gently closed the book.

'Another one, please,' Dot begged.

THE END

Lightning Source UK Ltd.
Milton Keynes UK
21 November 2009

146551UK00001B/1/P

9 781438 984070